FEEDING THE BEAST

SKYLER KENT

ISBN 978-1-63784-260-7 (paperback)
ISBN 978-1-63784-261-4 (digital)

Hawes & Jenkins Publishing
16427 N Scottsdale Road Suite 410
Scottsdale, AZ 85254
www.hawesjenkins.com

This is a work of fiction. Names, characters, places, and incidents are either the product of the author's imagination or are used fictitiously. Any resemblance to actual persons, living or dead, events or locations is entirely coincidental.

Printed in the United States of America

CHAPTER 1

When I opened my eyes, a naked man was in my bed, and I had no idea who he was or how he got there.

My head pounded, and I lay motionless as I tried to reconstruct the night before. How I'd made it home was a mystery.

I left work at 1:00 a.m. after a brutal shift. It had been a hot, sticky South Florida night. High humidity tends to bring out the worst in people, and I think there was a full moon out there somewhere. I'd had to deal with a few belligerent drunks and general assholes.

I needed to unwind, so I went to the Water Hole for a drink. Just one. But everyone was there, and that was about all I could remember. Except for a few snippets of naked bodies grinding up and down against each other.

My memory was muddled. *Had that been last night or some other time?*

I inhaled deeply to clear my mind and was instantly assaulted with the scent of men's cheap cologne and stale alcohol. I looked closer at the stranger sprawled on the bed next to me, searching for a memory. But I still had no idea who he was or how he'd gotten there.

It's times like this when I imagine that someone's played a cruel trick on me and placed a random stranger in my bed just to freak me out. But that rarely rings true. Well, actually, that's never happened.

I blinked and focused on the clock sitting on the end table, staring me in the face. It was nearly noon, and I needed to get back to work another shift.

I shoved the naked man and said, "Wake up."

He groaned but barely moved.

"Come on, let's go."

He mumbled something and sat up.

I wrapped myself in a sheet, hurried to the bathroom, locked the door, and showered.

I'd slept eight hours but was exhausted and hungover, and the steamy water felt good on my tired body.

I dried off and finally came around after a BC powder aspirin and a Diet Coke, my personal breakfast of champions. I dressed in my uniform: *tuxedo pants, white tailored shirt, and bow tie.*

When I returned to my bed, the stranger had fallen back to sleep.

"Hey, you?"

I poked him, and he opened his bloodshot eyes.

"Good morning, sunshine," he grunted. Then he asked, "Why are you dressed like a dude?"

"Let's go, big fellow."

He stood and smiled. My stomach flipped when I saw that he was missing an incisor tooth. Men I dated had to have all their teeth, at least when I was sober.

I wanted him out more than ever. I picked up his belongings and tossed them in his direction., but the clothes hit the floor with a thud. He wasn't even trying.

"Take it easy with my stuff," he said.

I usually have a snappy comeback, but I didn't know what to expect from this stranger, so I opted for the truth. "I've got to get to work."

"You're high-strung. Chill."

"Come on. I'm running late."

"You're late? Already?"

I gazed off. I couldn't spend any more time with this idiot.

"Just kidding around." He grinned childishly.

"I don't have time for this. Get dressed and get out."

Instead of picking up the pile of clothes off the floor, he sat back down on the bed and crossed his arms.

"I need to take a shower first."

"No time for that."

"I can't dress in my good clothes without a shower."

"Just wrap a towel around it and hit the road."

He got up again and stretched. We stood eye to eye, and I could see the jet-black mop on his head needed a touch-up. His gray roots were showing.

This guy was below my standards for so many reasons. If I'd been close to sober, I wouldn't have given him a second look. But apparently, I wasn't sober when I'd made that decision.

"Let's go, sport."

"You don't remember my name, do you?"

I couldn't care less.

"Come on, get out."

"I don't deal well with pressure."

"I've got things to do."

"Let me freshen, and I'll lock up."

"Not happening, my friend."

"So now we're friends?"

He smiled, and I got another glimpse of the missing tooth. Bile rose in my throat.

"I'll shower and be out of here in a fast minute. And maybe we can hook up later."

I glanced at the clock again. The seconds clicked by. As I saw it, I had few choices. I could cave and allow this stranger to stay in my home, and God knows what he'd do to my stuff. Or I could take drastic measures.

Drastic measures involved grabbing my .38 from its hiding place at the bottom of the grandfather clock that stood in the corner and threatening to shoot him if he didn't get out.

The gun is a bit of an antique, and I'd found it with the things my dad left behind when he'd abandoned my mother years ago. It worked fine most of the time, but the firing pin was worn down, so it occasionally misfires.

I agonized briefly over this, ran the legal consequences quickly through my mind, and thought that with a bit of creativity, I could actually get away with shooting this guy. He was in my home, and I had asked him to leave several times.

But I didn't plan to kill him. I just wanted him out of my apartment and out of my life.

Besides, if I did shoot him, it would take too long. The police would come around, asking questions, and I'd be late for my shift. I tucked the thought of pulling my gun back into my head. I needed to think outside that box.

So I picked up his clothes and threw them out the window. I watched as they fluttered downward. That amused me, and I smiled.

"What did you do that for?" he shouted.

"I told you to go, and I meant it!" I said.

"Now what am I going to do? I can't go anywhere like this."

I handed him a towel. "Go and do it quickly, or I'll call the cops."

His round moon face frowned.

"My name is Benny, just for the record. And I thought we had something going, but not anymore. You're a crazy-ass bitch."

He exited quickly, and I watched from the window as he picked up his clothes and climbed into an old green Ford Focus. A cloud of oily exhaust trailed behind as he sped away.

My headache rebooted as the sound of a puppy crying leaked in from downstairs.

I live on the second floor of a large house divided into four small apartments. The puppy appeared a few weeks ago, and the guy that lived below me left it outside tied to a rope. And it did nothing but whimper and cry.

I grabbed my backpack, locked up, and climbed the stairs down to the parking lot in front of the old building.

The whining puppy cried louder than ever when it saw me. Its tongue was hanging out, and its little eyes were begging for water.

This was all I needed. I hurried to the pup's owner's door and pounded.

The kid who rented the place looked fresh out of high school, and his name was Dale. He'd introduced himself to me when he was moving in.

After a minute without a response, I pounded harder. But Dale didn't answer.

The pup tilted its little head, and I noticed that it had blotches of missing fur. On top of its hunger and thirst, it had some sort of disease.

I ran back upstairs, grabbed a frozen hamburger patty from the freezer, and placed it into the microwave. While it was defrosting, I picked up a bottle of water and an old bowl from the cupboard.

The meat came out hot and watery. I cut it up and blew on it to cool it down, wrapped it in a napkin, and carried everything downstairs.

I placed the bowl in the grass and poured the water, and the pup lapped it up faster than I could pour.

And then I dropped the patty in the grass next to the bowl and said, "Take it easy with this. It's still kind of hot."

But the pup didn't seem to care. It devoured the meat like it hadn't eaten in days. And he wagged his tail so hard, his body shook with it.

I found a furred spot on its head and gave him a little pet, and then pounded on the downstairs door once more before giving up.

I hopped into my twenty-year-old Volvo. The air conditioner stopped working last year, so I drove with the windows down. It was the first day of October, and the weather was supposed to be cooling down, but we had an unusual heat wave.

As I pulled into backed-up traffic, my head throbbed, my stomach churned, and I vowed never to drink again. The five-mile drive seemed to go on forever.

I was looking forward to cooler weather. But even with the heat, you couldn't ask for a better place to live. The palm trees waved in the breeze, and birds flocked overhead from places up north soon to be covered in snow. I felt grateful to be living in *the land of sun and fun.*

I slowed down for backed-up traffic, and an empty Bud Light beer bottle rolled out from under my seat and under the brake pedal.

I tried to kick it away, but it was wedged in tight.

I leaned down and pulled the bottle out and tossed it into the back seat, and then looked up just in time to see a streetlight turn to amber. Instead of stopping, I floored the accelerator, barely making it through before the light flashed to red as I entered the employee parking lot of the River Beach Racetrack and Casino.

CHAPTER 2

River Beach is located in the northern part of Palm Beach County. It's not near the ocean, so there's no beach, and I've never seen a river. Who knows where that name came from? The enormous building was shaped like an ocean liner. At night, hotel windows light up, giving way to a magnificent sight that can be seen for miles. Thoroughbred horse racing occurs year-round at a beautiful track surrounded by green grass and a fountain in the center of an infield lake where flamingos bathe in the sun. But even though I was employed by the River Beach Racetrack, I hardly ever saw the horses run because I worked in the River Boat Club, located in another building with acres of parking in between.

As I got out of my car, Sally pulled in with her powder blue BMW, and I was surprised to see her on her day off.

I waited as she grabbed her backpack from the front seat, *hot pink with black straps with a secret compartment in the bottom.* One of a kind, just like her. We hurried through the employee entrance and punched in with seconds to spare.

"What are you doing here?" I asked.

"Thought I'd give a hand," Sally said. "And I need you to drop me at the airport later."

"Where you going?"

"Vegas, baby. We're tying the knot."

I furrowed my brow. "Congrats, Sal."

"I'm flying out tonight at seven. Gates has some business to take care of, so he's coming tomorrow. Maybe I'll get lucky at the tables before he gets there."

"Great," I said as I thought about what an odd couple they made.

Sally was tall and lean with a face that belonged in the movies. Gates was short, pudgy, and resembled Danny DeVito.

Whatever floats your boat was my feeling about this, and so many other things, when it came to Sally.

As we rushed into the break room, the manager, George, was giving out table assignments.

George looked more like a computer programmer than a poker room manager. Dark slicked-back hair bordered his nerdy thin face.

He looked up and said, "Just in time, girls. Annie, you're on ten. Sally, glad you're here. You are not on the schedule, but I'll find a place for you. We're slammed."

Ten is my favorite number and an excellent table to start with. My mood brightened.

Sally and I are poker dealers in the Boat Club. Not a bad gig. The pay is decent, I don't have to take my work home, and the hours are flexible.

As we stuffed our backpacks inside our lockers, George pointed to a list on the wall near the door.

"You're on the list, Annie. Get your state license renewed by the end of the month. And fingerprints are due this time."

"Great," I said, but I didn't mean it. Getting fingerprinted was always a hassle because I didn't have any. Somewhere in my mostly Scots-Irish family tree was a bit of Finnish. And from that, my father inherited a condition called adermatoglyphia. He was born without swirls and ridges on his fingers, and I was the only one of his four children to come out printless. *Lucky me.*

We grabbed tip boxes from the back room and headed out into the club.

Every table was full, and the place was rocking. We had viewed the jackpot amount flashing on the overhead monitor as we walked in. The Texas Hold'em bad beat had grown to $320,000 plus change.

"Unbelievable," I mumbled.

"Remember, we're sharing tips if we hit the beat, right? Fifty-fifty," Sally said.

"Sure, Sal."

Sally was an optimist. I had been working at the Boat for seven years and had never dealt it, and most of the 150 other dealers were just like me, including Sally. A few dealers had been lucky enough to hit it three, four, or five times, but not us.

We passed the security podium, and I nodded to Edsel Spears, a cop who worked an extra detail in the poker room. He's short but solid in stature and always had several weapons hanging from his belt with plenty of ammunition. He looked like he was loaded for bear or war, whichever came first.

At table ten, nine players sat playing Texas Hold'em.

Trevor was in the dealer's chair and had just finished the hand. He collected the cards and placed them into the automatic shuffler when I tapped him lightly on the shoulder.

He unhooked his tip box from the side of the table, and I hung mine in its place.

I glanced briefly at the dark circles under Trevor's eyes. He was twenty-three but looked close to forty. Short and lean, his skinny arms dangled inside the sleeves of his shirt.

He'd struggled with drugs and alcohol for as long as I'd known him, and it looked like he was losing the battle.

The whites of his eyes were bloodshot, and the blackness of his pupils had nearly filled the space where his light brown irises should be.

As he stood, I noticed some fresh ink on the back of his left hand. The ace of hearts had the waxy look of a new tat. And his earlobes were stretched thin by the round disks.

Trevor was a mess. But despite his appearance, I considered him a friend.

He smiled as he made his way to the next table in line, and I sat down in the dealer's chair.

I was happy to see Sam Jarvis at the table. Six feet something, with high cheekbones and stone dark eyes that you could get lost in. He had natural blond hair, always styled wonderfully. Good bones, not too thick, not too narrow, and his clothes fit like a glove over his well-built body.

"Annie, how's it going, kiddo?" Sam asked.

I smiled and nodded.

Sam was a flirt and went through women regularly; always shapely and beautiful, he had his choice.

Sally stopped next to Sam on her way to a table behind me. She reached over and plucked a red bird (five-dollar chip) from his stack and said, "Future tip. Good karma's important to your game, Sam."

Sam laughed as she dropped the clay disk into her tip box, and he handed her a green bean (twenty-five-dollar chip). She dropped that one too.

And then she winked at me before sauntering to her table.

Very few could get away with some of the things that Sally did.

"She's a trip," Sam chirped.

I grabbed the deck from the automatic shuffler and pitched two cards to each of the nine players at the table.

I looked around at the faces of good tippers. Ten was always the best table in the house, and I placed my hand in front of the guy at my right, seat nine, letting him know he was first to act.

Two guys folded.

Sam threw in two red birds and said, "Raise to ten."

The next guy folded, and two others called.

I burned a card by shoving the top card on the deck under the chips in the pot. And then I turned over the next three cards and spread them in the center of the table. Ace of spades, the ace of clubs, and a deuce of clubs. These cards are known as the flop and are community cards. The players can use their two cards and a combination of the community cards to form the best possible hand.

Walter was next to act. He was around thirty-five, with massive muscles bulging out of his tight T-shirt. *Good-looking too.* With his blue eyes and freckles, he reminded me of a little boy in a he-man's body—*a grown-up Huck Finn.*

Walter's eyes got big, and he led out with fifty. His muscles flexed, and I imagined an ace appearing on his forehead.

I can usually guess players' cards by how they react, and I'm reasonably accurate. You would think this would be an asset when I play, *but no.* I lose more than I win because I can't see anything except my own cards. I forget to look for my adversary's reactions and mannerisms. So, I can't afford to play too often.

Sam and another guy called.

I figured Sam for a club draw, and the other guy was donating, *chasing a dream with a pocket pair.*

I burned another card and placed the ten of clubs next to the flop. This card is the turn. I smiled at Sam, hoping he'd made his flush, and I was looking forward to a decent tip.

"What's the bad beat at?" the player sitting next to me asked.

I leaned back because his breath reeked of garlic and sour mash, and he smelled like he hadn't showered in a while.

"Just over 320," I replied.

Walter said, "All in," as he pushed two stacks of red chips into the pot.

I was sure he missed seeing the possible flush. His outs were to pair the board again or another ace, but the odds were against him. (Outs are possible cards that can improve a hand.)

"I've never seen the jackpot so high," Walter said.

Sam pushed two hundred into the pot, calling the all-in bet.

The last guy folded.

Gallagher, a short, stout middle-aged guy with huge teeth that looked out of place in his tiny mouth, inquired with his moaning little voice from seat eight, "What's the bad beat?"

A couple of the guys chuckled.

Sam chirped, "If quad jacks get beat by a better hand, the loser of the hand gets 50 percent of whatever the jackpot is. The winner gets twenty-five, and the table splits the rest."

"So if I lose with quad jacks or better, I would get over a $150,000?" Gallagher's eyes opened wide.

"Yeah, but it's hard, so good luck with that, Gale."

Gallagher frowned, flipped the hand attached to his limp wrist, and stated, "My name is Gallagher, Sam. And you should know that by now."

I imagined he was so sensitive about being called Gale because he's quite effeminate. If I had to make a guess, I'd say he was a gay man. He talks with a lisp, waves his hands in the air, and flips his head around when he wants attention. But I didn't care one way or the other, and he seemed to be sensitive about it, so I made sure I called him Gallagher because he's an adequate tipper.

I placed the river on the felt—a five of hearts. The river is the last card completing the group of five community cards. And it was a blank, helping no one.

Walter was quick to turn up his weak ace and six of hearts. Two pair —*I was right*.

Sam smiled as he turned over his king and queen of clubs, showing the nut flush.

Walter tossed his cards into the air as I pushed the pot to Sam. I smiled as he threw me two reds and a green.

A thirty-five-dollar tip was an excellent start to what I hoped would be a good day.

"Thanks, Sam," I said as I tapped the chips twice on the tray in front of me and then dropped them into my tip box.

The first tip always makes an irritating hollow ping against the metal, a harsh reminder that I had hours to go.

I gathered the cards into a neat stack and then pressed the green button on the shuffler. The metal door opened, and I placed the blue deck into the empty compartment and pulled out the red cards. The door automatically closed, and the shuffler hummed as it began jumbling up the deck.

As I pitched the next hand, Gallagher's father, Gates, walked by the table in his usual highborn manner.

The Honorable Gatlin Weekly played nearly every day. It was a well-known fact that Gates had been a traffic judge for years, and most offenders wished he was still on the bench because he was known for his carefree and loose manner when dealing out fines and penalties. An attorney who knew him once told me that his name should have been spelled W-E-A-K-L-Y because Gates favored the defendant, which was more than likely how he became wealthy, from all the bribes he'd received from defense attorneys and their clients. His long and fruitful career ended when he let a drunk driver off who celebrated by drinking a pint of whiskey in his car after leaving the courthouse. He headed for I-95, got mixed up, made a U-turn in the northbound lane, and headed south, going the wrong way. He ran into a family of four. Luckily no one died, but the mother of two lost a leg, and one of the girls got hit with fragments from flying glass, brutally scarring her and blinding her in one eye.

Judge Gatlin Weekly was asked to resign at the age of sixty-nine, and that was over ten years ago.

When Sally said she was engaged to the old geezer, I nearly choked on my drink and responded with a giggle. But she insisted it was true and held out her hand, revealing a massive diamond on her left ring finger.

She never wore her ring to work because she said it affected her tips—which was probably true.

Gates was wearing his usual mismatched outfit, and at the bottom of his skinny white legs, his feet were clad in floppy sandals. His long gray hair was wildly curly and pulled back into a sloppy ponytail. But he had a pleasant laugh and used it often, and he was a good tipper. Not just fair, but good.

Gates and his son, Gallagher, were not on the greatest of terms. Gates was a well-known homophobe and repeated his beliefs about the *gay lifestyle* being against the laws of nature as often as he could interject it into a conversation.

On the same token, Gallagher adamantly denied being gay and spoke often and obstinately about his conquests with the female gender.

After thirty minutes on table ten, the next dealer tapped my shoulder, an indication that my time was up.

On the way to my next table, I ran into Denny McCaffery, a sheriff's deputy working part-time security at the track. His six-foot-something solid body stepped aside to allow me to pass as he smiled.

"Annie, how've you been?" Denny's blue eyes sparkled.

I shrugged. "Good as usual. And you?"

Background noise droned as his radio crackled—*something indistinguishable*, at least to me. But Denny became preoccupied with the call.

He paused for a second and then said, "Really good to see you, Annie," and then rushed away with a radio to his ear.

Denny was one of the good guys, very friendly, and I had a longtime crush on him. But he wore a gold band on his finger that led me to believe he was unavailable. I watched him hurry away, and I thought once more about how it sucked that *all the good ones were taken.*

And then I turned around and had to step aside to let Shaka through. Another regular.

No room for both of us to walk in the aisle between the tables. Shaka stood at least six six, with jet-black skin, sporting an enormous belly and massive arms, all fat, no muscle. He struggled to walk, jiggling as he moved like a wave of lard through the room, bumping into tables and chairs. As usual, he was draped in colorful silk fabric that exposed layers upon layers of fat.

Shaka was a drug dealer and had cornered the market on most of the trade in the Boat and surrounding areas. Between hands, he'd hold court with the smurfs who sold for him.

Sometimes they'd leave the building and be gone for twenty minutes or so before returning reeking of skunk weed.

And they would laugh when I thanked them for the contact high.

After dealing for five hours, Sally leaned in as I pitched cards to a group of elderly men playing straight two.

"You're on the next break, so you can drop me at the airport," she said.

I nodded and continued running the game.

CHAPTER 3

The next few days were difficult. The room was crazy busy, and all I did was sleep, eat, and work. Management had asked everyone to work extra hours to fill in. I took advantage of the opportunity because I needed the money.

I was asleep after another hard shift when Sally's call woke me at 8:00 a.m., telling me to pick her up at the airport later that morning. She quickly spouted off the flight information, and then she hung up before I could respond.

I tossed and turned for another half hour before giving up. I made sure the pup downstairs had water, and I gave it another burger before dressing in my uniform and heading to the airport.

I waited outside Delta arrivals in a line of cars until an airport cop told me to move along. I circled in heavy traffic twice but still didn't see Sally or Gates outside. I pulled over, and the same cop motioned me away from the curb again.

Time ticked by as I drove, and I wondered if maybe I had missed them, and they found another ride.

I called Sally, and it went straight to voice mail, so I circled again.

She'd left for Las Vegas three days ago to meet Gates, and they were to get married. She flew out alone, and he was joining her there, and I assumed they would be returning together. Gates was wealthy, and I would have thought he'd have a car waiting instead of me and my old Volvo.

When I pulled up for the third time, the cop was already waving me away. But I spotted Sally wheeling her bag through the glass door, so I ignored him and double-parked next to an airport shuttle van. I popped my trunk and leaned over to open the passenger side door. Her backpack was slung over her shoulder, and she was wearing a stylish poncho and black slacks, and Gates was nowhere in sight.

Sally rushed behind my car and slammed her Louis Vuitton suitcase into the trunk so hard that my car shook. She glanced around before slipping quickly into the passenger seat.

"Sorry, my suitcase was the last one coming out," she said.

"Not a problem," I replied. "Where's Gates?"

She raised an eyebrow. "Not with me, that's for sure."

"What happened?"

Sally didn't answer. She was my best friend, but she had her secrets, and I knew she would tell me when she was ready.

I drove away as she looked out the back window. When Sally pulled the poncho off, I saw that she was wearing her uniform shirt.

"You going to work?"

"Why not?" She looked out the back again.

"What are you looking for?"

"I thought Gates might be here, but I guess not. I called you as a backup."

We pulled into the employee parking lot, and I parked next to Sally's Beamer, right where she had left it three days prior.

CHAPTER 4

The jackpot had grown to over $360,000, and everyone played fast to make as many hands as possible as the night moved on.

Time flew by, and at 1:00 a.m., I'd made it to an excellent no-limit table where the chips and action flew. And I noticed Sally was dealing at a prime high-stakes table full of good tippers.

I was fifteen minutes into my thirty-minute down when all hell broke loose at Sally's table.

I stopped pitching cards in the middle of the hand, but the players didn't care because they were all interested in what was happening behind them.

Sam jumped out of his seat and did the ridiculous floss dance, and he looked downright sexy doing it.

Another player had his cell out, taking pictures of the tabled hands.

A player from my table stood up, looked over the top of a group of guys, and yelled, "Bad beat!" And the whole room erupted. Some cheered. Others groaned and cursed because it wasn't them, and hoped it was a mistake and the bad beat was still up for grabs.

George ran up with Denny and Edsel at his side.

"Everyone, please stand clear!" Edsel yelled as he raised his hands.

George read the hands, nodded, and the celebration continued.

As the crowd parted, I was delighted to see that Sam was at the table, and the rest of the players were decent tippers, except for the evil Russian, Mik.

Mik hardly tipped and tended to blame dealers and other players for his losses. He was around fifty or older, his head was shaved to his pale skin, and he had a long jagged scar on his left cheek. His appearance and distinct Russian accent were menacing, and he tilted to one side when he walked.

I'd caught him taking chips off the table, which is against the rules, and he'd hated me ever since. Maybe he liked Sally. Most people did, but Mik was only one of the nine anyway.

I watched as Sam leaned in and whispered something in Sally's ear. She nodded as she caught me staring at her through the crowd. She winked in my direction, and I smiled back, knowing I would be getting a badly needed windfall.

My thoughts turned to money.

Ellie, my daughter, was in her last semester in college and needed money for her car payment and tuition, and my rent was a week overdue. These things were first on the list.

Maybe there'd be enough to fix the air conditioner in my car. I'd put something toward those credit cards that were so difficult to pay every month, and it would be good to have a few bucks in the bank.

I got back to reality and finished dealing the hand.

After the bad beat got hit, the jackpot went back to fifty thousand, and the place cleared out fast. Most of the dealers that were on break left. But when I approached George to see if I could go, he said I was pushing on to the next game.

I went back to work but found it difficult to concentrate.

I was distracted as I kept an eye on Sally's table, where she would stay until everything was verified and the jackpot was paid out.

I missed calling a winning hand, and a cranky man complained, "Pay attention!"

I apologized, got back to the game, and forced myself to concentrate.

As I pitched a card, Sally leaned in and whispered into my ear, "I tipped out at a little over eight grand. But don't worry, it didn't include Sam's tip. He's giving me cash. Probably over ten."

I furrowed my brow.

"I'm meeting him at the Hole. Get there as soon as you can, and I'll call you when I know the amount for sure," she said, and then she was gone.

Tip boxes are locked. Tips are counted at the end of each shift and turned in, and then paid back at the end of the week in a paycheck with taxes taken out. Personally, I would never have agreed to meet anyone afterward to get cash.

Even though it was tax free, it's a chance you take. The winner might have second thoughts and not show up. Or after they had time to think about it, you might not get as much as promised, and you'd have no recourse. It's against company policy to circumvent the system, and if you got caught, the penalty was termination. For me, not paying taxes wasn't worth the risk.

The standard tip for a jackpot is around 4 to 5 percent. I was thinking fifteen thousand, give or take. But Sam was a good tipper, and he was the one who got the big half, so his tip could be more if he held true to his word. Conservatively, half of the total tip could be around seven thousand, and I had already spent double that in my head.

I trusted Sally as much as anybody I'd ever known, but when it came to money, who really knows anyone?

My mind was overloaded, and my next table seemed to take hours. I couldn't read the cards, and the players were losing patience with me. I finally snapped out of my thoughts and came back to the dealer's seat again, staring at a table of angry men wanting to play Texas Hold'em.

At around two in the morning, I noticed something going on by the security podium. Three cops were standing together with their radios to their faces sporting looks of concern.

Denny looked up, caught me staring at him, and turned away.

Things began to happen in slow motion. My heart raced, and a sense of dread hit me. I looked at the players and couldn't understand what they were saying. It felt like I was out of my body, watching everything as if I were hovering overhead.

I finally got pushed out of my table and hurried over to George and asked if I could leave.

He didn't answer as he looked at the cops grouped together, still communicating on their radios.

And then Edsel and Denny rushed out the door.

He finally said, "Go ahead, Annie. Just be careful."

I exited quickly. As I stepped outside, an ambulance screamed down the dark road, followed by two police cars.

I ran to my car and fired up the engine, slammed the gearshift into reverse, and peeled rubber out of the lot.

The emergency vehicles' lights were still in sight, and I crushed the accelerator to the floor heading in the same direction. I followed the caravan around the corner and into the parking lot, where neon lights from the Water Hole shone brightly.

A crowd of people milled around as a group of police officers tried to maintain order.

An EMT rushed out of an ambulance with a big black medical bag hanging from his shoulder.

I parked in the first space I could find and climbed out of my Volvo. I got closer, but I couldn't see much.

I ran toward the scene and tried to push through the crowd. Someone grabbed me, and I fought to get free, but it was no use. I looked up and saw Denny's face. He wrapped his arms around me and said, "Stay back."

"Who…What…?"

His blue eyes turned uncomfortably downward, and I collapsed to my knees.

Through the sea of legs, I saw Sally lying on her side, and she was covered with blood.

Denny helped me up and pulled me off to the side.

He held me as I watched an EMT monitor vitals as another inserted a central line into Sally's arm. It took a few minutes to stabilize her, and then they lifted her onto a gurney.

"I need to go," I whispered.

"I'll drive," Denny answered.

We followed the ambulance in Denny's patrol car in silence, and I was grateful. There was nothing he or anyone could offer that I wasn't already thinking.

Denny pulled up to the sliding glass doors of the emergency entrance of Good Samaritan Hospital at the end of Flagler Drive. I jumped out as the howling wind picked up, and waves from the nearby Intracoastal lapped at the seawall.

Two paramedics pulled Sally from the back of the ambulance. Another EMT was on the gurney frantically pumping her chest. She had a mask on her face attached to an airbag. As soon as the stretcher hit the ground, an EMT began pushing air from the bag into Sally's lungs.

No one questioned or tried to stop me as I shadowed the team into the treatment area.

As they wheeled Sally into a trauma room, a nurse put a hand up, stopping me from entering. I stepped back and watched through the glass window as a doctor inserted a chest tube, and dark liquid flowed out from Sally's lung.

Nurses and doctors attached wires and clips on her fingers and chest.

A woman dressed in green rushed in with a bag of dark red blood, hung it from an IV pole, and attached it to a catheter. The crimson fluid dripped down the tube and into her vein, replacing some of what she'd lost.

They worked for what seemed like hours trying to save Sally, and all I could think about was how lost I would be without her.

When the doctor stood back, I knew it was over. A nurse looked up at the clock, and my eyes followed. It was ten past four in the morning, Sally was dead, and someone pulled a sheet over her head.

I jumped when a clerk touched my shoulder. Her name tag indicated she was Jill Lewis, and she said, "I'm so sorry."

I didn't reply.

"Are you related?"

I shook my head.

"Do you know anyone we should call?"

I stared back.

"Can you give me any information about her, please?"

"Okay, yes." My mouth was dry, and my words were barely audible.

I followed her to a workstation and took a seat across from her.

"Name?"

I looked at this woman for the first time. Around fifty, with a pear-shaped face. Prominent jowls and small inset pale green eyes. Her lips were pale, blending into her white face. *Cartoon character came to mind.*

"Sally Grover."

"Age?"

"Not sure. She was sensitive about that. But her birthday was in September. The eighteenth."

"Address?"

I had no idea where she lived and never realized how strange that was. The closest I'd been to her domain was a motor home that we took to other poker rooms up and down the coast, but I was pretty sure she didn't live in it.

"I don't know," I whispered. "Sorry."

"Phone number?" Jill asked with a smile, and I noticed a black spot in between her front teeth. Decay that hadn't been adequately taken care of. I looked down and saw she had a butterfly tattoo on her ankle. She had money for ink but not enough to take care of her teeth.

"Why do you want her number?"

"It's one of the questions on this form. She came in without any identification. Anything you—"

"Where's her backpack?" I interrupted.

"She didn't even have a purse."

"Sally never carried a purse. Someone must have her backpack. Maybe the paramedics. The Boat should have more information."

Edsel Spears stepped up. "Annie, it's me. You think this could have been a robbery?"

My mind raced in all kinds of directions, *none of them good.*

"I don't know, Edsel."

"The Boat?" the clerk asked.

"She worked at the River Beach Racetrack," Edsel said.

She handed me her card and said, "Call if you remember anything else. Sorry for your loss."

The thought of going on without Sally was not a good one, and I was sure I was never going to laugh again.

"Where's Denny?" I asked Edsel.

He tilted his head toward the exit sign. "He's in the waiting room."

CHAPTER

As Denny drove, my mind flashed in and out of the present and the past. Everything with Sally was exciting. And now things would change.

I looked at Denny. He had a sweet face, lean with a deep cleft in his chin, and good skin, smooth and fair. His eyes were set deep below his forehead, and he had a full head of brown hair streaked naturally by the sun. And he was there when I needed help.

"Thank you," I whispered.

He shook his head softly. "Wish I could have done more."

He reached in the back and pulled up a bottle of water. "You want some water?"

I shook my head, gave him directions, and he stopped in front of my apartment.

"Give me your keys, and I'll bring your car by."

I never gave it a thought as I unhooked my car key and handed it over. As I got out of his vehicle, I heard the puppy whimper from alongside my building. I leaned back in and whispered, "I'll take that water if you don't mind."

Denny handed me the bottle, and I made my way to the little dog and poured the water into the bowl I had left earlier. I noticed the poor thing had lost more fur.

And then I headed upstairs.

The next day I woke with a headache. I was on the couch, and everything spun around. I closed one eye, scanned the room, and was relieved to find that I hadn't dragged any strangers home.

On the dining room table was a half-empty bottle of New Amsterdam Vodka.

When I saw it was twelve thirty in the afternoon, I panicked.

What day is this?

And then I noticed that my laptop was missing. Apparently, my last one-night stand was a kleptomaniac. I quickly checked to ensure my grandmother's Wedgewood was in its hiding place in the secret compartment beneath my grandfather clock. I exhaled to find it was still there next to my revolver.

And all the while, I heard that damned pup whining from downstairs.

I showered and dressed in about five minutes.

I grabbed another patty from the freezer with no time to thaw the meat.

Downstairs, I replenished the pup's water and laid the frozen meat on the grass. The poor thing looked up at me and wagged its tail. I gave him a little pat on the head and then wiped my hand on the side of my slacks.

I kicked the door to the dog owner's apartment and yelled, "Take care of this animal!"

I didn't wait for a reply as I got into my car, where I found the key on the seat.

At work, with a few minutes to spare, I stopped in the ladies' room, looked in the mirror, and was stunned at my appearance. My eyes were bloodshot, and it seemed as if I'd forgotten to brush my hair. *Well, maybe I had.*

I ran my fingers through the tangled mess and splashed some water on my face.

When I entered the break room, I felt everyone's eyes on me.

"What?" I asked.

Kendra looked at me and said, "I'm so sorry about Sally. I know she was your friend, and…"

My knees buckled, my head spun around, and I couldn't catch my breath as I recalled the night before. And then everything went black.

When I woke up, paramedics were checking my pulse and taking my blood pressure.

"What happened?" I asked.

"You blacked out and hit your head on the table," one of the EMTs said.

I tried to stand, but a paramedic who looked to be about fifteen held me down.

"Don't even think about it, lady," he ordered in a voice that sounded as young as he looked. "Not until we're sure you're good to go."

After he finished checking me out, he told me to go home, put some ice on the lump, and take it easy for twenty-four hours.

He also told me not to drive, but I did anyway.

CHAPTER 7

I spent some time looking out my only window, blaming myself for everything imaginable, and wondering what I could have done to prevent the tragedy.

I should have stopped Sally from making the cash deal, but I was on another table and couldn't talk. And I was her friend, not her caretaker. Besides, I knew that even if I had been able to communicate my concerns, she never would have listened. She never listened to anyone. She never asked for advice, never even asked what I thought about anything. And I never questioned her. She oversaw her life and everything that surrounded her, including me. That was her way.

I noticed the light had turned to dusk, and I didn't know where the day had gone. I had a drink in my hand but didn't remember pouring it. But I was tipsy, that was for sure.

The puppy cried, and I managed to find more meat for him from my freezer.

I fed him from my hand and filled his water bowl, and then I noticed the lights were on in Dale's apartment.

I knocked hard on his door.

Dale's sunburned, pimply face appeared in the crack of the open door.

"What do you want?" he asked in a sleepy voice.

"You're not taking very good care of this dog you have chained up out here," I said.

"I don't want it." He tried to shut the door, but I leaned against it.

"You can't just leave it out here like this."

"It's yours…You can have it if it means that much to you."

"I can't take a dog right now. You need to let it back into your place."

"It's got some kind of disease. I don't even want to touch it."

"The poor thing needs to go to a vet."

"Then you do that. I was just trying to get my nut up to take it to a lake and put it out of its misery."

"You can't do that."

"Look, my girlfriend was moving and asked me to take care of it for a few hours, and then she broke up with me. I can barely make my rent. It needs medical care and food, and I can't keep the thing."

"Drop it off at the animal shelter."

"I don't even know where that is. If you're so concerned about the damned thing, you take it."

He slammed the door shut.

I kicked the door and shouted, "Don't you dare drown this pup."

I peered down at the little puppy. What was left of its fur was black and looked like it was vanishing before my eyes.

I gave the dog another pet, and it wagged his whole body. "Sorry, guy. I just can't take care of you right now."

And then I went back to my apartment.

I poured another drink and looked around at my dim, dull, sparse accommodations. If I died today, everyone would see that this is all there was to me. This was all I had to show for thirty-eight years of existence on earth, and it wasn't nearly enough.

Other than producing an offspring of considerable quality, I'd done absolutely nothing.

I drank the vodka straight up. I was just about to pour another when someone knocked on the door.

I froze. I was afraid it was Mr. Wong, my landlord, and I didn't have the rent money.

I snuck up to the peephole and looked. I was relieved to see Denny, dressed in his uniform, standing outside.

"Just a moment," I said.

I rushed to the bathroom and rinsed quickly with mouthwash, brushed my hair, and pinched my cheeks to add some color to my pale face.

Back at the door, I looked again to make sure I wasn't dreaming. He was still there, so I opened the door and dragged him inside.

"How are you feeling?" he asked.

"Okay, I guess." I tried to smile.

"I heard you took a spill at work."

"Oh, that. It was nothing." I rubbed my head, and it was still very tender. "Would you like a drink?"

He smiled. "Maybe later."

I didn't know why, but I leaped into Denny's arms.

I kissed him, and he kissed me back at first. But then he stopped.

I bit my lip and felt like crying.

"I dropped by to make sure you're okay."

I began to weep. "I forgot you're married."

He twirled his gold band around.

"I'm not really. I just can't seem to take it off."

I stared at the bottle of vodka and wanted a drink more than ever.

"I like you, Annie. I always have. But right now, well, I don't want to take advantage of…of a bad situation."

He led me to the couch and held me until I fell asleep.

CHAPTER 8

I woke up in bed with my head throbbing again in the darkness. I turned on a light, looked around, grateful to be alone.

Then I recalled that Denny had dropped by, and a groundswell of loneliness came over me.

My mouth was dry, and I needed something to drink, so I forced myself out of bed. I had to hold on to my head to keep it from exploding.

I grabbed a bottle of water from the fridge. As the door swung closed, I found a card under a magnet on the door from the Palm Beach Sheriff's Department, *Lieutenant Dennis McCaffery*. I flipped it over and saw that he'd written his cell phone number on the back with a note: *Call me.*

I smiled and then stuffed the card into the pocket of my backpack.

I gulped water while I checked my messages.

Mr. Wong had left two about the past-due rent, Ellie reminded me of her car payment and tuition, and then there was one from Sally.

"Hey, girl. Sam's on his way, and from what he said, it's going to be a big payoff for us. Meet me at the Hole as soon as you can, and we'll settle. Gotta go. I think I see him coming now."

The water suddenly turned acid in my stomach. I tossed it in the trash and opened the bottle of New Amsterdam.

CHAPTER

The next time I woke up, it was one thirty in the afternoon, but this time I didn't rush around.

I ambled downstairs, fed the puppy, and gave it water. And I took my time getting ready and then drove slowly to work.

I didn't want to go, but I had to. For the money, now that I wasn't getting the payoff from Sally, and I needed to keep busy. All I had done in the last few days was drink vodka and pass out.

I strolled in twenty minutes late and took time to select my tip box. Numbers used to be relevant to me. Ten was my favorite, but I didn't care. It was right there in front of me, but I settled for twelve.

I stood in front of George, waiting for him to say something about me being late. I was in a foul mood and looking for a fight.

"Are you okay?" George asked softly.

"I'm good. Why?"

"Because this is Wednesday."

I stared back.

"You don't work on Wednesday."

My shoulders rounded, and I sunk into myself. I wanted to disappear.

"Uh, can I work this shift? I need the—"

He interrupted. "Sure, Annie. You probably want to make up the hours because of the ceremony tomorrow. I understand."

"Ceremony?"

"The memorial for Sally."

I couldn't speak. I could barely nod.

"Go to table ten," he said.

My favorite number? *Not anymore.*

On my way to my table, I passed by the podium where the security officers congregated and was disappointed Denny wasn't there.

CHAPTER 10

Sally's memorial was held at the Casa Blanca Banquet Hall in West Palm Beach on the east side near the water.

Decorated with streamers, balloons, and party favors, the vast banquet room was jam-packed with people. Most were from the Boat. Nearly everyone was there. Players, dealers, and managers, and I wondered who was running the poker room and thought maybe they'd closed for this.

I looked around, trying to find family members, and I wondered how I could be such great friends with Sally and not know who they were. We did almost everything together, but we weren't joined at the hip. There were days when we didn't see each other, and even though there were times we spoke almost hourly, there were periods when we didn't speak at all. And she traveled a lot, most of the time without me, of course, because I could barely come up with rent. But that was not the case with Sally.

She was always jetting off someplace. In the last year, she had been somewhere in southern Mexico that I couldn't pronounce, and then she'd gone to Vancouver and London.

I didn't know how she did it. We made basically the same money. Granted, she probably made a bit more than me because of her spunky personality, but not that much more. When I asked her about it, she was vague and said she flew on standby and found exclusive deals on the Internet.

On the day she was murdered, I remembered that I had picked her up from the airport from her recent trip to Vegas, where she was supposed to get married. I'd forgotten about Gates and realized that I hadn't seen him since before they left. I looked around. As far as I could see, he wasn't there. *Strange.* She hadn't wanted to talk about what happened, and I wondered why. She was supposed to be celebrating her marriage, and now we were memorializing her death. I couldn't make sense out of anything.

I took a few steps inside, and a short brown-skinned man wearing a white server's jacket approached me. He asked in a Hispanic accent, "What is your name, please?"

He was holding a list appearing to be three to four pages long.

"Why do you need my name?" I asked.

"This affair is by invitation only."

"Annie. My name is Annie Laine."

"Oh, yes. We've been waiting for you. This way, please."

He led me to the front to a long table that faced the rest of the room with dinner place settings. I looked at the name tags. Sam and George had earned places in front on either side of me.

I asked, "Are we going to eat?"

"Si, I mean, yes. What would you like? Fish or steak?"

"I've never heard of a memorial that came with dinner."

"I'm here five years, and people do this sometimes. Mostly we do weddings, but we do these things too."

He pulled out a chair, I sat, and he gently pushed it underneath me.

"There is a bar in the corner." He pointed.

"Great. Thank you," I replied. And then I said, "Wait."

He turned back around, and I grabbed the list he was holding. He tried to retrieve it, but I turned away as I scanned the names in alphabetical order. I flipped it to the last page, to the Ws. Gates's name was on it but wasn't checked off. I turned back to the Gs. No one named Grover was listed either. And then I checked for Denny. I was disappointed that he didn't make the cut. But that made sense. Sally didn't know him that well and never knew about the crush I had on him. I never told her because she would have interfered, and I didn't want that, especially because I thought he was married and unavailable.

I smiled and handed the list back to the little man. He nodded politely and then returned to the door.

I looked to my right and saw George. We nodded at each other without exchanging a word.

I felt a twinge of guilt. I should have assisted in planning this. I didn't know how, but it bothered me that I didn't even try.

I headed toward the bar and ordered a double vodka on the rocks from a tall, thin man with pale skin. At first, I wasn't sure he understood what I had said. But he filled a glass with ice and poured a generous amount of Stolichnaya over the cubes. I pulled out a twenty, and he held up his hand.

As he gave me my drink, he waved and said in his Romanian accent, "No, pay. No tip. Everything taken care of."

I stuffed the twenty back into my pocket, grabbed my drink, turned around, and ran into Sam's rock-hard body. I gulped air into my deflated lungs.

"Sorry, I didn't mean to startle you," he said.

He was so good-looking.

"It's nothing, really," I spouted.

But it was something.

"She was quite a gal, right?"

"Do you have any idea what happened?"

He looked around before responding. "I met Sally a few minutes before it happened and took off right afterward. I think you know what we were doing."

I had more questions, but I became distracted because I had just noticed that there was no casket in front of the room.

"You want to get together later?" Sam asked.

"Uh, what?"

"Together, later?"

"Where is she?"

"Come on, don't play games."

"Where's the casket?"

"Didn't you run this whole thing?"

"I was too upset. How did you find out?"

"A guy came into the Boat and handed out notes to almost everyone. It gave an address and time and said it was a memorial for Sally. I don't know anything else." Sam shrugged.

I cringed. "Excuse me, but I need to find out more about this."

"Hey. I'm serious. Let's get together sometime soon."

I approached George in front of the room.

"I thought this was a viewing?" I said.

"Just a memorial, Annie," George replied.

"Why?"

"Apparently, this is what she wanted. I don't even know if she was buried or cremated, but she's not here."

"That's not what I'd imagined."

"That's all I know."

I gulped my vodka and took my seat.

Ryan, the poker room manager, walked up to the podium. He was a stylish man, handsome, in a George Clooney kind of way. Dark brown hair sprinkled with gray, slicked in a traditional cut. Not quite six feet tall.

He turned the microphone on, and almost as expected, it screeched through the room. He adjusted the volume and apologized, "Sorry about that."

The room quieted.

"Sally was a super gal, and I was proud to know her," he began.

Not true, Ryan. I thought about the numerous times he wanted to fire Sally for something she said or did. Most of the time, Sally was entertaining. Still, occasionally she would cross the line and hurt someone's feelings, and players would complain to Ryan. He'd written her up numerous times. And once, he set the paperwork up to have her terminated but was overruled by someone in upper management. That incensed him even more. He would watch her regularly on the monitor in his office as she dealt and made notes about every possible infraction.

I know all this because George kept her informed, and she told me about it. None of Ryan's methods worked because she was an excellent dealer. Sure, she could be impetuous at times, but she ran a good game. Eventually, he gave up. But they were never friends, that was for sure.

"I liked her from the moment we first met."

Another lie.

"Everyone here would agree that if nothing more, she was completely entertaining."

That was a diss.

"Enough from me. What I want to do is pass the microphone around and let everyone say something about Sally, and I want to start with her special friend, Annie."

Special friend? So sophomoric.

My mind whirled. I hadn't prepared anything.

Ryan handed me the mic. I stood and made my way to the podium.

I hesitated for a few long seconds as I gulped the rest of my drink. The room seemed to shuffle around in the uncomfortable silence.

And then I began. "I consider everyone at the Boat to be family."

Most everyone responded with a smile, nod, or "aww."

"But Sally was the finest person I ever knew. She had a way of putting things in perspective that was real. And she was honest. And she hit the mark every time. I learned so much from her, and I am grateful and privileged to have been her friend."

I choked up. But for some reason, I felt I needed to say more. I was more than Sally's *special friend.* We were best friends, closer than any two people could be.

It took me a few moments to recover, but it felt longer—*dead silence.* Everyone stared, the shuffling began again, and someone coughed. George cleared his throat as if signaling me to give up the mic. But I held on and squeezed harder. No one was going to take this thing from me before I got a chance to say more. I didn't know what, but I needed to say more.

I began slowly, "I don't know what happened to her…" My voice trailed off, and I shook my head softly. "Does anyone here have any idea what happened to Sally?"

I looked around at the sea of faces. Everyone blended together into something unfamiliar. A blob of eyes looked back, staring blankly. A few looked away, embarrassed for me.

"Who murdered Sally?" I exhaled and then asked, "Is that person in this room?"

Some people looked side to side as others probably wondered the same thing. But mostly, everyone stared downward, avoiding my probing eyes.

"I promise you. All of you." My voice escalated. "I will not stop until I find the person who took her life. I will not stop until I solve this! I will find you! I will find the person who murdered Sally."

Suddenly, I had everyone's attention.

"Whoever you are, be aware. Be very aware. I will find out who took Sally from us! And when I do, there will be hell to pay!"

Someone in the back clapped, and that set off a wave of applause that sent chills down my spine.

I was alone in front of the room as everyone stood, giving way to an ovation of magnitude.

I lowered my head, held the mic out, and someone grabbed it from my hand.

And then I wondered what I was going to do now. How was I going to keep my word and find Sally's killer? I didn't know what or how, but at that time, I knew I was going to do it. I was going to solve the mystery.

As someone else began to talk about Sally and her sense of humor, I headed back to the bar.

And that's about all I remember about Sally's memorial.

CHAPTER 11

The following day, I sat up in a strange bed and looked around. My eyes stopped curiously at the red wall behind a chrome bed frame. The other walls were painted bright white—*the room appeared in conflict with itself.*

I was naked, and everything was strange, except for the man lying next to me. It was Sam.

I lay back to ease the blood throbbing against my skull and waited for my stomach to settle.

Questions flew around in my head like bats in a belfry.

The last thing I remember was Sally's memorial, where I vowed to find her killer. A chill of foolishness washed over me. *The vodka had been talking.*

Sam was there, and he said he wanted to get together, but I ignored him. He was too hot for me, and I knew nothing good would come of it.

I'm good-looking. My dark blonde hair looked better when I had extra money to get a good cut and highlights, but it was long and silky. My body could use a little exercise, but I still looked decent in a bathing suit. People said I was a pretty girl, and when I dressed up and took time with my hair and makeup, I could be beautiful.

But Sam was way out of my league.

I picked up my clothes from the floor beside the bed and held them up to hide my body as I hurried to the bathroom.

I showered quickly and then wrapped myself in one of Sam's big fluffy towels. I found some toothpaste in a drawer and finger brushed my teeth.

I hunted through Sam's medicine cabinet and found an ample supply of hangover remedies. I grabbed a handful of TUMS and shoved them into my mouth, took a BC powder, and washed everything down with tap water from the sink.

When I got back to the bedroom, Sam was missing.

I wandered through his big house, found him in the kitchen wearing a pair of Ron Jon surfer shorts and a Florida Panthers T-shirt. On his feet were a pair of leather sandals. I watched as he scrambled eggs and fried bacon.

"What am I doing here?" I asked.

"You were pretty upset after the service. Nobody needs to be alone at a time like that," he said as he plated the food. "Let's take this out by the pool."

As we ate, Sam suggested I call out of work so we could spend the day together.

I was tempted but said, "I can't do that right now."

"Call in sick. Under the circumstances, they'll understand."

I had accumulated enough money for Ellie's car payment, but I still needed more.

"I've missed a lot of time."

"Okay, then I'll see you there. If you're not up to spending the day, I'll play some poker."

"Good luck." I picked up the dishes and headed back into the house.

My backpack was by the door, and I looked out the front window and was relieved to see that my car was parked in the double driveway. But I wondered how I'd driven myself in such bad condition.

I pulled out my keys as Sam walked up behind me.

"I almost forgot." He opened a drawer, pulled out a couple of handfuls of five-dollar chips, and handed them to me.

"What's this?" I wondered if I was being paid for sex.

"When I have a few chips left, I never cash out. I just leave. Something about standing in line bothers me unless I'm carrying a few racks."

Male egos can be a bitch.

"I never remember to bring them back. You'd be doing me a favor just getting them out of here. I'm tired of looking at them."

I hesitated slightly before deciding he wasn't treating me like a hooker and then thanked him and tucked the chips away.

I rushed home, changed into my uniform, and fed the ugly pup another frozen burger.

12

At work, my first table was a $1/$2 no-limit. Jean, a dark-skinned Haitian bulldog when it came to poker, was at the table. He spoke with a thick accent and liked to run the game.

I hated the thought of having him at my table. I was on the edge of combativeness, and he would surely give me a fight if I wanted. Only I wasn't sure I could win and couldn't stand the thought of losing anything else.

Jean won the first hand and threw me a white chip.

When I dropped it, I didn't hear that ping I hated so much, and that made me smile.

Even though I'd have to pay taxes on the gift from Sam, I was still ahead of the game.

As I dealt the hand, I looked around the room. I still hadn't seen Gates since Sally left for Vegas and thought it odd that he wasn't at her memorial. And he usually played every day.

Out of the corner of my eye, Sam stood staring at me, and I waved with my free hand. He walked away. At least I thought he did until I heard him whisper in my ear, "What are you doing later?"

I jumped.

"Huh?"

"Can we hook up?"

His words were crisp, his breath fresh, and he smelled of masculine lilac.

I couldn't remember last night, but evidently, it was good enough for an encore. He was asking me out after a one-night stand, which was a change of pace in my recent dating history.

"Where and when?" I replied.

"IHOP at midnight." Apparently, he'd given this some thought.

I nodded as I watched him strut out the door, and then I looked back at the table where everyone was staring at me.

I knew I was supposed to do something, *but what?*

"Up to you, anytime you're ready," Jean said with a sarcastic tone.

I burned a card and placed another one next to the flop as my mind took another lap around the room, still wondering about Gates.

Eight hours later, I cashed out feeling good. I'd made more than usual, and a big chunk of it came from Sam.

As I drove toward IHOP, my thoughts turned to Denny. He was my first choice. But I hadn't seen hide nor hair of him since I'd tried to seduce him in my apartment. And I was embarrassed about coming on strong.

I exhaled, exhausted from the fight. I wanted more, but I was always settling for less.

13
CHAPTER

IHOP was crowded. Apparently, it was the place to be at midnight, which made sense because it was across the street from the airport where people came and went at all hours.

I inhaled the smell of bacon, and it reminded me I hadn't eaten since breakfast. I looked around and spotted Sam at a table in the back. I took a step, but he waved and headed my way.

"Let me pay the check, and we'll get out of here," he said.

I was surprised that he'd eaten already. But when he looked at me with his dreamy eyes, the ping in my stomach moved to a lower spot between my legs, and I forgot about being hungry.

As I waited, my stomach began to growl, and a sickness overcame me that I couldn't ignore.

Sam laid some cash on the counter and pulled out his keys.

I said, "I'm sorry, but I'm not feeling well."

"Come on, Annie, I got whatever you need at the house."

I was so ill, I could hardly speak. "I can't."

I made it to the parking lot before throwing up.

On the way home, a wave of panic hit me when I realized I hadn't heard from Ellie. In fact, I hadn't received any calls from anyone. Something was wrong with my cell.

I grabbed my phone from my backpack and saw that the battery was completely dead. I'd been so preoccupied, I hadn't charged it.

I rushed home and plugged it in.

While it was charging, I fed the pup the last frozen burger and poured a drink.

When I looked back at my phone, the screen flashed with *You have twenty-seven messages.*

I heard the message from Sally again and cringed.

George had called about the memorial, and Ellie had left four messages.

My landlord informed me in his adorable Asian accent that my rent was two weeks late, and he would be by to collect.

A few dealers, managers, and players had offered condolences.

And then I heard the voice of a stranger. "This is Louis Ranger, attorney for Selma Grover, and I need to speak with you as soon as possible."

Weird.

It was too late to call back, so I refilled my drink and found a pen but couldn't come up with paper. So I wrote the number on the back of my hand.

I gulped the better part of the vodka without stopping, as I thought, *Selma Grover*. Had to be about Sally, but what? I had no idea.

My thoughts went back to Gates, and I scrolled through my phone pointlessly. There was no reason I'd have his number. The only communication we'd ever had was him as a player and me as a dealer on the tables.

Sally was engaged to him, and she said he lived on the island of Palm Beach on the ocean side.

I pulled up the county appraiser's office website, searched for Gaitlin Weekly, and found that he owned one property classified as residential. The address was on Ocean Boulevard, and that fit.

I entered a new contact for Gates on my phone and added his address. *I was making progress.*

I celebrated by pouring another drink, turning the TV on, and lying down on the couch.

CHAPTER 14

I woke up the next morning, sprawled on the sofa, and happy to be home and alone. I recalled the failed date with Sam from the night before, but the rest was a little fuzzy.

Then I noticed the phone number written on the back of my hand. I squinted at it for a few seconds before remembering the call from the attorney.

I dialed, and a pleasant-sounding young lady answered and said, "Louis Ranger's office, how may I help you?"

"Can I speak to Mr. Ranger, please?" I replied.

I waited on hold for a few minutes, got bored, and hung up. I redialed and left a message for the attorney to call me and then saved his phone number.

I showered and scrubbed the ink off my hand.

As I got out, someone began pounding on my door, and my cell rang simultaneously.

I wrapped a towel around me and grabbed my phone. I looked through the peephole at Mr. Wong standing in the hallway.

I veered away from the door and answered the call with a whisper, "Hello?"

"Ms. Laine?" a man's voice echoed from the phone.

"Yes."

From outside the door, Wong shouted, "I hear you! I know you in there!"

"This is Louis Ranger calling. I need to speak with you about the estate of Selma Grover."

"You mean Sally?"

"That's apparently the name she preferred."

Wong pounded again and bellowed, "Open door, I need talk now!"

Mr. Ranger asked, "Is this a good time?"

"Sorry, but I'll need to call you back."

I clicked off, opened the door, and Mr. Wong nearly fell inside.

"You no answer phone, you no return call, you no pay rent!" Wong yelled.

"I'm sorry, but I've had a lot going on lately. My friend—"

"No more story! You pay end of week or go!"

"That might be a problem because—"

"You always have problem. Ever since you come here."

"I eventually pay."

I crossed my arms on my chest and then recalled I was still wrapped in a towel. I stepped behind the door as Mr. Wong continued his rant.

"No more. You nothing but headache. No money, you leave by Friday!"

"Not sure you can do that without ample notice."

"This is notice! You not pay and not move by Friday, I take your stuff and throw it to the street!"

He huffed and then scurried away.

I hit redial on my phone, and Mr. Ranger came on the line right away. He asked if I could come by his office this afternoon, and we settled on a time.

As I dressed, my thoughts returned to Gates. He didn't show up for their wedding and didn't attend the memorial. I imagined they must have had one hell of a fight for him to shut her out like that.

I had some time before the appointment with the attorney, so I headed toward Palm Beach.

I followed the directions on Google to an enormous house painted in shades of flamingo and beige that bordered the water. Not the biggest on the island, but very nice. The grass was cut, and lavish landscaping neatly trimmed. And it had a wrought iron gate with a sign that read, *No Unauthorized Entry*.

I pressed a call button next to the gate but got no reply. After five minutes, I walked the length of the lot. The cement and brick fence was continuous and covered three sides of the property.

I rang once more, and then I looked up at the tall gate that came to sharp arrows on top. I took a breath and began to climb.

I got halfway up when a Mercedes Benz screeched to a halt on the road behind me.

I jumped off and encountered a red-faced well-groomed white-haired lady who had her phone out, taking pictures and dialing concurrently.

I held out a hand and said, "Wait, please. I'm here to check on a friend. I didn't get a response and became worried."

"Get away from that gate!" She insisted.

I stepped toward the open door of my car as I repeated what I'd already said. But she wasn't having any of it.

"Don't move. The police are on the way."

I jumped inside my Volvo and hit the road at full throttle.

I glanced in the rearview mirror, and she was still snapping pictures.

I trembled as I drove to Mr. Ranger's office, expecting the cops to chase me down and arrest me at any moment.

CHAPTER 15

Ranger's plush office was in a brown brick building in downtown West Palm Beach off Olive Avenue. I parked in a garage and took the elevator to the ninth floor.

When I introduced myself to the receptionist, she treated me to coffee. She led me to a conference room with a wall of windows that overlooked the city and Intracoastal.

I was still shaken up after my weak attempt at breaking and entering, but I began to relax in the warm surroundings of the law office.

I was back to thinking of why I'd been summoned but couldn't come up with much.

Mr. Ranger wanted to speak to me about Sally's estate, but I doubted she could have much of anything other than debt.

A man entered carrying a dense file that I assumed to be Ranger. He was short, stubby, and wore a quality hairpiece. Good, but it wasn't perfect because I could still tell it was a wig.

His face was ruddy red, and he had a fat neck. His tie looked to be looped too tight, and it appeared like it was cutting off the circulation to his head. But he wore a nice suit that fit him like a glove. Tailored, not off-the-rack, for sure, and he reminded me of a pig dressed up in good clothes.

He offered me a warm, sweaty hand, and we shook briefly before he sat down across the table from me.

"Why am I here, Mr. Ranger?" I asked.

"The reading of the will," he responded formally. "We need to execute it in accordance with Ms. Grover's wishes. This is the process."

"Where's her family?"

"She had no one. Just you. Shall we proceed?"

"Of course."

"Basically, Ms. Grover has left everything to you. The car, the bank accounts, the motor home, house, jewelry—"

"House?" I interrupted.

"I have all the keys. Each time she changed her locks, she sent me a new set. She was very precise about these things."

He handed me an array of keys on a *Hello Kitty* ring and a BMW key fob.

"She'd set up a trust, so it's easy and straightforward. Everyone should do these sorts of things, and I'll be happy to help you with your estate as well. At a more appropriate time, of course."

I remained silent, but my mind was wheeling. Information was entering into my gray matter at lightning speed and leaving just as fast.

"I need a few signatures, and my assistant will be happy to witness for you. The bank accounts are yours as soon as you go by and present a death certificate. I've supplied you with all the information and documents needed." He slid a large manila envelope toward me.

"What about debt? How much are the mortgage and the car loan?"

"Everything is free and clear. Ms. Grover had assets, no liabilities. We can transfer the car title right now over the Internet. Regarding the house, we'll submit the proper paperwork to the courts. It may take several weeks to see the change from the trust and into your name on the county appraiser's website. But you can move in right away."

He wrote an address with a gold fountain pen on white linen stationery.

I babbled a thank-you and headed out the door.

On the way down in the elevator, I thought about how private Sally was. I believed we shared almost everything; I assumed I knew her so well. But apparently, it was only the tip of her iceberg.

However, I had a house. Somewhere to live, free and clear, and that was a good thing.

And then I wondered where Sally's BMW was. I surmised that the police had probably towed it away from the crime scene.

I pulled Denny's number up on my cell and circled the send button with my thumb. Surely, he would know something about the car.

Even if we weren't going to be lovers, we could still be friends. I'd be seeing him at the Boat, and I thought I might as well get the awkwardness over with.

I pressed send, and the call went to voice mail.

I hung up without leaving a message.

On the way back to my car, I called work and told them I was sick.

16
CHAPTER

I picked up a couple of burgers from McDonald's and ate one as I drove. I dropped by the apartment and fed the pup the other one. As he ate, I filled his water dish.

Dale opened his door and stated, "I'm doing it later today."

"Look, I'll take him to the vet. Just give me some time."

"It's messing everywhere, and it smells out here. I can't bring anyone to my place because of that stupid shitting diseased animal."

"Please give me a few days. I'm on my way out right now, but I'll make sure to do it tomorrow."

"I've had it. This thing goes today, one way or the other."

I shook my head. There was no way I could deal with a dog, let alone one with health problems.

My shoulders rounded as I walked away.

As I started my car, the pup peeked at me from around the corner. It was so pathetic.

I got out and unchained the pup. I opened the passenger side door, and it hopped up and sat down in the seat. I shook my head as I mentally slapped myself in the face for making such a terrible decision.

As I drove, I googled the address Ranger gave me and was guided east toward the ocean. I crossed the bridge over the Intracoastal and felt a twinge of excitement as I found myself in the high-priced area of Manalapan. I headed south on Atlantic Drive with the Intracoastal and ocean on either side and looked for Big Pond Circle.

I found the street in a swanky neighborhood and drove slowly. There were many two-story homes with pillars in front, but most of them didn't have numbers or were hidden by shrubs and overgrown trees.

The voice on my GPS said my destination was on the right. But I didn't see a house.

I passed a church and tried to remember the last time I'd been. Easter? Christmas? *And what year was that?*

I found another number on a mailbox and whispered, "Damn." I'd passed it.

The pup gave me a look.

"Don't worry, I'm not taking you to the lake."

I turned around in a driveway and headed back.

GPS declared, *Your destination is on the left.*

I caught another house number and noted that the next one should be it.

But I was back at the church.

I parked in the lot and got out to take a better look. The pup jumped out and stood at my side.

A soft breeze washed over me, the sun beamed down, and the air smelled like the sea. And I instantly fell in love with the tranquil surroundings.

Sally had left me a church with a steeple and stained glass windows in the middle of a lovely neighborhood.

Everything looked orderly and proper. But it was still a church.

I climbed the steps to double oak doors and tried several keys on the Hello Kitty ring until I found one that turned. Finally, the dead bolt slid free of its housing, and with a slight pull, the door opened.

I stepped into a foyer with polished oak benches on both sides and a coatrack standing by the entranceway. The ugly pup followed.

We ventured further inside together and looked around. The front room was a square fourteen-foot area set up like a sunroom with a floral love seat, rattan coffee table, and matching end tables. The walls were paneled and painted a calming green. The room reminded me of a greeting room in a country home I'd seen in a magazine. It had probably been the narthex of the church.

The main room was massive, thirty feet by sixty. This area had been the nave. It was one great big room divided into three sections. The most prominent was an elegantly furnished living room with two white couches separated by a hand-carved oak table.

An earth-toned Persian rug covered the hardwood floor.

Off to the right side was a mahogany dining room table, matching high-back chairs, and a triple-door china cabinet. Everything sat atop a colorful Oriental rug.

The sizable area's left side was set up as a family room with a big-screen television, overstuffed chairs, and a roll-top desk. The rug under the furniture was darker, red with a black-and-white pattern. A gorgeous armoire sat off to one side. I opened both doors at once and found a bar stocked with liquor.

On the bottom shelf, stuffed way in the back, was a wooden box of Romeo y Julieta cigars encased in aluminum cylinders.

Next to the armoire was a small wine cooler filled with bottles.

Behind the main room, which had been the altar, was a kitchen equipped with top-of-the-line stainless steel appliances. The gas stove was extra-large and had a grill in the middle. The fridge was at least fifty inches wide with a see-through door.

I opened the refrigerator, and a blast of cold air hit me. I searched around, found a bottle of Fiji water, and twisted off the cap. I gulped half without stopping as the door closed by itself.

I went back into the great room and took another look. The ceiling was flat with golden brown knotty pine.

I stood in the middle of the big room with the puppy at my feet and circled around until I became dizzy.

The midafternoon sun shone through stained glass windows reflecting bits of color throughout the dwelling. I felt like I was in a fairy tale. I turned around and around, looking at every beautiful thing, and felt eerily out of place. This was Sally's house, and she gave it to me. I missed her terribly and was overwhelmed with guilt because I hadn't done anything to uncover what happened to her.

I was baffled. How could Sally afford a place like this? And why did she keep this part of her life secret from me?

When my head stopped spinning, I poured myself an abundant amount of vodka from a bottle of Stolichnaya and took a long pull. As I drank, I looked around for a bedroom. Stairs led upward to what was once the balcony of the church that had been enclosed.

"Stay," I said to the pup, and it sat down next to the bottom stair.

As I climbed, a feeling of trepidation overcame me. I opened the door and looked around at a huge bedroom.

A queen-size bed up against one wall was neatly made, and everything was in good order. The room was furnished with the same richness as the rest of the place. The headboard and dressers were lavish walnut bursting with wood-grain patterns. The legs and hardware appeared to be solid brass, and everything was highly polished. Over the top of the headboard was a shaded one-way window I hadn't noticed from the ground floor. I looked downward at the body of the house where I'd just been.

Everything worked. Everything was elegant. Everything was beautiful and perfect. Except for me. I looked at my clothes and crappy shoes, and I peered into the mirror at my face covered with cheap makeup. I was the only thing that didn't fit.

Everything was in good order, except Sally wasn't there. She was dead. She had secrets, and I wondered if her secrets could have led to her demise.

I opened a drawer of the nightstand next to the bed, not looking for anything particular, and found Sally's ZEV Glock 17 with a bronze slide, two magazines packed with bullets, and three full boxes of shells. Lightweight and compact, a beautiful gun.

Sally had let me shoot it when we went target practicing at the range. After handling my old pistol, this gun was a dream. It was nothing like my .38 Smith & Wesson with its long and heavy trigger pull.

I sniffed, and it smelled of oil, recently cleaned. I replaced it back into the drawer and exhaled, feeling safe.

I emptied the glass of vodka and then headed back down for a refill.

I sat on the couch with my glass full of clear liquor and stared at the yellow package that the attorney had handed me lying on the table. The pup jumped up and sat beside me as I pulled out the pages.

I flipped through copies. When I came to the death certificate, I took a lingering breath and another gulp of my drink. The next document was a copy of her Bank of America statement.

I'd forgotten what Ranger had said until that moment.

All I had to do was go to the bank and show my ID and death certs, and the money in these accounts was mine. *All my problems were solved.*

I poured another drink to celebrate.

17

The next day, I woke up on the couch with a massive headache and a killer upset stomach. If not for the empty glass and bottle of Stoli staring me in the face, I would have thought I had the flu.

It took me a few minutes to get my bearings in my new environment.

The pup sat in front of me, staring as my thoughts turned to Sally. This was my home, but it had come at such a substantial cost. She was gone, and I wasn't even looking for her killer as promised. My stomach churned as I asked myself once more, *What was I to do?* I had no idea.

I finally stood up and let the ugly creature out the front door. It handled its business and came back without any trouble.

I recovered from my flu a bit when I thought about the money in Sally's bank accounts.

After a long bath, I found a vial of OxyContin in the medicine cabinet and took one.

Before I left, I searched the Internet on my phone and found a local emergency veterinarian that welcomed walk-ins. It was early, and we got right in.

As I waited for the vet, I looked at the poor hairless creature and apologized. "Sorry, buddy."

I just knew the pup had some terrible uncurable disease and needed to be put down. But I couldn't stand the thought of it being drowned in a lake by pimply-faced Dale.

A short man entered and introduced himself as Dr. Ruiz.

And then he took a look at the pup and said, "I see you've got the puppy mange." He smiled as he picked up the dog and scratched its belly. The animal responded with a full-body wag.

"Puppy mange?" I asked.

"Probably from mites living in the hair follicles."

"Dear God."

"It's no big deal. Is he up-to-date on his shots?"

"I have no idea. It's a boy, huh?"

He smiled. "I guess you didn't notice. How long have you had him?"

"A few hours. The kid downstairs from me was going to drown it in the lake because he thought it had some incurable disease. All I know is he appears to be house trained, likes raw hamburger, and wags with his entire body when he's happy."

"We can handle all of the vaccines here, and I'll give you some shampoo to get rid of the mites."

I looked away.

"I'm sorry, but I can't keep him. Do you know anyone looking for a dog?"

"Even if I did, I couldn't place him in his current condition. Why don't you nurse him back to good health, and then we'll see?"

I felt sick, and I needed to eat. My stomach was protesting the Stoli from the night before.

"I can't do it right now."

"There's always the lake," he said with a smile.

I rolled my eyes.

I left with a leash, a bag of puppy food, pills for worms, shampoo for mites, the pup at my side, and a bill that I had promised to pay sometime in the near future.

I headed to McDonald's and ordered two sausage biscuits from the drive-through window, one for me and one for the ugly pup. After gobbling the food, I felt nearly human again.

At the bank, I leashed up the dog, and we walked inside.

The lady behind the desk leered.

I said, "Emotional support animal."

"Looks sick," she said.

"Puppy mange. No big deal, I have shampoo."

I transferred all of Sally's money into my own account, over thirty thousand dollars, and I did a happy dance inside my head.

And then I moved two thousand of the windfall to Ellie's account and withdrew a thousand dollars in cash.

As I walked out the door, I dialed Ellie's number, and we made plans to meet for lunch at one.

CHAPTER 18

I dropped the pup off at the house before heading back out to meet Ellie for lunch.

As I pulled up to the restaurant, my cell rang, and I saw it was Denny.

Excitement washed over me.

After a brief hesitation, I answered. "Hi."

"It's Denny. But I guess you already know that."

"How are you?"

"I noticed you called."

"Sorry to bother you, but I need a favor. Can you find out what happened to Sally's car after...? Well, you know?"

"Yeah, sure, I can check with the detectives handling that case. I'll give you a call back."

A massive redwood Buddha greeted me as I breezed into Rama's, decorated with Asiatic art and silk bamboo plants.

Ellie, my dark-haired beauty, was already seated but stood when I approached. She'd gotten her olive skin and dark hair from her father and her blue eyes and good looks from me. And I'd like to think her smarts came from both of us.

After a quick cheek kiss, I sat down and bit my lip, wondering how to tell her about Sally. I choked, not being able to find the words.

And then Ellie broke the ice. "I'm so sorry about Sally, Mom."

After I exhaled, I wrote my new address on a napkin and handed it to her.

"Sally left me a house, and I want you to see it. It's big, used to be a church, and it's kind of cool. You could stay with me if you want instead of in the dorm. Once you see the place, you can decide. And I got a dog. It's not really mine, and I don't know how long it's going to stay because it has puppy mange, but as soon as I get a handle on that, I'll put him up for adoption."

"Wow."

"I've got a few things to do, and I work tonight, but tomorrow's good. Or whenever you can. Just call to make sure I'm there."

After lunch, I gave her some cash and told her to treat herself. We parted with a kiss and a hug.

On the way home, Denny called back.

"I checked for Sally's car, and we don't have it. It wasn't reported impounded anywhere in the city. The D's working that case would be interested in taking a look if you find it."

"How would I go about doing that?"

"I'd start with where she was shot. Look around the immediate area, and then fan out. Can I ask, why are you looking?"

"She left it to me."

"Nice car. But I don't think you should handle this on your own. You could put yourself in danger."

Hearing his words sent a chill down my spine. I hadn't given a thought about being in danger.

"I'll be careful."

"Do you know when you might want to do this?"

I exhaled. "Maybe after work tonight."

"Mind if I go with you?"

"You want to?"

"I'm always up for an adventure."

"I get off at midnight. But I could leave if you want to go earlier."

"I'm on duty until eleven, so midnight is perfect. I'll meet you at your apartment if that's okay."

"Just meet me at the Hole."

CHAPTER 19

After my shift, I raced home to let the pup out and then headed to the Water Hole, where I found a guy named Pete standing behind the bar.

"Where's Finn?" I asked.

Finn was the regular bartender and would have been working when Sally was killed. I was curious about who was in the bar at the time she was shot.

"Don't know, don't care," Pete said. "Got a call from the temp agency, and they said to come here and serve alcohol."

He held a mug of beer to his lips, and he took a few gulps before placing a frothy glass of draft beer in front of me.

"It's on the house. First draft is free."

"How come?" I took a big swig.

"This place is working on a private label, and the distributor is supplying samples."

"Appreciate it."

Denny's big warm hand rested on my shoulder.

He was dressed in a white Tommy Hilfiger button-down shirt and faded blue jeans. And he was as adorable as any man could be, and I felt safe just because he was
there.

Pete placed a draft in front of Denny and repeated
what he'd said about the first one and the private label.

Denny looked at the pilsner of ice-cold brew but didn't
drink.

"Beer is beer as far as I'm concerned," Pete quipped.
"If it contains alcohol, I'm good. Free just makes it a whole
lot better."

Pete took another swig of his beer and then scuttled
away.

I took another long pull on mine, but Denny left his
beer where it sat and said, "Ready?"

"You want to finish your beer first?"

"I'm driving."

I reluctantly left the rest of my brew and followed him
out into the parking lot. He led me to a Chevy Impala,
beige with an impeccable shine.

Denny opened the passenger side door for me, and I
slipped in.

He drove around the parking lot, crossed Clearmont
Street, and circled through Wendy's lot.

All the time, I looked from side to side, hoping to get a
glimpse of the blue BMW for more reasons than one. Sure,
I wanted the car. My Volvo was old, faded, and the air conditioner didn't work. But I also wanted to find Sally's killer,
and I thought the car may lead to that end.

But since Denny mentioned the idea of me being in
danger because of something I knew, I'd been giving it some

thought. Sally and I were close. Not as close as I'd thought, but we spent a lot of time together. I knew nothing. But her killer wouldn't know that.

Denny turned around, made a right, and started a circular path around the Hole, covering every street. We'd driven for a few minutes before either one of us said a word.

He finally broke the silence. "How are you doing, Annie?"

"Better, actually," I answered, and honestly, I believed that I was. "At first, I was crazy," I admitted. "How could I go to work the next day without remembering that Sally was gone?"

"Denial is the first stage that most people go through when dealing with grief."

"Did you just make that up?"

"Look it up on your phone." Denny smiled. He had a great smile. Friendly, reassuring, and even though he was a big handsome man, the dimples in his cheeks made him cute as a young boy.

"Knowing the stages of grief could help you get through this."

"There are stages?"

"The second is anger. Then bargaining, depression, and, finally, acceptance."

"Think I skipped anger and went straight to bargaining."

"I hope you can skip depression and go to acceptance."

"You're a nice man, Denny. And I like you."

He blushed.

"Maybe when you get straightened around a bit, we can go out to dinner."

"What?" I quivered.

"Dinner, at a restaurant, you and me."

"I, uh, I think I might like that. When I get straightened around."

"I didn't mean you weren't straight. I mean, well, there's a lot of things going on in your life. I meant when things settle down. Just let me know when you're ready."

"Okay."

"Give me a call."

I was shaking like a schoolgirl with a crush. I hadn't been out on an actual date in a long time. Lately, it seemed like one hookup after another.

After my divorce, I still wanted a relationship, but nothing worked. Somehow, I got lost and settled for less. Much less. Sam was great-looking and kind to me so far. But I didn't trust him, and he went through women like a middle-aged Justin Bieber.

And just recently, I'd woken up in my bed with a complete stranger. I was on the wrong track, that was for sure.

Denny was a step up. A gorgeous man with a great job and, as far as I could tell, didn't have flaws. He was kind, cute, and everything any girl could want.

He circled a big white church when we got to Congress Avenue and came to a stop in front of Sally's Beamer.

Denny called the crime scene team, and they sent a tow truck. We spent another hour together waiting for them to finish processing the intake.

As he drove me back to my car, I texted him my new address. Meat Loaf's "Bat Out of Hell" ringtone echoed from his phone, and he quickly silenced the cell.

"Meat Loaf?"

He smiled. "He's got a tremendous voice. What about you? What kind of music do you like?"

"Not a big fan of hip-hop, but I like rock and roll, country music, and I like Meat Loaf too."

He gave me a peck on the cheek that sent a shock through me in a good way.

I returned with a not-too-passionate kiss on his lips. And then I watched him drive away, skipped to my car, and went back to the church house.

20

C H A P T E R

Denny called the next day to say that the Beamer had been processed and was ready to be picked up.

I asked, "Did they find anything?"

"Not that I know about, but I haven't had a chance to talk to the Ds working the case," he said. "I've been in court all day testifying on another matter, so I've been out of the loop. I'll be tied up for most of the week, but after that, we'll have dinner, okay?"

"Sure." I had a feeling dinner with Denny was worth waiting for.

After we hung up, I took an Uber to the impound lot, showed the paperwork from the attorney to a short Hispanic guy in a gray uniform, and he pointed to the back of the lot.

"Hope you got a key, 'cause we don't," he said with an accent.

I held up the smart key fob, and he walked away. I headed across the lot to the imperial blue BMW.

As I got close, the door automatically clicked open. My heart raced as I sat down in the driver's seat. The sun warmed the car's interior, and I inhaled a combination of new car smell and the musky fragrance that Sally wore. I checked the back seat for her backpack but came up empty. I got back out and checked the trunk. It was clean. I realized that even if the bag had been there, the police would have probably taken it as evidence that might lead to her killer.

I got back in, sat in the soft leather driver's seat, pressed the start button, and the engine purred to life.

The car handled great, and I liked the way I felt inside. I took the ramp to I-95 north and stepped on the gas. The car picked up quickly, and it was exhilarating. I passed cars like they were standing still. When I looked at the speedometer, it was rounding one hundred. I slowed to seventy and drove for another ten minutes. And then I turned around.

I loved everything about the life that Sally left me, except for the dark empty feeling.

Pup scurried over as I stood in the doorway of the house, looking upward, and made a promise to Sally that I wasn't going to give up. I would cut back on my drinking so I could spend more time at it. I wanted to find her killer, no matter what.

And then I thought about what Denny had said about the stages of grief. I was still stuck in bargaining and not looking forward to depression.

My stomach growled, reminding me I hadn't eaten since breakfast.

The freezer was loaded with prime fillets and chops. I grabbed a carton of ice cream from the back and got a spoon from the drawer. I opened the container but didn't find any ice cream. It was filled with cash instead—two bundles of hundred-dollar bills with fifty in each.

A strong urge to celebrate with a drink hit me. I took a breath instead because I'd promised Sally I wouldn't.

Instead of drinking, I gave the pup a bath with stinky shampoo and set a bowl of food and water out for him.

Afterward, I dialed up Lantana Pizza and ordered a large cheese.

As I waited, I showered and dressed in Sally's clothes. We were the same size, and she had good taste.

I let the pup out one more time and made a bed for him in the corner of the living area from a blanket.

When the pizza arrived, I paid with cash and tipped generously.

I laid the box on the coffee table in the family room area and turned on the big-screen TV. I grabbed a slice and took a bite. The place made good pizza, so I saved the number to my cell.

I found an open bottle of Cabernet Sauvignon, Caymus 2015, from Napa Valley, and poured a glass.

I sniffed. *Full body.* I sipped. *Very rich, bold, yet smooth.*

One glass of wine wouldn't hurt. And then I would get back to the things I needed to do. I finished the slice and drained the glass.

21
CHAPTER

I woke up with the sun shining through the stained glass. Colorful streaming beams of light decorated the house. I lay on the couch as I looked around, trying to get my bearings and wondering why it was so painful.

The TV was on, and my clothes were strung around on the floor surrounding me. And I was nude.

The pup sat staring.

The last thing I remember was eating pizza. Just one slice. The box was there, but the entire pizza was gone.

And I was sure I'd had unprotected sex. I searched my mind for a memory of who and what, but there was nothing. The only thing I knew was where. It had happened right here on this couch in this room.

And I was sick.

After covering myself with a silk robe, I let the dog out. And then I took a swab. Not sure why, but I did. I placed it in a plastic baggy and hid it behind a stack of tissue paper in the bathroom cabinet before taking the longest shower of my life.

I wondered what I would do with the swab. Probably nothing. I had woken up before and not remembered a lot about what had happened the night before. I always knew that it had been my choice, but not this time.

I looked through the upstairs window downward and realized I didn't even know where the back door was.

I had a bunch of keys and only knew where two went. One to the front door and one to the master bedroom.

I hurried downstairs and looked around.

The empty pizza box stared me in the face.

I picked it up, crushed it, and headed for the kitchen. Pup followed.

As I pulled the built-in refuse depositary out and crammed the box inside, the sound of pounding footsteps echoed from somewhere behind the back wall.

I screamed, and Pup yelped; we both jerked back as I slammed the drawer shut.

I tried to run but fell flat, hitting my chin hard on the floor. I began to crawl.

When I got to my feet, I ran up the stairs, grabbed the Glock from the nightstand, and headed back down. On the way, I caught a glimpse of myself in the mirror. Blood was dripping from the gash in my chin, but I didn't care. I was out to get whoever was there and probably responsible for other personal crimes against me.

I passed the table and glanced down at my phone. I wondered if I should call someone for help, but only for a second. There was no one. Denny's name passed briefly through my mind, but I didn't know what to say. *I heard someone behind the kitchen wall?* Or *I think I was assaulted, but I was too drunk to remember?* I couldn't bring myself to dial.

A feeling of loneliness ran through me. There was no one out there to help.

I began questioning my sanity. Did I really hear footsteps, or just imagine it?

I opened a door in the back of the kitchen slowly and led with the Glock.

No one was there, but I had found the laundry room with a big washer and dryer and four more doors.

I opened one and peeked inside and found nothing but darkness. I felt around, found a switch, and flipped it on. The space lit up, exposing a set of steps downward, and I was confused.

This house was so close to the water, probably just above sea level. No way this could be a basement. No one had basements in South Florida anyway. And then I realized there were twelve feet of steps out front leading to the front door. This wasn't a basement. I was looking at the first floor, probably used as the pastor's quarters or schoolrooms.

As I considered climbing downward, I remembered seeing a horror movie about a mother who kept her mentally deranged son in the cellar. My thoughts stopped short before I'd had a chance to speculate further into the dark fantasy.

I held the Glock and led the way as Pup followed down the narrow stairway to a hallway with two doors on either side.

It had a skunky smell, and at the end of the hall, a ladder hung under an overhead door.

I used one of the keys on the ring and unlocked the first door. The big room was empty except for a long metal table against the wall with a machine that looked like some sort of printing press. Next to a large cardboard box were stacks of money piled on top.

I stood silently with a strong urge to grab the money and run. But I needed to make sure this place was safe, so I closed and locked the door and continued my search.

Across the hall, I unlocked another door. Pup grumbled, and I knew before I opened it what was there. And it wasn't a family of skunks.

The room was brightly lit and loaded with greenery in full high blooms. I estimated the area to be at least twenty by fifteen, and it was jam-packed with marijuana plants. There was a small passageway between the stalks to make harvesting possible.

A thin watery mist sprayed with a hiss from an overhead sprinkler system.

"This can't be good," I whispered.

Pup sniffed the air, sneezed, and then ran back up the stairs.

I stepped inside and squatted down, looking around underneath the tables but saw nothing, no legs, no feet; no one was in the room.

I backed out and locked up.

And then I headed back to the end of the hall and climbed the ladder that led to the trapdoor.

I unlocked it and gave it a big boost. The door swung back and landed on the ground with a thud, and the sun shone in. I held the Glock as I climbed up, stood waist-high out of the opening, and circled around. No one was in sight, but I was surrounded by above-the-ground tombs in the middle of a graveyard.

CHAPTER 22

I stuffed the Glock into my waistband, climbed out of the door, and looked around at fifty or so crypts of various sizes and shapes.

Fifty feet to the right was a small building. I walked to the white concrete structure on a dirt road and tried a few keys on a side door until I found one that fit.

I pulled the Glock out and cautiously stepped inside. It was an empty garage with two double doors in front.

Off to the side was a stairway leading upward. I climbed the stairs and faced another locked door that I had a key for. I took a step inside and heard something hit the floor. I jumped and squeezed the trigger of my Glock, but nothing happened because the safety was on. I flipped it off and chambered a load as quickly as I could. Before I had a chance to shoot, I found the nature of the noise. A box of clothes had fallen over when I opened the door.

After I calmed down, I looked around. The room was loaded with furniture, boxes, and toys. Little girl's toys. Dolls, a pink Barbie car, and a ceramic baby that looked almost real.

I climbed back down the stairs.

Back inside the tunnel, I unhooked the ladder and laid it on the floor.

I ran back through the passageway and hustled upward. I closed the door and placed a chair under the knob so that it couldn't open.

I opened the next door with the Glock held high.

I gave it a push, and daylight shone inside. I'd found the back door.

Pup ran out, took a pee, and then returned.

As I opened the next door, a whiff of musty air hit me like a pillow to the face. I coughed, and Pup sneezed as I stepped into a room that looked to be about fifteen feet square.

And I was confused at what I'd found.

Canopy bed with Cinderella comforter. White furniture with a high-end Rosebery label. A poster of Cinderella with Prince Charming decorated one wall. Sleeping Beauty on another.

A little girl's room with a full bath—dusty, yet in good order; everything was in place, but apparently it hadn't been touched in years.

A jewelry case was the only thing on top of the dresser. I opened it, and a ballerina twirled as Swan Lake twanged.

I was prying into Sally's secrets. She was gone, and this was my house now, but this room made me shudder.

The next door sprung open to a staircase leading upward. I crept up the stairs lit with a spectrum of colors from a small overhead stained glass window. It was incredible and eerie at the same time.

And there was another bedroom identical to the one below, but it was decorated masculine with a dark wood poster bed and an earth-toned patchwork quilt.

I opened a drawer of a massive chest and found nothing. The closet was bare, and I was sure no one currently resided in the room.

A similar spectrum of colors shone along the opposite wall. And there was another see-through window that overlooked the main room in a hallway that led to the other side.

In the next chamber were a bed and an empty chest of drawers. The closet was bare as well.

I stuffed the Glock into the back of my jeans. I was becoming complacent, so distracted with what I was finding that my fear had dissipated.

Outside was another set of stairs that led back down. I anticipated that there was another room underneath, and I was not disappointed. There was an office with a desk, laptop computer, printer, and locked file cabinet. I used one of the smaller keys from the ring, opened the cabinet drawer, and glanced through copies of paid bills and service contracts.

I came across statements from Merrill Lynch, amounting to nearly two million. And then it hit me. If I was her sole beneficiary, this money could be mine.

I shoved the papers back into the cabinet, and then I hurried back downstairs to the underground room and grabbed the cash from the table.

Back in the office, I held several bills up to the light and examined them closely. They looked good to me.

I counted as I stuffed the money into the bottom drawer of the cabinet—ninety thousand dollars in one-hundred-dollar bills.

After hiding the cash, I pulled the statements back out and took a better look. I had no idea how Sally could have amassed all this money.

I made sure all the doors were locked, and then I dialed Attorney Ranger's number and left a message with his assistant to call back.

My stomach growled. I headed back to the kitchen and stormed through the fridge but found nothing fresh. I checked everything to ensure it didn't contain any hidden cash before throwing out old lettuce and sour milk. I found a small steak in the freezer and set it out to defrost.

I grabbed my cell phone to search for eateries in the area that delivered and found a Chinese restaurant that fit the bill, but before I had a chance to dial, Ranger called back.

I told him about the statements.

"I knew she had some investments," he said.

I crossed my fingers and asked, "Could this money be mine?"

"Send me a copy of the statements, and I'll look into it."

We hung up, and I tried to log on to Sally's computer, but it was password protected. The scanner/fax machine worked independently, so I was able to fax the statements to Ranger's office.

I placed everything back into the cabinet, relocked the drawer, and gave it a pull just to make sure it was secure.

I did a search on my phone for a locksmith and requested an emergency service call.

The lady that answered the phone said they could do that, but there would be an extra charge.

"Not a problem," I said. "I need someone here as soon as possible." I didn't care how much it cost.

With this money, I would never have to worry about anything ever again. I'd quit working, start a business, do something else.

I forgot about being hungry and poured myself a drink.

As I sat down on the couch, I remembered someone had been in my house, and my anxiety returned. I pulled the Glock out of my waistband and set it on my lap as I waited.

23
CHAPTER

I looked through the peephole and saw a tall, thin tan-skinned man with lots of black hair, and he was dressed in a locksmith's uniform, so I let him in.

He had a pleasant smile and spoke with a singsong accent I recognized as probably from Jamaica or the surrounding area of the Caribbean.

His hair was braided with colorful beads that clicked as he turned his head. He had a long face with a noble nose, and his name was Fareed.

I said, "I need all the locks in this place changed. And I need one key for all of them. Can you do that?"

"That is no problem, ma'am." He looked around. "This was a church?"

"That goes without saying. And use a quality lock, please. Start with the front door and work through to the back."

He changed the locks and followed me through the house and downstairs to the secret rooms. I left the door to the room with the marijuana alone. No way anyone could get to it if they couldn't get into the house. Fareed didn't mention the skunky odor, and that was fine with me.

As we headed toward the garage, Fareed did a double take at the graveyard. He didn't say anything about that either.

After working for just short of two hours, he presented me with a master and four copies, wrote out a receipt, and I paid him in cash. He gave me a card with a phone number written on the back and said, "This is my cell. Call me if you need anything else. And if you're serious about making this place safe, I suggest that you use the security system."

"Security system?" I looked around.

"You have the pieces." He pointed to a contact on the front door and the motion detector overhead. "But I don't see a control panel. How long have you lived here anyway?"

"Not long—can't you tell?"

He nodded.

"Hey, by the way, do you know a carpenter who can put in a small doggy door?"

"I know a guy."

After he left, I was utterly exhausted, and my jaw was aching. I glanced in the mirror. My shirt and chin were crusted with dried blood, and Fareed hadn't said a word about it.

After making an alarm service appointment, I got a call from a carpenter named Kline, who said he could come right over.

I had washed the blood off my chin and changed into a Miami Dolphins T-shirt by the time Mr. Kline knocked on the door.

He was fast and efficient, installed the door, cleaned up his mess, and was out of the house within forty-five minutes.

Pup watched him work and knew what to do. He went out and back in a couple of times just to try it out. I thought it was perfect. Large enough for this small dog but not big enough for a person. After the pup had healed and went to a good home, I planned to seal it up.

Kline mentioned something about the pup being the ugliest thing he'd ever seen, but I ignored him.

I locked the front door after he left and poured a glass of wine to the brim. And then I turned on the TV and settled on to the couch with my Glock stuffed in between the cushions.

CHAPTER 24

I opened an eye, and all I saw was a sea of grass. An ant crawled out of the forest of green and tickled my nose. I tried to wipe it away but couldn't move.

I felt someone's eyes on me, and with a lot of effort, I managed to transfer my line of vision beyond the grass.

From my angle, looking up, he appeared to be a colossal kid standing on the sidewalk in front of me. His eyes were wide, his mouth agape. He had a look any horror movie director would be proud of, and I wondered why he was staring at me.

A woman appeared moments later. I would eventually learn that this was the boy's mother. She gave me another kind of look and screeched, "What the hell's wrong with you?"

I wanted to answer but couldn't move my mouth because it was crammed into the earth.

With great effort, I lifted my head and stared at the woman as she picked up the boy. She used her free hand to shield his sight away from me.

I smiled and slurred, "Hello?"

She screamed inaudibly and ran away.

I rested my head back on the grass and dozed off. The next thing I saw were two sets of shiny black booted footsteps approaching.

Now what?

A cop grabbed me by the arm and lifted me up. Another draped me with a scratchy brown blanket.

Pup stood alongside and yipped.

I couldn't imagine what the fuss was all about until I looked down and noticed that other than the blanket, I was completely naked.

CHAPTER 25

The next thing I remember was waking up in a small drab room with a door containing a viewing window, and I assumed it was a medical facility.

I recounted the previous events involving my nakedness in the grass and dismissed the thought. *Lying on my lawn in broad daylight wearing nothing but a silly smile?* No way that could have happened. It just had to be one of those disturbing naked dreams.

But it had seemed so real, and what was I doing in a hospital? That was another question needing an answer.

I looked around for a buzzer to call someone, but nothing appeared within my line of sight. When I tried to move around, I panicked when I discovered that my arms were buckled to the rails on the hospital bed.

That's when my nightmare turned real, and I began to scream.

Dr. Bedad appeared at my bedside. Standing over me, he introduced himself with a thick Pakistani accent. "Hello. Ms. Annie Laine, I presume?"

He reminded me of the guy behind the counter at a local convenience store who'd asked me recently if I wanted a bag for my beer.

I exhaled and nodded.

"I am Dr. Bedad, and I am here to evaluate you." He pulled up a chair and sat.

"Before you do anything, you need to tell me where I am and what the hell I'm doing here!"

"You are in the psychiatric ward of the county hospital. You were brought here because you were found incoherent and without clothing in public."

"I would never do anything like that!"

He reexamined his notes before carefully replying, "That is what the report states here in your chart."

"Jesus Christ. Can you please remove these things?" I spoke with a shaky voice, referring to my arm restraints.

"Apparently, you became unruly when first presented."

"Do I look unruly to you?"

"A bit, yes."

"This is a mistake. When can I get out of here?"

"You are here on a twenty-four-hour hold. I must evaluate you to make sure you are not a danger to yourself or others."

He hesitated before asking, "How much alcohol do you drink?"

I gasped for air. "Not much," I lied. "I'm not an alcoholic if that's what you're asking. Sometimes I don't drink at all, and I have a job I need to get to. So please, you have to get me out of here."

He wrote something on his chart and then asked, "What types of drugs do you use, and how often?"

I took a deep breath and lied again, "I never do drugs."

He flipped through the pages on his clipboard and hummed slightly.

"Do you know what Rohypnol is?"

"Roofies?"

"You are familiar with this?"

"Only from a distance!"

"How so?"

"Like in the news. And I believe it's a topic in a popular movie. I know what roofies are, but that doesn't mean I use them. Why are you asking me about this?"

"Please bear with me. This information is necessary to discover what has occurred. What is the last thing you remember?"

I thought back.

"Last night. I was home watching TV."

"What day was that?"

"Friday."

"Today is Sunday."

Damn. I'd lost another day.

"How much did you drink?"

"One glass of wine. That's all."

"Based on what you've disclosed, I believe you were drugged with Rohypnol against your will."

My thoughts whirled around as my breathing began to get out of control. Everything got blurry.

I inhaled deeply, but I felt like I was suffocating, and my chest throbbed.

Dr. Bedad tucked my chart under his arm as he unbuckled both wrists.

"I am sorry that this has happened to you. I think you should file a report with the police."

That would be the last thing I needed.

"I want to go home," I was barely able to squeak out.

"If that is what you wish, I will sign your release. But once there or in a safe location, you must relax for at least twenty-four hours. No driving or operating machinery."

He laid his card on the rolling table and left the room.

One of the nurses let me use her cell phone, and I logged into my Uber account and ordered a car.

I was dressed in a hospital gown as an orderly wheeled me out. As I saw the light of day and the sun shining brightly, I felt a heaviness lift from my chest. The air thinned, and I could finally breathe freely. I imagined that this was how a prisoner felt when they were released from a lengthy prison stay.

It was dark by the time the Uber pulled up to my house, and the driver asked, "You going to church?"

I didn't bother with an explanation. I just nodded and got out of the car.

As I ambled up the steps, a neighbor stared at me as she walked by with a dog on a leash. I looked away and hurried through the unlocked door and then checked and rechecked every door in the house.

The ugly pup was licking his empty dish, and I felt terrible about leaving him without food or water. I took him to give him a chance at life, but I wasn't doing much better than Dale.

I loaded his dishes and said, "I'm a mess, you know? I don't know why you hang around here other than you're a mess too." I left him eating before climbing the stairs to the bedroom.

I tore the gown off and soaked in the tub for a while. Something needed to change. My life was falling apart, and I had no idea what to do about it.

I lay in hot water until it cooled with my eyes closed and thought of Denny. We may have had a chance. But not anymore.

He probably knew about my naked episode already. Cops shared everything with one another, and they were probably laughing about it by now. The police at the Boat probably knew all about it too. I didn't know if I could face them. I'd have to find another job.

I'd never felt so alone. I didn't want to do anything but crawl into bed and go to sleep. Sleep for days, weeks, maybe years. Sleeping forever sounded like a good idea.

Suddenly, I was wide awake and out of the water. I wrapped myself in a towel and ran down the stairs, taking three at a time. I stuffed my hand in between the cushions and was relieved when I pulled out the cold steel of the Glock.

And then I opened a new bottle of wine, carried it back upstairs, and locked myself in.

I found an ample supply of Valium in the medicine cabinet next to the OxyContin and took one of each and washed them down with the wine.

I lay down with the Glock under my pillow and fell into a deep sleep.

Sometime later, I had a dream. Not the annoying naked dream, this one was new.

I'm in a deep hole, trying to climb out. I get halfway up and fall back down to the bottom of the pit and hit the floor with a painful splat. And then I try again with the same results, except hitting the rocky ground becomes less severe each time, and my desire to climb wanes. The hole fills with water, and I can't breathe.

It was dark when I jerked awake.

I heard a noise that shook me, and my breathing became deep and rapid. I pulled out the Glock.

I stood at the window overlooking the great room as a child cried in the background.

And then I really woke up. My hair was wet with sweat, and I was breathing quick and deeply. I lay there for a moment, listening. Hearing nothing. I exhaled and calmed myself.

My thoughts turned to Ellie. She was a good girl, and I had to take some credit for how she'd turned out. I attended all her school events, was there when she played soccer, and never missed a game. Softball too. I was in the stands with a bat in my hand, the same as her. I hit the ball, ran the bases, caught fly balls, and made the plays. *We did it as one.*

She would never forgive me if I chose to sleep forever and not live out the rest of my life meant to be. Her children would never know me, and I would miss the best part. Growing old didn't seem so bad after all.

I gulped more wine and fell back to sleep.

CHAPTER 26

At first, I thought I was dreaming again when I heard someone pounding on the door.

I stumbled around in the dark and somehow managed to find my way out of the room. But I took a step and fell down the stairs.

I landed on my ankle, heard a crack, and felt a sharp, excruciating pain. Pup ran to me and licked my face as the pounding resumed, and it sounded like someone was trying to open the door.

I yelled, "Go away!"

But the pounding continued.

"Go away, or I'll call the police."

The noise finally stopped, and I hopped to the couch and fell back to sleep.

When I woke a few hours later, I was still on the couch, and everything hurt—my head, my back, and my ankle. But I was grateful I still had my clothes on.

With great difficulty, I pulled myself up. My ankle was so swollen, I couldn't tell where my leg ended and my foot began. And it was crooked.

I crawled toward the dining room table where my cell phone lay charging and pulled it down by the wire. It whacked me in the face so hard I knew I'd have a black eye.

I dialed 911 and gave a brief description of my condition. I managed to prop myself up enough to turn the bolt lock so that the door was open when the paramedics arrived.

CHAPTER 27

After x-rays, a nervous young medical resident, dressed in a white coat that was two sizes too big for his slight frame, entered the curtained enclosed area where I lay on a cot. He held up a tablet and said without introduction, "You have a type C fracture, a very volatile break." He pointed at an x-ray on the screen. "We'll need to reset the bone back…"

He continued talking, but all I heard was, *Blah, blah, blah.*

"I'm going to need something for pain, like right now," I stated.

He teased me by fumbling around in his pocket and then asked, "How did this happen?"

"I fell downstairs."

"And your eye?"

My hand drew to my face. I'd forgotten about getting whacked.

"I hit myself with my phone calling for help."

"What about your chin?"

"I fell."

"Are you prone to hurting yourself?"

"Not usually." I inhaled, thinking this wasn't going to end well.

"You were recently hospitalized under unusual circumstances and—"

I interrupted, "I was drugged, and I still can't remember exactly what happened, and I wish you wouldn't mention that."

"It's my job to ask these sorts of questions when someone comes in with the types of injuries you've displayed."

"I'm not hurting myself."

"Can you explain what's happened?"

"Bad luck."

"That's not good enough."

"That's all I have." He was getting on my nerves.

"I'm going to suggest a psych exam."

"Do whatever you want, but I need something for pain, like right away. And then make my ankle straight, and let me go home so I can heal."

"Nothing will happen until you speak to a trained mental health professional."

I rubbed my eyes with open hands.

"If you don't cooperate, I will have no alternative but to restrain you until the examination is complete."

"Just give me something, and I'll wait it out."

"As I said, no medication until you're cleared."

"Aspirin?"

"Nothing."

"Can't you see I'm suffering here?" I held my foot up.

"It won't be long."

He turned his back and exited through the curtains.

A man's voice droned from the next bay, "Everything okay in there?"

I wanted to tell the stranger to leave me alone but had second thoughts. I needed to appear sane and civilized to everyone if I was ever going to get out of here. And that had become a challenge.

"I'm perfect, thanks for asking."

"You can talk to me if you want. I'm a good listener."

"I would appreciate it if you would just let me rest."

The pain was so severe that I had begun to shake.

"Ignoring the problem will not make it go away."

I tried hard not to scream. "Please, just don't talk. I need quiet."

"God be with you."

"Thank you."

I turned away from the talking curtain and closed my eyes.

Less than a minute later, I was screaming my head off, begging for drugs. I oscillated between Percocet and OxyContin, and I didn't care which. I was sure I was headed for the loony bin but didn't care. They had meds there, and maybe that's where I needed to be anyway.

After screaming for two solid minutes, a trained mental health professional appeared at my side.

"Ms. Laine, I presume?" A red-skinned man that looked like he could have been Dr. Bedad's brother, with a similar accent, stood at the foot of my gurney.

"Yes," I was barely able to whine.

"I am Dr. Patel."

"Are you the psychiatrist?" I cried hopefully.

"Yes, and I wish to speak to you about how you're feeling."

"Fine! I'm all right, really. Except that my ankle's broken, and I'm in severe pain."

I threw back the sheet, exposing my ballooning leg.

Dr. Patel took a step back. "Oh my."

"Can you give me something for the pain, please?"

"As soon as I get some answers, I'll be happy to do what is best for you."

"Just make it snappy. I don't know how much more of this I can take."

"What do you mean by that statement, please?"

"Nothing. It's an expression. There's nothing wrong with me except for my injury. I'm not nuts and not hurting myself on purpose."

"This is your second hospitalization within two days. And the first one was…"

He flipped through a chart.

"Okay, okay! I was drugged and ended up naked on my front lawn. What does this have to do with that anyway?"

"I need to be assured that there is no pattern of self-abuse or any other type of exploitation happening here."

"Take my word for it. Nothing like that is going on. It's a new house, at least for me. I broke my ankle, and I need a cast, not a psychiatrist!"

"And your facial injuries?"

"It's just a series of unfortunate incidents."

"The staff has reported you've been begging for drugs."

"Because I'm in pain! Why can't you understand that?"

"Answer my questions, and we'll see."

"Okay, shoot."

"Are you in a relationship?"

"Maybe, possibly. Not sure about anything right now."

"When was the last time you were in a relationship?"

I gulped too much air and couldn't stop breathing. My voice weakened.

"I started seeing someone recently. But we haven't made any commitments."

"Do you feel unhappy or sad?"

"Right now, I'm not too happy, but usually I'm content or at least on an even keel."

"Do you sleep a lot instead of doing things you enjoy?"

"I sleep okay. Not too much, not too little. Can you just get me some aspirin, Advil, Tylenol, something?"

"Soon. Do you feel worthless?"

"No, never. I'm happy with myself and my life," I lied.

"You seem unhappy now."

"It all started with the death of my friend, Sally. She was always there for me. She was murdered in the parking lot, and I was at the hospital when she took her last breath. I didn't help plan her memorial service, and I was upset about that, but it didn't matter. She'd taken care of everything, and I miss her terribly. I guess I'm in mourning. Then I inherited her house, and I'm in a strange place."

Dr. Patel tilted his head as I continued. I carried on until I was sure I'd convinced him that I was downright nuts. "And then I was drugged and found naked on the front lawn."

He shook his head and said, "I'm sorry for you."

I placed my hands over my wide-open mouth and waited for the men in white coats to take me away. My breathing was fast and deep, and I became light-headed. I felt my eyes roll around, and then there was nothing but blackness.

When I woke, Dr. Patel was shining a thin beam of light into my eyes, and a nurse was at my side taking my blood pressure.

"What happened?" I asked.

"You hyperventilated, Ms. Laine," Dr. Patel said.

The nurse unfastened the cuff, and I cringed as the Velcro ripped apart.

"Has this ever happened to you before? Experiencing dizziness?"

"Maybe," I said as my head began to clear.

"What does it feel like when you've had this trouble?"

"Like I'm suffocating."

"Dyspnea. It's accompanied by agitation and a sense of terror. You are taking in too much oxygen. Quite simply, I believe that you have panic attacks."

Dr. Patel grabbed a latex glove and handed it to me.

"When this begins to happen, place something like this over your nose and mouth and breathe into it. A paper bag will work too. Keep something with you at all times. Do this before it gets to the point of fainting."

He placed his warm hand genially on my back. "You have been through a lot recently. It seems that these series of events are not the norm. I believe once you have solved your current issues and things slow down for you, the symptoms will dissipate. If not, you will need a more thorough exam and testing."

I covered my face with my hands and said, "My ankle is killing me. Can you do something about that, please? Before I go completely crazy!"

Instead of admitting me to the psych ward, he wrote me a script for Percocet and called the nurse who gave me a shot that put me into a coma.

I don't know what they did to me, but when I woke up a few hours later, my ankle was straight and encased in a boot. I got a set of crutches and instructions to stay off my foot and treat it with ice. They referred me to a few orthopedists in the area who would be happy to supply me with a cast.

I took an Uber to the drugstore, got the script filled through the drive-through window, and immediately took a double dose.

CHAPTER 28

Early the following day, I found an orthopedist who would see me right away.

Dr. Hilton was of average height, with both brown hair and eyes. His hair was neatly fashioned into a long tapered cut that stood high on the top of his head, making his square face appear longer. *Good style choice.* And he repeated what the ER doc had said about it being a bad break.

"You must stay off your foot completely for at least two weeks," he said.

I told him it was hard to get around with the crutches and they hurt my arms, so he gave me a rolling crutch and charged me two hundred bucks. But it was worth it.

I gave the receptionist my insurance card. She said it was good that I had insurance because I appeared to be accident-prone.

I remained silent as I handed her money for my co-pay and the crutch, and I vowed not to let the little things bother me anymore.

On the way home in another Uber, I called work and explained I needed some time off because of my injury.

CHAPTER 29

B ack at home, I took another Percocet and washed it down with a shot of vodka, and nodded off on the couch. I was awoken a short time later by an ADT technician pounding on my door. His name was Scott, and he was neatly dressed in a company uniform.

I was groggy, not feeling much pain, and wanted to tell him to just go away, but I was coherent enough to know that I needed this place safe and secure.

When Scott got a look at the pup, he asked, "What is that?"

"New breed of dog. I'm allergic to fur," I said without a smile.

"Maybe you should get a goldfish."

I ignored him as I made coffee. After a couple shots of espresso, I was almost back to normal, whatever that was.

It took Scott a few minutes to find the first keypad at the foyer wall hidden behind a panel.

He peered around the house and paid a lot of attention to the back area in the kitchen. I opened the door for him, and he checked the sensors and found another keypad under a panel next to the egress. There was another in the master bedroom hidden behind a fake cabinet door by the bed. He ended up where he'd started at the front door.

"I'll reprogram your system, and you can put your four-digit secret code in."

"It works?" I asked.

"It works just fine if you turn it on." He grinned.

Scott gave me a quick run-through. Then he tapped the LED screen and entered a bunch of numbers, symbols, and commands.

He turned his back and asked me to enter a master code, suggesting it not be my phone number, my house number, or birthday.

I entered 8190. Sally's birthday was September 18, so I reversed the numbers. I took a breath and began to relax.

He hit a couple of buttons, and the screen changed to a view of the front doorstep.

"I didn't know there was a camera out there." I tried not to slur my speech but was unsuccessful.

"If you're not looking for it, you'd never see it. It's connected to your doorbell. When someone rings, their profile automatically comes up."

Scott stepped outside, and his smiling image appeared on the screen.

"The display is also activated by stepping on the doormat."

I stuck my head out and looked up. I could barely make out the little eye peeking out between the wooden slats.

"Amazing."

"You don't have a recorder, but I can put one in if you need it."

"I think we're good for now."

He pointed out several smoke and motion detectors, glass breakage and CO_2 detectors, and methane and natural gas sensors in the kitchen.

"Everything's top-of-the-line. You have a designated phone line as the first line of communication with our central station. And you also have a cellular backup in case your phone lines are cut. All in working order. Whoever put this in paid plenty for this system."

Before leaving, I set up automatic billing through my bank account. And when he departed just before sunset, I felt safer.

I turned the system on STAY, leaned against the door, and exhaled. Pup stood in front of me, wagging his body.

I celebrated with two more pills. When I didn't get complete relief immediately, I kicked it up with a shot of vodka and passed out on the couch again.

30
CHAPTER

I woke up a few hours later with the doorbell ringing. I had a hellacious headache, an upset stomach, and my ankle was throbbing.

The ringing grated on my nerves as I shouted, "Who is it?"

No one answered, and the ringing resumed.

"Who's there, damn it? Answer me, or stay out there forever! I don't care."

I heard a muffled reply but couldn't recognize the voice or what was said. So I grabbed the crutch and rolled to the door. My ankle was so swollen, it felt like the cast was strangulating my leg.

I barely made it without collapsing. I opened the panel, looked at the display, and saw Sam standing outside. As I turned the thumb lock, the metal-to-metal sound of the bolt sliding open sent chills down my spine. I opened the door and sensed instantly that I was making a huge mistake.

The alarm began beeping as Sam stepped in. I placed a hand over the keypad and entered the code to shut it down.

"You don't look that good," he said.

"Thanks," I stated with a tone of sarcasm.

Pup growled at Sam as I rolled back to the couch.

"What's wrong with that animal?"

"What animal?" I answered as we sat down.

He furrowed his brow but didn't inquire more about the ugly pup. "Where have you been?"

"Why are you asking me that?"

"I missed you. I thought we had something going, and then you disappeared on me. Why shouldn't I ask?"

I had no idea what *something going* even meant. We'd had sex, but we'd never been on a date. Sam was a problem, and despite the mood-altering substances I'd ingested, I knew it.

I'd always stayed away from guys that were better looking than me. The whole jealousy thing, and people asking stupid questions behind your back, like, *What's he doing with her?* These things led down a path I didn't want to travel.

"I don't think we have anything going. We hooked up. That's it. And besides, I'm with someone else now."

"Nonsense. We have history and chemistry. I don't think you have anyone else, either."

"None of that matters. I don't want to see you. Not here. At work, we can be friendly, but I don't want a sexual relationship with you anymore. Please don't take offense, but I want you to leave."

"Let's have a drink." He ambled to the bar.

"I don't want a drink. I want to go to sleep. I have pain, and I'm not in the mood to see you or anyone else."

He ignored me and poured himself a vodka straight up. And then he made another for me.

He held it in front of my face, and my mouth watered. "Just go."

He handed me the glass, and I sniffed the finely distilled liquid. It was like an old friend I wanted to welcome with open arms.

I took a sip, and it burned nicely down my throat. And soon, it was gone.

My eyes became heavy. Sam spoke, but I couldn't understand what he'd said.

"What?"

"Sally and me. We had this thing, this project we were working on. I invested with her. Put money up for a press. That's what it looks like. And now she's gone, and I need to get it back."

"Machine?"

"Do you know where it is?"

I pictured the contraption I'd seen in the room downstairs and nodded.

"Sally got it for me, and I need to get it because she's... she's gone."

I tried to stand but fell backward. The pain had disappeared, but my head wasn't working right. Everything was moving in slow motion.

"It's downstairs," I slurred.

"Show me."

I pointed to my tricycle crutch, and he fetched it for me.

I tried to get up again but couldn't move.

Sam pulled me up and helped me roll through the kitchen and into the back room. I pointed at the door that led downward.

I felt like I was having an out-of-body experience, but somehow, I had enough sense not to give up my key. I unlocked the door and managed to say, "The room on the left. It's open."

I wheeled back to the couch and collapsed. Through my eye slits, I saw Sam carrying the machine out. And then he went back for the big cardboard box.

I could tell it was heavy by the way he was hunched over. And he had to stop and lean it on the table to get a better grip before heading back out the door.

As he did, something fell out, pinged on the floor, and rolled under the couch.

And then the door finally closed behind him, and I felt a huge weight lift.

I got up and grabbed my crutch as the chime sounded, and the front door opened again. I stared at Sam.

"You got everything?" I asked groggily as I slumped back down.

He sat next to me, shoved a bong in my face, and said, "Take a toke."

I pushed it away. "I'm subject to random drug testing at work."

"If they ask you to do that, tell them to test the managers first. They all get high, you know?"

"Actually, I've never been a fan."

"When was the last time you tried?"

I shrugged. "In college, it made me cough and paranoid."

"It's better now. Smooth and guaranteed to make you feel good. And let's face it, I think you could use some of that."

"No, thanks, really." I held up a hand again.

The next thing I knew, the pipe was in my mouth, and I was inhaling deeply. Sam was right. This stuff was good, and it didn't make me feel bad. I dozed off.

And then I jerked awake with a sense of urgency. And Sam was still there.

"Did we have sex?" I asked.

"What do you take me for? I don't fuck the dead." He kissed me.

"Time to go," I whispered into his ear.

"Let me stay. I'll make us some breakfast in the morning."

"No, please go. I'm in no mood for company."

He stood up, but instead of leaving, he said, "I'm hungry."

"No food in this house."

"I'll order something."

The mention of food made my stomach growl. But I needed Sam to go more than I needed to eat.

"I'll take care of you."

I stood and wobbled in place.

Pup growled at him again.

Sam scowled. "You really got to get rid of that thing."

"I'm lousy company for myself, let alone anyone else. I don't need to be taken care of. I just want to be alone."

"Okay, I'll go, but reluctantly." He sounded sincere. And then he added, "We're together now, right?"

"Just go."

"Promise you're not going to disappear on me again. I was worried when you weren't at work."

Sam left the bong and a baggy full of pot and blew me a kiss as he backed out the door.

After he was gone, I locked the door and set the alarm. I was happy to finally be rid of him and wondered why he hadn't asked what happened to my leg.

For the next couple of days, I didn't do much other than sleep and lie around, trying to heal with the help of the Percocet, Sally's OxyContin, and liquor.

I don't know if anyone broke in during that time because I was utterly incoherent and out of it and didn't care one way or another.

Somewhere along the way, I'd begun sleeping in the bedroom. The door had a solid lock, and I felt more secure there.

The rolling crutch worked well around the house except for the stairs. I had to crawl up and down and drag the crutch behind me.

31
CHAPTER

I woke up in pain and disoriented. The blinds were closed, and the light leaked through, so I suspected it to be daytime. And at first, I didn't know where I was.

My heart raced, my head hurt, and my stomach stirred. I stood up, and the room spun around a few times before I managed to pull myself up and hop to the bathroom in time to throw up. I splashed cold water on my face and then took two Oxys.

Making my way back downstairs took a lot of effort. I crawled downward, dragging the roller behind me.

By the time I reached the couch, I was exhausted. I lay down and fell asleep.

I woke to my cell phone ringing, and Mr. Ranger's voice sounded in my ear.

"I've got good news for you, Ms. Laine," he said.

"Great," I mumbled.

"The money will be coming to you. But it will have to go through probate, which will take a few months. And the IRA will create a taxing event. I have a good CPA that can help you with that. I'll also need you to come in and sign some paperwork to get the process started. When would you like to schedule an appointment?"

"I'll have to get back to you about that."

As I hung up, I wondered what was wrong with me. This was a lot of money, and it was mine. *Why wasn't I trying to get it?*

Drugs and alcohol were numbing my mind.

I tried to lift my hand to slap my face but couldn't make an effort. I closed my eyes and dozed off again.

When I woke up the next time, the light of the moon and streetlights shone through the stained glass, projecting colorful shards throughout the room.

It was 2:00 a.m., and my timing was off. I was sleeping when I should be awake and awake when I should be sleeping. And my ankle was throbbing.

Pup was out of food, so I gave him the steak I had set out to thaw.

And then I sat down at the desk, rolled back the top, and scribbled a list.

Stop drinking and taking pills.
Eat healthier.
Learn how to protect myself.
Deal with work: Quit/not quit?
Call Denny.
Sign papers.
Pay past-due rent.
Move out of apartment.
Get rid of pot.
Find Sally's killer.

My list was beginning to strangle me.

I crossed off *stop drinking and taking pills* and wrote *slow down* on the first item. And then I rolled to the bar, grabbed the open bottle of wine, and crawled upstairs. I took two pain pills, washed them down with a glass of wine, and turned on the TV, settling on a marathon of *Law and Order* as I drained the glass of wine.

And that's the last thing I remembered until the sun came up.

CHAPTER 32

Then came the day that my life changed forever.

I was very sick when I woke up the next day, and I knew something was really wrong.

I could barely open my eyes. Sitting up was a real chore, and my heart wasn't beating right. I dragged myself downstairs and drank some water.

The clock said it was ten o'clock, but I couldn't tell whether it was day or night until I looked up at the colorful windows and saw the moon shining through the darkness.

I drank more water and managed to heat up a bowl of soup. But I could hardly get the spoon to my lips without shaking most of the nourishment off. I finally poured what I could manage into a cup and drank the broth holding the cup with both hands to steady it enough to get it to my mouth.

I looked at the liquor cabinet and longed for a drink, but I resisted for about five minutes.

After a shot of vodka and a pill, I felt better. Not good, but better.

And then my phone beeped.

As I lifted the cell, I noticed there were numerous missed calls over the last few days.

I didn't recognize the most recent number, and it had registered less than half an hour earlier. And before that, Ellie had called. Before that, I'd gotten a call from work and several from Denny. My heart skipped a beat.

I called Ellie back, and it went straight to voice mail.

I called the number I didn't recognize, and a woman's voice answered, "Palm Beach Sheriff's Office, how may I direct your call?"

"Wrong number," I answered.

As I hung up, my phone rang. It was Ellie, and she had been arrested.

I dressed quickly and called for an Uber and mentally patted myself on the back for knowing enough not to drive.

CHAPTER 33

On the way to the police station, I gave the driver an extra twenty to make a quick stop at a convenience store. I picked up a couple of packs of NoDoz and a diet soda because I could hardly keep my eyes open.

I popped four tablets into my mouth at the register and chased them with the soda before paying.

The clerk looked at me and said in a Middle Eastern accent, "Eye drops."

"What?"

"You need eye drops too. Very red. And breath mints."

I nodded, and he added a small bottle of VISINE and mints to my purchase.

At the police station, I identified myself and said I was here to pick up Ellie.

A hefty female wearing a uniform too tight for her bulk sat behind the bulletproof enclosure. The name tag pinned to her chest indicated she was Sergeant Aberdeen. She smirked, pointed at a row of uncomfortable-looking chairs lined against the wall, and said, "Wait there."

I followed her directions and took a seat. Despite the NoDoz and the hard chair, I dozed off.

I was awoken by a man and a woman yelling at Sergeant Aberdeen. He was at least six feet tall, black, and towered over her. She was thin as a rail, white, and disheveled. Their clothes were ragged and dirty.

Apparently, they were in dispute with another street person about a grocery cart full of their stuff.

He opened his mouth, exposed rotten teeth, and stated, "He wants to put his stuff with ours. I don't want it, and I'm not having it!"

The woman didn't speak. She hid behind the man as if she wasn't even there.

He said, "I picked up the cart, and he has no rights to it. He claims grocery carts belong to everyone. But I own it 'cause I'm the one that wheeled it up from Winn-Dixie."

Aberdeen stated, "The cart doesn't belong to either one of you. It belongs back at Winn-Dixie."

"No, it don't! Everybody knows that carts are for everybody to use, dumb bitch."

"Look. We can go back and forth about this until I reach my limit and I come out there and arrest you, or you can get out of my lobby and deal with this on your own."

"You can't arrest me for filing a complaint."

"I can arrest you for the theft of a grocery cart valued at around one hundred dollars. Or you can leave right now. Those are the only choices you're going to get."

He smiled stupidly and replied, "I'd like to see you try."

The woman behind him grabbed the man's arm and pleaded, "Come on, Adahay. We don't need no trouble."

He should have listened to Sergeant Aberdeen and his girlfriend, but instead, he pounded on the glass and screamed, "You ain't got the balls to do it! You ain't even got balls!"

Aberdeen pressed a button on the console in front of her. Within seconds, a squad of four uniforms raced out of a door from somewhere in the back. They grabbed hold of Adahay, slammed him to the floor, handcuffed him, and carried him away. The woman ran out of the door, and I was alone again.

It wasn't long after that the door opened, and Detective Warren walked over and took a chair next to me. He was past sixty, gray haired, and wrinkled.

"Are you Ms. Laine?" he asked politely.

"Do you have news about my daughter?" I asked.

"She's in lockup and will have to stay until morning when she'll be arraigned before a judge."

"Why?"

"She's charged with drug trafficking with intent to sell."

"There must be some mistake. My daughter doesn't even do drugs."

"There's always a first time. Parents are usually the last to know."

"She's never been in trouble."

"The judge may have mercy on her and set a low bail."

"How much is that?"

"Depends on the circumstances. My advice to you is to contact a bail bondsman. He'll know what to do."

"Can I see her?"

"Not tonight. Looks like you could use some sleep anyway."

I rubbed my eyes. "You're probably right."

"Do you need me to call someone for you?"

"I can handle it."

He pursed his lips and said, "Whatever you do, don't drive."

"I Ubered here, and that's how I'm leaving."

He nodded. "Good luck."

I rolled to the street. As I waited, I felt the pulse in my neck. My heart was beating crazily. I was dizzy, and I sat down on the curb.

I was happy to see the same Uber driver as before, and he was all too willing to take me wherever I wanted to go because of the big tip I'd laid on him for my earlier trip.

I'd entered my address as my destination on the app. But when I climbed into the front seat of the car, I told the driver to take me to the all-night walk-in clinic around the corner instead.

CHAPTER 34

I lay on the examination table in a small room. A dark-skinned medical assistant with a Spanish accent took my blood pressure and then drew some vials of blood.

"How did you hurt your ankle?" she asked.

"I fell downstairs." I was so weak I could barely speak.

She gave me a cup and asked for a sample. I climbed off the table with great effort, and she helped me roll to the restroom.

Soon I was back dozing in and out as I waited for the doctor. After what seemed like hours, a very tall, thin woman appeared at my side.

Her face matched her body, slim and long. Her name tag indicated "Hatfield, MD." Other than her white coat, she wore a look of concern.

"What's up?" I asked. "Am I dying or something?"

"No," she answered frankly. "But you may want to make some changes to your lifestyle if you want to reach old age."

I gulped. "I drink a bit but usually don't take pills." I held up my cast leg. I didn't think I needed to say more.

"You're pretty run-down and anemic. I'm going to give you a B_{12} shot that should help you feel better. And I've got some iron tablets for you to take."

She paused as she looked away.

"And you're pregnant."

Her words hung in the air like a bad smell.

"Jesus Christ," I mumbled.

I began breathing deeply, tried to calm myself, but couldn't.

I pointed to a nearby box of latex gloves. She handed me one, and I held it over my mouth and nose.

Eventually, I relaxed and could breathe normally. But it still felt like I'd just taken a punch to my chest.

"Now let's talk about options."

"Options?"

"You may want to consider termination."

My mind whirled.

"It's apparent that you've consumed a lot of alcohol and been taking other powerful pain meds."

"They were prescribed by a doctor."

"And that doctor didn't know you were with child. These things can have a detrimental effect on a fetus."

"But not for sure. Isn't that right?"

"Are you planning to maintain your lifestyle or to keep the baby?"

I couldn't answer right away, and she stood silent for a few seconds.

I finally replied, "I don't know."

"If you do decide to continue the pregnancy, you'll need to discontinue all pain medications and quit drinking at once. Do you think you can do that?"

I blew out a gust of air. Thoughts raced through my mind. But not about termination. I was concerned about what I'd done to the baby.

And who was the father? I hoped with all my heart that it wasn't Sam's. He had the looks and was reasonably intelligent, but I didn't want him in my life. And I prayed it wasn't the other recent mistake, Benny. But who else had there been? Denny would have been my choice, but we hadn't had sex, so it couldn't be him. I'd been drugged with roofies and was sure I'd been with someone but couldn't remember who.

And then I thought again about all the bad things I could have done to this poor child.

I was crushed with dread.

"Do you know how far along I am?" I was barely able to squeak out the words.

"Does it matter?"

I looked away. "I don't know anything right now."

"I'll give you a referral for an ob-gyn. They can help you with that."

After she left, I called another Uber. A different driver showed up, and I gave him a twenty to make a stop at an all-night Burger King. I bought two Whoppers, one for me and one for him.

Back at home, I took an iron pill and forced myself to eat. I could barely finish a quarter of the sandwich, but it was better than nothing—more food than I'd had in over a week. And a Whopper was meat, cheese, lettuce, and tomatoes, so in my opinion, that covered most of the food groups.

I gave Pup the rest of my sandwich, and he was so grateful that he wagged his body as he scarfed it up.

35
CHAPTER

It was 4:00 a.m., and I needed to sleep. I wanted a drink and a pill, but I took a long shower instead. It seemed like that was one of the few places I didn't crave for mood-altering substances.

And then I tossed and turned for a while before I finally gave up and made coffee.

I found a loaf of bread in the freezer and toasted, buttered, and ate quickly.

The alarm rang at eight, but I was already dressed and ready to go. I gathered my backpack and stuffed it with cash. I looked around. My eyes focused on the bong and the baggy of pot still on the coffee table. I shoved the paraphernalia into a desk drawer and ordered another Uber.

I arrived at Best Bail Bonds, conveniently located around the corner to the courthouse, and met with Gordon Best.

"Call me Gordy," said a robust man dressed in a wife-beater and jungle-shaded combat pants. "The charge is 15 percent, which you never get back, even if the client keeps their word and appears in court at the designated time. And I'll need collateral. What do you own?"

"Why?"

"Here's how it works, lady. Say the judge has mercy on your daughter and sets bail at fifty grand. I tell the court I'm good for it, and they say okay. But first, you gotta prove you're good for all of it, or there's no deal. I can't hang myself out for the whole enchilada unless you give me an assurance of assets enough to cover my ass."

He hesitated and stared at the ceiling before asking, "Capisce?"

"Sure. I've got cash. Is that okay?" I pulled a bundle out of my backpack.

He smiled broadly and answered, "Cash is good. But hold off until we find out what's happening. Now what about collateral?"

"I own a house."

"What's your name?"

"Annie Laine."

He typed on his keyboard. "I don't see anything."

"It was recent."

"Not good enough, Ms. Laine. I need to see it on the county's appraiser website to believe it."

"But I have cash."

"Her bail could be high. You got fifty grand or more?"

"Maybe." I wanted to save the money for a defense attorney. But getting her out of jail was the most important thing at the time.

"Maybe don't cut it. I think we're done here."

"Please help me. My daughter is innocent, and it'll all get straightened out. It was a big mistake."

"If I had a penny for as many times as I heard that, I'd be a wealthy man."

"I have a relatively new BMW." I took the key fob out of my bag.

"Got the pink slip?"

"It should be in my name by now."

"Let me take a peek."

He typed feverishly on his keyboard and found that Attorney Ranger had done a stellar job transferring the Beamer into my name. It turned out that the Blue Book value was around ninety thousand dollars. *I had no idea.*

He told me to call when I knew more, and I was off to the courthouse.

CHAPTER 36

I was surprised to see the state of my daughter as she was led into the courtroom through a side door. She was dressed in a wrinkled T-shirt and sweatpants, and her hair was stringy. Her eyes were red, and her makeup was smeared.

This was my child, my claim to fame, the only thing I'd gotten right in my life. My heart ached for her, and my heart broke for me. I had failed her. Somehow this was my fault. I hadn't given her enough advice, or maybe I'd given too much. Whatever it was, the blame fell on me, and it was a heavy burden.

Ellie glanced around the courtroom. When her eyes found me, she seemed to exhale with relief. And then her shoulders slumped, and she shook as she wept.

The bailiff called the court to order, and the Honorable Judge Barry Carp entered.

He was tall, nearly six and a half feet, and his hands were blemished with brown age spots. He had gray hair and eyebrows that shadowed his eyes like the visor of a baseball cap. And he had rosy cheeks. As he passed the court reporter, I noticed his belly protruding under the robe draped across his body.

I recognized him as a regular at the five-ten no-limit table at the Boat. He drank Dewars scotch, straight up, and plenty of it. And over the years, he'd lost a lot of money.

He was always pleasant to me, and we'd shared many smiles and winks along the way. He'd flirted even though he wore a wedding band. I didn't mind because he tipped well.

But eventually, he would reach a limit after five or six of his double shots, and there would be no more winks or tips. When Carp became intoxicated, he hated everyone. He'd been asked to leave on a couple of occasions because of his verbal abuse and threatening behavior.

So we had a bit of history. But under these circumstances, I had no idea whether that was good or bad.

And I would soon find out that Judge Carp was intolerant of drug dealers and drug abusers.

A few defendants were summoned before Ellie, and I began to see a pattern forming. He would listen to the charges and hear the defense attorney, which was the same tired-looking public defender for the most part, and all defendants pleaded innocent. He would then set bail based on if it was first, second, or many more offenses. Then he would pound his gavel loudly and shout, "Next."

And in my layman's opinion, Judge Carp's idea of reasonable bail was unreasonable.

My hands were shaking, and I felt like bugs were crawling all over me.

Finally, Ellie stood before Carp with the same worn-out public defender at her side. His name was Enrico Diaz.

She leaned over, whispered something to him, and they both looked in my direction.

The bailiff read aloud, "Defendant is charged with willingly and knowingly trafficking illegal drugs on public school property, Your Honor."

I took one big breath, but it didn't satisfy me. I had no idea Ellie was selling drugs at school.

Judge Carp asked, "How do you plead."

Ellie replied softly, "Not guilty."

I took more air into my lungs, wanted to scream, but somehow found the strength to restrain myself. It felt like a hundred-pound gorilla was sitting on my chest as I pulled a latex glove from my pocket and breathed into it.

As I calmed, I quickly searched my phone. I found that trafficking drugs in schools was a first-degree felony punishable by up to thirty years in prison, and I nearly fainted.

Diaz added, "Ms. Laine doesn't have a record and has strong ties to the community. She is a college student in good standing, and her mother is in the courtroom today, Your Honor."

Diaz turned and pointed in my direction. I wanted to slide down in my seat and disappear, but I sat tall, so he could see me. Carp's eyes opened wide, and I sensed he recognized me. But I still didn't know if that was good or bad. Whichever way things turned out, I was going to accept my responsibility as her mother.

Judge Carp hesitated and then shouted, "Bail set at one hundred thousand dollars!" My chest heaved as I placed the glove over my face again.

I can do this, I reassured myself. I'd give Gordy fifteen thousand in cash to post bail and have plenty left to pay for a first-class attorney.

I stood as they led Ellie back out the door she'd entered earlier, and then I raced out of the courtroom.

Back at Best Bail Bonds, I unloaded fifteen thousand dollars from my backpack onto Gordy's desk. He fed the bills into a cash counting machine and nodded. He gave me a receipt, we signed paperwork, and then he told me to go to the county jail next to the courthouse and wait.

It took two hours before Ellie burst through the door. My daughter was safe, and I was going to do whatever was necessary to clear her name.

As we stood waiting for an Uber, Ellie cried and said, "I'm so sorry, Mom."

"What happened?" I asked, hoping she had some explanation that would exonerate her. I waited for her to say it was a mistake or that she'd been framed.

But instead, she said, "I shouldn't have agreed to do it in the first place. I was so stupid. After I had time to think, I said no. But I couldn't get out of it."

37
CHAPTER

As the Uber drove, my cell rang. It was the human resource manager, Anita, and she asked me if I'd gotten her messages about stopping by with a doctor's note before returning to work.

I replied, "Sure. It's just that things are a little hectic for me right now. I need a few more days."

"We're busy, Annie. The season is here. We've got a big tournament coming up, and we need you working."

I promised I would be by soon. I had plenty of cash, but I didn't know how much Ellie's defense would cost. And I still needed to go to the attorney and sign those papers before he could start the probate process for big money, which would take a while.

I handed the driver a twenty and asked him to stop at the grocery store.

I gave Ellie cash for a large bag of puppy chow and to get whatever she needed, and she was back in no time.

As the driver took off toward our final destination, Ellie asked what had happened to my leg.

I told her a short version of the long saga that involved my recent misadventures.

As we pulled up to the door, Denny was standing outside. He was dressed in a sport coat, tie, and matching slacks. He grabbed the puppy chow from Ellie and followed us inside.

The ugly pup met us at the door, and Denny gave him a look but didn't say anything.

Ellie said, "I need to take a bath and soak the last two days off me."

I directed her to the room with the canopy bed.

And then I got back to Denny.

"I've been trying to reach you, Annie. How are you?" Denny asked.

"Not too good, I'm afraid," I said. "It feels like my life is falling apart before my eyes. Do you know anything about what Ellie's involved in?"

"I talked to the arresting DEA agent. Apparently, she was caught with a backpack jammed full of CRYOVAC packs of OxyContin."

"Dear God. Why?"

"She's the only one that can tell you, but I'll do what I can to help."

I looked him up and down and said, "You look nice."

He smiled. "I was in court on another case. Did she say anything to you?"

"Only that she was sorry and that she tried to get out but couldn't."

"Well, that's something. Is there anything I can do for you?" He looked at the cast on my foot.

"You have no idea."

"You want to get something to eat?"

I stared back. He knew nothing about my problems, and if he did, I was sure he would be hightailing it out of there.

"I've got a lot of things going on with me right now. And I don't think it would be good to drag you down with me."

"Drag me down? Not very likely."

"You don't know what you're saying. I've done some—"

He interrupted. "Try me," he said as he drew me to him. "You're important to me, and I want to help any way I can."

I melted as I tried to compose my thoughts. If I told him everything, there was a good chance he would be sympathetic, leave, and never come back. If I didn't, when he found out, he would never trust me again. Either way, there was a good chance this romance was over before it began.

I led him to the couch, and we sat down.

I began with the small stuff. "I'm pretty sure I'm an alcoholic. And I've taken too many pain pills. You probably know by now that I was found naked on the lawn and woke up in the psych ward of the local hospital."

He said nothing.

"Cops talk, I know. But I can explain. I was drugged with roofies. I don't know how it happened because I can't remember."

"It doesn't matter," he said.

"How can it not? I'm probably the big joke of the sheriff's office."

"No one thinks that."

"A little kid saw me naked on the grass."

He smiled and shrugged. "Things happen sometimes. Hopefully, it'll never occur again."

He squeezed my hand. "You've got to do better than that to get rid of me."

I exhaled. "I'm pregnant."

He didn't let go of my hand, but he sat back a little. "You're certainly full of surprises." Denny raised an eyebrow.

"I knew that would be a deal-breaker." I pulled my hand away and ran my fingers through my hair.

"I didn't say that. What now?"

"I'm going to have it," I said as I realized I'd made the decision.

"Okay."

"Okay, what?"

"You're going to have a baby. Want to celebrate?"

I laughed. "How do you want to do that? Champagne? Vodka, straight up? Apparently, I'm having a lot of issues with withdrawal symptoms from alcohol and opiates. It feels like bugs are crawling on me. And it's only been a few hours. Anything you can do about that?"

"Have you given any thought to rehab?"

"That takes time. I don't know how much Ellie's defense is going to cost, and I need to get back to work."

He leaned close like he was about to disclose a big secret and whispered, "I have friends who can help you."

I scoffed. "What kind of people help with these sorts of things?" I began scratching. The bugs were back, and they were worse than ever.

"Good friends. And especially someone who helped me when I was in the same way as you are now."

"What are you saying?"

"I've been there."

"Wow."

"You're not the only one with surprises."

He kissed me, and I forgot about my pain, and my skin stopped itching.

CHAPTER 38

I left food and water for Pup and checked on Ellie before going to get something to eat. She was sound asleep with pictures of fairy tales dancing on the walls.

Denny drove my car to Chili's, and we ate hamburgers and fries, and at first, we talked about everything except our lives.

After eating half a burger and a few fries, I was done. I settled back and watched Denny finish his food.

His eyes were bright and sea blue with flecks of yellow—beautiful eyes—and I imagined him as the father of my baby. That would make everything okay. But I was jerked back to reality when Denny said, "Tell me."

"What?" I asked innocently.

"Tell me about you. Your life and family."

"Why is that important?"

"I'm curious. I want to know all about you. But if you're not ready, that's okay."

I bit my lip. I didn't know where to begin.

"I'll tell you what," he said. "Let me fill you in with a few details about me, and then you can decide."

I nodded, thinking his story would never compete with mine.

"I was married to Olivia and delighted with my life and my wife. It was wonderful. I thanked God every day."

He looked out the window and then back.

"I graduated high school at sixteen and started college right away. After graduation, I enrolled in the police academy."

"As a cop, I was on a fast track to the top. I aced the sergeant and lieutenant exams, and I was promoted to detective. I dressed in a suit and solved crimes. I came home one day, and Liv told me the good news. She was pregnant. Life couldn't get any better."

His eyes turned downward in silence.

I asked, "What happened?"

"They found a lump. Turned out to be a very aggressive form of cancer. The doctor told her to abort because she would never make it if she didn't. She didn't want to, but I begged her. She was my world. I told her we could have more babies after she was well but that I would never make it without her."

"She got the abortion," Denny went on, "but it didn't matter. Three months from diagnosis to death. And it was painful, depressing, and so very hopeless."

"My life crashed, and I tried to drink myself to death. I nearly lost my job. Got caught driving drunk and got demoted back to uniform, but it didn't stop me. I still drank. Every day, all day long."

"How did you quit?" I asked.

He smiled. "How do you know I didn't?"

"You don't drink now."

He shook his head. "I've been sober for five years. Working back took a lot. It was really hard. But I had to do it or die."

"I quit the first time for six months and celebrated with a couple of beers. I ended up with my car wrapped around a tree—a one-car accident. I broke my leg and hurt my back, and ended up in the hospital. My Captain came to see me, and he said that I was history. My life as a cop was over.

"I thought I didn't care. On the third day there, I began to itch, and then I had a seizure. They put me on Dilantin.

"While I was recovering, someone came to see me. And I wasn't too happy that this guy was interfering with my life's mission to obliterate myself.

"At first, he dropped off literature. I never looked at it and threw it away as soon as he was out the door. But he came back, and he kept on coming back.

"I was depressed, and I asked the stranger to do me a favor and bring some pills and booze next time so I could just end it.

"After I got out, I started right back where I'd left off. A week later, I ended up in a watery ditch. Somehow, I'd managed to pass out with my head above water. I should have drowned.

"I pulled myself out, muddy and soaked to the bone. I could barely walk. I couldn't find my car, my wallet was missing, and I had no idea where I was.

"I tried to get a ride, but no one would pick me up looking like that. So I walked until I came to a gas station. I was in Texas, near Lubbock, and didn't know how I got there. The guy behind the counter was about to call the cops. He wanted me out of his store. But I talked him into letting me use his phone.

"He finally agreed. Then I couldn't think of anyone to call. I thanked him and started to walk away. And then I remembered the man in the hospital. It took me a few minutes to remember his name. He'd said to call him, and he would come and get me no matter where I was or what I'd done—but I doubted it.

"I dialed information, and he was listed. He answered the phone, and I told him I was in a bad way, both physically and mentally, and I wasn't very handsome. I was covered in mud and soaking wet."

"He said to give the phone back to the clerk. They talked for a few minutes, and then he wrote down a credit card number. After he hung up, he ran the card, handed me three hundred dollars, and then pointed me in the direction of the bus station. But first, he gave me the key to the men's room and said to clean up.

"His name is Perce Murphy. I call him Percy, and he's my best friend."

A chill ran through me.

"He's also my sponsor with AA."

I swallowed hard. "Do you want me to go to AA?"

"You have to be willing."

"I still want to drink and take drugs," I admitted.

"It's hard. I fight the urge every day. But it gets easier. If you're serious about having this baby, you'll need help. Percy helped me, and he can do the same for you."

"Is that why you're here? Am I your project? Are you here to save me from myself?"

"No, Annie." He smiled. "I care about you." He looked away. "I'm not good at this because it's been a long time since I tried, and I'm really not sure how to go about it. But I want to be with you. I'm here because I really like you, more than just a friend."

I had to force myself to take a breath.

"I've had one relationship in my life. And that was years ago, and I'm out of practice. I've always liked you. But you were one of the in crowd, and I was just me, hanging out, watching from the sidelines.

"You're the first one," he continued. "You're the first one since Liv passed away."

"I hope I don't disappoint you," I said because it was the only thing I could think of.

"Don't worry about me. Take care of yourself."

I scratched my arm.

"Still feeling itchy?"

"Yes."

"It's going to get worse. You're in danger of having seizures, and you're not going to be able to do this on your own."

"I can't go to rehab. I need to work."

"No, you don't," he stated firmly.

"I need to help Ellie."

"You're sick. They'll wait for you, and if not, so what? You'll get another job, but you only have one life, and now you have another that needs taking care of."

My mind whirled as thoughts bombarded my skull.

"Would you like to meet my friend?"

CHAPTER 39

Denny drove to the Evangelical Lutheran church off Federal Highway, where we entered an AA meeting in full progress.

The smell of coffee brewing sickened me. I stood against the back wall listening but not actually hearing members giving testimonials as others applauded at their horror stories and offered support.

Darkness surrounded me as I slid down the wall to the floor. Denny sat down next to me and put his arm around me.

Finally, the meeting was over, and I watched as legs and feet passed by and disappeared out the door.

A small, thin freckle-faced man with a friendly smile sat down on the other side, took my hand, and I began to sob.

"I'm sorry," I babbled.

"It's okay. Everything's going to be fine," the man said.

"But my heart doesn't beat right, and I'm really sick, and I want a drink so bad, it hurts."

"What's your name?"

"Annie Laine."

"Hello, Annie Laine. My name is Perce Murphy, and I'm an alcoholic. But you can call me Percy."

"Can you help me?" Tears streamed down my face.

"Time is an issue," Denny said. "She doesn't have twenty-eight days, so conventional methods won't work. She needs special handling."

Percy nodded. "I'll take it from here."

"Call me when she's ready."

Denny kissed me on the top of my head, stood, and walked away.

Percy reached up to a nearby table and grabbed a piece of candy. As he handed it to me, he said, "Have a piece of fudge."

"No, thank you. Candy's never been my weakness."

"It'll make you feel better. Sugar and chocolate help."

I took a bite of the fudge and swallowed quickly. And then another bite. And then another piece. Eventually, I did feel a little better, but I was nowhere near back to normal. I was still shaking, and my brain felt like it was on fire.

After my sugar fest, Percy began, "You can't do this alone."

"I do most things alone."

"Not this. And I'm going to call someone to help. You need to detox."

"How long does that take? I have to be at work in the morning."

He laughed.

And then I began babbling about my friend being murdered, my job, and the money needed for my daughter's legal difficulties. "I drink because of my problems," I stated.

"I hear that all the time. But the truth is drinking causes more problems and solves none."

I knew he was right, but it didn't matter to me at the time.

I blurted out, "And I'm pregnant."

"Dear God." He laughed and handed me a tissue. "Let me make a call. And you must promise not to drink anymore while you're pregnant."

"I promise."

He laughed again. "That's what everybody says."

CHAPTER 40

We left the building through the back door. Percy led me to his van, and I got in without reservations. He was a stranger, but I was confident that he was going to help me.

I slept for a few minutes on the way to a storefront, and when Percy helped me out of the van, my legs felt like rubber.

He knocked on the glass door, and I met another stranger.

Grace Klein was short, chubby, and cute with wild curly hair. She had a permanent look of concern on her face and was wearing a white blouse with a doctor's coat over the top.

"This is her, huh?" Grace asked rhetorically.

"The one I called you about," Percy replied as if I wasn't there.

She glanced up and down at me. "You're a little thin."

"I've lost weight recently, but I think I've regained my appetite. At least for burgers and fudge."

"Add some fruit, and you're good to go."

Grace led me into the back. She handed me a cup and told me to give her a sample. When I returned, she took some blood and instructed me to lie down on a gurney.

She inserted a needle into my arm, and fluids dripped into my veins.

I began feeling better almost instantly. "What's in the bag?"

"Saline. You're dehydrated."

She shoved a release at me, and I signed it without reading.

"I'm pregnant," I said.

"Congratulations. I hope the father is supportive."

"Is this conversation confidential?"

"Of course."

"Can you do an HIV test?"

"I can do that."

"I don't know who the father is, and I've had sex at least once without consenting. I was drugged."

"Oh my."

She inserted a needle into the line, and I fell asleep.

I woke up a little later, and Grace was there by my side. She'd changed into green scrubs.

"How are you feeling, dear?"

"Good," I said.

"Here's the deal." She leaned against the wall as she explained. "You've got to eat regularly. Even if you're feeling sick, force it. If you throw up, eat some more. You'd be surprised how much nutrition the body retains. And drink plenty of water."

"That's it?"

"I'm not finished. Take these." Grace handed me a bottle of prenatal vitamins. "Take a couple right away. Get plenty of rest. Even if you can't sleep, lie down for at least eight hours out of a day. And you're going to need a lot of chocolate."

"You and Percy are big on candy."

"Chocolate increases the levels of endorphins. It should make you feel better."

"Anything would be an improvement."

"No doubt. Some say that yoga helps."

"I'm not a big fan of organized exercise."

She handed me another bottle of pills and said, "If things get bad, take one of these."

I looked at the amber bottle of little orange pills without a label and asked, "What is this?"

"A mild tranquilizer."

"No, thanks." I handed them back to her. "No more drugs. I'm not taking anything that could hurt my baby."

"That's what you say now. But the symptoms will return, and you may become distressed to the point that it will put your health and unborn child at risk."

She gave them back. "Just in case."

I stuffed them into my backpack, just in case.

She stopped the IV, pulled the needle out of my arm, and placed a Band-Aid over the hole in my skin.

"Getting through this isn't going to be easy."

"I'll do what's necessary."

"You say that now."

"You said that before."

"And I meant it both times."

"How much do I owe you?"

"The supplies and tests cost about five hundred dollars."

I reached into my bag and pulled out my debit card.

"Sorry, cash only."

I looked at my watch. "I have some at home but need to go now and get ready for work. Are you going to be here later?"

"It's okay."

"I have money, and I will pay you. I'm so grateful and can't begin to tell you how much better I feel."

"Call Percy if you want to give us something. He'll handle it." She handed me a piece of paper. "These are the results of your tests. Take them with you when you go to your ob-gyn. Good news is the HIV test was negative. But you'll need to be retested again in a month. Your doctor can handle that from this point on."

I sprang from the storefront, where Percy was waiting. He escorted me to the open door of the van, and I slid inside.

He sat down in the driver's seat, smiled, and said, "You look almost human."

"That's something," I replied.

"You're going to go through a lot. For months, you'll crave hard. Please consider attending meetings." He handed me a paper with a list of locations.

I stuffed it into my backpack, knowing I would never go.

"Also, it helps to have a happy place to go to in your mind. Think about a time or place where things were joyful and peaceful for you. If you can't come up with anything, make something up. A beautiful garden, a beach, or a calming lake. Water has a soothing effect on most people."

A happy place. I thought about the beach. When Ellie was a girl, we'd escape there when things were terrible in my marriage. I knew I would never attend meetings, but the happy place seemed doable.

Denny was waiting in the parking lot when we returned to the church.

I hopped out of the van and limped to Denny's car.

I got in and asked, "What time is it?"

He raised an eyebrow and said, "Nine AM."

"I've got to go to work."

"You know you went through detox, right?"

"And I feel so much better, thank you."

"It took a little longer than you think."

I bit my lip. "How long?"

"Three days," he said sheepishly.

"How could that happen without me knowing?"

He took my hand and gazed into my eyes. "I misled you, and I won't apologize for it. I will honor your decisions from this point on, and I make no excuses for what I did. And you have to believe me when I say I'm going to be here for the long haul."

"You don't care that I might start drinking and taking drugs any minute? You don't care about how I've lived my life up until now? How many mistakes I've made? How can you—"

He placed his finger on my lips to silence me.

"I don't care about anything except us. I'm here for you in whatever way you want or need."

He pulled me toward him and kissed me.

CHAPTER

41

Denny said he'd called into work and lied about where I was. He told George that I had pneumonia and would need a few more days. He also presented me with a note from Dr. Klein as proof of the lie.

On the way, we stopped at the grocery store and bought a lot of food.

At home, Pup wagged his body, happy to see me.

Denny cooked breakfast. And then he picked me up and carried me upstairs.

Keeping busy helped the urge to drink dissipate, and sex sure did the trick. But afterward, my skin was crawling again, and I thought, *If I could just have sex and live in the shower, I'd be fine.*

We camped out in bed most of the day, making love and talking.

And I shared some things about my life. "After I finished college, Hank, my ex-husband, continued on and got his master's in English and began teaching at the local college. We split up because he couldn't stop humping his female students. He said the girls came on to him, and he couldn't resist. He eventually impregnated one of them and left when Ellie was ten."

I took a breath, and then I continued, "Ellie tried to call him and found out he'd moved away without telling her."

I told him I had two brothers and a sister, but I left out the part about my mother being a real bitch. I never knew why, but she'd always treated me poorly. I was afraid he'd think there was something wrong with me if my own mother hated me, so I thought I'd save that for another time.

Eventually, he had to go to work.

"Are you going to be okay?" he asked.

"I'll be fine," I said, but I wasn't sure. My ankle was aching, and I was craving hard.

"Oh, and there's one more thing I should mention, and it's a big one."

"This has got to be good." Denny cringed.

"There's a room underneath us that's filled with marijuana plants growing like crazy. And I don't know how to get rid of that mess."

"Got to hand it to you, Annie."

"Any ideas?"

He furrowed his brow and shook his head. "Let me give it some thought."

After he left, I hobbled downstairs and wheeled around the big room with Pup trailing along behind me. I palmed a couple of Tylenol we'd picked up at the store and grabbed a bottle of water. I turned on the TV and sat down on the couch.

I was a little shaky, and when I tried to put the pills in my mouth, I dropped one, and it rolled under the couch.

I leaned down and felt around for the pill but came up with a round clay disk.

I stared at it as I rubbed it between my fingers. I'd touched hundreds of thousands, maybe millions of these. I didn't know the exact dimensions, but I knew it was a blank chip.

Pup sat down in front of me.

"What do you think?"

All he offered was a throaty rumble.

This was what I heard pinging as it hit the tile floor when Sam picked up the heavy box from downstairs.

I thought back and wondered how he'd known where I lived. As far as I knew, I'd never told anyone my new address except for Ellie and Denny.

I tossed the chip aside and spent the rest of the day trying not to think as I kept busy straightening up around the house.

When I became shaky or the cravings returned, I ate chocolate.

I had a salad and a bowl of soup for dinner, went to bed around ten, and tossed and turned, craving alcohol, drugs, and Denny.

42
CHAPTER

The following day, Ellie made breakfast. I don't know what it is about bacon, but it always makes me smile.

I tossed Pup a piece, and he was so pleased about it that his whole body shook with joy.

We ate in silence at first until she asked, "Do you want to know what happened?"

"I'm listening," I said.

"I didn't know I was transporting drugs."

I bit my lip and held my tongue.

She looked away. "Well, I may have had an idea that it was something that might have been illegal. But no one came right out and said it."

"You didn't ask?"

She shook her head. "I was being paid a lot of money not to ask questions."

"Who are these people?"

She looked at the floor. "I don't want to tell you."

"After the first time, I told him I didn't want to do it anymore. But he insisted. Said I needed to finish what I started or else."

"Who is he?"

She looked away. "A menacing voice on the phone. And I'm still scared."

"No one can get to you if you're here with me. I won't let anyone hurt you."

She cried and shoved her plate away.

I pulled her toward me. "Denny said he'd help. I'll call my attorney, and he'll refer us to someone specializing in this sort of thing. Everything's going to be all right."

CHAPTER 43

When Denny returned the next day, he asked to see the grow room, and he followed as I crept down the stairs.

At the bottom, Denny looked around, sniffed the air, and said, "This is amazing."

"You haven't seen anything yet," I said with a grin as I opened the door.

"Right where you said it would be."

"It really stinks."

"Good stuff."

"You come up with an idea on how to get rid of it?"

"I got a guy."

"What about the legal ramifications of having drugs in my house?"

"You moved in without prior knowledge of this, is that correct?"

I nodded and tried to smile, but my ankle was throbbing.

"I'll handle it."

He tilted his head and grinned. "Or you could go into the business."

"Thank you, but I'm good. I don't need any more problems."

"I've got a friend. A cop that owes me one. That's the way we work sometimes. He'll dispose of it without reporting."

My chest relaxed, and I began to breathe again. We got back upstairs and sat down on the couch.

He smiled and kissed me with a beautiful, passionate kiss that sent me whirling.

Pup yipped.

"That's enough from you, Pup," I said.

"He's going to be a good one when his fur grows back," Denny stated.

"Everyone thinks he's got some terrible disease. The previous owner was going to drown him."

"And you saved him. You're a hero, Annie Laine."

"I wouldn't go that far."

Denny picked me up and carried me up the stairs.

We kissed and touched softly, still getting familiar with each other. He caressed me, and my cravings turned from drugs and alcohol to Denny. When he entered me, I gasped. This was my dream come true. This was everything I ever wanted.

We made love slower and more tenderly than before. And afterward, we fell asleep in each other's arms.

CHAPTER 44

I woke up later in pain and alone. I hobbled to the bathroom and took another Tylenol. It was still light outside, and the doorbell was ringing.

The ringing continued as I crawled downstairs and hollered, "I'm coming."

I looked through the viewer at the face of a stranger. He was tall, very dark, and bald. His head shone in the setting sunlight.

I pressed the speaker button and asked, "Who are you?"

"Danzel White. Denny sent me."

I unbolted the door and let him in.

Danzel towered over me. He was tall enough to be a basketball player, but he was soft. And he moved slowly.

"Denny told me you found the mother lode of cannabis in a secret room downstairs."

"Let me show you."

I rolled through the kitchen to the door in the back with Danzel and Pup in tow.

"It's the door on the right. Sorry, but I don't think I can make it down there again." I handed him a key.

Danzel nodded and disappeared downward.

I hollered, "There's a light switch on the wall when you get inside the room."

I heard the door open, and I heard a gasp.

"You sure do got a lot of cannabis down here," Denzel's voice echoed upward. "It's going to take a while to get all of it."

I rolled back to the table, picked up Pup, and waited. I rubbed his neck and noticed that his fur was growing back.

"You're going to be a real dog soon," I said.

Pup rumbled.

Danzel came up with an extra-large garbage bag stuffed with pot. As he skirted by me, I got a whiff of skunk and hoped it wouldn't linger for long inside the house.

After numerous trips back and forth, Danzel finally reported, "Got it all out. Just got to clean up a bit."

"Thank you. I really appreciate this."

It was another forty-five minutes before I saw him again.

He sprayed the house with an odor eliminator that made me sneeze.

"I left the door open to air out the room. That stuff was pretty strong."

I thanked him again and asked, "How much do I owe you?"

"It's been taken care of."

Danzel left, and I bolted the door shut.

I wrapped my cast in plastic and took a long hot shower. It helped ease my urges, but I knew I couldn't spend my life in running water.

I finally got out and climbed into bed.

After tossing and turning for an hour, my cell rang. I answered groggily without looking at the caller ID, "Hello?"

Denny's voice echoed in my ear, "How are you doing?"

"Having a bad night."

"Want me to come over?"

"Absolutely."

I sprayed myself lightly with one of Sally's expensive perfumes and dressed in a sleeveless white top. I covered it with a lovely lace shirt that Sally had never worn. The price tag was still attached.

I slipped on a pair of baggy pants that fit over my cast and exhaled.

I needed a distraction from my urges for self-destruction, and Denny had called at the right time. I was ready and waiting for him by the time he arrived.

45

Keeping busy was an effective deterrent for addiction and pain control. I cleaned my bedroom, scrubbed the bath, and had tackled the kitchen by noon. And then I looked around the main section of the house. All it needed was a little dusting and a run with the vacuum.

I sat down at the rolltop desk and found the list that I'd written days ago in a drunken drug-filled haze. It was nearly indecipherable, and I almost gave up trying.

But then I made out the first item, and the rest seemed to follow an identifiable pattern.

Stop drinking and taking pills.

I smiled as I crossed it off. I'd accomplished that, at least for the time being.

The next thing was to *eat healthier*, and I was doing that too.

Learn how to protect myself. That was important, so I circled it.

Deal with work. Quit or not. And I had decided that I would continue working. At least until Ellie was in the clear.

I crossed off *Call Denny* with vigor.

I still needed to get with Ranger and sign papers.

I'd gotten rid of the pot but needed to pay my past-due rent and move my stuff out of my apartment.

As for *finding Sally's killer*, I circled it twice.

My list had gotten smaller and more manageable.

Percy had said things would get better when I stopped drinking, and he was right. I wasn't drinking because of my problems; my problem was drinking. It still seemed too easy.

I jotted *Percy* at the bottom of the list because I still needed to pay him.

And then I added, *Find baby daddy* in big bold letters.

I imagined that it was Sam. Maybe I would move away, and he would never find out.

And then I thought of my relationship with Denny. I was carrying someone else's baby, and worse yet, I wasn't sure whose.

No matter how hard I tried, I couldn't get past the big mistake I'd made. *Benny*. I was too messed up to remember if we'd used protection.

I took a couple of breaths into a bag.

Benny wasn't bad looking, but he had a lot of issues. Dishonesty, thievery, and bad teeth, just to start. He was a jerk. But my child wouldn't be like him. I would raise him or her to be better.

Then my thoughts turned to what having a baby would mean. Responsibility. Day care. Bottles and diapers.

Questions whirled through my head like a tornado. Was I ready for this? I closed my eyes as I remembered all the drinking I'd done and drugs I'd taken.

I came out of my funk as Ellie entered, pulled up a chair, and sat down next to me.

"How are you doing?" she asked.

"Not too good, I'm afraid," I said.

"You want me to get you a pain pill?"

I shook my head and swallowed hard. "I quit drinking and taking pills."

She smiled. "I'm glad, Mom. Because I need you more than ever."

"I'm pregnant."

"Holy cow! I've always wanted a sister."

I laughed. "What if it's a boy?"

"I think I can deal with that."

I stroked her long dark hair. "I love you, my child."

"Me too, and I'm not done needing you."

CHAPTER 46

I called an Uber and stood outside, but when I looked at my Beamer, I decided I would drive.

As the Uber driver pulled up, I gave him a twenty for his trouble.

It was difficult, but I managed to use my left foot to maneuver the pedals.

I drove carefully as I ate my breakfast in my car from a McDonald's bag I'd purchased from the drive-through window.

I knocked, Mr. Wong's eyehole shaded, and he opened the door hostilely.

"You show up after partying for many weeks! You think I do not know what you do with money instead of pay rent?"

I handed him a fistful of cash, and it silenced him.

"I'll need a receipt, please."

He stared at the money for a moment and then turned and waved me inside his studio apartment, vibrantly decorated with Asian silk and paintings of orchids and slanted-eyed women dressed in long colorful kimonos. Wong's place was small but neat and furnished with a TV, desk, and a light green couch, which probably pulled out to a bed. Alongside the kitchenette was a breakfast bar with two chairs.

Mr. Wong's mauve walls reminded me of Sam's bedroom, and my stomach stirred.

"I'm moving out," I said. "I'll be back with a truck."

"Your stuff is trash!" He handed me a receipt.

"Thanks for your input."

Before I turned to leave, he held the bills up to the light, making sure they were real.

I rolled to my apartment and turned the key.

When I opened the door, the familiar smell of old vodka hit me. Everything was the same but felt different. This wasn't home. It had been a place to sleep and drink and nothing more. Being there made me lonely.

I took my gun and the Wedgewood out from its hiding place and left it on the kitchen counter.

I opened the closet door and looked at my clothes. There was nothing I wanted. Sally's closet held better things, and they all fit. I would never wear any of these things again. Even her uniform shirts were whiter and brighter than mine.

I slid the Northwestern University diploma off the wall. After spending four years at this excellent institute, I'd planned to go forward to law school, but life got in the way.

Other than River Beach, I'd had one job. I worked for a law firm where I kept the books, did research, and occasionally followed people to confirm or dispute their credibility.

I would need a truck for the grandfather clock, but that was it. Mr. Wong was right. I didn't need anything else from this place. Especially the memories.

I wrapped the Wedgewood in a dish towel, shoved the gun into the waistband of my jeans, tucked the diploma under my arm, and left to continue my fresh start.

CHAPTER 47

I was in a melancholy mood when I called Percy, and we agreed on a time and place to meet.

He was waiting at Starbucks when I rolled in.

I sat down, and he smiled warmly.

After asking how I was, the next thing out of his mouth was "Did you go to a meeting yet?"

"Not yet," I answered. "But I will." It was hard to lie to this man, and making eye contact with him was difficult while doing so. He had done so much for me, but I was doing okay without meetings.

"I want to pay for what you and Grace did for me. She said it was all right to give you the money." I handed him two thousand dollars in cash.

He didn't count it. He just folded it and placed it into the top pocket of his shirt. "I'll make sure Grace gets it," he assured me.

He put his hand on mine, and his warmth radiated up my arm.

"You promised," he murmured.

"I've had a lot of things going on, but I haven't been drinking and no drugs. And now I'm taking care of things. It's a good sign, right?"

"Grace will appreciate your donation. She usually doesn't get anything if they leave before paying."

"How often does this happen?"

"A lot of people need this sort of help instead of typical methods because of time constraints, flying under the radar, or other personal reasons."

"You're a good man, Percy. And I appreciate what you did for me."

"The worse may be yet to come."

"I'm committed to kicking this beast in the nuts."

He laughed. "I sincerely wish you the best."

As I rose to go, he gently grabbed my arm. "Go to meetings. I don't think I could have gotten through my tribulations without them. I relapsed five times in fifteen years because I didn't have the support."

"Five?" I sat back down.

"It's not unusual. With AA, I've been drug and alcohol free going on ten years. It works if you work it."

I looked at his boyish face and asked, "You look young."

"I know. With the amount of booze I've consumed in my life, I should be a dried-out old prune. But I started early. I come from a long line of serious drinkers who left their Irish whiskey out for an eight-year-old to devour. I went to school drunk. Couldn't ask a girl out unless I had a few. And taking a test was a nightmare without half a pint. I was good at it. And no one knew."

"What about the smell on your breath?"

"I chewed a lot of gum, ate a bunch of Tic Tacs. I missed my childhood, so I'm making up for it now. Tell me about Annie."

"You mean like when everyone gets up in front of the group and admits they're alcoholics and tells terrible stories about embarrassing things they've done when they were drunk?"

"It can be helpful to hear that you're not alone."

"But I don't need it."

"You may not realize it now, but you do. As embarrassing as it may seem, it helps."

"I appreciate what you've done for me, Percy, but I need to be perfectly honest about this. I will not be going to meetings, and I will probably never call you again. Don't take it personally, but I don't want to rehash my transgressions. We've both come from families of drinkers. We have that in common. But in my family, we tend to handle problems by ignoring them. I've never been able to blurt things out in a public forum, and I doubt I'll change at this point."

"It has nothing to do with you or your family. How you feel is all part of the persona of an alcoholic."

I felt the blood rush to my face. I hated that word and all it implied.

"Why put a label on it?"

He pulled a small pamphlet from his pocket and laid it on the table.

"I want you to have this. It's a little book that will help you understand your illness."

I looked at the word on the cover: *Serenity.*

"The steps to recovery are listed and outlined here. The words in this book have saved hundreds of thousands, and it will save you if you let it."

"So easy." I shook my head.

"It's not easy. It's very hard. But it's a good program."

He opened it to the first page and read, "The first step is to admit you are powerless over alcohol. That your life has become unmanageable. Can you admit that?"

I gulped air and nodded. "Yes, but I'm doing better now."

"Trust me, it's short-term. You'll need more help. And when you do, please read this. You can always call me. And I won't ask again about meetings because I realize it makes you uncomfortable."

"I'll try."

He took my hand and said, "Recite the serenity prayer with me, please."

I read from the book as he narrated from memory:

"God, give me the grace to accept with serenity the things that cannot be changed, the courage to change the things which should be changed, and the wisdom to know the difference."

CHAPTER 48

I was psyched when I walked out of the coffee shop. I had crossed three more things off my list, and I picked up my phone to call Ranger's office, but something stopped me.

I stood in front of the Bruce Lee Karate Center.

I opened the door and watched a class in progress.

The instructor was a slight Asian man, and as he spoke, his group of students listened intently.

"This is not to be used to play games. You use these techniques to defend yourself only. Remember, danger is everywhere."

A short Asian lady behind the counter asked, "May I help you?"

I said, "I want to take that class."

She gave me a form to complete with a disclaimer at the bottom. I paid for a month in advance and enrolled in a Krav Maga class without knowing what it entailed. But I knew danger was everywhere, and I liked the confident tone of the instructor's voice.

One more thing off the list.

CHAPTER 49

I wheeled into the HR office at work. Anita, the HR manager, asked me what had happened to my leg.

I looked into her dark brown eyes that matched her skin. She was around thirty-five, but her chubby round face gave her a youthful appearance. She wore a sleeveless floral top and black capris. Her arms were flawless, but her face was marred and bumpy with adult acne.

"Fell downstairs," I said.

"Sorry to hear that, but the season is here, and we need everyone working if at all possible."

The thought of returning to River Beach overwhelmed me. I considered giving my notice and walking away, but then what?

I apologized and said, "I've been through a lot."

"I can't imagine how difficult it was losing your friend like that. Is there anything we can do to help you?"

I exhaled and coughed when I remembered Denny had said I'd been sick.

"I'm doing much better, thanks."

She glanced down at the cast on my leg. "Are you going to have any problems moving from one table to another?"

"I think I can manage. But I need a few more days."

She gave me another week off, and I crossed one more thing off my list.

I rolled out of the office with a busy mind. I needed to find an attorney for Ellie and get with Ranger to sign paperwork.

Finding Sally's killer was losing priority.

I called Mr. Ranger and explained that a friend of mine needed a criminal defense attorney referral. He gave me the name of someone and said he was the best. And then he added, "You need to sign those papers. The sooner you do, the sooner you get that money. It's going to take several months as it is."

I still had an appointment with the baby doc, so I asked, "Can I come by after five?"

"Try to make it by tomorrow, and I'll have everything ready. My assistant can handle it. You don't even need to see me."

I hung up and called Defense Attorney Cletus Jenson and left a message with his receptionist for him to contact me.

As I drove away from River Beach, I looked in the rear-view mirror and noticed a black sedan seemed to be following me. I made a quick turn, the car continued onward, and I exhaled.

50
CHAPTER

As I drove to the baby doctor, it felt like my skin was moving around on my bones.

Dr. Ricky Jones wasn't tall, nor was he handsome. He was slightly tan and had green eyes. His face was round, and his light brown hair was straight and covered his forehead. I examined his diplomas on the wall and noticed that he'd attended medical school at UAG, the Universidad Autonoma de Guadalajara in Mexico.

I didn't care for the idea that my doctor had attended medical school in Mexico but was reassured when I saw that he'd completed his residency at Johns Hopkins here in the USA.

He asked with a smooth Southern drawl, "How've you been feeling?"

"Pretty good," I lied.

"Let's take a look under the hood, shall we?"

As he examined me, he made me laugh as he sang Bruno Mars's "When I Was Your Man." And he was a pretty good singer.

After a thorough examination, he asked openly, "How old are you?"

"Thirty-eight."

He picked up my file from the nearby counter and flipped through.

"You've got another child, age twenty?"

"Yes, and she's fine. Perfect, in fact. Real smart, and she was a wonderful child."

"You should get an amniocentesis."

"I was expecting that."

"My nurse will help you with scheduling. Any problems I should know about?"

I was reluctant, not wanting to verbalize the sins of my past, but I knew it was necessary.

I looked away as I spoke, "Well…I didn't know I was pregnant, and I drank. And I was drugged."

I took a breath.

"Sorry to hear that."

"As soon as I realized, I quit."

"What was the drug?"

"Roofies, without my knowledge. And I took pain pills for my broken ankle. I've been clean ever since I found out, and I've been eating healthy."

I paused and then added, "I had sex without my permission when I was drugged, and I don't know who the father is. Amniocentesis should be helpful to compare DNA. Correct?"

"Yes, definitely. How much were you drinking?"

I avoided his eyes. "A lot."

"Any problems quitting? Withdrawal symptoms?"

"Yes. All of that."

"Hum." He placed the file back on the counter.

"What does that mean?"

"First trimester is an important one."

I squeaked out, "I know."

"We'll need to draw some blood. And we'll need to test for HIV right up until the birth."

"I know about that too."

"Okay then."

"What if I've done something dreadful to this baby?"

He put his hand on my shoulder and said, "Having a child is like taking a trip to Europe. There are different ways to go. You have a wonderful child, a great trip, and something you'd want to do again. And I sincerely hope that this one will be similar. But sometimes, things turn out differently. You may end up going another way, backpacking, or just not having a plan at all. The route is the same, but the mode of transportation and accommodations may change. Just remember, after the baby is born, the choice is not yours anymore. There'll be no upgrades. If you're ready for this journey, then we're all set."

"How bad can it be?"

"Congenital disabilities and deficits are challenging. But everything might be fine. Before we go off the deep end, let's get some images and see what's what."

"Can you tell from a sonogram?"

"We can see if the spine is closing like it should and if the baby's heart is beating correctly. We count the fingers and toes. And it seems to me that you're prepared. So are you packed and ready to go?"

"Let's do this."

CHAPTER 51

The room was dimly lit, and I lay on the table with my belly exposed. The tech was a disheveled middle-aged woman who appeared to have given up on herself. She was overweight, and she wore a faded stork-printed smock. Her hair looked like it was once colored light auburn, but it had been a while since her last dye job. She had a good inch and a half of gray growth.

Her name was Alice, and when she spoke, her frumpy appearance faded. She had the voice of an angel.

"I'm going to introduce you to your baby," she said.

Alice went through the preordained list of checks, and she appeared extraordinarily confident and competent. She showed me all five fingers and five toes on both hands and feet. She said the baby's heartbeat was strong, and then she asked, "Do you want to know the gender?"

I nodded.

"It's a little girl."

I gasped softly, "A girl. Is she healthy?"

"Doctor will go over the important things, but she looks good to me."

I let out a sigh that echoed through the room.

Dr. Jones came in and reviewed all of Alice's findings and agreed that everything appeared normal. But he cautioned that there may be other things that may not show up on a sonogram.

I wiped the goop off my belly, made an appointment for the amniocentesis, and skipped out the door. My baby looked good, was the right size, and had a strong heartbeat. So far, so good.

CHAPTER 52

The pain in my ankle was constant as a toothache as I rolled into the break room at work. The swelling was down, but the skin inside the cast itched like crazy.

Someone asked, "What the hell happened to you?"

I shrugged and said, "I fell downstairs."

Everyone laughed, which in most cases would seem insensitive, but dealers are a rare bunch.

I rolled around, picked up a tip box, and checked in with George, who said, "Good to have you back."

I smiled and requested an early out as soon as possible.

"I'll do what I can, but it's busy." And then he asked, "You okay?"

I nodded and rolled away. The place was a zoo with lots of regulars and plenty of snowbirds.

I parked my trike cane on one side of the table and hung my tip box on the other. I started at a large table without an automatic shuffler. It was more work than other cash tables, and the action was intense.

As I shuffled up, it felt clumsy, and I clumped the cards—nothing like the way I usually do things. As I pitched, it felt like a chore. I'd always done well expertly placing the cards in front of each player, but on that day, I was more like an amateur.

I managed to get through the down without incident, and as I rolled to my next table, I felt almost normal. Working was keeping my mind busy.

I dealt six tables in three hours before I got a break.

As I rolled toward the break room, Sam surprised me with a hug and a kiss on my cheek.

"You don't look so good. Why don't you go home?" He seemed genuinely concerned.

"Every table is full."

"They'll make allowances."

"They've already made plenty. As soon as the room starts breaking down, I'll be the first one to go."

"Let's get something to eat. How about a steak? And I've got a few pills you might be interested in."

"I told you, Sam. There's someone else."

"Okay," he moaned. "But I still want to get those pills to you. It looks like you can use something."

"Thanks for the offer, but I'm getting by without drugs," I answered as I tried to roll away.

"Look, get rid of whoever you got on the line. I want to take you out and show you off."

I bit my lip.

Sam added sincerely, "I'm in love with you, you know?"

I gawked back without answering.

"Call me when you're ready." He made a *call me* sign before rushing away.

I didn't have any idea what he was talking about. We'd had a one-night stand, and nothing about what he'd said made sense.

It was two more hours before George allowed me to leave.

As I rolled slowly to my car, I felt itchy. I was shaking and sweating, and it felt like my heart was going to jump out of my chest.

On the way home, I looked in the rearview mirror, and the black sedan was back.

I took a quick turn, the car proceeded onward, and I added paranoia to my list of ailments.

I got home and took a shower. As I stepped out, my phone was ringing.

It was Denny asking if I wanted company.

I was dressed and ready in a matter of minutes.

I opened the door for Denny, but before we had a chance to sit down, the doorbell rang again.

I opened the door to Sam holding a bag of white take-out containers.

He sidestepped me, took a look at Denny, and blurted out, "Who called the cops?"

"I think you both know each other from the Boat," I said.

"Is this the guy you told me about? The one you tossed me aside for?" Sam laughed.

"Sam, please leave and don't come back," I pleaded.

"You can't be serious. I'm better than him."

Sam looked up and down at Denny. "A lot better in every way."

Denny furrowed his forehead, and Pup growled.

"Get that thing away from me," Sam grumbled.

I took a deep breath and scratched my skin until it began to bleed.

Sam had illegal business with Sally, growing and selling pot, and probably more than that. He didn't care about me. He was using me to get what he wanted from this house. The sad part was he didn't need to romance me or lie about falling in love. Other than sex, I would have given him whatever he was looking for. All he had to do was ask.

Denny opened the door and told Sam that it would be best if he left.

Sam shambled out and disappeared into the gloomy darkness of late afternoon.

As soon as he closed the door, Denny asked, "Are you hungry?"

"Starved," I answered.

"What do you feel like?"

"Cheeseburger. With lettuce and lots of onions."

"I know a place," Denny whispered like it was a deep, dark secret, and it made me laugh.

And I wanted him more than ever in my life.

CHAPTER 53

We ate at Duffy's. Afterward, Denny stayed the night, and in the morning, around six, he dressed in his uniform and left for work.

I was making coffee when the doorbell rang, and I halfway expected Sam again, probably wanting the marijuana.

But I looked at the viewer on my keypad and saw Trevor's image lurking outside.

I couldn't remember the last time I'd seen him.

I opened the door, and he nearly fell inside.

He stunk of body odor, chemicals, and urine. His clothes were dirty and spotted with grease, and his shirt was missing buttons.

Pup sniffed around him as I helped him to the couch.

He sat in silence for a moment as I continued my examination. Dirt was encrusted in the creases of his neck. His fingernails were dark with filth, and the folds in his arms were speckled with bloody needle holes.

"What's up, Trevor?" I asked.

He twitched a weak smile and whispered, "I'm in a bad way, Annie."

"I can tell just by looking at you."

"I need help."

"Obvious as well. What can I do?"

"I need to get into a program." He closed his eyes and drifted off.

I looked at my cell phone screen with Denny's number on it.

He'd been willing to help me, but this was a little over-the-top.

I had a filthy drug addict in my home, and I didn't know what illnesses could have tagged along with him.

I finally pressed "Dial," and Denny answered on the first ring. I filled him in on Trevor's condition, and he said to hold tight, and someone would be there soon.

Forty-five minutes later, Percy Murphy appeared at my door with a big black man at his side he introduced as Elijah Jones. He was dressed in green medical scrubs and looked like he had just left an operating room. Elijah wasn't much taller than me, but he was bulging with muscles.

After introductions, Elijah gloved up with latex and pulled a medical mask over his face. He picked up Trevor with ease and carted him away.

Percy asked, "What's his deal?"

"He's been in numerous programs before," I said. "And it's obvious that he's hooked on heroin."

Percy said he'd call me when he knew more and rushed away.

CHAPTER 54

It was pouring down rain as Ellie drove my BMW to Attorney Cletus Jensen's office. I'd told Louis Ranger that I wanted the best, but I had no idea what that entailed.

Jensen's office was in the high-rent area of West Palm Beach, just north of CityPlace on Olive Avenue. Everything was sopping wet, and a group of thunderheads gathered above as Ellie drove the Beamer past the downtown shops and restaurants with a fountain spouting in the center of the square.

There were many good memories from this place. Ellie and I had celebrated at Saito's Japanese Steak House when her good grades got her a partial ride to Florida Atlantic University. And when she made the softball team, we had dinner at Brio's Bistro and ate fillets. We'd gone to movies and festivals here. Food and CityPlace played a significant role in good things celebrated in the past.

Another kind of memory was being created, and it didn't come with the same warm and fuzzy feelings.

Ellie pulled into the parking garage. The gate went up, and we forged ahead, and I got a glimpse of another black car passing behind us. More uneasiness followed.

We rode the elevator up to the top floor in silence.

As I pulled the door open to the outer office, I began to believe that my statement to Ranger might have been a bit overstated. I didn't really know if I could afford the best after all.

The reception sector was perfect, with beautiful natural wood flooring covered with silk Persian rugs and high-end furniture. Live orchids were expertly arranged in lead crystal on a carved wood pedestal next to a reception desk. A gorgeous blonde, a twenty-something-year-old woman, sat waiting with a smile that could make hearts melt.

From the bronze plaque placed strategically on her desk, I discovered that her name was Melitsa, a classy name for an elegant girl with a flawless face accompanied by sea blue eyes and perfect white teeth.

She spoke softly with a sweet Southern intonation, "Annie Laine?"

I nodded.

She sashayed from around the desk, and I noted that she had the perfect body to go along with the face. A complete package, and I wondered what she was doing here. She belonged in Hollywood, auditioning for starring roles in blockbuster movies.

She led us down a hallway and into the well-decorated private office of Cletus Jensen.

Cletus had an oval face with a square jaw. He smiled warmly as he stood to welcome us. He held out a hand, offering me a chair, as he said, "Won't you please have a seat?" He looked at Ellie and said, "And you can sit right next to your mama."

His voice was warm and friendly.

As I sat down, I blurted, "When we talked on the phone, you said you had some good news regarding Ellie's defense."

"Ellie is a good girl caught up in a dangerous game," he began. "She's charged with bringing drugs into a school with the intent to distribute. This carries a mandatory minimum of thirty years in prison and up to a million-dollar fine."

I gasped and found it hard to catch my breath. I cupped my hands around my mouth and tried to calm myself.

He held up a reassuring hand. "However, my staff and I have been working diligently and believe we have found a way to get around this severe punishment."

"How?" I was barely able to squeak out the single word.

"The courts are a bit more lenient to addicts."

I heard the word *addict* and began to breathe madly. I pulled out a paper bag and held it over my face.

"Are you all right?" Jensen asked.

I waved a hand through the air.

"I'm fine," I gulped.

"You don't look fine to me."

I muttered, "I have panic attacks. Sorry. Please continue."

"What I have to say gets better."

"Better than my daughter being a drug dealer and an addict?"

Ellie said, "Mom, I'm not—"

"She isn't an addict," he interrupted as he held up a lab report. "I know this because Ellie was drug tested after her arrest, and she passed. Not the slightest sign of pot, cocaine, or heroin. So our initial strategy is out."

"Initial strategy?" I asked.

"Like I mentioned before, the courts are lenient toward addicts. They tend to send them to rehab instead of jail."

"So if my daughter were a drug addict, she would be in less trouble?"

"It seems unfair, I know. But I've spoken to the assistant state's attorney handling Ellie's case, Madge Bello. She agrees that the system is flawed. And she's fairly open to a deal."

"What's the deal?" Ellie asked.

"House arrest and probation. We've whittled it down to one year, and I'm trying to reduce it to six months."

"I can't leave the house for six months?"

"With some exceptions. You'll be able to attend college classes. Your areas of study are subject to approval by the SA's office. And no night courses. And you can attend family functions with prior authorization."

"How long is the probation?" I asked.

"We're at ten years but still negotiating. I want five, but I'm not sure we'll get it. Bello's already bent over backward in this case as it is."

He looked at Ellie and said, "I have to emphasize that this deal means no jail time, and that's huge. But you will have to admit to the judge that you are guilty and apologize to the court. And you will be a convicted felon."

"No jail time, and I'll be able to attend school?"

"Yes."

She exhaled audibly. "I think I love you."

"My wife will be thrilled." He smiled and then added, "This is what Bello's offering. But there's a stipulation. You need to give the judge a name."

Ellie's eyes hit the floor.

"This condition is nonnegotiable. If you don't come up with a name, there's no deal, and you will go to jail for a long time."

"Do I have to tell you right now?"

Everything became clear. Ellie was trying to protect me. I didn't need to hear her say it to know who it was.

"I don't need an answer today. But we'll want to get this done and over with before the ASA changes her mind. I think I can get a hearing scheduled for an initial court appearance next week. We've worked hard on this. Bello doesn't want to prolong this process, and we don't want to piss her off."

"I need to check a few things out first to make sure I've got my facts right."

"Don't wait too long," Cletus cautioned as he rose from behind his desk and offered Ellie his hand.

He looked at me and said, "Now we've come to the hard part."

"Is cash okay?" I asked.

"Cash will be fine." Cletus smiled warmly.

We left the office in reasonably good spirits and hopeful for a promising future. And my backpack was fifty thousand dollars lighter.

55
CHAPTER

The night before Ellie's court date, I tossed and turned and barely slept. When I did doze off, I had a bad dream about going to work naked, and I woke with a headache.

I dressed quickly and then stumbled around the house looking for food, but nothing appealed to me. I drove to McDonald's in the rain and ordered a couple of Egg McMuffins. When I returned, Ellie was gone.

I ate in the car on the way to the courthouse and arrived a few minutes early. ASA Madge Bello sat at a table on one side of the room. She was thin and tall and appeared well-groomed.

On the other side, Attorney Jensen sat alone. He spotted me and waved me forward.

I tried not to panic as I rolled toward him, but with every inch came more apprehension.

He made a weak effort to smile as if nothing was wrong and then asked, "Where's Ellie?"

"I'm sure she'll be here soon. Traffic's bad, you know?" My tongue was thick, my mouth was dry as a desert, and I could hardly speak.

I grabbed my phone and noticed a missed call from Denny. Probably offering support. I ignored it and dialed Ellie's phone. It went straight to voice mail.

I started breathing heavily, pulled out a baggy, and put it over my face.

Jenson offered me a bottle of water, which I gulped quickly.

I redialed Ellie's phone, and it just rang and rang.

I babbled, "She's not answering. Maybe I should go look for her."

"Where?"

I shrugged. There wasn't anywhere.

I looked around the courtroom and spotted Gordy Best in the back like a vulture, ready to pounce.

My whole body shook like I was freezing, but I was burning up and dripping with sweat. I was over the edge and needed a drink in the worst way. My pulse raced, and I was exhausted beyond belief.

"Do you need a doctor?" Jenson asked.

I choked out, "I'll be okay."

I closed my eyes and tried to go to my happy place. I was at the beach with sand between my toes and five-year-old Ellie playing in the sand.

But my happy place disappeared when the judge began to speak, "Is your client here, Mr. Jensen?"

He stood. "Her mother has indicated that she will be here shortly, Your Honor."

I glared at Karp from my seat.

"We've waited long enough. I don't care what her mother says. She's in contempt, and I have no alternative but to revoke…"

Gordy edged over to me and held out his hand. "I'll take that key to the Beamer now."

Judge Carp squinted and asked, "What's going on there, Mr. Best?"

"Just picking up my property, Judge. She put her car up for bail, and I plan on driving it away from the courthouse so that she doesn't try to hide it from me."

Carp frowned and said, "I haven't finished ruling yet. I would appreciate it if you would allow me to complete the process before proceeding with your business. And in the future, you will address me as Your Honor."

Gordy smiled and nodded.

"Step away from that woman until the order's entered," the judge said with a lot of indignation in his voice.

I bowed my head and closed my eyes.

Carp cleared his throat.

The door to the courtroom opened, and I hoped that I would look up and see Ellie, but Denny stepped inside instead. His eyes searched the room. He found me and nodded.

Judge Carp gave him a look and asked, "Lieutenant McCaffery. Can I help you?"

Denny took a few steps and said, "Your Honor, Ellie Laine is not here—"

Carp interjected, "That's fairly obvious."

"She's been in an accident." Denny looked at me.

I stood up fast and nearly fainted.

Denny winked. "But she's okay. Some minor bruises and cuts, I'm told. But her phone was damaged in the crash and wasn't able to call her attorney or her mother."

"How did you receive this information when she hasn't got a phone?"

"She had the responding officer contact me because I know the family personally. I tried to call your clerk, but he informed me that you were in session and couldn't be disturbed. So I came straight here."

"Where is Ms. Laine now?"

"She should be here any minute."

Jensen said, "Your Honor, I respectfully ask to delay these proceedings to allow her more time."

Gordy sunk back in his seat, frowning.

Carp moved his mouth around like he was adjusting his teeth.

Bello frowned and threw up her hands. "We had a good deal in the works. Too good, as far as I'm concerned. And now this?" She shook her head. "This was a very grave crime. At this point, even if she shows up, I'm tempted to pull the deal."

I whispered, "No."

The door opened again, and a uniformed officer entered and whispered something in Denny's ear.

"Ellie's coming up the elevator and will be here within seconds," Denny said. "Your Honor, and respectfully, ASA Bello, she's a great girl with a good head on her shoulders."

And then Ellie entered with a white bandage covering her forehead.

I jumped up, we hugged quickly, and she took a seat next to Jensen.

I sat down behind them, and Denny slid in next to me.

Judge Carp looked at Ellie and asked, "Are you all right?"

She nodded, stood, and said, "Yes, Your Honor. I apologize for being late, but my car was T-boned by a guy who ran a red light. I did the best I could." She began to cry.

"Enough." Judge Carp waved a hand in the air.

I couldn't tell if he was upset because Ellie was late and crying or if he was just ready to get things done and over with. I was hoping for the latter.

"Proceed with the deal on the table." Carp looked at Madge Bello.

"Like I said, I'm inclined to pull the—"

He interrupted, "The deal, Madge. Let's not play games."

Bello picked up a sheet of paper and read, "The state will stipulate to one year of house arrest and nine years' probation. During her house arrest, she will be permitted to attend college and become employed but will not be allowed to enter any drinking establishments, including nightclubs or any such institutions. She will be tested for drugs her entire probation and will be responsible for all costs."

Carp appeared to be reading and not listening to the prosecutor.

When Bello finished, she sat down and waited.

Carp cleared his throat and looked down at Ellie. "Young lady."

"Yes, Your Honor?" Ellie whispered.

"What were you doing in the library of a local college with twenty pounds of packaged illegal drugs in your backpack?"

"I was told I was delivering study guides for less fortunate students."

Carp frowned.

"But I was stupid," she continued. "I should have known what I was doing wasn't right."

He read from a file in front of him. "Says here you were tested for drugs, and there was none found in your system."

"That's true, Your Honor." Jensen nodded.

"I have one question before I approve or disapprove your deal, Ms. Laine. Who gave you the drugs?"

There was so much silence that I could hear my heart pounding loudly in my ears.

Ellie glanced at me. Blood had leaked through her bandage, and she looked even more pathetic.

She said, "I'm sorry, Mom."

Carp was clearly riled. "The court has asked you a question. Now answer."

"Sally Grover gave me the backpack." She bowed her head.

I knew Sally had to be involved.

"I tried to stop. But then Sally died. Afterward, I threw the bag into my trunk and forgot about it. But then I got an anonymous call. I didn't recognize the voice, but he said I needed to complete the task or else. Those were his exact words."

"That's it?"

She looked sadly at me. "It was a man's voice, and he said my mother would die a painful death if I didn't deliver."

I gasped.

"The only reason I considered it was to make things easier for my mom. She paid for everything and was struggling to keep up. Sally said she'd pay my tuition if I dropped the bag off."

"Did you receive compensation for this action?"

"All I got was arrested."

This got a few chuckles from the gallery.

Judge Carp pounded his gavel and told everyone to be silent.

He inhaled deeply, bit his lip, and then said, "You didn't know what you were carrying?"

"Honestly? I could have guessed that something wasn't right. But I was so focused on school that I didn't care. I'm very goal oriented, and I felt I needed to graduate on time."

"Can you prove that Sally Grover is deceased?"

Ellie shrugged as Denny approached.

"Her murder is still being investigated by the sheriff's office. I can pull the information up on my cell phone if you'd like."

But Carp's clerk was on the spot with an iPad. He handed it over, and Carp read in silence as I shifted around in the hard wooden seat and breathed into the baggy.

When he raised his head, he asked Denny, "Drive-by?"

"There had been some other shootings in that neighborhood. So far, there's no apparent motive."

"Drug related?"

"I don't believe that drugs were a focus in this case. But I'll make sure to fill the detectives in on these new developments."

Judge Carp nodded, looked at Bello, and said, "I don't like this deal."

I slumped in my seat as Denny sat back down next to me.

Carp looked harshly at Ellie and asked, "What are your plans, young lady?"

"Regarding, Your Honor?"

"For your life."

"I want to finish my bachelor's degree, master's, and then my doctorate."

He shuffled through a file in front of him and then gave Attorney Jensen a look.

Jensen asked, "Is there anything I can help you with?"

"Do you have her college records?"

He tore open a file on the table in front of him. He unbuckled a clasp and thumbed through.

It took him less than a minute to produce several pages of Ellie's transcripts.

I leaned toward Denny and whispered, "He's very organized."

Jensen handed it to the judge.

Carp scanned quickly, flipping pages back and forth.

He cleared his throat and mumbled, "Majoring in political science. What are your plans after college?"

Ellie looked downward. "It was the law. But I don't see that happening now. I'll have to find something else that I can feel passionate about."

"I'm impressed by your diligence. It appears you've maintained a near-perfect average throughout your collegian career. However, this is a serious situation."

He looked at Bello and said, "Drop the house arrest. And five years of probation sounds more reasonable, don't you think?"

I watched as Bello nodded reluctantly as her face reddened.

"And monthly drug testing at your expense," Carp said to Ellie. "Stay out of bars and nightclubs until your twenty-first birthday."

"Thank you, Your Honor." Ellie's rounded shoulders squared off.

"I'm not finished. And this is most important."

He paused for a couple of seconds and then continued. "If you stay in school, finish a degree in whatever you decide, and complete all requirements of your probation, your file will be sealed, and you will no longer be a convicted felon."

Denny squeezed my hand as Ellie whispered, "Thank you."

"Go and do good things. And whatever you do, don't disappoint me. Because if you do, there will be hell to pay."

Ellie rushed to me, and we embraced as she wept in my arms.

When I opened my eyes and looked back, I caught a glimpse of Sam rushing out of the room.

CHAPTER 56

As we left the courtroom in the drizzling rain, Ellie whispered, "Thank you, Mama."

She hadn't called me that in many years.

"I will never disappoint you again," she promised.

"This was just a little hiccup in your life." And then I asked, "How are you doing?"

"It looks worse than it is," Ellie said as she felt the white bandage on her head. "Just a scratch, nothing serious." And then she thanked Denny for his help.

He smiled. "Do what Judge Carp said, and we'll never mention this again."

"Where's your car?" I asked.

"I think it's totaled. They had to tow it away."

"How's the other driver?"

"Eighty-year-old guy. He was taken to the hospital. The responding officer told me he's shaken up, but he'll survive." Denny said.

I asked him, "Got time for lunch?"

"I'm still on duty. We'll catch up later?"

57
CHAPTER

Clouds covered the sun, but after days of downpour, the rain had finally let up, and the temperature was in the seventies.

Pup's fur had grown in nicely, and he was turning out to be a fine-looking dog.

The holidays were approaching, and Thanksgiving was on my mind. As I drove, I made plans and a mental list of things we needed for dinner. I wanted to spend the holiday with Ellie, Denny, and my family. But I cringed at the thought of extending an invitation to my mother. Her idea of a family get-together was to dwell on the past inequities and every terrible thing my father did to her. He'd left her the day before Thanksgiving, and she hated him and everything about the holiday. She'd told us that she preferred to be alone because she had no desire to give thanks for her pain, but she'd said that every year and always showed up. My sister, Beth, confirmed that she wouldn't make it, and both of my brothers had already made plans.

I was on my way to work when I passed a white truck on the side of the road. The back door of the dually was open, and Sam was bent over halfway inside.

I had mixed emotions about stopping. But I pulled over and backed up toward Sam's truck. I needed to determine why he was at Ellie's hearing and didn't want the confrontation at work.

I regretted my decision as I got out and stepped into a puddle of fallen rain. I was tempted to get back into my car and drive away. But I didn't.

I wheeled my crutch over muddy rocks as I approached, and Sam didn't see me at first.

I was just a few feet away as I heard him curse to himself as he fumbled with something in the back cab of his truck.

"Hey!" I surprised him.

Sam jerked up and hit his head on the top of the open doorframe. As he did, a rack of black hundred-dollar chips crashed to the wet sand and gravel. More chips and racks were strewn on the crew cab's floor.

"What's going on?" I picked up one of the chips.

He blanked a look and shrugged.

I took a step backward. "Did you make these?"

Without a word, he bent down and picked up chips from the wet ground.

"What are you planning?"

He answered with an anxious tone, "You don't understand anything, Annie. Just get the hell out of here."

I felt a few drops of rain and heard thunder from a distance.

"You can't be serious, Sam. They do a count every day. You'll be seen on camera cashing in all these chips."

As traffic zoomed behind us, he grabbed my arm. I was instantly terrified. He could push me back into the path of an unsuspecting vehicle, and I'd be dead.

His face reddened with anger as he screamed, "You're a stupid pill-popping drunk! You disgust me! And if you tell anyone about this, you'll be sorry."

He exhaled, rubbed his face with his other hand, and let go of my arm. "I'm sorry. I didn't mean that, Annie. But I have to leave! I'm dead if I stay here!"

"What are you saying?"

"Don't tell anyone about this until tomorrow. By then, I'll be gone. After that, I don't care what you do or what anyone sees on the cameras!"

He begged with terror in his eyes, "Please don't tell anyone." He lowered his voice. "I like you, Annie, and I'm sorry it didn't work out. Under different circumstances, maybe things could have been good for us."

I backed up, tripping over rocks and stumbling through the wetness. And then I turned and hurried to my car.

CHAPTER 58

The sky opened up, and rain poured down as I drove, and I was having palpitations again. I felt dizzy, so I pulled off the road into a parking lot and waited for my heartbeat to return to normal.

As I sat there, I contemplated my options. I could go to work and pretend nothing happened or tell what I'd seen and face whatever came from that.

Maybe I would be considered an accomplice. I'd given Sam the printing press and the chips. I shook the thought from my head, called Denny, and told him everything.

I expected him to ask me why I'd stopped in the first place, but he didn't. And I was glad.

He told me not to do anything. He was on his way.

After hanging up, I sat for a moment staring at the rain and breathing hard. I felt my neck for a pulse to make sure my heart wasn't going to explode. The beats were still erratic.

I closed my eyes, sat for a few minutes more, waiting for my stomach to settle, and my heart to start beating the way it should.

I forced myself to breathe in and out slowly. And then I went to my happy place where the sun was shining, and Ellie was bouncing a ball along the shore.

I finally opened my eyes, took a deep breath, and pulled back onto the road.

The rain was really coming down as I rolled my crutch and held an umbrella over my head on my way to the employee entrance.

As soon as I got inside, I put the umbrella away and trailed water down the long hallway to the poker room.

I entered the break room just as George was putting in the push. Our eyes met, he looked away, and I got a bad feeling.

I was the only one that wasn't in the lineup. After everyone left the room, George said, "Need to talk. In the office, please."

I rolled into the office behind George, and Denny was already there. Ryan was behind the desk, and he smiled and asked, "How are you doing, Annie?"

"Good, thanks. Had a lot of things going on, but hopefully, the worst is over."

"Denny just got here, and he says we've got a big problem with one of our players." He motioned toward an empty chair, and I sat down.

George backed out and closed the door behind him.

"Tell me what happened."

I recited everything I knew as Ryan took notes. Sam had picked up the machine that looked like a printing press and a box of blanks. And I told him about seeing the chips he had in the back of his truck that I assumed were counterfeit.

"What's Sam's last name?"

"Jarvis."

"You had this machine at your house?"

"Sally's house. She left it to me after she…after she was killed."

"You think Sally was involved somehow?"

I shrugged. "I don't know." But I knew she had to be the catalyst.

"How many chips do you think Sam has?"

"They were all over the place. A few racks of reds, but mostly blacks. If I had to guess, at least twenty racks."

"Two hundred thousand dollars, huh?"

I nodded.

"How did they look?"

"Good. If I didn't know any better, I'd say they were real."

Ryan leaned back in his swivel chair. He put his index fingers together, forming an upside-down V, and placed them on either side of his mouth. And then he looked at Denny.

"No penalty for counterfeiting chips," Ryan said. "This is a tough situation. Currently, there's no crime."

"Federal counterfeiting laws don't apply because the value of a chip is nominal. It's only a crime when the perpetrator trades them for cash. And then we don't usually know it's happened until we do the nightly count. We'd have to look at the tapes to see who cashed in large amounts."

"If he cashes some or all, the charge could range from petty theft to grand larceny," Denny stated.

"And Annie will have to testify against him."

I asked, "Am I in trouble?"

"There's no problem with accessory before the fact," Denny said. "I was there at the time when he picked up the material. Neither one of us could tell what it was. And his deal was with Sally. Annie had no knowledge about the overall plan."

Denny was lying to protect me.

"What do you want me to do?" Denny asked.

"Let me think." Ryan rocked in his chair. "For a place like this, most of the time, publicity is a good thing. Getting our name out there is important. But this type of publicity—telling the public about a scam involving fake chips…" He trailed off and then said, "It might just give people ideas."

Ryan rubbed his forehead as if he was massaging his thoughts, looking for the correct answer.

"Consider this. Say Sam walks in with the chips. I imagine he'll have them in a backpack or bag of some kind. George is already informing everyone to keep a lookout for him. When he shows up, we'll let him know we're on to him, talk him into turning over the fakes, and ban him for life."

Ryan looked at me. "How well do you know Sam?"

"At one time, I thought we were friends. But not anymore."

"Let's keep this as quiet as possible. The fewer people that know, the better."

Ryan's eyes bounced back and forth between us.

"So are we good with this?" he asked.

I nodded right away, but it took a few seconds for Denny to agree.

And then he picked up my hand and asked, "How you doing?"

"Better than ever," I lied. My stomach was churning, my heart was beating too hard, and I was a wreck.

Sam had threatened me, and I hadn't heeded his warning. I tried not to shake. But I had a bad feeling this was not going to end well.

There was a knock on the door, and George stuck his head in and said, "Sam's here."

Ryan's eyes opened wide. "Already?"

"He's at the cashier's counter."

George closed the door, and Ryan gave Denny a look. "I'll leave this in your capable hands. Get him in here without alarming the entire room if you can."

Denny nodded and exited.

CHAPTER 59

Sam showed little emotion and offered virtually no resistance when Denny grabbed him by the arm, confiscated his heavy backpack, and escorted him to the manager's office.

I stood across the poker room, watching the closed door and wondering what was happening inside. Sam came out a few moments later with the backpack. I could tell it was empty because it appeared deflated, just like him. His shoulders slumped with his eyes focused on the floor. He headed toward the door with Denny following close behind.

As Sam passed tables, players' heads turned in his direction, finding the action off the table more interesting than the cards. But no one said anything. The usual buzz diminished to silence. The tables were full of regulars, and most knew Sam. A lot of them were friends.

Before leaving, Sam stopped, turned, and scanned the room. His eyes settled on me, and his face burned with anger.

Denny stepped up and said something, and they disappeared out the door.

I was shaking as Ryan approached and said, "Go home, Annie. Take it easy for a few days. Do you need a ride?"

I shook my head and answered, "I'll be okay."

"Thank you for coming forward. And please be careful."

I nodded and left.

On the way home, I stopped at Walmart and picked up about a hundred dollars' worth of chocolate, bottled water, and fruit.

As I was checking out, Denny called.

He apologized for leaving me, but he wanted to make sure Sam didn't circle back to the track.

"I followed him home. But I just got a call to investigate a traffic death, so I'm leaving now. Looks like he's there to stay."

"Did he say anything?"

"He wasn't too happy. And he said you need to watch your back. I'm sorry, Annie."

I had trouble getting my words out.

"Are you coming by?"

"Traffic deaths tend to take a while. I'll call you later. I'm off for a couple days, so we'll do something." He said and then added, "I don't think I need to say this, but lock your doors and make sure the alarm is on."

At home, I lay down but couldn't sleep. I tossed and turned but didn't get up.

The feeling of dread was still with me. I was worried about Denny and how this thing with Sam had affected our relationship. I'd been nothing but trouble for him since the beginning.

And then I realized that I was falling into the same pattern of depending on others to make me happy.

Sally had swayed me more than I'd realized. She dictated when and where we went, at what time, and what we did when we got there.

I vowed to change. To be independent. To find myself, whatever I was. And if it was with Denny, all the better. But I needed to become secure with myself first.

I looked around in the dimness of the room. The colorful shadows from the stained glass windows shaded the darkness. It was beautiful. I felt content here, and this was my home now. But I needed to work on me.

Around 6:00 a.m., I was wide awake and raring to go. But I remained in bed in a supine position until eight. And then I sprang from my bed, determined to work harder to put my life in order for the sake of my own physical and questionable mental health.

Thanksgiving was right around the corner, and we had a lot to be grateful for. I wanted to make a pleasant family meal and to create some good memories.

Things were turning around in my life in a decent way. I had money, Ellie was out of trouble, and I was with Denny. *What else could I possibly want or need?*

CHAPTER 60

I showered and dressed in stretch pants and a white button-down shirt. I found a pair of Fatbaby boots that Sally had worn often and pulled the left one onto my foot. *A good fit.* Just like everything else that Sally left me. And wide enough for the Glock to fit inside if I needed to carry it.

I muffled my steps as I crept downstairs.

My phone rang, and the sense of trepidation returned when I saw the caller ID.

"Hello, Percy," I answered.

"How are you, Annie?" he asked.

"Everything is going well. How about you?"

He ignored my question.

"I'm calling about Trevor."

"I figured as much."

"He's in bad shape, but of course, you know that. I've done all I can for him. He barely made it through detox, and he's struggling with rehab. Apparently, he's been using heroin and other drugs for a long time. His only hope is to get him into a long-term program."

"What can I do?"

"I don't have the resources locally, but I've contacted a friend in northern Utah. He runs a drug camp in the middle of nowhere, and I think it would be a good fit for Trevor."

I bit my lip and asked, "How much?"

"As I said, he's a good friend. The usual cost for the three-month program is fifty grand. But I got him to hold a place for Trevor for twenty."

"What are the chances this will work?"

"Same as everyone in his condition. Less than 25 percent remain drug free for five years. But it's the only chance he has."

"I know he's bad."

"That's an understatement. He talks a good game, says the right things. But he's a veteran. Been in and out of several programs already, and he knows what we want to hear. But he has never been to a long-term program like the one in Utah. He'll be isolated from the world, forced to live a healthy lifestyle during his stay. It's in the middle of the desert. The only way in or out is by helicopter. And if he walks away from the place, he'll never make it back to civilization. Everyone has to pass an examination to rule out major health issues like heart or major organ problems. Trevor's borderline when it comes to his health. He'll have to sign a waiver, and he's willing to do that."

"He has a heart murmur. I can tell you because he assigned you as his health-care surrogate and gave you power of attorney. His exact words were *I trust her with my life*. Said there was no one else that cared about him more than you. Not even his family."

"Jeez. We're just friends. That's sad."

"He wasn't very forthcoming at first. But after detox, he became depressed, and the stories just seemed to pour out. He's had a troubled life."

I was silent for a few seconds. We'd said enough. Handing over the money was the only thing left to do.

"I can drop by tomorrow."

"That's fine."

"Thanks, Percy. And Happy Thanksgiving."

Another can of worms. It was becoming a habit that I wished I could break.

I needed a distraction, so I finally sorted through the pile of mail I'd picked up from my apartment. Then I logged into my bank account and paid bills.

As I sorted through the rest of the junk, I became aware that I hadn't received any mail in this big house that burned electricity and gas and used water like crazy. A feeling of urgency resounded. I didn't want to live without these conveniences.

I stood in front of the house and looked around for a mailbox but found nothing on the road. There wasn't anything by the entryway either.

I went back to the street and stood facing the house. And then I saw it—a big iron box attached to an oak tree. I stared at the keyhole in the back.

Out of the keys Ranger had given me, I'd found locks for all but one.

I stuck the last key on the ring into the hole, but it didn't turn. I tried it upside down and sideways, but nothing happened. And then I pressed the button, and the door opened. Apparently, the keyhole was a fake distraction.

I was a little disappointed that the last key was still unaccounted for.

The mailbox was so stuffed, it was hard to pull everything out.

Back inside, I sorted through the pile and disposed of the junk. I found Sally's American Express statement, three pages of charges, but no payment was due. No household bills, but there was personal mail for Gates, which made sense because he and Sally were getting married, and he was moving in with her. I wondered again what went wrong.

I examined the statements from the bank accounts that Ranger had given me. There was nothing there, no signs of payments for credit cards or utilities.

I ended up back in the office with the statements from Merrill Lynch. I discovered that an amount was transferred every month from interest and gains into a separate account, and the proceeds were more than enough to cover expenses.

I eyed the debits and credits and noted that the electric bill ran more than I made in a week. Sally's credit cards, taxes, and insurance were all paid automatically.

I looked back during the year and was shocked at the property tax bill, over twenty thousand dollars, and the homeowner's insurance was nearly as much.

I had enough money for a few months, but not enough to afford those kinds of costs for long. I decided to leave well enough alone. These accounts would transfer to me soon enough, and in the meanwhile, bills were being taken care of.

61
CHAPTER

Plans for Thanksgiving materialized remarkably. As expected, Mom didn't make it. Beth showed up, and to my surprise, she brought the twins—the two babies that her estranged husband, Carl, had conceived with a dancer that caused the destruction of their marriage.

But they were adorable little creatures, and Beth repeatedly apologized for bringing them. Carl and his paramour were working. She'd stopped dancing and started waiting tables at the restaurant where Carl worked as a chef. They were called in at the last minute and asked Beth to watch the babies. Odd, but true.

At that point in my life, I didn't care. I just wanted everything to come together on a good day and for us to become more of a family.

The twins were a big hit. Everyone took turns doting over them.

Ellie and I cooked turkey and all the fixings, and we all overate until we had to unbutton our pants.

62
CHAPTER

A week later, I was feeling great. My ankle had finally stopped throbbing. I hadn't had a drink, and I hadn't been to a single AA meeting.

I wheeled into the orthopedist's office with a smile. The technician piled a blanket over my midsection to protect my baby and then took x-rays of my ankle. While I waited for the results, I called Denny and made dinner plans, and we agreed on seven.

I rolled down the hall to a room and waited. The doctor entered, holding a DVD. He shoved it into his laptop and pointed at the image of what I assumed to be my ankle.

"See this?" he asked. "This is your talus. It's the bone that connects your foot to the tibia. This white spot is calcium built up, and it appears that it's healed crookedly. You'll need to have surgery to correct it."

"What happens if I don't?"

"You'll walk with a limp. May cause arthritis." He squinted carefully at the black-and-white image. "We need to talk seriously about surgery right now. I can go in and reposition the bone—"

"I can't," I exhaled as I interrupted.

"It'll be worse later." He popped the DVD out.

"Don't take it personally, Doc. I'm pregnant. And I need this thing off."

I picked up my leg and held it high.

He shrugged. Without another word, he grabbed an electric saw and began the process.

And I walked out of the building with a limp that would remain with me for the rest of my life.

As soon as I got in my car, I closed my eyes, thanked God that the burden of the cast was gone, and scratched the itch that had driven me crazy for weeks.

And then I drove to my first Krav Maga class.

CHAPTER 63

I learned that Krav Maga was a system of self-defense that was developed for the Israel Defense Forces. It was comprised of a combination of several combat techniques and was derived from street fighting.

My instructor, Yen Foo, was from Vietnam. The short, petite middle-aged man was highly proficient in his art. Despite his small stature, he could take down the toughest students in the class and demonstrated this ability often.

Foo was not to be fooled with. He was leery when I disclosed I was pregnant, and at first, he said absolutely not.

And then I did something that was way out of character for me. I revealed that I'd been drugged and assaulted, and his resistance ceased. We worked it out where I would be primarily an observer.

Mr. Foo spoke in his Asian accent throughout most of our first class.

"The original concept of Krav Maga is to take the most simple and practical techniques of other fighting styles and to make them rapidly teachable to military novices," he explained.

"Krav Maga is an aggressive philosophy emphasizing simultaneous defensive and offensive maneuvers, and several military organizations teach these techniques.

"First, try to avoid battle. Always be aware of your surroundings because danger is everywhere. However, if avoidance is impossible or unsafe, you must act quickly and aggressively. Here, you will learn the most vulnerable parts of the body and how to attack. And you will learn the methods you need to cause injury and/or death to the enemy.

"It's like shooting a gun. Not shooting for fun. If you point a gun at an adversary, you must shoot to kill. No messing around. This is the same. You fight to kill. If you disable in the process, that's okay too. As long as you achieve the goal to incapacitate your opponent."

I learned that the most vulnerable points of a human body are the eyes, neck or throat, face, solar plexus, groin, ribs, knees, feet, fingers, and liver. Mr. Foo said to zero in on the most accessible target and hit hard, fast, and often.

Foo also covered the area of situational awareness to identify potential threats before an attack occurs.

"As you observe your surroundings, you must also have the intelligence to know when you are in a dire situation. Control impulses, and do not do something reckless like attacking an innocent.

"Also, never strike for revenge. Confucius said, *Before you embark on a journey of revenge, dig two graves.* It is a beast that will eat you from the inside out. Forgiveness is the lamb that will allow you to sleep at night.

"Krav Maga is for protection. Do not use it unless you are prepared for someone to die."

If I'd heard someone say that a few months ago, I would have been terrified. But I had discovered anger within me. I was mad as hell about being drugged helpless and whatever had happened without my permission.

When the class was over, Mr. Foo asked me to stay.

After everyone had left, he said, "You have been hurt."

I stared at the floor, not knowing how to react and wishing I hadn't told him about my attack.

"You are taking a big step to regain your sense of self. Just remember that you are the master of your fate and the captain of your soul."

I whispered, "Invictus." It had been a long time since I thought about the words of one of my favorite poems. *Out of the night that covers me, Black as the night from pole to pole...*

He smiled and said, "I hope you find peace, and one day you will be unafraid."

I stopped at the grocery store on the way home and picked up food for a romantic dinner I was planning for Denny.

As I parked in the lot, I thought I saw a truck that looked a lot like Sam's pull around the corner. I kept my eye on it as it drove away, and I realized I hadn't thought about him in days. He had made a threatening remark, and I needed to watch my back.

Mr. Foo reminded me, *Danger is everywhere.*

As I placed items in my basket, I couldn't get Sam out of my head. The most obvious question I had was *Why?* He appeared to be successful in his business and personal life, but now he was desperate to get away.

And I was troubled that Denny and I hadn't spoken about it after Sam was banned. We just let it go.

We talked a lot, but mainly about the past and the mistakes we'd made.

I wanted to look toward our future, but our pasts had so many unresolved loose ends.

64

I cooked shrimp with a light sauce. I added more but-ter, skipped the white wine that the recipe called for, and tasted. It wasn't bad. Not as tasty as usual, but still quite good.

As I watched the water come to a boil for the linguini, nagging paranoia returned. *Black sedans, Sam's threats, and Sally's death. Danger was everywhere.*

And then there was the question of the paternity of my unborn child.

I was scheduled for amniocentesis in a few weeks, and it would contain the necessary DNA. I still had the bong that Sam sucked on and planned to use it to assist in my search.

Then there was Benny, my big mistake. But the swab I'd taken from the unknown person sent chills down my spine.

Denny hadn't asked, and I wasn't going to mention it, at least until I was sure.

I dressed in a low-cut lace top and a pair of designer jeans that seemed to accentuate my good features and hide my pudgy belly. I'd gained a few pounds since I quit drinking and started eating better. And I wasn't experiencing so many withdrawal symptoms—*what a relief.*

I tossed a salad, set the table, and finished the pasta with a few sprigs of parsley. I hadn't cooked a complete meal by myself in a while, and it felt right to do so.

But Denny was late, and the pasta was getting cold when he finally showed up and apologized. He and his partner had to pick up a shoplifter from Marshalls and drop him off at the county jail.

I heard what he said, but the word *partner* stuck in my mind.

"We need to talk more," I blurted out. "I didn't even know you had a partner."

"Her name is Gina. She's divorced and has two children. We'll have her over for dinner if that's okay with you. You can meet her, and you can meet all my friends."

We sat down at the table to slightly warm pasta, and our meal began with a kiss.

And then Denny said, "I love you."

I gasped for air as he smiled and kissed me again.

"Too much too soon?" he asked.

"I love you too," I said as I exhaled.

"Tell me about your day."

I couldn't keep the smile from my face as I twirled pasta on a fork. "I've started a self-defense training program."

"Good for you. What kind?"

"Krav Maga."

He sat back. "Is there something I should know about?"

"I want to be able to protect myself."

"But Krav Maga?"

236

"You're familiar with the concept?"

"Somewhat, but not entirely."

"It's founded on the idea of self-defense and being aware of your surroundings. Sally died because she didn't know what was happening around her."

Denny took my hand. "I understand that you were personally and profoundly affected by her death, and I want to help you through this. I can protect you."

"You're not with me all the time."

"That's true, but this is a bit extreme. Are you sure this is the way you want to deal with it?"

"Yes."

"If this is what you want, I'm all in."

"You're perfect, better than I'd ever dreamed of," I said. "But there's something I've been avoiding. Something I need to tell you about myself."

He smiled and said, "Shoot."

"My mother hates me. I don't know why, and I hope you don't think less of me because of this."

He furrowed his brow and looked away.

"First of all, there's a lot of that going around. Difficulties between mothers and daughters, that is."

"Huh?"

"Please don't think I'm making comparisons, but Olivia's mother was never happy with anything she did, except me. She loved me. Her daughter? Ah, not so much. Her mother expected perfection from her and never settled for less. Liv grew up terrified of her."

Same as me.

"She became neurotic about everything. Our home had to be spotless just in case Harriet stopped in. And she did all the time, unexpectedly. It was as if she wanted to see something bad so she could criticize Liv because she enjoyed it so much.

"But Liv was perfect, so much better than me. I was the flawed one.

"During our marriage, even though I loved Liv, I did things to her that she didn't deserve. I drank a lot, not as much as when I reached rock bottom, but quite a bit. I didn't come home when I should have and lied about it. I'd say I was on a stakeout, but I was really at a bar around the corner." He hesitated for a beat.

"And I cheated on her."

I tried not to react, but I was stunned.

"With my previous partner. We got together a couple of times, and I felt horrible about it afterward. I wanted to confess to Liv, but I knew it would hurt her, so I left it alone. When she got cancer, I was glad I didn't say anything. She didn't need to be unhappy in her last days. It was the best thing I ever did.

"There are many things I regret, but one thing that gnaws at me is that I didn't stand up to her mother for her. I witnessed the abuse and did nothing about it. And it was brutal. According to her mother, Liv was either too thin or too fat. The food she cooked contained too much salt or too little. Our home was always super clean and orderly, but Harriet would find other things. Like the furniture didn't go with the carpet, and the ceiling fans were never at the right speed."

"That's ridiculous," I said.

"I should have stopped it," he said as he shook his head. "But I took the easy way. Conflict avoidance was my mantra. At work, I could break heads, but at home, I just wanted peace and quiet so I could keep on doing whatever I wanted. Even if it was at my wife's expense, I just wanted to drink and not deal with the errors of my ways."

"I'm far from perfect, so we're a good pair," I said but instantly regretted it.

He smiled and said, "I've been attracted to you since I first saw you at the track. There's something about you that made my head turn when you walked by. But I was in recovery at first and afraid of rejection afterward. I tried to get your attention several times, but you never seemed interested."

"I thought you were married and too good for me," I admitted.

"We've wasted a lot of time." Denny smiled with his whole face.

I took his hand and led him upstairs.

CHAPTER 65

I was back in the pit, and it was more frightening than ever. I tried to grasp on to something, anything to pull myself out, but the walls were slick as ice. And I feared there was no way out of this one.

I woke up soaked with sweat.

I lay still for a moment beside Denny as I calmed. And then I heard what sounded like someone walking on the ceiling above me.

At first, I thought the noise came from the roof, and then I realized that the ceiling above me was flat, but the actual top of the church came to a peak. I didn't know why I hadn't noticed it before, but there was an attic in this place, and someone or something was up there.

I shook Denny, placed a finger to his lips, and whispered, "I think someone's in the attic."

He found his gun, and I grabbed the Glock from the nightstand next to me.

He dialed his cell and said, "Stay put."

But I didn't listen.

Curiosity drew me into the closet. I shoved the clothes aside. As I stared at the back wooden paneled wall, the footsteps became louder.

I could hear Denny whispering to dispatch in the background as I touched the wooden barrier. I shoved it sideways, but nothing budged at first.

I pushed the clothes to the other side and gave it another try. This time the wall moved, revealing a stairway. I was shaking like crazy and glad I wasn't alone.

And then I realized that I was in charge of my fate. The fear disappeared, and I stopped shaking. I sensed danger, but I was ready for it.

I inched quietly upward, stood just below the wooden floor above, and I felt Denny behind me. He crept up beside with his gun in his hand. We peeked out together, side by side.

The dim moonlight lit through stained glass windows. At first, I couldn't see anything except shadows and furniture.

And then a man stepped out of the darkness opening cabinets and tearing through the contents.

I edged back as I heard the faint but welcoming sound of sirens in the near distance. *Help was on the way.*

I took a step back down, and the wood creaked. I froze as I heard a pop, and a bullet whizzed overhead.

Denny fired back, jumped into the attic, and rolled to a ready position.

He shouted, "Stop or I'll shoot!"

But the intruder didn't heed the warning. Footsteps thundered through the attic.

I flipped the light switch on a wall, and the place lit up. I crept back up and saw Denny staring at the far corner of the room. He moved quickly from wall to wall, leading with his gun and me shadowing behind.

We ended up gawking downward at a spiral staircase that led into darkness.

Denny asked, "Did you recognize him?"

"It was too dark."

Sirens echoed from outside, and red-and-blue lights flashed through the stained glass.

I ran downstairs and opened the door.

Two police cruisers were parked haphazardly at the curb. Four cops approached with their weapons out.

Pup greeted everyone with a wagging tail and a friendly yip.

As the house filled with uniformed police, Ellie emerged from her room and asked, "Was that a gunshot?"

"Someone was in the attic," I replied.

"We have an attic?"

"Apparently."

One of the uniforms with a name tag stating his last name as Hardy approached. "How do you get up there?"

Denny led the way as a parade of cops followed with weapons drawn.

After a few minutes, Denny returned and said, "Stay here."

And then he was gone again, joining the rest of the searchers outside.

More patrol cars and unmarked cruisers pulled in as I stood with Ellie. She was shaking. But I wasn't, nor was I afraid.

I was ready to defend myself and my daughter. Mr. Foo was doing his job.

After a long and thorough search, they didn't find anyone. They examined the spiral staircase leading downward but couldn't figure out how to open the door at the bottom. I gave up the last key, but they were still unsuccessful.

The CSI team arrived and pried bullets out of the wall and fingerprinted the attic. And we gave statements about what had occurred.

The sun came up, and everyone left except for a single patrol car that remained outside on the street.

Denny stayed home until the locksmith showed up again.

CHAPTER  66

Because of the recent issues, Fareed suggested I replace all the locks with something called EVVA MCS. He said it was a magnetic lock and very complicated and almost impossible to infiltrate.

He showed me an oddly shaped key with a row of round holes.

I answered quickly, "Replace them all and give me six master keys. And we have one more door to deal with." I showed him to the closet, and he followed me upward.

When we reached the landing, Fareed was already moving toward the far corner.

As he disappeared into the darkness, I took a better look at the room. It was spacious, with a bathroom next to the entryway. Large enough for a couple of people to live in.

It was also equipped with a kitchen area, sink, stove, and small wood-paneled refrigerator. The little icebox was packed with drinks: water, beer, and soda.

I opened an overhead cabinet and found an abundance of vacuum bags of Patriot Pantry food. Other cupboards contained cases marked "Emergency Survival Kit." Three months' supplies in each box, twenty in all. Enough for a person to live for years.

I was so engrossed by what I'd found, I wasn't paying attention to Fareed.

The sound of his voice made me jump.

"I'm here in the circular stairway. Meet me outside so we can locate the door."

I heard him, but I wasn't really listening. My eyes settled on a bed behind the boxes and other junk stored in the room. The covers were thrown around, and it appeared that this bed had been slept in recently.

"Ms. Laine?" Fareed interrupted my thoughts.

"I'll meet you down there."

I hurried around the house to where I'd imagined the door should be in proximity to where Fareed had indicated. I expected him to be standing outside, but he was nowhere in sight.

I heard pounding and followed the sound around the corner toward the back of the house. Dark hardwood covered every inch of the exterior, and the door was hard to find. Eventually, I found a dimple in the wood. I pressed it, the panel opened, and I faced another door with a keyhole.

Fareed's voice leaked through. "You need to unlock from outside. It's dark, and I can't find the knob. Hurry up. It's hot in here."

I used the final key, inserted it, and tumblers fell into place. The door opened, and a wave of musty heat hit me in the face. Fareed stepped through, drenched in sweat.

I peered inside at a small dark landing yielding to a spiral staircase.

After he was done, he handed me the bill. The bottom line was more than I had paid for my used Volvo ten years ago.

"Thank you, Fareed," I said. "Now I need you to do me a favor."

He answered with a stare.

"Teach me how to pick a lock."

CHAPTER 67

I gave him more cash, and Fareed gave me a lock and a pick set, and he showed me the basics.

"Stick the tension wrench into the bottom of the keyhole, apply light pressure, and then use the pick of your choice to move the tumblers into place," Fareed said.

He noted that the rake pick was his go-to, but I should try each tool to determine my own personal favorite. And then he told me to be careful and to never tell anyone where I'd gotten the kit or advice on how to use it.

I tried the rake pick first and did what he had shown me. It took a couple of times, and I managed to open the lock in just short of fifteen minutes. *Too much time.*

My efforts were interrupted when Denny dropped by. He entered carrying an overnight bag, and I greeted him with a kiss. Sex was a huge part of our relationship, and I didn't have any complaints. He excited me just by standing near me.

He placed his bag on the floor and made sure the door was secure before leading me upstairs.

Our lovemaking had become more familiar. We had become comfortable with pleasing each other without the clumsiness of new lovers. And it was good.

Afterward, I said, "Move in."

"I'm already here most of the time."

"Bring your clothes and whatever else you want. This place is big enough for you and your things." I paused as I waited for an immediate affirmation, but he didn't say anything.

"Where do you live anyway?" I realized I didn't know. He'd never taken me to his place. A chill of insecurity washed over me. *He had secrets, just like Sally.*

The sides of his mouth turned up, and dimples dented his smooth cheeks. And his eyes—beautiful blue eyes—sparkled with happiness. *I was in over my head.*

"I have a house. Not as big or as good as yours, but it's okay, and it's paid for. The best thing I like about it is that it has a pool. And I like to exercise by swimming laps."

"I could put one in."

He laughed and said, "Where? In the middle of your graveyard?" And then he pulled me to him. I laid my head on his chest and listened to his heartbeat.

He ran his fingers through my hair and massaged my scalp, and it felt good.

And then his phone rang.

He examined the number with interest and let it ring four times before answering. "This is Lieutenant McCaffery. May I help you?"

As he listened to the voice on the line, I headed for the shower.

The next thing I knew, Denny was right in there with me.

I laughed. "You're a pretty frisky fellow."

"My captain has requested a meeting. And when the captain calls, a speedy response is imperative."

He washed quickly, kissed me goodbye, and said he'd see me later.

"Keep the Glock with you at all times and double-check the doors and the alarm, please," he insisted.

I furrowed my brow.

And then he said, "Yes, I'll move in."

I did a happy dance inside my head.

CHAPTER 68

The morning sun had lightened the colorful windows, and I heard Ellie moving around in her room.

I made breakfast, and I gave her the funny-looking new key.

I told her about what I'd found upstairs—the food supply, kitchenette, bed, sofa, and even a TV and DVD player.

"It's a small apartment, like an efficiency," I said.

"Survival food? What was Sally into?" She shook her head.

I shrugged and hesitated for a few seconds before I asked, "How close were you?"

"Not close at all. Sally called and said she wanted to help me. I was surprised. I don't even know how she got my number."

"When was that?"

"Shortly after the last time I spoke to you about needing money. A couple of weeks before she was killed. We met in a Walmart parking lot. She gave me the pack and told me what to do."

"Was there anyone other than Sally involved?"

"Just her at first. The voice on the phone that threatened me was a man, but I don't know who that was."

Something I did had set Ellie's troubles in motion. I had met Sally for lunch at the Okeechobee Steak House on our day off a few weeks before she was killed, and I had mentioned that I needed money for Ellie.

And then we ate steaks and drank martinis. Sally paid, of course, and we laughed throughout the meal. But for the life of me, I couldn't remember what was so funny. That was the day she told me she was planning to marry Gates.

And that led back to the question. *Where was Gates?* I still hadn't seen him at the tables.

Ellie looked down and then away, avoiding my eyes.

"What is it?"

"I lied to the judge. I dropped off backpacks twice before they caught me. Sally paid me five hundred cash each time. Do you think I'm a terrible person?"

I caressed the side of her face and said, "You're good, Ellie. Money makes a difference in people's lives. As much as I hate to admit it, I don't feel good when I don't have enough. I found some cash when I moved in here, and I can't remember being happier. At work, money makes the games. People want it, and that's why they come. And they turn up in droves. Hundreds of thousands of dollars pass through my fingers each night. People get happy when they win and become miserable when they lose. It's the way things are."

"For me, it's just a vehicle to get what I want?"

"What do you want, Ellie?"

"I want to finish my education and teach at a good university. And then I want to meet the right guy and have a family. Big house and lots of kids."

She reminded me of my similar plans from years ago, and my heart ached.

"I've been missing for a while," I said.

"I was older, and it was all right. I didn't need you so much. But I need you now, and you're here where you should be."

And I remembered being there too. I hadn't been drinking all my life. I hadn't started my destructive behavior until Ellie began to pull away when she was in high school, just like most kids seem to do. Then she left home, went to live in the dorm, and I was alone. That's when I'd started my downward spiral. She'd kept me sane and sober.

And then she dropped a bomb. "Aunt Bethie called and asked if we have room for her."

I gulped. I loved my sister, but she was so very needy. She talked too much about her problems and didn't have a filter of any kind. I could only take her for the short run.

"Sure, Beth can stay with us," I said.

Family is family, and it was a big house.

CHAPTER 69

Denny was working, Ellie and Beth went shopping, and I was alone. But I didn't need anyone to help me with what I was about to do.

It was a dark chilly day that threatened rain as I stood out back of my house and looked at my sad little Volvo sitting in disrepair, parked next to the garage. On the other side, nestled next to a slatted wood fence, was the motor home.

I walked through the graveyard and opened the door to my old car. I cringed as the smell of stale alcohol and aged upholstery hit me.

Old beer and soda cans littered the floor. I cleaned the car out, throwing everything into a plastic grocery bag I found stuffed under the seat.

It had been months since I tried to start it, and was reasonably sure the battery was dead. I sat down in the driver's seat and turned the key. Nothing happened, just as I had expected.

I searched the garage for jumper cables but didn't find any.

As I trudged back toward the house, something caught my eye. A tomb with a headstone with the image of a young girl etched into the granite. Underneath the image, the words and numbers brought me to my knees. "Born 8-1-50, Died 10-20-56." This little girl died just after her sixth birthday. And her name was Amanda Grover.

Sally's daughter? I wondered. And then I noticed the stone next to it. "Selma Grover. Born 9-18-51, Died 10-1-2020." Sally was buried in my backyard, and I didn't even know it. I'd vaguely remembered asking someone where she was, but no one knew. She had planned her own ceremony and burial. And I was surprised to learn that she was nearly seventy. I would have never guessed.

She was in total control of her life and her death and everything else, even me.

I sat down on the crisp grass for a while and thought about my feelings of anger toward her. How could she have gotten Ellie involved with illegal drug trafficking? *Was she a friend or a foe?*

We'd traveled in her motor home, and she paid for everything and even staked me in poker tournaments. She threw a lot of money at me. I came in fifth and won seven thousand dollars two years ago. Her cut was half. But she wouldn't take it.

Why had she chosen me as her friend? She could have hung out with anyone. I thought back to my first day at the Boat, and she picked me out of the crowd and offered friendship. That was over seven years ago, but it seemed like she'd been with me all my life.

I looked at the big house she'd left behind and the Beamer sitting in the parking lot next to it, and all that money, ill-gotten more than likely. And now my family was secure inside, and we were all reaping the benefits from her endeavors.

When I finally stood up, I was less angry with Sally.

After purchasing a set of jumper cables from an auto parts store, I pulled the Beamer next to the Volvo. I left it running as I opened the hoods of both cars. After attaching the cables, I got into the Volvo and turned the key, and the old car started smoothly.

I threw the cables in the garage and looked around. There was enough room to park two cars in there. So I pulled the Beamer inside.

On the way out, I noticed a ring of keys hanging on a hook by the door.

I'd finally found locks for the keys on the Hello Kitty ring and wasn't up for more mystery.

I pulled them off the hook and examined them, eight small keys and two big ones. One large one looked like an ignition key, and the other had a rounded head. I was confident this set was for the RV.

Sally upgraded her motor home last year from a Coachmen Freelander to a Canyon Star class A with a garage. We'd taken several trips in the Freelander but only made one trip in this one.

I unlocked and opened the RV door and stepped up into the living area. The place smelled of booze, pot, and Sally. I climbed into the captain's seat, put the key into the ignition, and turned. To my surprise, it started up right away.

I did a quick look around and found more of Sally's clothes hanging in the closet. And I found a money belt

SKYLER KENT

in one of the drawers. I remember Sally using it when we went on our gambling trip, and it still had a few hundred dollars in it.

I locked the motor home, thinking about traveling as a family. We could go to the mountains or spend time on a lonely beach somewhere and just relax.

I drove the Volvo to Jiffy Car Wash. Four short dark-skinned men detailed the old car and almost made it shine.

It was past dark when I'd finished with the distractions and chores and returned home. I dressed in black and then slid back into the Volvo behind the wheel.

256

CHAPTER 70

I parked in front of Gates's house and approached the fence pillar with the message to ring for entry.

I pressed the button, not really expecting a reply.

I got back in my car and drove up the block looking for a property without fencing or walls. I stopped at a vacant lot covered with palm trees and sea grapes with a sign posted on the road, *Private Property, Intruders will be prosecuted.*

So I broke the law.

I walked in the sand, through the dense vegetation, to the water. And then I jogged down the beach to the back of Gates's house.

He had a screened-in pool with a Jacuzzi, waterfall, and cabana, all colored in hues of greens and blues.

I pulled on a pair of latex gloves and knocked on the French doors. I didn't have fingerprints, but I worried about DNA. It seems they can get it from anywhere nowadays, even sweat.

Receiving no reply, I lit up my phone and peeked through the window at Italian tile, wool rugs, and expensive furnishings. Cardboard boxes were stacked along the wall, but I sensed no activity whatsoever.

I looked around for signs of an alarm system but didn't see any.

I edged to another set of French doors and glanced inside at the master bedroom, where I spotted a little green light on a panel on the wall. Gates had a burglar alarm, but it wasn't activated.

The door was locked, so I removed the pick set from my pocket and went to work.

I was inside within a matter of minutes, and the smell of putrid meat greeted me like a punch to my face.

I coughed and gagged as I looked around.

In the master bedroom, there was a partially packed suitcase sitting on top of a white down feather comforter.

The buzzing sound of insects caught my attention coming from the master bath. I pushed the door open and found Gates rotting away in the sunken Jacuzzi tub in front of a huge picture window with a beautiful view of the ocean behind him.

His head was above the blood blackened water, and his mouth and eyes were wide open. Maggots and flies were feasting on his swollen tongue, crawling in and out of his nose and what was left of his eyeballs.

As time went on, the putrid smell was getting easier to take, and I resumed my investigation.

Nothing was unusual in the kitchen and living areas.

I found a packed box labeled "Financial Records" and tore the tape off. Closing papers for the house were on top. I was surprised to see that Gates's home sold for a whopping $12.5 million. But the payoff figure between the first and second mortgages was more than $13 million. He'd had to pay to sell his house.

His latest Charles Schwab statement showed the withdrawal. After that, he'd sold everything and withdrew two million, leaving a balance of seventy-four thousand.

After a closer examination of the closing papers, I found that the new owners lived in Europe and had handled everything through an attorney. They had no idea that their house smelled of death, and the previous owner was rotting in the tub.

I put everything back, re-taped the box, left the same way I'd come in, and drove home.

CHAPTER 71

I parked next to the garage and walked through the graveyard to the back door.

I undressed and stuffed everything I was wearing into the washer, dropped a double Tide pod into the water, and started the machine.

The stench of death was still with me as I wrapped myself in a towel I found in the dryer and hurried toward the stairs.

When Denny said, "Hello, Annie." I nearly jumped out of my skin.

I turned on the light and said, "Gates is dead."

"Take a long bath, and I'll spray the house with a deodorizer."

"You always know the best things to do."

I soaked at first and then scrubbed every inch of my body. And then I emptied the tub and refilled it and washed again and shampooed my hair repeatedly.

After a while, Denny appeared at the door.

"Talk to me," he said as he sat down.

"Sally's fiancé. Gatlin Weekly. He plays at the track, at least he used to, and he was a judge."

"What does he look like?"

"About eighty, I'd say. And wears his gray hair in a ponytail. Kind of eccentric, and—"

"That old guy that wears sandals and food-stained shirts?"

I nodded.

"He was engaged to Sally?"

"Odd, but true. Sally went to Vegas to get married, but he didn't show up. She was upset when I picked her up at the airport. He didn't make it because he was dead."

"How'd you find him?"

"He used to play poker every day, but I hadn't seen him since Sally was killed. I went to his house to see if he was all right. But I found him in the tub with maggots crawling in and out of his orifices."

"You broke in?"

"I picked the lock," I said as I looked away.

Denny took some time to gather his thoughts. "I sensed that you may be searching for resolve, and I understand. But I must ask you to please consider all the risks before acting in the future. It's not just you anymore. Ellie, the baby, and I love you very much and would truly miss you if you were to end up on the wrong side of the steel bars or, worst yet, dead."

He took a breath. "I don't mean to lecture. Let me help you. If there are similar things that you feel you need to do, just include me. I have some authority, and I can keep you out of trouble."

"What can you do? You're a police officer. How would you feel about picking a lock and entering someone's home? That's illegal for both of us."

"Sweetheart." He bit his lip. "I love what I do, and I'm good at it. I solve crimes. But sometimes, I cross lines. And I don't have a problem doing that if the net result is favorable. For me, justice is the bottom line." He paused. "I hope that doesn't scare you."

I shook my head.

"I think we make a hell of a team," he said as he grabbed a towel.

I agreed, but I doubted I'd be able to keep my word. Not totally, at least. I would never let Denny help me search for everything that I was looking for, which included the identity of the father of my child. That was my personal mission.

Denny held out the towel and said, "You're shriveled. Time to get out."

"I can still smell it."

"You're the only one who can. It's in your nasal passageway, and it will be with you for a while."

I got up and wrapped myself in the towel.

"So here's the story," Denny said. "Your friend, Sally, was killed recently, and her fiancé hasn't been seen since. You became concerned and asked me to drop by his place to check on him."

"I don't want to be alone. Can't you just call someone?"

"And tell them what? My superhot girlfriend decided to play detective and broke into his house and found his rotting body in the bathtub?"

My jaw dropped.

"So…you think I'm superhot?"

He smiled.

"I've got to go, but I'm warning you, I'm going to come back smelling just like you did."

"I'll hold my nose and run you a bath."

He kissed me, and I said, "Stay safe, my dear."

CHAPTER 72

I assumed Gates's and Sally's deaths were connected. And maybe everything had something to do with Sam and his troubles, but I wasn't in the mood to fret over the madness. I was feeling more secure, but the past was more vexing than I could ignore. As hard as I tried to convince myself that it didn't matter, it did.

I left the house on a mission.

I drove faster than I should have to the Hole. I hadn't been there in a while, but I was still surprised that Finn wasn't there. I approached the stranger behind the bar with unnatural dark red hair and dull brown eyes. The skin sagged around his chin, and I guessed him to be in his midfifties, maybe rounding sixty.

"Where's Finn?" I asked.

"Quit" was all he said as he drew a beer from the tap.

"Do you know where he went?"

"No idea. One day he was here. The next he was gone like the wind."

He moved away and slapped the draft down in front of a guy on the other side of the bar.

My lungs deflated, and I inhaled deeply. The too-familiar smell entered my nostrils, and I craved a beer.

My hands shook, and I was sweating like crazy as I asked him, "What's your name?"

"I'm Tab. Just like the old Diet Coke drink in the pink can," he said with a bit of a grin.

I took a seat at the bar and trembled, "Hello, Tab. My name is Annie, and I need a draft."

He sauntered directly to the tap, picked up a cold glass from an ice bath, and drew the amber liquid.

As he slid the brew toward me, my mouth watered, and my pulse raced. I was excited about the prospect of infusing my system with alcohol and felt a bit of a sexual tingle.

I quickly picked up the glass and lifted it to my lips. I sniffed. The only thing better would've been to guzzle the brew and get another and another and two more. I took a big swig into my mouth and swished it around without swallowing. It never tasted so good.

I put my hand on my stomach and spit the beer back into the glass.

I left a five on the bar and departed. Once out the door, I crammed a piece of gum into my mouth as I rushed to my car.

CHAPTER 73

I hurried into the Lutheran church, where I had met Percy. I hadn't noticed before, but the place was beautiful, and it reminded me of my home.

Except for a few technical design differences, the buildings were the same.

I looked around and saw the balcony that was much like where my bedroom was. And the windows were colorful stained glass, just like home.

Take out the wooden altar and the form-fitting pews, build a kitchen up there on the landing, and this could be my house.

Unlike when I was there last, there was no meeting going on. No coffee brewing, no one admitting the errors of their ways in front of a crowd of troubled strangers. No fudge and no Percy.

But I wasn't disappointed. A feeling of calmness washed over me. I felt comfortable within the peaceful environment, and I realized what was important. I was here. I'd taken a critical step toward my recovery and had found comfort within this sanctuary.

I sat in a pew, stared at Christ in the center of the high place, and whispered to the figure nailed to a cross with bloodied hands, "I am powerless over my desire to drink, and my life has become unmanageable."

I searched my bag for the little book that Percy had given me and opened it and began to recite.

"God, give me the grace to accept with serenity the things that cannot be changed, the courage to change the things which should be changed, and the wisdom to know the difference."

CHAPTER 74

Sally had been murdered, Gates was dead, and my stomach was upset. But I had leaped over a massive hurdle by resisting the urge to swallow the beer.

I dialed, and Denny answered on the first ring.

"What's up?" he asked.

"Just curious. Do you have the time and cause of death on Gates?" I asked.

He hesitated. The silence lasted only a few seconds, but it seemed longer.

"Could have been a couple of months. The body was badly decomposed, and we hope to get the details from the ME later today. Why are you asking?"

"I assumed his death was the reason he didn't meet Sally in Vegas, and I just wanted to be sure. And it's fairly obvious that he was murdered, right?"

"It's a real possibility. What are you planning?"

"I'm just speculating on how the pieces of this puzzle fit together."

"Keep me in the loop, hon."

"I promise," I lied.

"Thanks, by the way. You're helping me look good with the Ds working this case, and I can always use the brownie points. Especially if this turns into something."

"Glad I could help."

"I love you," he said.

I melted.

"Me too," I managed to squeak out.

CHAPTER 75

After I hung up with Denny, I wanted to celebrate with alcohol. I closed my eyes, wished for the desire to go away, and I wondered how long it would take to not want to drink myself into a stupor.

When I opened my eyes, I stared at the rolltop desk across the room and remembered that I had stuffed the mail in it. Sally's mail. And Gates's mail was there too.

I sorted through the pile and pulled out a small yellow padded envelope with Gates's name written, but it didn't have any postage on it.

I opened it, and a key fell out along with a card for Extra Storage off Military Trail. On the back of the card were two numbers, the first one was seven digits, and the other was four.

As I drove south on Military Trail, I became aware that the desire for alcohol had dissipated. I realized more than ever that staying busy was a big part of staying sober. I vowed to keep as active as possible in the future. Or at least until I could control my desire.

I entered the seven-digit code written on the back of the card on the keypad to open the gate. I found a unit with four digits that matched the other number.

The key I'd found opened the heavy-duty padlock without a problem. And I began to think that this was too easy. I turned around and looked, halfway expecting a killer to be lurking behind me. Someone was looking for something, and people were dying because of it. *Danger was everywhere.*

I closed the door behind me to the small unit and turned on a dim overhead light. The area was sparsely filled with boxes of books and old furniture. I picked up several books and leafed through nothing but paper and words.

I stuck my hand into the folds in the furniture's crevasses and came up with lint and a few coins.

I turned on the flashlight on my iPhone and looked in the shadowy area behind a couch.

Shoeboxes piled halfway up to the ceiling lined the back wall.

The top row was filled with cheap shoes. Not Sally's style, for sure. When it came to leather, she wore the best. I wasn't even sure what they were made of, but they were all brand-new.

The second row was different.

The boxes were filled with money—*hundred-dollar bills.*

I counted quickly and estimated the amount to be two million dollars.

Finding money made me happy, but not this money. This cash smelled of trouble.

And another thing about this unit bothered me. There was no film of dust on any of the contents. It was as if these things were recently and randomly placed here for one reason: to hide the bounty of cash.

I had more questions than answers.

I put everything back as it was and locked up. As I drove away, the black car showed up again. It turned off when I looked in my rearview mirror.

I drove home the rest of the way with a tightness in my chest and an awful feeling in the pit of my stomach.

CHAPTER 76

I still felt a need to find Finn from the Hole to question him about the night Sally was killed.

I looked online and found the most recent address for Finnegan Dikes and drove to a duplex with cars in both driveways.

I approached unit B and knocked. As I waited, the sound of a baby crying leaked through the door.

A Hispanic woman holding a bawling infant answered abruptly. "Como?"

"Is Finn here?" I asked.

"No, Finn, no live here. Me, I only here," she said as she slammed the door.

I took a breath, moved to unit A, and knocked.

A dark-skinned man answered, dressed in work clothes with "AAA Mechanics" and the name Shack embroidered in cotton above his pocket.

"Hi," I said.

"What do you want?" Shack asked.

"Do you know Finn Dikes? The man who lives next door?"

"He don't live there anymore." He tried to close the door.

I put my best foot in between the door and jamb, and it didn't hurt much when he tried to slam it because he held back.

"Do you know where he went?"

"No, but if you find him, let me know. He owes me for rent."

"When did he move out?"

"Couple of months back. And Finn left everything. Ratty furniture, food in the fridge. I had a mess in there when I cleaned up. Had to store his stuff according to the law and put an ad in the paper, and then we auctioned it off. Didn't cover anything. But it's the legal process. I go by what's legal. Just in case you come from the county."

"I'm not from the county."

"Good thing, now take your foot out the door before I really close it."

77
CHAPTER

The amniocentesis wasn't altogether painless but wasn't nearly as bad as I'd expected. But I hoped that I would never have to go through getting a needle inserted into my stomach again.

After it was over, I requested DNA results in addition to the other stuff they checked for.

There was an additional charge for this, but I didn't care, and they said I'd have the results within five days.

I also asked where I could get a DNA test on items such as a toothbrush or a pipe, and they directed me to a local lab.

I rushed home, collected the bong that Sam had sucked on, and headed for the door. But something stopped me. I thought about the swab. I ran upstairs and pulled out the baggy I'd hidden behind a column of tissue in the back of my cabinet. It had to be Sam, I told myself.

I stuffed the baggy back. *One test at a time.*

I locked up and drove to Rapid Testing.

A tall, lanky brunette with white streaks in her shoulder-length hair sat at a desk behind a sliding glass window.

She greeted me with a smile, and the tag pinned to her blouse indicated that her name was Amber.

It was a drab place without much atmosphere, plainly painted dull beige walls lacking pictures of any kind.

And I was relieved that no one else entered the waiting area while I was there.

It wasn't long before Amber led me to a small room, handed me a swab, and told me to rub it around the inside of my cheek. I gave her a control number from my amniocentesis test and the pipe.

I didn't know why I felt the need to explain, but I said, "Just to be sure."

She bobbed her head and asked me for ID, six hundred bucks, and my signature on a standard form that gave them permission to obtain the results. Amber flipped her hair away from her shoulders and said, "It'll be about a week total. We'll call you."

The next seven days didn't move quickly enough for me.

I finally got a call from Dr. Jones, and he said he had good news. "There were no chromosomal abnormalities, and your HIV test was negative."

I felt relieved and said, "Thank you." And he asked me how I was doing.

"Fine, and better since I heard from you," I replied.

"Hang in there. We'll see you next month."

Work was decent. I was in a good mood, and the cards seemed to fly off my fingers. I made better-than-average tips, and life seemed good. I worried less and began thinking that the baby would be healthy and everything would be all right. *This trip to Europe might just be first class.*

I was convinced Sam was her biological father, and he had good-looking genes. But I wouldn't tell him anything about her. I would raise her myself.

CHAPTER 78

The next day, I was awakened by a call from Rapid Testing. A technician by the name of Pablo blurted out that there wasn't a match.

I lay in bed with my phone to my ear, hearing the words but not understanding totally what was being said. I had relied on it being Sam. Aesthetically, he was perfect, having every trait anyone could ever want in a child. *But...*

"Are you sure?" I asked.

The tech was polite as he replied, "The only DNA on the pipe was yours."

"Huh?" I sat up.

"That's all I know. Sorry, we couldn't be more helpful."

He hung up, and my world was spinning again.

CHAPTER

79

After washing my dark clothes several times, I could still smell Gates's decomposing body. So I threw everything out and purchased a black sweatshirt and baggy sweatpants from Walmart, along with a new pair of gloves and a ski mask.

Denny was on the job, and Ellie was in her room studying for exams when I drove my Volvo down the street where Sam lived. The car was still a bit smelly, and I noted that I should have it professionally cleaned again and soon.

I passed by once, parked up the street, and waited. *No lights, no movement in or out.* I wrapped a leather fanny pack around my expanding waist and shoved my Glock in my boot.

I approached the front door and rang the bell, and Michael Jackson sang "Beat It."

Cute.

No one answered.

I looked through the etched glass window in the door and confirmed there was no movement within.

I pulled the gloves on and tried the door, but it was locked.

I moved in the shadows around the house to the back. The pool emitted a swampy smell, proof that no one had been there for a while.

I looked through the sliding glass doors that led to the bedroom and saw nothing out of the ordinary, *same big bed and red wall.* My stomach flipped.

I tried the door and was surprised that it wasn't locked. As I slid it open, the smell of death hit me. I pulled a hand towel from my bag and covered my face before stepping inside.

I wasn't here to find another dead body, but I could do nothing about that at the time.

I headed for the bathroom, picked up the electric toothbrush from the counter, and shoved it into my bag.

I could have left at that point, but I just had to be sure.

I followed the smell through the house and found the body in the kitchen. But it wasn't Sam. I couldn't recognize him because there was a hole in his head where his face should have been, but I could tell the body was a male, and this man was shorter than Sam and not as buff.

I had no idea who I was looking at.

I jumped when I heard the phone ring. I looked at the caller ID on the house phone and read that ADT was calling. I glanced at the keypad by the door, and the red light was blinking.

Stupid. I hadn't checked.

I hurried out the door and back down the street.

Suddenly, I felt eyes on me. I stopped and scanned the street, didn't see anyone, so I continued to my car.

CHAPTER 80

After disposing of my clothes, scrubbing myself, and spraying the house, I crawled into bed and waited for Denny.

I tossed around beneath the covers for hours before I heard the door open and footsteps coming up the stairs.

I blinked and rubbed my eyes as if I'd been asleep.

Denny turned on the light, and I was surprised that he stood in front of me in his underwear. My surprise turned insightful as the dead-body smell hit me, and I knew.

"How's it going?" I asked.

"We should talk," Denny said.

He sprinkled the room with Smelleze before stepping into the bathroom, where he soaked. I sat down on the edge of the tub and looked into his eyes.

"You don't have to ask," I said. "I know you saw me at Sam's house. And I thought I was hiding so well."

He smiled.

"I had to do it. Sorry, but I have so many questions without answers."

I didn't bother to explain that I was there to get a toothbrush when I came across the rotting corpse.

"Do you know Mikhail Vazov?" Denny asked.

"I don't think so. Why?"

"Played at the track. He's Russian."

I pulled away. "Mik?"

"I believe that could be the name he went by."

"I know who he is, but not very well. Why?"

"He's the DB in Sam's house."

My mind went somewhere else. Denny was still talking, but I didn't hear what he was saying. I remembered the last time I'd seen Mik. He was sitting next to Sam at the table when Sally dealt the bad beat the night she was killed.

Sam needed to get away so urgently that he risked everything. He was desperate, trying to cheat the Boat to amass enough money to start over. And now Mik was found dead in Sam's house. Another link or coincidence? I dismissed the idea of it being a coincidence almost immediately. All these things had to be connected.

"That's not all," he said.

"I'm afraid to know."

"Gates didn't die of natural causes. He was shot in the stomach, but that's not what killed him. He drowned. After being shot, there was a struggle. Someone held his head below the water until he stopped breathing."

"Merciless."

"Annie, can you tell me why you went to Sam's house?"

I lied. "I wanted answers. He's connected to everything, just like Gates. The door was open, the smell was overwhelming, and I was curious."

I couldn't admit that the real reason was to get Sam's DNA to solve the mystery about my unborn child's paternity. And finding Mik was a bonus.

Denny dipped down below the surface and then emerged, spitting water out of his mouth and nose. "I can't stand the smell of death."

"Sorry."

"I thought we had an agreement to keep me in the loop."

"It was the spur-of-the-moment. But after you're done there, maybe you can help me find somebody."

"Another connection to this case?"

"Finn Dikes. He was the bartender at the Hole when Sally was killed. He left his job right after, and he may know something. I looked him up on the Internet, but Finn moved out and left no forwarding address. Left his furniture and food in the fridge."

Denny stood up, and I handed him a towel.

Back in bed, he had his law enforcement laptop open and was searching.

"Find anything?" I asked.

"Finnegan Dikes recently changed his address to a PO box."

Denny showed me a copy of Finn's picture on his driver's license, and it bore a remarkable resemblance to the man that poured my drinks and drew my beer.

"That's him," I said. "Barbed wire tattoo around his neck and all."

"We can check local watering holes close to where he picks up his mail. Might be working or drinking around there."

CHAPTER 81

I snuck off and dropped Sam's toothbrush off at Rapid Testing in the morning and did a little Christmas shopping.

Shortly after noon, Denny and I checked out all the local bars in the immediate area around the postal store that Finn had listed as his address. No one recognized him from the driver's license photo that Denny had printed out.

We ended up in Denny's Impala, staking out the postal store. After three hours, I glanced at my watch and said, "I'm bored out of my mind, hungry, and need to go to work soon."

He laughed and said, "Stakeouts are not my preferred task either. But they're necessary."

We picked up cheeseburgers from McDonald's and headed home.

At work, I asked everyone if they'd seen Gates's son, Gallagher, and they all had the same answer. No one had seen him in weeks, maybe months.

I hoped that he hadn't fallen victim to the increasing death toll and thought I'd look up his address and check him out too. With Denny this time, as I'd promised.

But tomorrow was Christmas Eve, and everything would have to wait until after the holiday.

CHAPTER 82

Christmas started out to be a good day. We opened presents in our pajamas. I gave Denny a Glock, the same model as mine, the one that used to be Sally's and the one he had admired. I also gave him *The Very Best of Meat Loaf* DVD, and I wasn't sure which one he liked the best.

He gave me a beautiful gold medallion, and I got a pair of earrings for Ellie. But the hit of the day was the used car I'd purchased for Beth. I had it parked out front with a big red bow, and she was overwhelmed with gratitude.

We cooked but not nearly as much as Thanksgiving. I'd picked up a ham from Honey Baked, and Beth made mashed potatoes and peas. Ellie baked a cake. Even though I'd invited the rest of my family, most of them didn't show up at first.

Carl made a surprise visit with the twins shortly before noon, and Beth was elated. She'd always wanted children, but it never happened.

Ellie had once asked Beth about her acceptance of the twins, and she responded that they were babies and hadn't done anything wrong.

Dinner was ready and served just after one, and we stuffed ourselves and laughed at one another's quips and talked about things that happened long ago. And then my mother knocked on the door, and everything changed.

She entered with a downturned mouth. At one time, my mother was considered a beauty. She had all the right features: an oval face, smooth skin, button nose, and large eyes. I remembered her years ago in a bathing suit at the beach, and she had the shape to go along with the looks.

But now her eyelids sagged along with her butt. Her waistline bulged, and she had developed a decent set of jowls. Her hair was gray and looked like she'd hacked it off with a dull pair of scissors.

Everyone stared, waiting for her to reveal her mood, which could be ordinarily bad, sometimes really bad, and rarely good.

"Your brother's drunk again," she said.

"Where is he?" I asked.

"My house. I had to leave because I couldn't stand the smell of him anymore."

My brother Bill had struggled with one substance after another all his life. Divorced, no kids, couldn't keep a job for long. But when he was around, my mother picked on me less. So I missed him when we were all together.

She looked at me and said, "I hope you're not drinking because I don't think I could put up with any more of that today."

Denny furrowed his brow at her remark and sat up in his seat like a lion ready to pounce.

I patted him on his knee, and he relaxed.

"Mom, this is Denny," I said.

He stood up and offered his hand. Mother eyed him up and down and turned away. "I think I'm coming down with something, so I'm not shaking hands today." She added, "And don't try to kiss me, any one of you. It's for your own good."

She looked around, and her eyes settled on Carl.

"You have a lot of nerve showing up."

Carl cowered. Beth headed for the kitchen because she knew she was next.

But she didn't say anything more, and I was relieved. She'd always sensed weakness, and I had been weak. I considered her lack of criticism of me as a compliment.

We served her a plate full of what was left from our dinner, and she complained that we didn't have any turkey.

I snuck upstairs and found a blouse in the back of the closet with the tags still on it. It was a beautiful silk blend, and I wanted to keep it for myself. But I wrapped it in Christmas paper and gave it to my mother.

She opened the gift with care and held out the shirt.

"Hmm," she said.

"I hope it's your size. If you don't like it, I'll take it back and get you—"

"I think this will be fine."

That was as close to a compliment that my mother ever came to give.

Ellie and I had a tradition of watching *A Christmas Story*, and had set the channel on the TV to change as it started.

My mother moaned through the first ten minutes about having to watch that awful movie again and then said goodbye and left abruptly.

After she was sure Mom was gone, Ellie said, "Now we know what to do to get rid of Grandma."

We all laughed and enjoyed the movie for the umpteenth time.

Later that night, Denny and I took a short walk to the ocean.

The night was clear, and the sound of the waves beating against the shore was relaxing.

"It was a good day, don't you think?" I said.

"I assume your mother was on her best behavior."

I laughed. "Probably because of you, thank you very much."

He kissed me.

"She needs to size you up first," I said. "Mom has to find a weakness before exploiting it."

"And I have plenty."

"Your secrets are safe with me."

"I have another gift for you. But I didn't want to do this with the rest of your family around."

As he removed a small ring box from his pocket, I began to shake and breathe deeply.

He handed me a baggy and I covered my face with it.

"I used to be a Boy Scout, so I came prepared." He smiled.

I calmed, opened the box, and it was exactly what I expected. A diamond ring, white gold, big center stone with baguettes circling halfway around the band. And it was beautiful.

"Will you marry me?"

"Are you sure?"

"Never been more sure of anything in my life."

"What about us both being alcoholics?"

"I hate to mention this, but I think we've been in a serious relationship for a while. And I've been in recovery for a long time. It'll be okay."

I answered him with a kiss, and he slid the ring on my finger.

83
CHAPTER

The day after Christmas, Denny and I returned to the postal store and waited again. We had packed ham sandwiches with leftovers. After two hours and three bottles of water, I decided to take a break.

I walked a couple of blocks to Publix Supermarket and used the facilities. On my way back, I got a call from Denny. He said to hurry up because Finn had just entered the postal store.

I jogged back in time to see Finn, out of shape with an overextended stomach, dressed in a Margaritaville T-shirt and Bermuda shorts coming out of the store.

Denny had the car running and ready to follow. I slipped into the passenger seat, and we waited for Finn to lead the way.

Finn swaggered down the first side road heading north off Forty-Fifth Street.

We watched from the road as he limped into a one-story horseshoe-shaped small apartment complex with eight units. He lived second from the front on the south side.

"Ready?" Denny asked.

"You bet." I grabbed the handle and opened the door.

When we got there, Denny knocked on the aluminum door slatted with jalousie windows.

The windows opened slowly, and Finn asked, "Who's there?"

"It's me, Finn. Annie from the Water Hole."

"What do you want?"

"I'm with a friend, and we need to ask you some questions."

"About what?"

"Can you please open the door and let us in?"

The door cracked open; Finn peered out and looked around. "Hurry up, get inside."

We scooted in.

"Good to see you," I said.

"What is this about?" Finn asked.

"What's with the apprehension?" Denny asked.

"This isn't the best of neighborhoods."

We stood by the door and looked around the small apartment with one chair and a small end table. An old TV with a converter attached sat on a tiny kitchen table crowded with dirty dishes and takeout containers. And the place reeked of alcohol.

I took a better look at Finn and noticed his skin was more yellow than before. The whites of his eyes were blood-shot and tinted custard.

The table behind him was crowded with beer cans and empty bottles of Jack Daniel's.

Denny extended a hand and said, "Denny McCaffery. I'm Annie's friend."

"So?" Finn said as they shook.

"We're here to ask you about what happened on the night that Sally was killed," I said.

Finn threw up his hands. "I don't remember."

I thought back to when I'd frequented the Water Hole when Finn was tending bar. He knew everyone's name, what they did for a living, and their drink of choice. He'd shown interest in people's lives and could recall the slightest of details. He remembered everyone's problems and joys and asked about their personal lives like he was a friend. I was sure there was nothing wrong with his memory.

"Just tell us who was there."

"Annie, I always liked you. My time at the Hole was good. Good people, good times, and lots of booze. I was very intoxicated at the time of the shooting."

"I know it was a difficult time, but—"

"But nothing. Some cops came by and told me to disappear. I'm amazed you found me. They gave me some money to relocate and said not to talk to anyone about it."

"Cops?" Denny asked.

"That's what they said."

"I've never heard of that happening with the police. How much money did these guys give you?"

"Enough to make it worth my while and get me away from all of that. And let me tell you, I liked Sally a lot. I was heartbroken about what happened."

"Did these so-called cops give you an idea where those funds came from?"

"I asked about that, and they said it was slush money funded by a group of concerned citizens who help people get away from tragedies. I thought that made sense, so I didn't ask any more questions."

"Remember their names?"

"No."

"What did they look like?"

"White and average."

I asked. "How did they sound?"

He shook his head. "I knew something was up when they gave me money. They both spoke with European accents. Russian, if I had to guess."

"Ever see them before?"

"No. But they had this menacing tone that scared the hell out of me." He hesitated and then added, "They weren't cops, were they?"

Denny asked, "What were they wearing?"

"White shirts with the sleeves rolled up. Kind of sloppy."

"Getting back to Sally," I said. "Did you hear the shots?"

He closed his eyes. "Yes, and it was horrible. I knew something bad had happened. I could tell it was a gunshot. Bam, bam, bam. A series of three, and then three more. I hit the floor before the second series, scared to death."

"Who was in the bar before you heard the shots?"

He looked away and lied. "I don't remember."

"Come on, Finn."

"Just like I told the cops, or whoever they were, I didn't see or hear anything and can't remember who was in the bar at the time. I swear. I must have blocked it out because I was in shock."

"Which cops? The ones at the scene or the ones that came later?" Denny asked.

Finn shrugged. "I don't remember anything."

"Who are you afraid of?" I asked.

Finn's eyes grew wide. "No one."

"Did they threaten you?"

Finn stared intently at a chip in the linoleum floor. "I just don't remember anything."

Denny came on stronger. "Are you serious?"

"Look, most of the time I worked at the Hole, I was out-of-my-mind drunk. I don't know how I made it to work. I remember very little about what I did when I was there, and a lot about how I got home is a total blank. I'm away from all that now, trying to get sober."

My eyes glanced at the whiskey bottle on the table.

"That? Well, I'm cutting back slowly. I've done it before, and it works for me. I'm down quite a bit, as a matter of fact, so I know it's working."

I looked at Denny, and he gave me a shrug.

He took out a card and handed it to Finn.

"Call if you think of anything."

Finn glanced at the card, sneered at Denny, and said, "You're with the police. Why didn't you tell me that in the first place?"

"I'm sorry if I didn't make that clear."

Finn threw up his hands. "Annie, I miss you and the gang from the Boat. But you should have been honest about him. You both have to leave."

Denny said, "We're not here on official business. We just want to—"

Finn interrupted. "Go! Just go. I don't have anything to say." Finn wrapped his arms around his chest like he was being trapped in an imaginary straitjacket.

CHAPTER 84

As Denny drove, he said, "As far as I know, we don't have anyone with a Russian accent on the force. But I'll make some inquiries just to make sure."

"He lied about almost everything," I said. "The only thing I heard that made sense was that he hit the floor when shots were fired."

"I don't think I'm the one to get the truth out of Finn."

"What are you suggesting?"

"Nothing. Well, I don't know yet. But I've alienated him, and there's no going back after that."

I was silent for the rest of the ride as I ran options through my head.

We stopped and ate burgers at Chili's and mainly spoke about family things and the baby. And then I said. "I want to go back tonight."

"Back where?"

"To Finn's, by myself."

"I can't let you do that."

"You want me to include you in the things that I do, right?"

He took a sip of his water before answering.

"You can go back, but I'll be outside the door, and the window has to be open, so I can hear and see if you're in trouble."

When we got home, we made love and then showered together.

After it was dark. I grabbed some cash from my stash, and I backed the Volvo out. On the way, we stopped at the liquor store and bought a bottle of Jack Daniel's.

I parked in the empty lot at the postal store, and we walked back to Finn's apartment.

I tapped softly on his door, but he didn't answer. I looked through the open jalousies and saw a figure lying on the floor.

"Passed out or dead?" Denny asked.

I tried the door, but it was locked.

I pulled out my pick set from my backpack, and forty seconds later, the door was open. A new record—but I held back on a fist pump.

Denny whispered, "You're amazing."

He stood back as I opened the door and entered the room. The smell of urine and feces hit me immediately, but I was grateful that it wasn't the stench of death.

I saw another bottle of whiskey on the table. *Empty*.

Finn lay on the floor with his pants down around his knees, naked, for the most part. I noticed he hadn't been circumcised. I'd seen a few of those, and it was always a surprise.

His pants were soiled, so I'd imagined that's why he'd taken them off. At least halfway.

I placed a finger on his neck and felt for a pulse. Weak, with an occasional erratic beat.

I poked him with my boot.

"Finn, this is Annie. Are you all right?"

He didn't move one iota.

I kicked harder, and he grunted.

"Wake up, Finn."

He opened his eyes.

"Hey, are you okay?"

"What?"

"You remember the night Sally was killed?"

"I'm not 'posed to say." Finn slurred his words.

I pulled out the bottle of booze. "I brought you something."

His eyes opened a little more.

"Who was at the Hole the night Sally was killed?"

He reached toward the bottle.

"Tell me who was at the bar first, and you can have this."

"'Fraid to say. Those guys told me not to talk about that. Said not to, 'specially don't tell anyone 'bout who was in the bar and what they were doin'. Said it a few times."

"You said Sally was your friend, right?"

He nodded and grabbed hold of the bottle, but I held on tight.

"You want to find out who killed Sally?"

"Yeah. But I don't want them guys after me."

"I need your help."

"Lemme have a drink."

"If you tell me, I'll let you have it all."

"I'm 'fraid."

I pulled the bottle away and held it up just out of his reach.

"How much money did they give you?"

"Can't 'member."

"I'll give you more, and you can move again so they can't find you."

Finn swallowed hard and then said, "Well. Let me see."

He closed his eyes. "That ugly local couple that comes in and gets drunk every Saturday night. You know 'em. They was there." He opened his eyes and gazed off.

I nodded. Sure, I knew them. A middle-aged couple that drank draft beer, ordered snack food, and occasionally danced to the music. A bleached blonde who was letting her dark hair grow out, and he was homely and dark haired, sprinkled with gray.

"And then there was…" He hesitated.

"Go on."

"Shaka was there with that kid that hangs 'round him," Finn continued. "I need a drink."

I cracked the bottle open, and Finn sat up enough for me to pour a shot in his mouth.

"Ahh. Cuttin' back tomorrow."

"Who else was in the bar, Finn? Tell me about the kid."

"You know, that guy who wears his pants 'round the knees? Always showin' his underwear. Calvin Klein."

I knew exactly who he was talking about. Everyone called him Pepper, and he hung around with Shaka. He was a shady-looking black guy who rolled up his sleeves to show off his muscles heavily tatted with ink. It was hard to distinguish the design because it blended into his dark skin. His pants sagged down, and I could tell his choice of briefs was Calvin Klein because the label was forever exposed, like *a badge of honor.*

I'd suspected Pepper was one of Shaka's smurfs.

"I've seen him," I said. "Shady-looking fellow."

Finn nodded.

"Anyone else?"

"Sure. There were others, regulars, but I wasn't payin' much attention to 'em. I was fairly loaded at the time."

"Nothing unusual going on?"

"Uh, there was someone else. Never saw him before and looked out of place."

"How so?"

"Dressed in 'pensive clothes. Dapper. Good hair. Styled. And had a big diamond ring, thick gold chain 'round his neck, and wore a good watch."

"White or black?"

"White guy with light hair. His skin was dark from the sun. He looked like a golfer. Wearin' a golf shirt and looked the type that played the game."

"Anything else that you remember about him?"

"Talked like one of those Queebies."

"Queebie?"

"From Quebec. Or somewhere up there."

He pointed to the ceiling.

"Canadian?"

"Surrrre."

"What happened after the gunshots?"

"Everyone took cover. Me too. Hid like a chicken. I'm a lover, not a fighter. Gimme a drink."

I poured more liquor down his throat.

"After the gunshot? He told me not to say nothing."

"Who?"

"Shaka pulled me up. I was dangling off the floor in his arms. And...and...I thought he was gonna kill me. He's huge. But he didn't. Just told me what to do. *Be quiet, don't say nothin'.* Tell everyone you don't 'member, and if I told anyone who was in the bar, he would find me, cut my balls off, and stuff 'em down my throat."

"And then what happened?"

"I still got my balls."

"What happened after Shaka made his threat?"

"They left out the back door."

"Shaka and Pepper?"

"Yeah."

"What was everyone doing just before you heard the shots?"

"Just before? Uhm. The ugly couple was smooching at the table. *Disgusting.* I hate to see them do that. And people were playing pool, nothing unusual. The golfer was lookin' in the mirror a lot and sippin' his drink, nursing it, like he didn't wanna get loaded.

"Shaka and Pepper, they were waitin' for someone. Watchin' the door and lookin' at the clock."

"Who were they waiting for?"

"Think I overheard Trevor's name. Your friend, right?"

"Are you sure?"

"Yeah. Pretty sure they were waitin' for him."

"And you didn't tell the police that either?"

"No. Nothin'. I want to keep my balls and don't want to be dead."

"Where did the golfer go after you heard the shots?"

"He followed them out. Shaka and Pepper. I don't think they were together though. They were from different paths. Later, after the real cops left, the fake ones came 'long. They gave me the bread and told me to disappear."

"How much money do you have left?" I asked.

Finn smiled stupidly. "You thinkin' about robbin' me, Annie?"

"No. But you may want to move again."

"Don't have that much. Things cost lots."

"You want to get sober?"

"Surrrre."

"I'm going to call someone to help you. They'll dry you out and get you into a program."

I gave Finn the bottle, and he gulped like he was dying of thirst.

Denny stepped inside, and we wiped down two kitchen chairs before taking seats. He looked at me and said, "You're good at this."

I gazed off as I wondered how I'd become entwined in a circle with so many people who were of questionable character and suffered from substance abuse.

As we waited for Percy, Denny helped Finn pull his pants up. And then Finn faded back into his stupor.

Just before Percy arrived, Finn's eyes opened, and he asked, "Annie? What you still doing here? Told you before, I'm not sayin' nothin'."

"Don't worry about it, Finn. We're here to help you."

Percy arrived, and Denny greeted him with a bear hug.

I gave him a bunch of cash and said, "You don't have to tell me it's a hard case. I know that already. Let me know if you need anything else."

Denny helped Percy carry Finn to his van.

After they drove away, Denny said, "You're a good person, Annie."

"You would have done the same thing."

He shook his head and said, "I'm not that good."

I smiled and kissed him.

"I need you to do something for me," he said.

I answered with a sideways look.

"Teach me how to pick a lock."

85
CHAPTER

Back at home, Denny quickly dressed for work and left me with an overactive brain and my yellow pad. I sat at the table with a pen in my hand and wrote names on a flowchart, Sally, Gates, Sam, Mik, Shaka, and Pepper, and then I wrote Trevor with a question mark.

In the middle of the page, I wrote two million with a dollar sign on one side and wrote "drugs" with a question mark on the other.

Money for drugs made the most sense. A lot of money meant a lot of drugs.

But I had been wrong about so many things in the past. Maybe I was wrong about this too.

What was Sally's connection to Russians? Someone had instigated this deal with something for a massive amount of money. But who? Mik? Which side was paying, and who had the merchandise?

It had to be drugs if Shaka was involved. I pictured a truckload of heroin, cocaine, or a combination. Very large, hard to hide. I imagined a semitrailer or a shipping container full of white powder hidden in a garage some-where—*a definite possibility.*

I didn't know much about Shaka other than he sold pot to the players at the Boat, but maybe he was spreading his wings. *Getting into the big times?* Perhaps he was the facilitator, along with Mik.

Pepper was Shaka's smurf, a minion, and it was hard to believe either one could be a significant player.

Sam didn't have any money, and Trevor had less than him. I couldn't figure how either one of them could be architects involved in this master plan.

I scribbled Gallagher's name on the yellow sheet but quickly crossed it out because I concluded he didn't have the intestinal fortitude for anything of this nature.

I sat back and looked at my handiwork. I was missing a connection.

I picked up my pen and wrote *Golfer.*

CHAPTER 86

Denny's shift ended at 6:00 a.m., and I was up when he entered the house.

"What's up?" he asked.

I showed him my yellow pad and said, "I think it has something to do with a big drug shipment. Shaka is a dealer. If he's involved, it has to be. And a considerable quantity, not easy to hide."

He examined the yellow page of names, circles, and arrows.

"A whole lot of drugs and people are getting killed over it. And a bunch of money." I was tempted to tell him about what I'd found in the storage unit, but I held back and asked, "Can you get some information on Shaka and Pepper?

"Probably." He sat down at the table with his laptop and typed information into the law enforcement database.

"Well. This is interesting," Denny quipped.

"Tell me."

"Shaka's real name is Thomas Jefferson Carver. Parents immigrated from Jamaica. Thirty-three years old and has an extensive record of dealing drugs, petty theft, and assault, dating back to age seventeen. Probably a lot more sealed in his juvie record. Most of his cases were pleaded down. Not much jail time. Must have a good attorney because some of these drug arrests were serious. But in the last two years, he's managed to stay clean."

"He got smart and began using smurfs to peddle for him," I said.

Denny typed some more. "Known associate, Warren King, AKA Pepper. Drugs and drug dealers go together. That definitely seems to be the connection."

I thought back, trying to remember the last time I'd seen Shaka or his gang.

"I haven't seen these guys at the Boat since Sally was killed. And we need to find the golfer."

"I've got a list of cars left in the parking lot after the shooting. I asked for this when we were looking for your Beamer." He tapped more keys. "I would imagine he'd be driving a fairly expensive vehicle, but I don't see anything that could belong to a guy like Finn described. Mostly compacts and midsize cars."

"How do we find this guy?"

"First thing tomorrow, I'll talk to the Ds working on this case."

"Do you have Shaka's address on that thing?"

He shut the laptop. "Don't even think about it, my love. I want you around longer than next week."

I looked away.

"Drugs and murder are police business. You've done enough, please. Let me handle this from now on."

"Okay," I said. But I didn't mean it.

87
CHAPTER

The circus was in town, and I was dealing a table full of Romanians. Most of the time, they drink and laugh and joke and lose money. But occasionally, their shenanigans lead to fights, both verbal and physical. On this day, they were happy-go-lucky, and I was glad about the lack of conflict.

I'm not sure why the Romanians like to play with one another, but they do. Most players want to play against strangers or acquaintances instead of friends, but these guys were different. They come in and ask to sit together, and then they proceed to take one another's money.

Simon and Octavian, both tall, thin, and fair skinned with dark hair, enjoyed aggravating each other. As I shoved a pot to Simon, Octavian wished for Simon to go to hell in gasoline-burning pants.

Their banter made me smile until something else caught my eye. Benny walked up the aisle toward the cashier.

As I ran the game, I watched him buy chips and then head for a table on the other side of the room.

I worked until ten, and then I asked to leave.

I drove to the front entrance and waited.

Benny exited two hours later, and I almost missed him because I was close to dozing off.

He took off in his old Focus, and I followed in my Beamer.

I stayed back. It was just after midnight, and very few cars on the road didn't leave much in the way of cover.

The Focus made a right turn off Van Buren Street onto Emerson Drive and then made a left onto a dead-end street.

I killed my lights and pulled off onto the grass at the top of the road.

I huddled down and watched as Benny's car turned into a driveway at the fourth house on the north side.

I sat up to catch sight of him as he entered a small wood-framed box house on the shabby neighborhood street.

I drove by slowly with my lights still off. On the side of Benny's house was a rusty jacked-up junk car with one wheel missing, and the front yard was full of overgrown weeds.

At the end of the road, I maneuvered a three-point turn.

I stopped in front of Benny's and looked up the street with sixteen homes, eight on either side, a quiet little neighborhood nestled in the middle of a larger city. Nothing extravagant here. I had a feeling if I'd sat there much longer, someone would notice my overpriced car and become suspicious. But I lingered for a few more moments.

The lights went on in the little house. He had stolen my laptop, and we had sex that I couldn't remember.

I winced at the thought of the mental image. I'd stooped low. So low, I had nowhere to go but up.

A porch light came on across the street, and curtains separated in the window. I put the car in gear and inched my way out of the dead-end road.

CHAPTER 88

I spent most of my time the next few days trying to dismiss the turmoil going on in my head. Denny wanted to handle the investigation, and I was going to try to let him.

On top of murder and mayhem, the paternity of my unborn child occupied my thoughts. I knew where Benny lived now, but I would wait until I got the results on Sam's toothbrush back before doing anything about that.

And I didn't have to wait long.

I was driving when Amber from Rapid called and gave me the news. Good or bad, I wasn't sure, but Sam turned out not to be the father of my child.

Now I knew I would have to deal with Benny. But it would have to wait. It was New Year's Eve, and I was food shopping for another celebration.

Traffic was heavy and a little scary. I drove cautiously on the lookout for drunk drivers. Last year, I was one of them; now, I feared them. *Ironic.*

I checked the rearview mirror and saw a black sedan two cars back. I made a quick turn and kept my eye on it. The black car went straight, and I exhaled.

I finally made it home unscathed. Ellie and Beth helped carry groceries into the house, where we prepared a feast to ring in the new year. We cooked a rib roast and everything that went with it.

I was setting the table when Denny came home from work. He grabbed my hand, and we sat down on the sofa next to each other. He said he was going to have to ditch the uniforms.

My thoughts turned to the worst of scenarios, as I imagined that he had gotten fired.

"What happened?" I asked.

"I retook the detective's exam, and this time they didn't pass me by. They made me a detective again. I wanted homicide, but no openings. I had to settle for burglary for now." He smiled big.

"That's amazing. You worked your way back."

Pup rushed over and sat down in front of us. His fur had grown back, and he'd turned into a fine-looking dog.

I gave him a pet. "You're a real dog now."

"You should probably name him."

"He has a name. He's a dog named Pup."

Dinner was served, and we ate like pigs.

We spoke very little at first, and then Beth expressed her dissatisfaction with her job search.

"You should stop by the college and see if you can get some financial aid," Ellie offered.

"Good idea," I said. And then I picked up my water glass. "I want to make a toast. To happiness. We're going to have a baby within this new year, and Denny and I are going to be married."

I smiled brightly, and Denny beamed.

"I'm so happy for you," Ellie said.

Beth furrowed her brow. "Seems kind of fast, if you ask me."

As she cut her steak, Ellie, Denny, and I clinked glasses of water, toasting our good fortunes and a bright future.

And then Percy called.

Finn was in bad shape.

"End-stage cirrhosis of the liver," Percy said. "His only hope is a transplant, but that's not likely with his history of alcohol abuse. What do you want me to do with him?"

"What does he want?" I asked.

"He asked me to drop him off at the nearest bar."

I suggested he call an Uber.

CHAPTER 89

The next day, I dropped some money off at Finn's so he could be comfortable as he drank himself to death, and then I headed back home to pick up the Volvo.

I had done a reverse address lookup and found that Benny's full name was Bernard Simpson, and I had to admit that he looked more like a Bernard than a Benny to me.

As I drove, I looked side to side along the dark dead-end street in the run-down neighborhood, bypassing the house at first. Then I turned around in someone's driveway and doubled back.

Lights were on, and I could see a shadowy figure moving around inside through the front window.

I parked a few houses down from the old house on the swale and kept an eye on the beat-up Ford Focus parked in the driveway next to the sagging porch. I pulled a cap over my head and settled back, determined to stay alert until he left his house unattended.

It wasn't long before the porch light came on, the inside lights turned off, and Benny came through the front door. He locked up and quickly made his way to his jalopy and drove away.

My heart pounded as I considered what I was about to do. I'd been lucky so far, but if I got caught breaking and entering, I'd be in a lot of trouble. Nonetheless, I couldn't deny my desire to find out if this idiot could be the father of my child any longer. Not that it would make a difference, I just needed to know.

I drove around the corner and parked on the street behind Bernard's house.

I opened the car door, took off the cap, and pulled a ski mask over my face. I grabbed a bag from the back seat and kept my head down as I limped through the side neighboring lawn toward his backyard. I was gaining more confidence until I stumbled on a root from a ficus tree that had pushed up through the grass.

My hands hit the ground with a thud that hurt, but the pain wasn't severe enough to deter me. I rose more determined than ever.

I ducked down and moved quickly through the yard toward the back of the house and came face-to-face with a four-foot-high chain-link fence. I put my good foot in between the wires, swung my other leg over the top, pushed off, and landed gracefully on the other side. Smooth, but a little painful. My ankle was still sore.

The back door was old, and the top half had a window. I slipped on the black leather gloves, pulled out the lock-pick, and got to work. In a matter of seconds, the tumblers fell into place.

I leaned against the wall, shaking badly. I wanted to give up and get the hell out of there. But I closed my eyes and imagined a quick trip in and out.

I opened the door and was relieved that no bells or alarms rang.

I hurried through the house, down the hall to the bathroom, and pulled a plastic baggy from my pocket. I grabbed the only toothbrush from the holder, dropped it into the bag, and then hurried back out.

I glanced through the front window. The street was still quiet, and Bernard's car was nowhere in sight. I looked around and saw my laptop sitting on a small kitchen table. I grabbed it and pulled the wire from the wall, and tucked it under my arm.

Before leaving, I took one last look around. This old house was more of a shack than a dwelling.

And then I spotted Sally's backpack hanging on a hook next to the front door. There was no mistake; it was her bag.

I hadn't seen it the first time through because it was partially covered by a jacket, but there it was, black with hot pink straps.

I grabbed it before heading toward the door.

And then I stopped. If I took it, then that would taint evidence in a police investigation.

I placed the laptop back on the table, sat down, and dumped the contents out on the dirty tile floor.

All standard stuff, nothing I hadn't seen before. But I knew about the secret compartment at the bottom and felt around from the inside.

Something was there. I turned it over and unzipped the flap that encircled the bottom of the bag. The sound of the slider gliding across the elements gave me chills.

It opened, and a bundle of cash fell out—fifty one-hundred-dollar bills. Five-thousand dollars stuffed snugly in the secret compartment.

Apparently, Bernard wasn't bright enough to find it, so he wouldn't miss it. I stuffed the bills into the waistband of my slacks and took a second look at the items lying on the floor. *Nail clippers, four lipstick tubes, blush, an old flip phone, a paperback novel, a few coins, an old cigar, and a Post-it note with three numbers separated by hyphens.*

I opened the phone and tried to turn it on, but it was dead. I fanned through the book before throwing everything except the money back into the bag.

But the cigar was a problem. The outer leaf had broken, and bits of tobacco fell out over everything. Brown specks marked the tile floor.

I scooped up the particles as best I could and flushed them down the toilet.

And then I hung Sally's backpack where it had been and placed the jacket over it as good as I could remember.

Lights shone through the window from the Ford as the car pulled back into the driveway, and I froze in place for a fast second.

I took a quick look around. Everything seemed okay and in place except for the laptop. I hadn't plugged it back into the socket, and the wire was sitting on top of the cover. I gave the cord a push, and the plug landed with a crack on the floor near the outlet. And then I turned and ran.

I opened the door and closed it quietly behind me.

I leaned against the outside wall, and it took some effort, but I controlled my breathing and didn't pass out.

The front door slammed, and I waited for Bernard to settle inside or for him to find something askew and come looking. If he were to come out the back door, I'd have to fight him. And I was prepared because Foo had trained me well. I visualized disabling him.

I was covered from head to toe, so he wouldn't have any idea it was me. And then I'd run away, hop the fence, and be home free.

I heard him rattling around for a few minutes, and then the light came on in the back of the house where the bathroom was located. I took it as a good sign and a perfect time to make a run for it.

I stepped swiftly down the steps to the sparsely sodded yard and then moved to the four-foot fence.

I hopped over, landed softly, and didn't look back as I jogged through two neighboring yards. I exited on the sidewalk, paused to take a hurried breath, and looked back at the little house. The light in the bathroom was still on, and I imagined Bernard searching for his toothbrush.

The following day, Amber at Rapid Testing smiled with recognition as I walked through the door.

I signed the consent form and handed her the toothbrush encased in the plastic baggy.

"Probably six to seven days. We're running behind a bit," Amber informed me. "That will be six hundred dollars, please."

I asked, "Do you give a discount on repeat services?"

"Sorry, no. But a lot of our customers ask about the same thing."

I left wondering if what she had said was to make me feel better or if it was just a private joke.

CHAPTER 90

On a sunny January day, the relentless heat had given way to coolness. The wind had picked up, and the breeze felt good.

Denny and I left the house to run some errands and ended up at a jewelry store owned by Herman Chase, one of the Boat players from the high-stakes game known as a *fish*.

A fish is an unskilled player who plays fast and loose and usually loses more than he wins. And Herman was known for loose play and significant losses. There's a saying in poker, "If you can't spot the fish within the first half hour at the table, then it's probably you." Fish or not, Herman didn't seem to care one way or the other. He enjoyed the comradery and didn't seem to mind passing his wealth around. And he tipped the dealers well.

Chase's Fine Gems and Gold was in a storefront shopping center in Palm Springs.

Herman stood behind the counter and said he was glad to see us. His full head of salt-and-pepper hair was styled magnificently, not one hair out of place. His nails were manicured and glossy.

He pointed us to several trays of men's wedding rings in various shapes and sizes enclosed in a glass case.

Denny picked a thick white gold band with a set of five diamonds totaling 1.2 karats. Herman pulled the tag off and slashed the price in half.

Afterward, we ate lunch at Okeechobee Steak House, and I couldn't keep the smile from my lips.

And then the smile disappeared as I realized the last time I was there was with Sally. A chill ran through me as I wished I could share the news with her. She had been my friend for years, and I couldn't let her go. Even with the bad, I still missed her.

"What's up?" Denny asked.

"The last time I was here was with Sally," I answered. "I feel kind of empty about not having her around."

Denny raised an eyebrow.

"I'm furious with her for what she did, but I still miss her," I admitted.

He smiled, placed his hand on mine, and said, "We'll make new memories. Sally will become a flicker in your past."

"I'm not sure it'll be that easy."

"I understand."

"Let's talk about something else," I said as I bit my lip.

"Whatever you want."

"Let's set a date."

"You decide." He grinned full faced.

"Tell me how it was with you and Liv."

He looked away before answering, and I thought I'd made a mistake. But he finally said, "We had a big wedding. Olivia wore a white dress, and I wore a tuxedo. She had lots of friends, and I had almost as many. The guest list was over a hundred. And she was beautiful." His eyes welled up.

I took a breath and said, "I don't know if I can live up to her."

"I adore you."

"But you're still in love with her."

"You're different. Sure, I loved Liv, and sometimes I miss her. But she was too good for me, and she never let me in. I don't think I ever knew her. Not the real Olivia. We were married, but I always felt like an outsider. It's not the same as you. We've both been in the same dark places and understand what that's about. I get you, and you get me. I love you, and I want to spend the rest of my life with you. Let's make this happen as soon as possible. I want to be married before the baby comes. I want everything to be perfect."

I grimaced. "I'm not perfect."

"No one is. We have our pasts and our mistakes, and we'll have to deal with all that. But I want us to be as good as we can be together." He took a breath. "I want us to be a family. I want to be your husband and Kaitlyn's father."

We left the restaurant but didn't go straight home. We took a side trip to the courthouse and applied for a marriage license. And it took longer than we had anticipated. The forms, prenuptial handbook, and the questionnaire took some time.

We giggled our way through the silly questions, paid the fee, and exited, smiling brightly.

On the way home, I got a call from Rapid Testing and found out that Bernard was not my child's father. I was relieved, but it meant that I still had work to do.

CHAPTER 91

The sun shone brightly in the cloudless sky. It was the Saturday after Valentine's Day, and I was nearly five months pregnant. I'd had my hair trimmed and highlighted, and I wore flat heels and an off-white dress with a matching beaded jacket. I must say, despite my belly bump, I looked quite attractive when we rode the courthouse elevator upward.

Denny dressed in his favorite navy tweed sports jacket with matching slacks. His tie was red with blue and white sideways stripes. And he was absolutely handsome.

My family was there. Ellie, Beth, and my mother. My brothers were both too busy to attend, but that was okay. We hadn't been close in a long time.

Denny's mom, Susan, stood a good five inches taller than me, and I could see where he'd gotten his good looks. She was a stately woman in her early sixties but looked years younger. Smooth, tight skin, bright eyes, and a rose-bud mouth.

Denny's father died when he was ten of heart problems. Denny was okay, but his brother, Darby, had inherited his father's tendency for cardiac issues.

Darby was thin, pale, and sickly. He'd developed congestive heart failure in his twenties, and it was a medical miracle to have lived as long as he had.

The ceremony went off without a hitch, and we all made our way downtown to CityPlace to Saito's Japanese restaurant. We took seats around a large hibachi in the back room and toasted everything and everybody with sparkling cider.

We ate and joked and told trivial stories about silly things. And Ellie took pictures.

I was never happier. It was just a few months ago when I had been down so low, drinking, and misbehaving. I pinched myself just to make sure I wasn't dreaming. How this happened was a mystery. I went from being a drunk, sleeping around with anyone I could find, to a person of virtue. My life was nearly perfect.

Except I still didn't know the father of my baby. And I was running out of possibilities.

And other questions needed answers. Who had murdered Sally? And what about Gates? And where was Sam? And what about the money in the storage unit? These things nagged at me continuously.

But not on that day. I did my best to tuck my thoughts away.

Denny needed to get back on the job, and two days was all he could squeeze in for a honeymoon. But it was all right. Two days of bliss were precisely what we needed.

We spent our time at the Chesterfield Hotel on Palm Beach Island, overeating, sleeping twelve out of twenty-four hours, and walking hand in hand in the sand along the ocean.

Time flew by as we made love and spent every minute at each other's side.

But even as we spoiled ourselves with pleasure, and as hard as I tried not to think about it, the need for answers gnawed at me.

92
CHAPTER

The day after we returned from our brief honey-moon, I dropped by Mr. Ranger's office and signed the papers to transfer the investments. He scolded me because I had waited so long and said there would be an additional delay because he would have to order current death certificates.

But it didn't matter much to me. I had cash, and I was making money. The household expenses were handled, and Denny was sharing other costs.

After signing forms, we spoke about a will. I filled him in on the new developments in my life, and he seemed genuinely pleased.

And then the hard part came.

Ranger said. "Your estate is sizable, and you don't want to leave beneficiary decisions to the courts.

"Also, guardianship is another big concern. Who would you want to raise the child if you were not here anymore?"

"Huh?" I never gave any thought to what would hap-pen if I was gone. I would have two children, and both would need financial assistance. Ellie had to finish school, and my baby would need support for at least eighteen years. And what about Denny? What would happen to him if I was gone?

My thoughts went briefly to the money in the storage unit and what it would mean to my family, but I quickly shook that thought away. I knew it was trouble.

I asked, "How would you suggest I do this?"

"You've got a lot going on." He glanced at my belly, getting larger by the minute.

"Give some thought to the division of assets. We could set up a revocable trust to supply income to help support your children. And you should consider life insurance to help cover estate costs."

I had thought I was making progress, but my head was spinning by the time he was done with me.

93
CHAPTER

I was dealing a good game. Walter was in seat five, and his friend Harry sat in seat one. Harry kept everyone upbeat and laughing with one-line jokes. He was also a generous tipper, and it seemed contagious. The players laughed as I smiled, tapped, and dropped chips into my box.

And then Gallagher sat down in an empty seat. I stopped pitching cards. I hadn't seen him since before Sally was killed. I'd found his father dead in the tub and didn't know what to say. I finished dealing the cards and looked away.

No one spoke until Harry broke the ice. "Sorry to hear about your dad, Gale."

Gallagher looked at me with his little beady eyes. He opened his mouth but didn't say anything at first. And then he smiled slightly, and his teeth seemed bigger than ever.

"I need to speak with you, Annie," Gallagher said with a sinister tone.

"Ah, sure. Should be on break in a bit. If you're here, we can talk," I replied.

He threw his cards into the muck without looking. "I'll be at the bar."

The table exhaled in collective relief as Gallagher left.

"Did I say something wrong?" Harry asked.

"You called him Gale, asshole," Walter said as he rolled his eyes at Harry.

"That's his name, right?"

"It's Gallagher, and he hates being called Gale."

Harry shrugged. "Well, he needs to get over that."

"We only call him Gale when we want to put him on tilt. You know he's a fish, and you just let him slip away."

"Sorry."

An hour later, I approached Gallagher at the bar. He smelled like a liquor store and was well on his way to being drunk, if not there already.

"What's up, Gallagher?" I asked.

"You know my father was murdered, right?" he said.

"I'm so sorry. I always liked your dad." The smell of his dead body was still etched in my memory.

"He was killed because of the bitch, your friend, Sally."

"What are you saying?"

"About her being a bitch or that she killed my father?"

"They were going to get married."

"Liar, liar! She used him. And she stole my dad's money! My money! And I want it back!" Gallagher's little eyes bounded around in their sockets.

"Be specific, Gallagher. Tell me everything you know."

His hands turned to fists, and I flinched as my stomach twisted in knots.

"He gave her two million dollars!"

"I don't know anything about that."

"No, no, and no! He sold his house and emptied his brokerage account. Withdrew everything, and it's gone because she took it!" His voice escalated. "I don't know why I'm even talking to you! You were in on it!"

"Why would you think that?"

"Two peas in a pod. You're the same as her! Thieving bitch number two!"

"I don't like where this is going."

"You know where it's going because you've got my money!"

"Let me make this perfectly clear," I stated. "I didn't have anything to do with this, and I don't believe Sally stole your dad's money."

"Surrrre!"

"Calm down and tell me what happened?"

"He cashed everything in—and let me emphasize cash! That conniving bitch robbed him!"

I was reasonably sure he was referring to the money in the storage unit. Still, I needed to make sure before handing it over.

"Now is not the time, nor is this the place for this. Let's meet somewhere tomorrow—"

"No! Here and now!"

I made a mistake and turned my back on him. And then Foo's voice screamed in my head, *Danger is everywhere.*

A cold sensation ran down my spine.

Just as Gallagher raised his hand to strike me, I buckled my knees and leaned forward. His fist barely swiped my back.

I turned around and retaliated by grabbing the index finger on his right hand and twisting it, just like Mr. Foo had taught me. Grab the most vulnerable target available and cause the most damage before the enemy has a chance to act. Get the upper hand, and don't give up.

Gallagher cried, "Stop, stop, you're hurting me!"

I twisted hard until I heard bones crack. I had the urge to twist the digit off but was stopped short when Walter took over.

He grabbed Gallagher's arm and wrapped it around his back. He took hold of a fistful of hair with his other hand and smashed his head onto the bar. Glasses clinked.

He fell to the floor, thrashing in pain.

I yelled for security, and two cops came running.

Gallagher screamed as a crowd gathered. "She broke my finger! Arrest her!"

"He tried to punch Annie," Walter said. "She was defending herself."

They pulled Gallagher up and dragged him away in handcuffs.

George pushed his way through the crowd that had gathered and motioned for me to follow him.

I took a seat in the manager's office as Edsel Spears joined us.

Edsel took a detailed report about the incident and asked me to sign it.

As I reviewed what I had said, I became aware of an increasing tightness in my abdomen. And then came a cramp that bent me over.

George asked, "Are you okay?"

Edsel pulled up his radio and called for an ambulance, and then assured me he would get ahold of Denny.

On the way to the hospital, I noticed I was breathing fast and deep, hyperventilating again. I squeaked out, "Bag, please."

The paramedic handed me a plastic bag, and I covered my face with it and then asked, "How far along are you?"

"Not far enough. Barely six months."

"I'm going to give you something to calm down." He held up a needle, ready to stab it into the central line that he'd stuck into my arm earlier.

"No drugs. I'll be okay." I thought about the beach and the sun and Ellie running in the sand. But she was older, and a little girl was running next to her. The girl had sun-streaked hair and bright blue eyes. She smiled, and her dimples dented the smooth skin of her cheeks. I began to breathe normally, and the pain in my belly ceased.

Denny was waiting under the overhang at the emergency room entrance when we arrived. He escorted me inside, holding my hand and whispering that he loved me.

He waited outside a flimsy curtain as an ER doc examined me. The doc picked up a clipboard and asked, "You're thirty-eight?"

"I know it's late in life to be having a baby. But I'm going to do this. No matter what." I didn't know why I had become so defensive.

"What brought this on?"

"The baby? The usual way, I imagine."

He smiled. "I meant this particular episode."

"A customer got angry with me at work and tried to punch me. I avoided his fist and retaliated by breaking his finger."

He nodded.

"Tell me about the baby. Is everything okay?" I asked.

"Baby's fine. Everything seems good, for now. However, you should try to avoid that degree of stress in the future."

"What do you mean?"

"All factors considered, I believe this is a high-risk pregnancy. You should begin treating it as such."

"What should I do?"

"Less. Don't put yourself in an adverse situation. And relax as much as possible."

"Can you ask my husband to come in here, please?"

"Sure. I guess this is a dismissal."

"No, it's not. He needs to be involved."

The curtain separated, and Denny stepped inside.

He held out his hand and said, "I'm the husband, Denny McCaffery."

They shook hands, and Denny kissed me on my forehead.

"My feisty little wife," he quipped.

I grinned as I placed a hand on my protruding belly. "Not so little anymore."

The ER doc said, "I'll have the nurse bring in your discharge papers. Please make an appointment with your baby doc within the next few days. And take it easy. No more brawling!" He smiled and exited.

Denny raised an eyebrow. "I heard you're quite the street fighter."

"I was lucky," I said.

"You going to quit working?"

"What do you think?"

"Up to you. But I wouldn't mind if you did. At least until after the baby's born."

I smiled and waved Denny toward me. We huddled as I told him about Gallagher's accusations concerning stealing his father's money.

He grinned. "Where are you hiding it, Annie? Come on, you can tell me."

I bit my lip as I thought, *In the storage unit, silly*. But I didn't say it out loud.

CHAPTER 94

The next day I made an appointment with Dr. Jones. I got right in after I told the receptionist about my recent episode.

The first thing they did was another sonogram. Alice squeezed the warm goop from the tube on my belly and applied the probe. She said, "You're just about twenty-four weeks, and your baby should weigh around six hundred grams. Up until now, we've measured from her crown to rump. But from now on, we'll measure her crown to heel."

Alice moved the probe around. She clicked a button at specific points in the examination. "She's about twelve inches long, right on target. You have a name for her yet?"

"Kaitlyn. We'll call her Kate or Katie, I imagine," I said.

"Kaitlyn can hear you now. You might want to start reading or singing to her. Unless you're an awful singer."

"You're funny, Alice."

"And Katie seems to be right on target with every-thing. Don't tell Dr. Jones I said that. He likes to be the only one to deliver good news. But you seem like you could use some sooner rather than later."

"Thank you."

She printed out a picture and handed it to me. The image had a face, arms, and legs. I could even see her tiny fingers.

"She's kind of thin, don't you think?"

"She'll start fattening soon."

Dr. Jones repeated the same information, almost verbatim.

"What about the problem I had? It felt like I was in labor," I asked.

"You more than likely experienced a Braxton–Hicks contraction. False labor. A sign that your body's getting ready for the big event."

"What should I do?"

"Take it easy. No bed rest for now, but it may come to that if you don't reduce your stress level," Dr. Jones said as he thumbed through my file. "Your latest HIV test was negative again."

I drove away from the doctor's office with a smile on my face. Happy, healthy, and more hopeful that Kaitlyn was not marred by my self-indulgence.

95
CHAPTER

After putting my paperwork in for the leave, I drove home, dropped off the BMW, and picked up the Volvo.

My head was swirling. I had begun dreaming about what was in the storage unit. The cash I'd found in Sally's house was dwindling, and this could be my family's to do with as we pleased. But I had a feeling that it would come with a price. It had to be returned to its rightful owner and stop the string of deaths and suspicion. If it belonged to Gallagher, the man who tried to punch me and accused me of thievery, I would give it back. But I needed to make sure.

I was still preoccupied with searching for the father of my baby, but what I'd found in Bernard's house added more questions.

What was his involvement, and why did he have Sally's backpack?

My brain was on overload again. I wasn't working and didn't have that distraction. I couldn't ask Denny for help because I was too embarrassed by the sordid encounter between a stranger and me.

It was crazy that I was heading back to the dead-end street where Bernard lived in his dilapidated house with Sally's backpack hanging on a hook behind a jacket and my stolen laptop sitting in plain sight on his kitchen table. But I was.

It was dark when I pulled up to the curb and parked a couple of houses away.

The Ford wasn't in the driveway, a good indication that he wasn't home. I backed out and parked one street over. The same place I'd parked the last time I'd broken in.

And I took the same path through neighboring yards and over the fence to the back door.

I picked the lock and entered without incident.

I waited in the dark for what seemed like hours, but when I checked my phone, it had only been twenty minutes before headlights graced the front window.

I pulled my Glock from my boot and placed it on my lap.

The door opened, and Bernard swaggered in.

He turned on the light and, at first, didn't see me.

When I said, "Hello, Bernard," he nearly jumped out of his skin.

"What the hell?" he said.

I picked up the Glock to make sure he saw it.

"Have a seat." I motioned to a chair.

"What do you want?"

"Sit!"

He sat down.

"I need information."

He fidgeted.

"First, that backpack that you have hanging behind your door. Tell me how it came into your possession."

"I remember you now. We had a thing. You're friends with the bitch."

"You really shouldn't do anything to anger a person with a gun. Especially when you don't have one. You get me, right?"

"Calm down. You're high-strung, as I recall."

"This is not about me, but you're in big trouble, Bernard. You have evidence involved in a murder. Now tell me about the backpack."

"What backpack?"

"I know it's there. You know it too. So don't be a dick."

"It's mine."

"Pink? I don't think so."

"How do you know what's in my house?"

"Trust me."

"You've been here before. You stole my toothbrush. Why would you do that?"

"Don't know about your toothbrush, but who's the thief here? I believe that's my laptop sitting on your table behind us. Now tell me about the backpack." I pointed the barrel of the gun at him.

He swallowed hard. "I found it on the road."

"The truth, Bernard. And I'm losing patience."

"That's the truth."

"I deal with liars all day long. I can tell when someone isn't truthful, and you're lying. Tell me where you found it. Now."

I pointed my gun at his chest.

"Okay, okay. Put that thing away, and I'll tell you everything."

"I'm not putting anything away until I'm satisfied you've told me all you know."

"Well, first, I apologize for not calling you after we—"

"Shut up!"

"Okay, I know you're sensitive about the way I left things, but I just didn't think we clicked."

"You've made it clear you didn't like Sally. At some time in the past, did she piss you off? How angry at Sally were you, Bernard? Enough to take her backpack, and maybe mad enough to kill her?"

"I would never do anything like that."

"You're a thief and a slimeball, but you'd stop at murder? Convince me."

"Taking a life would be sinful."

"Face it, Bernard, you're a bad guy. Crossing that line should be a standard progression for you."

"Okay, I took your laptop. But I needed it. I'm not working, and I wanted to get my résumé—"

"Don't piss me off."

"I've never felt sorrier about anything I've done. I even went to church and confessed." He looked away, and I knew he was lying.

"Take the laptop back." He threw up his hands. "Forgive—"

"Tell me about the backpack!"

"Okay, okay." He exhaled audibly. "I was there, and it was terrible."

"How so, Bernard?"

"Stop calling me that. I go by Benny or Ben."

"Asshole would be a better fit."

"Don't be cruel."

"Being cruel would be to shoot you in the face, leaving, and letting your body rot until your neighbors smelled your decaying flesh."

He cringed. "I'll tell you. Just let me get my thoughts together."

"You don't have to think about anything if you're telling the truth."

He zeroed in on my belly.

"OMG! You're pregnant. That's why you stole my toothbrush! You think it's mine."

He chuckled, and the sound annoyed me.

"Not even close, Bernard." I stared straight. No way was he going to catch me in a lie.

"I'm not responsible for that. I had too much to drink, and we never did it. And I just wasn't into you anyway."

I flinched and instantly regretted it.

"Answer the question!"

"I think I just did."

"The backpack, Bernard." I waved my gun, so he knew it was still there. "This is your last chance, and don't leave anything out."

"Okay, maybe I didn't like her. But she thought she was better than everyone else. At the bar, I tried to sit next to her, and she moved away. She was an uppity bitch. But when I saw her lying there in the parking lot bleeding like that...it was awful."

"You saw Sally?"

"I was on my way into the Water Hole, and she was doing some sort of deal with a guy."

"What guy?"

"I don't know his name. But you know, the good-looking one. They call him *Romeo*. He's always at the Boat. She was sort of with him, but he had his pick and got passed around a lot."

My cheeks burned. "Go on."

"I saw them kissing. Sally was in Romeo's truck, and I thought he was going to do her right there. I was close enough to see."

"Where were you?"

"I was walking toward the Hole and got distracted when I saw them. I stood beside the car next to them so they couldn't see me."

"You thought they were going to have sex, and you wanted to watch?"

"Well, anyone would. But they didn't get that far. She opened the door and hopped out of his fancy ride. Double cab and all. Big dick in his big truck."

"And she had the backpack with her?"

"Yeah."

"Continue."

"That's it. She got out, and he sat there for a minute watching her as she swayed toward the bar. You know, her *come-and-get-me walk*? Her and the kid."

"What kid?"

"The drugged-out stoner that hangs with you guys."

"Trevor?"

"I don't know his name. But you know who he is. He works with you."

"Where was he when Sally got in the truck?"

"I told you, he drove her there in that piece-of-shit car of his."

"No, you left that part out, Bernard."

"Don't call me that."

"Then what? After she met Trevor."

"They were heading for the Hole. And then a big maroon car drove up, an SUV of some kind, and whoever was inside let her have it. Three shots, blood sprayed all over the place. They fired three more times. She was lying there in the road, right next to me."

"The kid ran away. The SUV and the truck took off at the same time. The jalopy split a few seconds later. In different directions, all of them. No one was left but me and her. I grabbed the backpack and hightailed it out of there.

"Sure, I took it. But it didn't have anything in it. Nothing but junk, I swear!"

"Did you call for help?"

"I figured someone would come along. Somebody had to hear the shots."

"You didn't try to help her? Stop Sally from bleeding to death when it could have made a difference?"

"I wouldn't know what to do. Besides, I wasn't going to touch her. Blood was spurting out everywhere. She was with everybody, and I could've been infected with something."

"You should have called for help and stayed and told the authorities what you saw."

"The kid didn't stick around. Romeo skated. They left her, and she was friends with them. I didn't even like her. I got the hell out of there just like everyone else."

"Did you see anyone besides them?"

"Just the ones I told you about." He looked down at the Glock. "Put that thing away and get out of my house!"

"Not yet. First, you have to promise not to call the police or tell anyone about me being here."

"Don't worry about it. Trust me."

"That's a problem, Bernard, because I don't."

"I don't want anything to do with this."

He stood up and approached me, not near enough to grab my gun but too close for my comfort.

"I don't think you got the guts to pull the trigger anyway. You're not going to shoot me."

He took another step, and I kicked, hyperextending his knee. He howled and fell to the floor.

"Mistake, asshole, and not your first."

Tears streamed down his cheeks as he cried.

"Shut up." I held the gun to his temple and patted him down. I felt the oblong hardness of a cell phone and nothing more—no needles, knives, or anything else that could hurt me. Mr. Foo had warned us about sticking hands into pockets without checking first.

I pulled the cell phone out with a gloved hand.

"Just call 911!" he begged.

"Has to be your voice, not mine."

"My leg…it's swelling up, and the pain is terrible!"

"If you say anything about me, I will find you, and you will no longer be a witness. You will become the next victim. And I'll make sure the police know about what you did. The story is that you ran into the coffee table in the dark."

"Yes, yes. Now get out of here!"

"Count to sixty, and then you can scream your lungs out. But not before that, you got it?"

"Yes! Just go!"

I grabbed Sally's backpack and looked back at the whimpering man.

"Remember, your fingerprints are all over this."

On the way out, I heard him screaming as my bad foot hit the back porch. He didn't bother counting at all, and that pissed me off a little.

I made it over the short fence without incident and hurried to my car.

Bernard's howl was loud and steady. Lights turned on in neighboring houses as I drove away.

There was nothing in the backpack but junk. But I just couldn't bring myself to toss it. Maybe I wasn't as smart as the crime lab technician who could find evidence. But Bernard's prints would lead the police to him, and he would lead them to me.

I was weaving a web of lies and deceit. I'd created a beast, and I hoped I could keep things straight enough not to destroy everything worthwhile in my life.

At this point, I didn't know if I cared if Sally's murder was ever solved. I didn't care about Sam anymore, and I hardly knew Gates. He was a mere acquaintance. I wanted out of this downward spiral. If my family was safe, I decided I was okay—no more playing detective. No more taking chances and breaking into houses and threatening people with guns. *Who did I think I was anyway?*

I parked on the road behind my house and hid the backpack in the room over the garage inside a box of toys. Sally's daughter's toys. Amanda Grover, six years old plus a few months when she died. My heart ached. Emotions for Sally swung like a pendulum.

I drove around the block, parked in the lot, and limped toward the house.

As I walked around the Volvo, I stopped as the trunk stared me in the face. I stuck the key in the hole and turned.

And there it was—Sally's suitcase.

The half-moon shone enough light for me to see the Louis Vuitton logo on the bag. I'd forgotten that she slammed it into my trunk when I picked her up at the airport.

I tried to close the trunk but couldn't bring myself to do it.

My curiosity got the best of me. I carefully unzipped the bag and looked through clothes, makeup, and other toiletries, and found nothing out of the ordinary.

When Denny got home, I told him about the suitcase, and he had someone from the department pick it up.

CHAPTER 96

It wasn't until two weeks later that I was finally able to relax. By then, I was reasonably sure Bernard hadn't reported my breaking and entering and assault crimes to the police.

At first, I jumped at every knock at the door and expected a gang of cops ready to take me to jail. I wasn't entirely sure he'd never reported it, but I did breathe easier as time passed.

Bernard's story about Sam and Trevor being at the scene of Sally's murder stuck in my craw.

I wanted to tell Denny. But what was I going to say? I was looking for the man who fathered my child, which led me to break into Bernard's house? And by the way, the creep's a material witness to a murder?

So he might ask, how could I be with a guy like that? And I would have to admit that, actually, we hadn't had sex after all. He was too drunk and just not into me.

I was confused and insecure about how much Denny would take without thinking I wasn't worth the trouble.

The question of who fathered my child was still up for grabs. Denny hadn't asked up until now, and I hadn't offered. I wondered what he thought. He probably figured it was Sam's, and apparently, that was okay with him.

I had given up the suitcase, and the crime team went over it with extreme vigor but didn't find anything.

The pricey bag was returned to me with thanks for the donation of useless things that amounted to nothing in an unsolved murder case. But Denny seemed pleased I was trying to help.

If only he knew.

Our relationship was thriving, regardless of my secrets.

I was nearly seven months pregnant and had one last sample. But I didn't want it to be a stranger and leaned toward not finding out as the best course of action.

I was on my way home and took the exit off I-95. As I passed restaurants and storefronts, heading for the bridge that led to Manalapan, I noticed a beige Taurus half a car length behind me with Sam at the wheel.

I swallowed hard as he pulled up beside me, showed me a gun, and motioned for me to make a turn at the next intersection.

I made the turn but then floored the accelerator instead of stopping. His sedan was no match for my Beamer, and I left a wide gap between us.

But I slowed to a stop when I found I was driving on a street that went nowhere. It dead-ended in a cul-de-sac abutting up against the Intracoastal. I slammed on the brakes, and Sam's car skidded to a stop sideways, blocking me from backing up.

What now? I thought as I wished I had my Glock. I made sure the doors were locked as he approached the driver's side window.

He screamed, "Get out!"

"Go away, Sam!" I yelled back.

He shot the window out. The bullet missed my head by inches and blew a hole in the floorboard.

He reached inside and grabbed me by the hair. He opened the door and dragged me back to his car as I screamed for help.

Two big houses on either side of the road were set back deep into their lots, and my screams went unanswered.

He slapped a piece of duct tape across my mouth and shoved me into the driver's side of his Taurus.

I was terrified as he pushed me over the middle console and punched me in the face. He wrapped the tape around my wrists in front of me and pointed the gun at me as he jumped into the driver's seat.

It happened so fast that I couldn't fight back. But then my mind geared up to hyper speed, trying to figure out how I would escape.

I recalled that Mr. Foo had said if captured, try to befriend your abductor.

Sam's face was unshaven, and his hair hadn't been trimmed in a while. His clothes were wrinkled and sloppy with dirt and spattered with dried blood.

As he skidded away, I pulled the tape off my face and asked, "What's going on, Sam?"

He held the gun to my head and said, "Shut up!"

As he drove, the gun didn't move from my temple.

I calmed and remembered Mr. Foo's words. *Keep your eyes open. Be patient, but do not wait too long. You must strike at the first opportunity because you may not get another.*

And I hoped I hadn't missed my chance already.

Sam pulled the Taurus into a narrow driveway around the back of a small strip of stores.

He grabbed my hair again, pulled me back over the console, and led me to the rear door of a vacant storefront. I could feel the gun sticking into my ribs.

He was so close I could smell him. Bad breath, body odor, and stale cologne. Nothing like he once was.

Pieces of a doorknob lay on the ground; a hole remained where the knob once was.

"Open it," Sam ordered.

I pulled the door open and stepped inside.

The room was spacious, and the sunlight dissipated as Sam closed the door. The only light that shone in was from the round hole in the door, and the space smelled dirty, just like him.

Sam turned on a camping lantern, and I saw a blanket in the corner and fast-food wrappers all around.

He ran his hand up and down my body, found my cell phone, threw it to the cement floor, and crushed it with his foot.

"What's happened to you, Sam?" I asked.

"Shut up, Annie!" he said as he moved his hand to hit me. I veered away; he missed and became off-balance. But only for a second.

I was close enough to hit, but I froze. Sam moved away before I had a chance to strike. And I heard Mr. Foo's words in my head again. *If you fail to take advantage of any opportunity to disable your captor, it will more than likely be the last thing you do.*

I was shaking and losing the ability to remain calm. I thought I was tough enough, but I was wrong. My breathing became rapid, and I placed my hands over my face.

Sam looked at me, seeing me for the first time.

"Are you pregnant?"

I squeaked out, "Big lunch."

He snickered. "You don't think it's mine, do you?"

"Why wouldn't it be yours?" I was hoping for some compassion.

"I never wanted any fucking brats. I had a vasectomy right after college."

So much for compassion.

"I found a body in your house."

He looked away, and I noticed he had a white bandage wrapped around his left hand.

"Do you know anything about that?" I asked.

"No idea." His eyes veered to the left, an indication that he was lying.

"Did you break into my house?"

"It's not your house!" Sam pushed me backward.

I hit the wall and allowed my body to slide to the floor. If Sam got close enough, I'd kick him in the knee, just like Bernard.

"What were you looking for?"

He held up his hand. "This is all because of you. You ruined my chance to escape this disaster!"

"I'm sorry. If you'd told me what was going on, maybe I could have helped."

Sam laughed. "You couldn't work your way out of anything. Then you hooked up with that cop, and lo and behold, I'm supposed to trust you? Since I've known you, you've been a stone-cold drunk. And he's got a past too. Holy cow, you guys make quite a pair."

He was right. I was a drunk saved by another one. Separately, we were flawed. Together we were strong. I was healthy now, not what Sam thought, and that gave me an edge.

"What happened to your hand?"

"Oh, this?" He held it up high and began unwrapping the bloody bandage.

I watched as he got closer to the flesh and saw he was missing his pinkie finger.

"Oh my God! What happened?"

"What do you think?"

"Who cut off your finger?"

"The fucking Russian threatened to kill me if I didn't come up with the money."

"For drugs?"

He ignored me.

"Are they watching you now? Do they know where you are?"

"I hope not. And I doubt it because if they did, I'd be dead by now." He shook his head. "And so would you."

"Tell me so I can understand."

"The only thing I need from you is money. I don't need you to understand anything."

"I'll give you all the money I have, but you have to tell me what we're dealing with so I can keep my family safe."

Tears rolled down his cheeks.

"Mik came to my house and threatened me. He said he would kill me if I didn't tell him what he wanted to know. And I had no idea what he was talking about. All I knew was Sally was into something big, and that was from the horse's mouth. I asked her what she was doing with that old geezer, and she said they were going to make a lot of money. Millions. That didn't surprise me because she was always up to something. She's the one that got me involved with growing pot and making fake chips.

"Her love of money was so obsessive. She had plenty, but she always wanted more," Sam cried.

"She got that machine and supplies, and I was supposed to get cash from the chips a little at a time. I'd play with fake chips and then add just three grand a day to my stack. No one would ever know, and we'd make over a million in one year. And she had someone lined up to sell the pot."

"Shaka and his crew?" My voice was shaky.

"What does it matter now? She ruined it with that deal going on with that old man. Christ, how could she?"

"She was a user," I said with more confidence.

"Oh, yeah, and you should know more than me!"

"Sure, she used me. But she gave plenty too."

"She gave, all right. Like getting your daughter involved." He laughed. "She wanted the leverage."

"What?"

"She's the one that called the cops!"

"Why?" I could barely speak.

"Sally's way. Everything she did was for her benefit. She needed you to work for her, transporting or something else. I don't know what, but I knew why."

I forced myself to remain calm. If I was ever going to get out of this, I had to rein in my hysteria.

"She used you too."

"Shut up," he screamed.

"I'm sorry. I know you were there when she was gunned down. Do you know who or why?"

"I have my suspicions." He looked away. "When Sally disappeared, everyone thought she turned on them."

"When she went to Vegas?"

"Mik thought she was running away with the money. And he had other people to answer to, other Russians. That's all I know. And when she got killed, he came after me! He said I was in on it, but I wasn't. I still don't know! Mik cut my fucking finger off because of you and your boyfriend. All I had to do was leave and never come back! This is your fault!" He held up his bloody hand again.

"I can help you now, Sam. I have enough so you can still get away."

"Where's the money?"

I had cash at home, but no way was I leading him to my family.

"Take me to the bank," I commanded.

He glanced at the clock on his phone.

"Banks are closed. But I know there has to be cash somewhere in Sally's house."

"I found it and put it in a safety deposit box," I lied.

He blinked hard.

"What happened to you?" I asked again. "You always appeared to be a successful businessman with lots of excess cash to burn at the tables."

He shook his head. "Shut up!

He closed his eyes, and I cocked my leg, but he was too far away and still holding the gun. I mentally kicked myself for not acting when I had the chance.

"I'm sorry," I said, trying to sound as sincere as possible, but I was raging inside.

"Keep your sorry and cram it up your ass! If you don't come up with some serious cash, I'll call them right now." He pulled a flip phone from his pocket and held it high. "I still have Mik's phone, and it's got his Russian contact number programmed in it. Get me cash, or I'll tell them you know everything."

"You wouldn't do that."

"What makes you think I won't?" He grabbed me by my hair and pulled me to my feet. I kicked his leg, and he veered back. I leaped toward him, but he rolled away, avoiding my blow. He jumped up, pushed me back against the wall, and shoved me to the floor.

Sam stood over me and shouted, "Wrong way to go, Annie." He put the gun to my head.

"What would you expect? You kidnapped me and threatened my life, and you think I'm not going to fight you for it?" I was shaking like crazy.

I felt a sharp kick inside my belly that reminded me I had a lot to live for.

"Where's the money?" Sam screamed.

"Okay, okay. I know a place I can get cash right now."

I had my doubts that this was the best possible plan, but I had nothing else.

"It's in storage."

"How much?"

"A lot. But what guarantee do I have that if I give you money, the risk will be over?"

He stared back and scoffed. "Guess you just have to trust me."

I blew out a whiff of air and thought, *This is never going to end.*

I jumped to my feet and darted toward him.

"Sit down!" Sam screamed.

He gave me a push, but I stayed on my feet.

He swung at me, but I ducked and came back up with fisted hands and struck him in between his legs. He fell and moaned as he held on to his crotch.

"You're dead!" he screeched.

I kicked him in the arm, and the gun went flying across the room.

I jumped toward the weapon, but he was closer and got ahold of it first.

Before he had a chance to aim, I kicked him in the head.

Stunned, he gazed back at me.

I took advantage of his stupor and jumped on his neck with my good foot. The creepy sound of bones breaking moved the bile from my stomach into my throat.

I stared at the man I once considered a friend, and now he was dead at my hands. I had killed a human being.

I dropped to my knees and felt for a pulse. Nothing. But how could there be any life when I'd flattened Sam's neck to the floor?

I quivered at the sight of him lying there and remembered what Mr. Foo had said. *Killing is easy. How you feel about it afterward is often difficult to get past.*

I bit at the tape until my hands were free. And then I searched Sam's pockets and found his iPhone and Mik's flip phone. I turned on the flip phone, and there was one recent number.

I sent a text. *I know where the money is.*

A return text registered almost immediately. *So do I. I want diamonds.*

I furrowed my brow. *Diamonds?* I never would have guessed.

I texted back. *All I know about is the money. That's the best I can do.*

I waited a few minutes and almost turned the phone off because I didn't want anyone to track the signal.

The phone pinged, and I read, *All Two Mill still in storage?*

I answered, *Yes.*

I read, *No cops.*

I answered, *No cops. Never bother me again.*

And then I broke the phone into pieces.

I picked up my broken cell but couldn't get it to turn on.

By the time I hurried out of the storefront, the sunlight had transformed into dim dusk.

I was perplexed as I walked away. *Was Sam just an innocent bystander? Bystander, maybe, but definitely not innocent.*

97

My car was still parked where it was left with the door wide open. I picked up the key fob lying nearby on the road and cleared the broken glass out of the front seat of the beamer. I looked around. The street was empty. Two big houses, but no cars or people. No one was there to see my car and become suspicious and call the police. It could have sat here undetected for hours, maybe days.

I drove over the Intracoastal bridge and tossed the broken flip phone out an open window as I pondered what to do next.

I had planned to cook dinner, but that was out of the question for so many reasons.

I struggled with the idea of how to tell Denny about Sam. I tried to think up a way to make things sound better than they were. *How would he react to the fact that his wife had just killed someone?*

As I saw it, I had two choices. I could tell Denny the truth or not say anything and let Sam's body rot until someone called the police. There wasn't much of a chance of connecting me to that storefront because I didn't have fingerprints to leave, and I had taken my phone and duct tape with me.

But what about DNA from skin cells or hair? That was entirely possible.

I stopped at Grana Pizza on the way and picked up a couple of pies before heading home. The aroma of the food gnawed at my stomach. I wasn't in the mood to eat, but other people needed feeding.

And I pondered how I could be doing this with all that had occurred just a short time ago. *I was kidnapped, nearly killed, but I turned the tables and escaped.*

Denny's car was parked in the lot, alongside Ellie's and Beth's.

I stood for a moment at the door, took a breath, and then entered the house.

Ellie, Denny, and Beth sat at the table. As soon as I entered, all eyes focused on me.

"What's up?" I asked as I sat the pizzas on the table.

No one replied.

"Dinner is served," I said.

Denny took my hand and said, "We need to talk."

I nodded, and we headed upstairs.

Once inside our bedroom, he said, "You have a bruise on your face, and I can tell something awful has happened."

"You're a pretty good detective." I stared off.

I told him almost everything. Being kidnapped by Sam, Mik cutting off his finger, his fear of the Russians, and the diamonds. But I failed to mention the money in storage and that I was mad as hell at Sally for what she did to Ellie.

"I killed Sam," I said. "I knocked him down and stepped on his throat until his neck was broken, and he's dead."

"You're in shock."

"Actually, I'm thankful to be alive, and I'm truly grateful for your love and support."

"Where did this happen?"

I told him the storefront's approximate location, and he made some calls and repeated what I'd said.

He ended the call with "I'll meet you there."

He hung up and pulled me to him. He hugged me hard before he left.

The next day I went to the nearest T-Mobile store and purchased a new phone.

CHAPTER 98

As my stomach expanded, so did my confidence. I showed up early for every Krav Maga class, watching and listening to every word.

Eating better became a way of life. The hardest thing was salt, and I just couldn't give it up. And I cheated with an occasional cheeseburger and Egg McMuffin.

But whatever I was doing was an improvement. I was feeling better than I had ever remembered and less afraid as time moved forward.

A sense of empowerment mounted within me, and I knew I was becoming *the master of my fate and the captain of my soul.*

Ellie was at school, and Beth had taken a job at Burger King, and it seemed to be working out for her.

Denny was on the job. Since being promoted to detective, his solve rate was above average, and he was a star once more.

I was alone in my huge house and utterly bored out of my mind.

I stewed about it for over an hour, staring at the swab in the baggy.

Gritting my teeth, I stood. Like a Ninja Warrior, I became focused. I grabbed the swab and headed for Rapid Testing before I had a chance to change my mind.

The sky was dark with rain-filled thunderheads as I drove the Beamer with a plastic garbage bag taped around the gap where the driver's side window should be.

I dropped off the swab and babbled something about being sorry for bothering Amber again.

She smiled the same as before and said it wasn't a problem.

I turned to leave and then stopped.

"I was drugged and assaulted," I said.

She furrowed her brow. "I'm sorry to hear that. But you don't have to explain anything here. We don't judge."

"I feel like I'm becoming a potential guest on the *Jerry Springer Show*."

"We get people with a lot more samples than you, and I hope that you eventually find what you're looking for."

Humbled, I bowed my head.

"Would it be helpful if you knew the ethnicity of this sample?" she asked.

"It would be good to know."

I thanked her and rushed out into the dull light of midday. The sky had begun to drizzle with a misty rain.

As I drove, I glanced in the rearview mirror and saw the black sedan a few cars back. I had thought the paranoia would have subsided, but there it was again.

Millions of dollars and a lot of diamonds. I gave the Russian his money back, but that didn't solve the mystery.

I made a quick turn and glanced back again. The black car was gone, and I pulled over and eased back off the edge of my seat.

Thunder cracked, and rain flooded across my windshield. The garbage bag leaked around the edges, reminding me that I needed to get the window fixed.

As I pulled back out, I passed a KIA dealership and changed my mind about the window repair.

I turned around and traded the Beamer in on a Kia Sedona minivan. Despite the missing window and the bullet hole in the floorboard, they gave me a nice big check to boot.

Back at home, Denny greeted me at the door with a kiss. He seemed surprised that I'd traded in the Beamer.

I said that a minivan seemed more practical, and he agreed.

Ellie and Beth were cooking, and the house smelled wonderfully of tomatoes and garlic. My stomach growled— *hungry for food and answers.*

CHAPTER 99

The call came seven days later.

I had picked up my cell numerous times to call Amber to cancel the test but never dialed. This one was the worst of all.

What if the genes of violence were passed on? I would always be watching, wary, and wondering if evil traits would appear.

What about ethnicity?

I would love her unconditionally. But how would Denny react to a child that was noticeably different than us?

I was home alone when the phone finally rang, and I let it ring four times before I answered.

This time, Amber asked me to stop by. She said she wanted to go over the results with me in person.

She was short and to the point and hung up before I had a chance to protest.

I was in the car and on my way within a matter of seconds.

As I entered the facility, Amber greeted me with a smile and said, "I'm sorry I wasn't more specific on the phone. You must have all kinds of questions."

I didn't reply as she led me into one of the small rooms, not much different than the rest of the place. *Plain and dreary.* White walls instead of beige were the only exception.

A small table and two chairs sat center of the room. I sat down and folded my hands on the cheap Formica tabletop.

"Tell me," I said.

"First, and I think most importantly, this sample is not from the father of your baby," she said.

I exhaled. "Why did you make me come down here?"

"The sample is from someone with a gene abnormality, and I thought you should know this. This unknown has the gene for Tay-Sachs. He probably has difficulty walking. It's a good thing he's not the father."

"Great."

"And he's clearly of East Slavic descent. Ukrainian or Belarusian-Russian. All indicators point in that direction."

The word *Russian* stuck in my craw, and I thought immediately of Mik. He walked with a limp and was Russian. That made him an excellent candidate for being the one. But why him? And how did he get into my house? Other than work, I would never let him anywhere near me.

I gulped air and put my hand over my face trying to stop the hyperventilation attack.

Visions of horrible sex bombarded my brain with me passed out and helpless with Mik on top. I gritted my teeth and vowed never to be weak again.

I couldn't catch my breath, and I felt my face burn red.

I knew Sam had to be behind this. I was stupid, such a fool for letting him into my life. I was glad both were dead. Sam and Mikhail, the creepy Russian, were burning in hell.

I was sick. And it took a lot to keep the bile in my stomach down. I felt faint, and it made me mad that I wasn't in control of my emotions again.

"I'm sorry," Amber said. "Are you okay?"

I laid my head on the table, so I wouldn't fall and hurt myself.

When I woke, Amber was holding a bag of ice on my forehead. A short light-skinned Hispanic with a scar from surgery for a cleft lip stood nearby. I assumed this was Pablo, the voice on the phone that called with test results.

"Calm down, miss," Pablo said. "We called for help."

"I don't need anyone. I just need to go home, that's all."

"Are you sure you're okay?"

"I have panic attacks, and I'm all right now."

"I have more information for you," Amber said. "Are you okay to receive it?"

"Tell me, please."

"We did the genetic test on the DNA from your fetus. It could be helpful."

She showed me a pie chart with a few colors. The most significant portion was blue; two slivers were green and yellow.

"What is this?" I asked.

"Blue is Great Britain, England, Ireland, Scotland, or surrounding areas. The green is Eastern Europe, France, and Germany. The other tiny portion is from Western Europe."

I stared at the colors. This was basically the same as me. My ancestry was here, and Kaitlyn's father was similar. At least ethnicity would not be an issue Denny and I would have to deal with.

I picked up the chart. "This information is very helpful. How much do I owe you?"

"You've already paid too much." Amber bit her lip and looked away. "If there's anything more we can do for you, don't hesitate to call."

I passed the ambulance as I drove away.

I couldn't get Mik's image out of my head. I pulled over and tried to think of good things. I made an effort to go to my happy place, but it wasn't working.

I began reciting the AA mantra. *God, give me the grace to accept with serenity the things that cannot be changed...*

I stopped midsentence as the sudden sickness overwhelmed me. I opened the door and threw up on the road.

CHAPTER 100

I was breathing fire and shooting bolts of lightning from my eyes as I entered the door. No one was home, and I was glad. *Good for them.* If I'd encountered anyone just then, there would be hell to pay.

I wandered around, searching for something, anything that would alter my mood. I needed drugs or booze, or both. To hell with sobriety. I was far enough along that a bit of stimulant wasn't going to hurt my baby. I was convinced the placenta would do its job and keep bad things away from her.

Rationalization is a beautiful thing, and addicts and alcoholics use it often. But I didn't need to rationalize. At that moment, I didn't care about anything or anyone but myself.

The doorbell interrupted my pursuit of vodka and pharmaceuticals, and that infuriated me even more. I glanced at the image in the viewer and saw Trevor frowning back at me.

I wanted to scream, but I opened the door instead. Trevor hugged me hard, flung me around, and whispered in my ear, "I'm sorry, Annie."

He caught me off guard, and I got distracted from my mission of self-destruction. At least for the moment.

"It's good to see you, Trevor," I said, but I didn't mean it. All I wanted was to get rid of him and to get back to my mission to drink or medicate myself into oblivion.

"I owe my life to you, Annie."

"You did the work." I tried to sound sincere, but it was difficult. Trevor was involved somehow with Sally and her scheme, and he'd kept it from me.

"If not for you, I would have died on the street." He grimaced, and I noticed the needle tracks on his arms were well healed.

This bit of good news lightened my mood just a little. I had saved Trevor, and he may have returned the favor without knowing. My desire for drugs and alcohol waned.

The baby kicked, and I caressed her little foot. I was almost okay again.

"You're not out of the woods yet, let me tell you."

"You're pregnant," he stated and looked away.

"Are you okay?"

"I'm sorry. After everything you did for me, you don't deserve this."

"What's up?"

He ignored my question.

"You're very pregnant," he repeated but didn't smile, nor did he appear happy. He furrowed his forehead and cringed instead.

An uneasy feeling crept into my head.

"Listen, Trevor, I was just getting ready to go out," I lied.

The uneasiness exacerbated to near panic. I knew I needed to get rid of Trevor and bolt the door immediately.

A shadowy figure moved behind him, and I pushed Trevor aside and used all my force to attempt to close the door.

But I was too slow. Something was braced against the massive oak.

Trevor joined me as we shoved harder. And then somebody pushed back, and we lost the battle.

The door flew open, and Shaka stepped inside. He was dressed in an orange and red silk shirt with matching slacks.

He grabbed me by the throat and pushed me.

The momentum carried me back, and I flopped down on the couch. I was grateful for the soft landing but petrified for my life.

Pup ran up to Shaka and growled. Shaka kicked him, and Pup yelped as he slid across the floor and cowered in a corner.

"That wasn't necessary," I said. "You're nothing but a coward!"

"Shut up, bitch, 'cause you're next!" Shaka shouted.

I stared up at him. Shaka was a mountain, and Trevor was lost from sight somewhere behind.

"What do you want?" I asked but knew that this was the Armageddon I had dreaded and hoped would never come.

Trevor stepped out from behind the big man and said, "Just tell them, Annie, and they'll never bother you again."

"What do you think I know?"

"Where is it?" Shaka growled.

"I have no idea," I said as I searched for a vulnerable spot to kick. He was well padded with rolls of flab, so I knew I'd have to use a lot of force. And if it didn't work, he would retaliate and probably kill me.

Shaka backhanded me.

"I, I don't know. All I know is whatever you're looking for is not here."

Shaka laughed.

"Give it up, Annie," Trevor interjected. "Take my advice, and don't mess with him!"

Shaka looked at me. His eyes opened wide like he was seeing me for the first time.

And then he began laughing loudly. His colossal stomach shook like Jell-O as he bayed.

"This is gonna be easier than I thought. I'll just kick the bitch in the stomach and see how she likes it."

He picked me up, and my feet left the ground. Face-to-face, I could feel his breath on my skin.

"I'll kill your calf if you don't tell me!"

"I was never involved in any of this," I said. "It was all Sally. I don't know anything."

I tried to imagine kicking Shaka between the legs, but I doubted I could hit his gonads. It seemed every vulnerable area was covered with a thick protective layer of lard.

So I kept talking.

"Sally and I spent a lot of time together. Tell me what you're looking for, and maybe it'll ring some sort of bell. I'll help you figure this out."

"Don't play games!" Shaka screamed in my face.

"It's drugs, right? There was a grow room—"

"It's not drugs, Annie," Trevor said.

"Okay, I was thinking along those lines. But if it's not drugs, what else could it be?"

Shaka dropped me back on the couch and glared at me. I felt like his eyes were boring a hole in my chest.

"Let's start with a little information. Is it bigger than a bread box?"

I was trying to appear calm, but it was nearly impossible. I expected Beth and Ellie to walk through the door at any moment, and that would make everything more complicated.

"No, Annie!" Trevor screeched. "It's not that big. The diamonds would fit in a box or a can or something like that!"

Shaka's eyes left me and landed hard on Trevor.

"Shut the fuck up!" His enormous voice resonated.

"Diamonds? I would have never guessed," I lied.

Shaka lifted his hand to hit me, and I shrunk down, giving him a smaller target.

"Sally had a storage unit," I managed to squeak out.

The big man stared back.

"They could be there. I checked it out once, but all I saw was junk. But I wasn't really looking for anything in particular. There's just some old furniture and boxes."

"Where?"

I needed to find a way to disable the big hunk of lard and do it soon, but it was going to be tricky. All I could think about was Ellie and Beth.

"It's on Military Trail, and I have the key somewhere around here. Let me find it."

My Glock was upstairs in my room. But I didn't think it was possible to get away and grab it before Shaka killed me.

I tried to stand.

"Don't move!" Shaka yelled.

I eased back.

"Tell me where 'tis."

"In the desk."

As he moved, waves of flab waggled underneath his colorful sheer attire. He tore open the rolling wood and began searching.

"There's a business card with writing on the back along with the key. I can help."

"Shut up!"

I heard Mr. Foo shouting, *Find a weakness! Now!*

I watched as Shaka pulled open drawers and threw the contents from the desk on the floor. But I knew it wasn't there. The key and the card were tucked away in my backpack, and I wasn't about to disclose that. I was sure I'd be dead if I was no longer needed.

I glanced at Trevor. His face showed terror as his eyes bounced around, and he shook his head.

He wasn't a villain; he was a victim. Captured, just like me.

I wondered why they waited so long. And then I realized Trevor was far away in a place they couldn't get to. He was the link to Sally. When he returned, they were right there to pick up where they left off, looking for the diamonds. He had to give them someone. That's why he was sorry.

I figured that Shaka wasn't working with the Russians. He was on the other side that brought the diamonds. *Small enough to fit anywhere.*

"I know what it looks like," I said. "I can find it quicker than you."

Shaka looked back at Trevor. "Keep her quiet!" And then he got back to his search.

I looked for the most vulnerable spot, and then I made my move.

I slid across the room quickly and kicked the back of Shaka's knee.

The hit was on mark and effective. He fell backward, and I had to move fast so he didn't land on top of me. He hit the floor so hard it shook the house.

He took a breath, reached into his waistband, and pulled out a revolver. I kicked his hand, and the gun clanked across the floor.

As Shaka floundered around like a big fish out of water, I kicked him in the side of the head as hard as I could. Blood spattered on the wood floor as I kicked again and again until I was sure he was unconscious or dead, and I didn't care which.

And then Trevor grabbed hold of me. He hugged me and whispered again, "I'm so sorry."

"It's okay, Trev. We're safe."

"No, we're not."

I turned around and faced two more men. And they both had guns.

CHAPTER 101

The men were both fair skinned and had round faces, light hair, and brown eyes. They looked so much alike that they could be brothers. But one was short, about the same height as me, and the other was tall and slim.

And they had guns, 9-millimeter SIG SAUERs. I knew this SIG because I'd almost bought one like it at Sure Shoot, and that particular one had caught my eye. But the price tag was out of my range.

They looked around, and their eyes focused on Shaka's massive body lying on the floor, bleeding into the wood.

"We need to get him out of here, aye?" Shorty said. I'd dealt cards to many snowbirds from the north, including Canada, and they tended to finish a question that way.

Finn said the guy in the bar at the time Sally was killed sounded Canadian. The pieces were coming together, but I didn't like my part in this puzzle.

Slim held a gun to my head and said, "Tape her up."

He threw a roll of duct tape at Shorty.

What now, Mr. Foo? He'd never covered this particular scenario in class.

Slim looked at Shaka and said, "So you know how to defend yourself?"

Shorty pulled me up by my hair as Slim aimed his Sig at my stomach.

He pulled my hands behind my back and taped them together, and then pushed me back onto the couch.

I looked around, and Trevor was nowhere in sight.

The door opened again, and another man entered, dragging Trevor with his arm twisted behind him.

The third guy was tanned like he was out in the sun a lot—*the golfer*—and he didn't have a gun.

He looked at Shaka and asked, "Is he still alive?"

Shorty placed a hand on Shaka's throat and said, "Got a pulse."

"Get him out of here," Slim ordered. He waved his hand at Trevor and said, "You too."

"Where are we going to hide him? He's huge!" Shorty said.

"In the dark around the side. Make sure no one finds him until morning."

The men struggled to drag Shaka out of the house, leaving a trail of blood as they went.

I took a breath and tried to stay calm. *There is no value in panic*; Mr. Foo had said that too.

After a few minutes, the three men returned red faced and sweating from the strenuous job of dragging the big man out.

Slim said, "That information you told Shaka about is in the desk, aye?"

I looked away. "It's not there," I lied. "When I searched the place, I didn't see anything of value, so I tossed it. But I remember where it is and the code to get in."

And then they forced me outside and into the back seat of a light gray SUV.

Shorty got in next to me, and the golfer forced Trevor into the back next to Shorty.

Slim drove as the golfer rode shotgun in the front. I was relieved when the SUV pulled away from my house because my family was safe, at least for now.

"Where's this storage unit?" the golfer asked.

"It's on Military. North of Forest Hill, I think."

"Don't play games."

"I was only there once."

"Look, I respect your condition, and we don't need to hurt you or your child. After we find what belongs to us, we'll drop you off, and you will never hear from us again. You'll go on with your life as if nothing happened."

"Sure," I said with a disbelieving tone.

"You sound doubtful."

"You killed people. Why would I think things would be different with Trevor or me?"

"We didn't kill anyone." His voice echoed in my ears.

"What about Sally and Gates?"

Slim laughed as he floored the accelerator. "Their deaths complicated everything!"

"I wouldn't have wanted that in my wildest dreams," the golfer proclaimed.

"If they had followed through with the original plan, we would all be happy and have what we wanted, and none of us would be in this situation today!" Slim yelled.

"Nothing was gained from their deaths," the golfer said.

"Everything we worked for is gone!" Slim added.

"You sent Shaka to kill me," I said.

"We hired the big guy to scare, not to kill you," the golfer insisted. "He's a credible threat, wouldn't you agree? I was surprised that you overtook him—and, quite frankly, impressed. I hope he makes it through the night. We have scruples, after all."

His speech was refined, and his mannerisms were a blend of class and good breeding. Almost convincing.

"Our initial contact was Gates. And then that woman, Sally, got involved, but we didn't have any particulars about her. We didn't even know her last name," the golfer admitted. "Your so-called friend, Trevor, was sort of a go-between. We knew more about him. He was easy to find. But then he disappeared suddenly, and we had to wait until he returned from his extended vacation."

"And when he did, he led us to you," Slim stated. "He gave you up without much effort. Even asked for money in return!"

His words rang in my ears. Trevor stared at the floor as tears dripped from his face.

Slim looked away from the road and glared at me. His eyes fluttered, and then he lied, "You help us, and we'll let you go. You can trust me."

I had a feeling that *trust* was the furthermost thing from his mind.

I'd seen their faces and heard their voices. I could easily pick them out of a lineup and describe them to a police artist precisely enough to produce accurate portraits that anyone who knew them would recognize. I knew I was never going to get out of this alive unless I took charge. But my hands were tied, and now they knew I had self-defense skills.

"If you want me to trust you, un-tape my hands," I demanded.

Slim smiled slyly. "Get us to the storage unit, and I'll think about it."

We were at an impasse.

"Bring up your GPS and search for the nearest Extra Storage location," I said.

"You've been there before, aye?" the golfer asked.

"Yes, but only once, and it was in the daylight. And I came in from a different direction. I used GPS to find it, so I suggest you do the same."

The GPS led us to the nearest storage location, but I knew it wasn't the right one. There were several on Military Trail, both north and south.

We pulled up to the gate, and I tried to look confused. "This doesn't look familiar," I stated as I sought more time to figure a way out.

"You're playing games!" Slim said. "This is not the way to get on the good side of me!" He hit the dash with his fist and pulled up a little Sig with a faux wood handle grip, tiny in his large hand. Another gun, but not one I'd preferred. Too small and sometimes unreliable.

Three guns so far. Slim had two, Shorty had one, but the golfer hadn't brandished anything yet.

And I sensed that Slim oversaw this operation.

"Pointing a loaded gun in my face is not going to make me want to help you."

He pulled the gun back. "I needed to make a point!" he barked.

I noticed the golfer was shaking. His partner's aggressiveness had put him on the edge of his seat.

"Stop it. We don't need to provoke her further," the golfer said as he held up a hand. His skin was soft, definitely not into heavy lifting. No doubt, he had a lot of hired help surrounding him.

"Look," I said. "I'm afraid of you. You don't have to threaten any more than you already have. I know where the storage unit is, and I have the combination you need to get inside the facility. So let's make a deal."

"You're not in any position to make deals!" Slim shouted.

"And you're in no position not to."

Slim remained silent for a few minutes and then said, "What's your deal?"

"I don't want your diamonds. I have everything I need. My deal is to let us go, and I'll give you the information, in that order."

"That's laughable."

"Not really. I don't want to live my life worrying about what's around the next corner. I don't want to drive around with one eye behind to see if I'm being followed, and I don't really enjoy being woken in the middle of the night with someone breaking into my house. And on top of that, bodies are piling up, and the killing needs to end. I'm exhausted."

Slim looked at the golfer. "She's lying. You can't trust her."

"Shut up!" the golfer barked.

"Let us go, and I'll text you the information," I bargained.

The golfer looked away as he pondered my words. "What if the money isn't there? What if it's not in the storage unit?"

"It's there," I lied again. "Two million dollars. I saw it myself."

Slim slammed his fist on the back of the seat.

"Two?" he screamed. "It's four million! It had to be four or nothing!"

Numbers bounced around in my head. *Two plus two.* The diamonds and half the money were missing.

"What will you do if it's not all there?" I asked.

"We'll go back and search your house. We'll tear the thing apart if that's what it takes!" Slim said.

"There's nothing there. I've looked from top to bottom even before I knew what I was looking for. Sam had access numerous times, and he didn't have any luck either. It has to be in the storage unit."

The golfer looked straight at me and asked, "Who is Sam?"

I stared at the back of the seat. Sam hadn't lied after all. He got caught up in it because of Sally.

I assumed that Gates had instigated the plan. He found an opportunity, approached Sally, and she promised to marry him as part of the deal. Sally had more than likely gotten the Russians involved through her contact with Mik. Trevor was somehow helpful, and she used him. She had the connections and could have pulled everything together.

"Sam is nobody. Let us go," I repeated. "If you don't find everything you're looking for, you know where I live, and I'm not going anywhere."

"Trevor told us your husband is a policeman," Slim said. "You think I'm stupid?"

"My husband is on my side, in the same position as me. He wants this madness to stop just as much as I do. So here's the deal, plain and simple. You let us out on the street somewhere with one of you to watch us. I'll text you everything you need, and you can search the place. Either way, we walk, and you get the goods or eliminate one more location. If you don't find everything you're looking for, you'll need to keep on searching. I'll assist you any way I can."

Trevor had remained silent throughout our exchange, and then he opened his mouth. "Annie is the most honest person I know. Whatever she says, you should believe."

"Of course, you'd say that," Shorty said. "You're in the same position as she is."

"Then keep me and let her go. I'll be your insurance policy."

"Shut up!" Slim said. "Let me think."

"What exactly do you have to gain from killing us?" I asked.

He looked at Trevor and said, "You told us she would spill her guts without any problem. And now we're being led around like idiots, listening to liars."

"We're the only hope you have."

"If we don't find anything in the unit, I will kill him," Slim said, referring to Trevor. "How about that?"

"You kill Trevor, and it's all over. I'll—"

Shorty slapped a piece of tape over my mouth.

"No more talking," Shorty said as he looked at Slim. "Just make the call."

They let me out and kept Trevor. Slim and the golfer remained in the car, and Shorty stayed with me. Slim handed his partner a pay-as-you-go burner, and the SUV sped off.

CHAPTER 102

I stood on the corner of a quiet residential street with my hands taped behind my back.

Shorty ripped the tape from my mouth. It stung, but I refused to react.

I considered my options. I could disclose the correct information and hope for the best. Or I could fight.

I chose both. I recited the location, the combination, and the number of the storage unit from memory. As Shorty was busy texting, I kicked him in the knee. He fell to the ground, and before he had a chance to raise his gun, I jumped on his chest. All the air escaped from his lungs, and bones cracked.

I ran down the street until I found a chain-link fence with wire prongs sticking upward. It was difficult to reach with my hands behind my back, but somehow, I managed to tear the tape away from my wrists.

I hurried back and grabbed the gun and phone from the ground. I checked on Shorty one last time; he was wheezing and still out of it.

I called Denny and told him where I was and what had happened.

He said to hold tight. He would send help.

I re-texted the information about the storage unit to Denny and pressed send. And then I checked the gun to see how many shots I had. It was empty.

I looked down at the comatose man I'd laid out on the sidewalk. I'd done a lot of damage to a defenseless man. But I didn't know that at the time. *Better be safe than sorry,* Mr. Foo would have said.

103
CHAPTER

The police response to the storage unit was almost immediate, but Slim and the golfer never showed up.

As I waited for the ambulance and cops to arrive, I dug through the wallet of the guy gasping for air on the sidewalk.

Brian Beasley, 58, Canadian citizen, currently living in the exclusive Ibis country club community in North Palm Beach.

His wallet also contained pictures of a woman, probably his wife, and three teenage boys.

Beasley was transported to the hospital in critical condition. His lungs had collapsed, and despite the paramedics' efforts to pump air in, he died anyway.

However, I googled him and found that he'd recently retired from a cushy government job with the Natural Resources Canada (NRCan) department. He was a director in the green mining division.

I searched the Internet and found that there was a bit of controversy involved in his sudden retirement. His close friend and fellow worker, Harold Steiger, was called into question.

Steiger's name popped up in association with the ministry of the Canadian Environmental Protection Department. He was one of the analysts who approved a mine expansion in Northern Canada that caused severe pollution in the Mackenzie River. He and his cohort were charged with crimes against the government.

Beasley was later cleared, but the scandal had prompted his untimely resignation.

Steiger was not as lucky. He was arrested, and his assets were frozen. Months later, he was granted an interim release pending trial. He and his family were ordered to surrender their passports and not leave the country.

But they disappeared, and Steiger was currently a fugitive at large.

I stared at the picture of two men leaving the courthouse. I knew them both. I didn't have to read the caption to recognize which one was Steiger. He was tall and slim, the most aggressive of the three men who had kidnapped me. Beasley was the short one.

I speculated that these guys, Steiger and Beasley, were compensated by overlooking environmental dangers and got paid off with diamonds. A lot of diamonds worth millions of dollars.

At home, I pulled out Sally's bank account records and credit card statements for the months before being killed.

Ten days before she flew to Vegas, there were a lot of charges for gasoline and food. Starting in West Palm Beach. The first charge was over two hundred dollars at a Wawa station on Belvedere Road just off I-95. And there were similar expenses in Jacksonville, Charlotte, somewhere in Virginia, Columbus, and finally Niagara Falls, Canada. All totaled, the time from West Palm to Niagara Falls was just over thirty-two hours and took a lot of gas.

The return trip had started almost immediately and had taken less than twenty-seven hours. Sally had to have had some help with the drive. *Maybe Trevor?*

Sally said she was going to Vegas to marry Gates, but he didn't show because Gates had been murdered before he had a chance to get on the plane. I saw suitcases packed for the trip on the bed in his house. He needed to complete the trade first, cash for diamonds, but nothing happened— neither Vegas nor the deal. He never showed up because he was dead.

And the likely scenario was that Sally had smuggled the fugitives into the United States from Canada in her motor home.

Things were finally coming together.

Finding Steiger was going to be a problem. I had no idea who the golfer was, and Beasley was dead. I had killed the only link that might have answered the rest of the questions.

Sally returned from Vegas without Gates, and she kept her eyes peeled for danger as I drove.

I had wondered why she parked at the church and hitched a ride to the Hole with Trevor, but now it made sense. Someone was looking for her, and they probably knew what kind of car she drove.

Gates had sold his investments and taken out the cash. Two million, not four. Half of the funds.

I knew more, but everything I'd learned led to more questions.

I was sure that Steiger was the diamond broker, and Gates had pulled Sally in, and she'd gotten Trevor, Mik, and the Russian involved. But why Trevor and not Sam? Another question I'd probably never have an answer to.

Sam was close to Sally doing other shoddy deals but wasn't included in this one, but Mik didn't know that.

Had Sally found a way to double-cross everyone?

I had a feeling that the Russian I spoke to on Mik's phone had answers, and I was a little sorry for tossing the burner.

Shaka lived through the night and spent a week in the hospital recovering. He was questioned at length but said his memory was impaired by the kicks I delivered to his head, but I didn't believe that for a moment.

I still felt a bit of remorse about killing Beasley. But I got over it when Trevor's body turned up with a bullet in his head, floating in the shallow waters surrounding the Lake Worth Pier.

CHAPTER 104

Most of Trevor's family had tired of his addiction and the heartaches that came with it long ago. No one cared enough to pick up his remains and give him a proper burial—*no one except me.*

I invited everyone from the Boat, and a big crowd showed up. I scheduled a viewing at a local funeral home, and then he was driven to my house in a black hearse and entombed in my backyard. And then we had a celebration of life in my home with loads of catered food and lots of alcohol. I didn't have a problem with not drinking because the smell of the libations and occasional whiffs of cannabis made me sick.

I delivered the eulogy with a morose account of Trevor's young life. He was intelligent, energetic, and addicted to drugs. An illness that every one of us had been affected by one way or the other. And he was a friend.

I didn't say I was going to find his killer like I did at Sally's celebration. *No more promises. The time had come for actions to speak instead of words.*

As I plotted my next move, Denny rubbed my back and said, "We're looking into all known associates. We'll come up with something."

"Keep me in the loop, please," I asked as I gave him a peck on the lips.

When it was over, I was exhausted. My mind was overworked, and my body was weak. I climbed the stairs and slept as the caterers removed their pots, pans, and Sterno and cleaned up.

Denny woke me the next morning to tell me that they tore apart the storage unit and found nothing but old furniture and cheap clothing. No money or diamonds.

He asked me what I wanted to do with the junk, and I said to donate it or throw it out. I didn't need to dwell on dead ends. I had more important things to deal with.

We'd never be safe until this business was resolved.

I placed a call to Attorney Ranger and told him to set up the trust and let me know what else he needed.

I was making bad decisions and doing dangerous things. I wanted to make sure my family was taken care of if something happened to me.

105

I climbed the stairs to the storage space above the garage and found Sally's backpack where I'd thrown it after picking it up from Bernard's.

At first look, I didn't think there was any clue inside, but I was beginning to think I may have been wrong.

I cleared a space on the hardwood floor and dumped it out. More tobacco flakes fell from the cigar.

I zeroed in on the Post-It note with the numbers written on it. Sixteen-twelve-sixteen. It was a code for a combination lock.

I tossed the romance novel aside and took the cheap phone.

Back in the house, I searched for a universal charger but couldn't find one. I shoved the phone into my backpack, and then I drove back to the Boat.

I said hello to all my friends in the break room and stayed until they headed out to their assigned tables.

I was finally alone and able to complete the task that I'd come for.

It wasn't hard to find the purple combination lock still hung on the locker that had once belonged to Sally. She used this locker back when I thought she was my best friend, and I believed I knew everything there was to know about her. But I was so stupid. Following her like a lost puppy, one drunken day after another. But that was on me, not her. *I was the master of my own fate.*

I dialed the lock around and back and around again until it stopped at the last number. And then I pulled. I wasn't surprised when it opened. I unhooked the cheap combination lock and opened the metal door.

Four aluminum cigar cylinders were the only contents. Romeo y Julieta, just like the box at the bottom of the liquor cabinet in my house.

When I picked them up, I felt the contents jiggle against the metal.

I slipped them into my boot, closed the locker, and tossed the lock. I walked quickly out of the Boat, knowing I would probably never return.

106

CHAPTER

I waited until I got back home before dealing with the aluminum tubes. There was no hurry. I knew what they contained, and it wasn't cigars.

I dumped out the diamonds on the smooth surface of the dining room table and stared at the stones. Big and round. At least four carats each. I took a close look at one and couldn't detect any flaws.

I counted them as I put them back into the tubes— 210 beautiful diamonds.

But I needed an expert opinion to determine that they were real and not cut glass.

I called Herman Chase to make sure he was in, and then I drove to his store.

He was bright and chipper as always and asked about Denny.

After I filled him in on a few things that were happening in our lives, I pulled one diamond out of my pocket and placed it on the glass counter in front of him.

He stared at it for a moment before picking it up and placing it on a piece of black velvet. He viewed the stone through his jeweler's loop and shook his head.

"Is it real?" I asked.

"It's real, all right. And it's magnificent. Where did you get this?"

"I inherited it from Sally, and I'm just getting around to dealing with her estate." I had become quite a proficient liar.

He took another look. "Clear, no flaws at all. Brilliant cut. Very good. Excellent quality."

"How much is it worth?"

He put the stone down and tilted his head. Thirty, forty, maybe more."

"Thousand?"

He nodded and grinned. "You want to sell it?"

"I'm not sure."

"I'll give you thirty-five for it right now. I've got a buyer that would just love to have this."

"What if I had a few more to sell?"

"A few I could handle. But it would take time. I'm not in that type of business."

"What type of business would that be?"

"I'm in retail. I'm not a broker, nor do I have the underworld contacts."

"Underworld?"

"Diamonds are the black market currency of choice. Better than cash, they can be transported easily, and they're totally untraceable. Even better than bitcoin."

I pocketed the rock and said, "Thank you, Herman. If I decide to sell it, I'll be back."

In my car, I pulled my Glock out of the glove box, checked the clip to make sure it was full, and then shoved it into my boot.

107

CHAPTER

Spring had morphed to summer somewhere along the line, and I'd gotten the AC fixed in my Volvo as I drove to the sheriff's office.

Seven months pregnant, sober, and I was still fighting my way through life.

My stomach bulged, but I hadn't gained much weight and was still quite agile for my condition and size.

We didn't need a drawing of Steiger because we already knew who he was and what he looked like. But the golfer was another story.

I sat down with a police sketch artist and had given him a slightly different view of the man known as *the golfer*. A more prominent nose, thinner face, and I said he had a receding hairline, but that wasn't factual either. As a matter of fact, the rendition looked nothing like him at all.

And then I called an artist friend I knew from the Boat and hired him to change the sketch. We put together a perfect drawing of the man I was after.

"This is exactly what I was looking for," I told him.

And he said it was good to see me, too, and it was also great to get paid.

I stopped at a cell phone store and purchased a universal charger, and plugged the phone from Sally's backpack into the lighter socket in my car. It was so dead it didn't turn on right away, so I just let it charge.

I took I-95 to Northlake Boulevard and then drove west until I arrived at the Ibis Golf Club entrance.

It was exclusive and expensive to play there and advertised as the best place for golf in Florida. But I didn't come to play.

I stopped at the gate and expressed my desire to join the club.

The guard eyed my twenty-year-old Volvo and said, "Leave me your number, and I'll have someone call you. And just so you know, you'll need a recommendation from a member in good standing."

I bit my lip and held up the portrait of the golfer.

"You ever see this guy before?"

He grabbed the paper and took a closer look.

"You're the second person this week to show me a sketch. I didn't recognize the other one, but this one, I might just know."

"This guy may have played golf with Mr. Beasley, the resident of Ibis, who was recently killed."

"Maybe," he said as he handed it back.

"Got a name?"

"Hum, perhaps."

"How much to jog your memory?"

"Show me what we have to work with, and I'll let you know."

I pulled a hundred-dollar bill out of my backpack. "Come to think of it, I don't think so."

I added two more bills, and he snatched the money and said, "I never saw this guy before. And by the way, your buddy, Beasley? Never played golf."

He walked back into the guard shack and slid the door shut.

I drove away, feeling stupid. Beasley and Steiger were fair skinned, unlike the golfer; neither one played outside games.

The golfer had money, and I knew where people with money lived. I pulled up my phone and did a search for golf courses on Palm Beach Island.

The first one I found was the Palm Beach Par 3. I booked a tee time for later that day and headed toward the beach.

As I drove up the coast, I passed by Gates's mansion. I pulled over and looked through the wrought iron gate. Two cars were parked in the driveway, and a child's bike lay on the lawn by the front door. And I wondered how they'd gotten the putrid smell out of the house.

Harold Steiger had said he was after the cash. Four million, not two. That meant half the money was missing. If it was still in Gates's house, it was lost forever.

The diamonds I'd found could be worth as much as eight million. Gates had put up two million, and the Russian put up two more with plans to double their money. And Gates had dangled the carrot in front of Sally, and she grabbed it with both hands.

I drove away thinking about all that money.

The Par 3 golf course was on the water and absolutely beautiful. The grass was bright green and flawless, and the sand dunes were pure white. A cool breeze blew in from the east, and the sun was high in the sky.

As I walked around, aromas from the restaurant gnawed at my stomach. But I had no time to eat.

I headed to the pro shop, where I pretended I was interested in a set of golf clubs. And then I showed the clerk my drawing.

"Sure, I know him. He used to come in here all the time. But I think he plays at the National now," he said.

"Do you know his name?"

"Not a clue, sorry," he said as he hung shirts and straightened displays around the place.

I left and drove to the Palm Beach National Golf Course.

The course was beautiful, and I headed straight for the pro shop. I skipped the facade and just whipped out the picture.

And the salesman said, "That's Jeffery Upton. I'd know him anywhere. He's here all the time."

After thanking him, I drove to Dunkin Donuts and pulled up Jeffery Upton's info on the county assessors' website. Come to find out, he lived next door to Gates.

108
CHAPTER

I parked off the road in front of the empty lot next to the house where Gates had once lived.

I walked along the side of the road to Upton's residence. There was a call box next to the six-foot wrought iron barrier similar to the one at Gates's house, and I lay on the button until a woman's voice with a Spanish accent squeaked out.

"Who is there?"

"Annie Laine, and I need to speak to Jeffery Upton," I insisted.

"Let me see mister here," the voice answered.

"I'm sure he's there, and I'm quite certain that he'll meet with me."

A few seconds later, the Spanish voice returned.

"Oh, si, mister is here. He say stay. Meet you at gate."

I didn't answer, nor was I surprised. The last thing Upton needed was me at his doorstep.

I watched as he exited the big house and hustled down the long drive in his bathing suit, partially covered with a robe. The flip-flop of his leather sandals got louder as he neared.

His forehead furrowed, his mouth formed a frightful grimace, and he didn't look happy to see me at all.

"What the hell are you doing here?" he whispered through the gate.

"We have unfinished business," I said.

He looked back toward the house, where a woman dressed in a bathing suit stood with her arms folded across her chest.

"Meet me later."

"No. Right now. In the light of day."

"I have a family. Leave them out of it."

"I have a family too. Tell me everything."

"It's too involved. It'll take too long, and I can't stand out here talking to you much longer before my wife gets suspicious."

"I don't care what she thinks. As a matter of fact, that might work out better. Let's tell her too."

"You don't understand. It will ruin my life."

"No, I don't understand. But I want to. So start at the beginning. Let's have it right now."

"Okay, okay, but first, let me get rid of her."

The woman had started walking toward us. As she neared, I saw that she was absolutely stunning. Her skin was bright and creamy white. Her face was perfect in every way, and her eyes were the color of jade.

She spoke in an elegant New England style. "What is going on, Jeffery? Who is this woman?"

He took a deep breath. "This is a business associate of Chaz. He sent her to see if we would be available to golf with them tomorrow. Says we're not answering our phones."

"Tell her that we have plans, and let's get back to the pool. The children are alone."

"I don't know anyone named Chaz, and I'm not here about golf," I said. "I'm here to get the details on some shady business deals that your husband is involved in, and I'm not leaving until I get answers. Or you can call the cops. And in that case, I'll let them figure it out."

Upton bowed his head.

Her eyes sprang from him to me and back again.

"Well, dear. Don't be long," she said before turning around and hurrying away.

Upton exhaled. "That wasn't necessary."

"It wasn't necessary to kidnap me or to kill Trevor," I answered.

"I didn't kill him. I didn't even have a gun, and the other guns weren't supposed to be loaded. But apparently, one of my associates didn't listen."

"Steiger killed him?"

"Where did you get that name?"

"There are few secrets when you have Internet access. I know some of them. Now tell me the rest. Start with what happened to Trevor."

He took a deep breath and then began. "We drove past the location you sent us to, but the police were there. Steiger got mad and began beating Trevor with his gun. He told me to stop at a bridge by a canal. He dragged him out of the car, shot him, and threw him in the water. I was horrified and truly sorry."

"Where is Steiger now?"

He rolled his eyes and looked up to the heavens.

"They're staying in my guest house. Him and his family."

"What's your connection to all this?"

"It wasn't my doing. Steiger sent word down through Brian, who I know from back home. We grew up together in Canada. He was trying to work out a deal and thought I would know people who would be interested. He presented an invitation to join a syndicate that was guaranteed to make a lot of money. He had accumulated some diamonds from his association with a mining company and needed to liquidate his holdings. And time was of the essence.

"He also required transportation out of Canada for him and his family," the golfer went on. "That was imperative to cement the deal. I had to come up with investors and a total of four million dollars. And that's not easy when it comes to the circle of friends that I have available to me. They all have money, but most are above reproach. But my neighbor, Weekly, I knew was somewhat shady. He wasn't really a friend. More of an acquaintance.

"He was once a judge, so I thought he could be trusted. But personally, I didn't care for the fellow. He appeared to be a pompous ass, and he was always trying to breach the wall between us.

"But when I approached him with the deal, he said yes right away. And then he told me about this woman. I met her, and she said she had a motor home that was big enough to smuggle the family of six out of Canada.

"Gates said he could get a hold of two million. But Steiger said he wouldn't take half; he needed four. The woman said she could find someone else to put up the rest.

That's when she came up with the Russian. He said he had friends that could bring in the other two.

"Steiger was desperate, and he agreed.

"I didn't like where it went after that, but I was in too deep. I said I wanted out, and they sent that Russian after me. Mik, they called him. He said he would kill my family if I didn't finish what I'd started. He'd already made promises to his friends. The ball was rolling, and he said it couldn't be stopped.

"What was your cut out of this?" I asked.

He swallowed hard. "Ten diamonds, free and clear. I saw the stones, and they were beautiful. Four, five hundred thousand, easy money for me. But I didn't plan to sell them. I'm a collector, and I wanted to give one to my wife for our anniversary.

"Well, let me just say that didn't happen. Suddenly, poof! Everything fell apart, and the whole thing went to hell."

"And Sally and Gates were killed," I said.

"I don't know how any of that happened. You must believe me. All I wanted was to set up the deal and to get rewarded with a few diamonds. Sally dropped them off here, Steiger and his wife and four kids. Gates was supposed to make the exchange later. But he never showed."

"He was murdered," I said.

"Yes, yes, I know. But that woman had to have had something to do with it. I knew she was trouble from the beginning."

"She was murdered too," I stated.

"I didn't have anything to do with that either."

Upton looked back toward the house. "Steiger and his family have been here ever since."

"How did Sally end up with the diamonds and the cash?"

He looked away again. "Steiger was dead drunk and stoned when we got here. That drug addict, Trevor, was supposed to be the extra driver, but he was bad business. He brought a bunch of marijuana with him, and all Steiger did was smoke and drink on the long trip home. We had to carry him off the motor home. When he woke up, he noticed the diamonds were not in his suitcase. He accused Sally of stealing them. But I called Gates, and he said Steiger gave them to her for safekeeping, and they were to settle up later.

"I got Steiger calmed down, and we made plans to meet that day to complete the transaction, and like I said, that never happened." He shook his head. "Steiger got mad. He said he was going to kill everyone, starting with Sally. But we didn't know anything about her."

"When Trevor told us she was murdered"—Upton exhaled—"I thought Steiger must have done it. But he couldn't have because he had an alibi. I remembered that at the time it occurred, he was here, ranting about killing her. I don't know what happened to the woman."

"I have to ask," the golfer hemmed as he stared away. "Do you know where the money went?"

"I gave the two million back to the Russian. I don't know where the rest of it is. But I have 210 high-quality diamonds hidden, and they will never be found if anything happens to me."

"That's only half. The total was 400 plus 10 for me, and they were going to split them, 200 each. Two million for 200 rocks times 2—that was the deal. Four million for Steiger. He wouldn't settle for less, and he would never be heard from again."

The gears in my head were turning. Forty thousand each is what Herman said. I had thought that Sally and Gates were set to double their investment. But I was wrong—two million dollars for stones worth four times as much. They stood to clear six million. I tried not to react, but I was a bit taken aback, to say the least.

I was thinking maybe I could buy them. The house was worth a lot, and I wondered how quickly I could get a loan. And then I snapped out of it. If I made the deal and cut out the Russian, I feared they would follow my family and me for the rest of my life, and I doubted that would be long.

"Now he's stuck in my guest house," Upton continued. "He wants his money, and he's not going to stop until he gets it. They can't live here forever. My wife is threatening to leave if they stay much longer."

"All I have is what I told you about," I said. "I'll give them back, and Steiger can make the deal with the Russian or find another buyer."

"He needs the cash now. None of us knew anything about how to get in touch with the Russian. Sally kept that information to herself. She played her cards close to her chest. And I don't know anyone else that will buy the diamonds. It takes time to put deals like this together. Time he doesn't have." He looked up to the sky and then continued with his babble. "Half is better than nothing. Can you think of anyone with money who could make this kind of deal?"

"Steiger's a killer and a thief. You should turn him over to the police and let them handle it."

"I'm involved too. And if Steiger even thinks I'm talking to you, I'm afraid he'll kill my family. You have to help me," he begged. "Do you know how to get in touch with the Russian?"

I didn't want Upton's family added to the victims. I just wanted it to end.

I mentally kicked myself for destroying Mik's phone with direct contact with the Russian, but I still had Sally's flip phone, and maybe his number was there.

"How can I get in touch with you?" I asked.

"You think we're going to stay in touch?" He scoffed.

"I may have a plan."

"Tell me...No, don't tell me." He held up a hand. "I don't want to know anything. Just make it go away."

"The last time I was in contact with the Russian, he was still interested in the diamonds."

He kicked the asphalt under his sandals and said, "I told you not to tell me." And then he reluctantly recited a phone number.

CHAPTER 109

As I drove away from Upton's big house, I tried to think of other places the rest of the diamonds and money could be but came up empty.

I parked alongside the road and listened as the ocean waves ebbed softly against the sandy shore. I pulled up Sally's flip phone, and it had charged enough to turn on.

I scrolled through messages between her and another unknown number I assumed to be a pay-as-you-go phone that Gates was using.

Gates's text to Sally: *St is pissed. Says you stole the glass. He said you took everything.*

Sally to Gates: *He was drunk. They had to carry him out.*

Gates to Sally: *Where is everything now?*

Sally to Gates: *Our money is in safe; you know where and how to get it out. Rus cash S/B in storage by now. Check before you do anything. Key in mailbox with info to make a trade, Rus stones where you said to put them. Trust me, love. Getting on the plane now. See you in Vegas, baby.*

Gates to Sally: *Almost ready. Can't wait. Where are our diamonds?*

Gates to Sally: *Tell me. I need to know.*

Four hours later, Sally texted back.

Sally to Gates: *Just landed. Our glass is safe as a baby in the womb. You take care of Ruskie?*

Sally to Gates: *Everything go as planned?*

Sally to Gates: *Did you get my text????*

Sally to Gates: *Psycho Mik threatened me. You need to take care of this.*

Sally to Gates: *The psycho said terrible things would happen if he didn't get his cut.*

Sally to Gates: *I'm waiting. Where are you?????*

Sally to Gates: *Answer me!!!!! Mik called again. Just pay him. He's scaring me.*

Sally to Gates: *I'm going to work when I get back. They have security, and I'll be safe there until we get this sorted out. Love.*

And then there was an incoming call that went unanswered.

I assumed Gates hadn't replied to Sally's texts because he was dead by that time. He'd never made it to Sally's house because the key and storage information was still in the mailbox.

Killed by the Russian? That didn't make sense if Gates had access to what they wanted, and he was willing to make the trade. But Mik was a loose cannon.

Half of the money and diamonds were missing. If Gates hid anything in his house, it was lost, at least to me.

I pulled up next to the garage and stared at the motor home. I grabbed the keys and opened the door of the

Canyon Star. It was warm inside, and there was still a hint of booze, pot, and Sally's scent left behind. I thought there could be a safe in here because she had one in the other RV we'd taken trips in. And she'd said it wasn't part of the standard package and had it installed. It made sense that she'd done the same thing to this one.

And this is how Steiger was transported out of Canada.

It could also be in the house, but I'd hoped not. That would be a nightmare, like searching for a needle in a haystack.

The other safe was hidden under the bed behind a panel. I lifted the mattress, but there wasn't anything that resembled a safe. I searched the rest of the place, went through the kitchen and living area, and looked in the small washer and dryer.

In the back was a little garage that contained a motorcycle. I'd never seen Sally ride it, and just thinking about her on the bike made me smile.

I ended up in the bedroom again. I held the ring of keys and imagined all the doors they'd unlocked. The big one was the ignition key, the smaller ones were to the outside storage, garage, and then there were two left, a round-headed hood key and a funny crimped key. The crimped one had to belong to the safe.

Then I tried to imagine the most logical place for it. Easy access and not too high for Sally to reach. I bent down and looked around. I found a panel with an odd-shaped fastener under the headboard. I unhooked it, and the board sprung open. And then I used the funny key to open the metal door.

I had to get down on my knees to pull out the money crammed tightly into the steel-encased area large enough to hold two hundred bundles of cash—ten thousand dollars per bundle. *I'd found the missing two million.*

I sat back and took a long look. This bounty was Gallagher Weekly's inheritance. But its intended use was to purchase diamonds.

Gallagher would have to survive without this money because everyone needed to be free of Steiger and his cruel nature. I stuffed the money back into the safe and walked to the house.

Once inside, I picked up Sally's cheap flip phone and dialed the unknown incoming number. It rang twice, and then I heard a message that sounded Russian. I didn't know what it said, but I assumed it was something about leaving a message and getting back. I hung up without saying anything.

The phone rang instantly.

I pressed to answer but remained silent.

The Russian-accented voice from the other end was soft and low. "You have news?"

"About?" I asked.

"You know."

"Where are you?"

"Not important."

"You want the diamonds?"

"You have them now?"

"Do you still have the money I gave back to you?"

"I have money."

"What's my guarantee that you will not kill me?"

"I am businessman. I do not kill. I trade only. Canadian is killer. He is bad man."

"What was your connection with Mik?"

"He is no good too, but was family. I did not like to deal with him, but we have a saying, money is thicker than blood."

"I thought you'd leave the country."

He scoffed. "I am American citizen. I am here, always close."

"How can we do this?"

"Meet in public place. Airport is good. I give you big bag of money, you give me small box of lovely diamonds."

It took me about two seconds to agree. "What time?"

"Now is time for everything. Meet at Spirit arrival. Baggage turntable, north side. I wear blue shirt with American flag pin on collar. I have black pants and big shoes because my feet are very large. Hands too."

"I'm—"

"I know what you look like."

"I'm leaving now."

I headed toward the airport, wishing and hoping I wasn't driving to my death. I left my car parked in the short-term lot, felt inside my boot to make sure the cigar tubes were still there. But before getting out, I took ten diamonds from one of the tubes and placed them into my glove box—*Upton's cut*. But I had my doubts I'd be handing them over. And then I made my way to Spirit baggage pickup.

The Russian was easy enough to pick out. His description was spot-on, right down to his big feet. He shoved a large duffel on wheels toward me, and I handed him the tubes.

Neither one of us said a word nor checked our packages before going our separate ways.

I expected to be shot in the back as I hurried to my car, but that didn't happen. I got in and drove away.

CHAPTER 110

I called Upton and told him I had the money.

"All four million?" he asked hopefully.

"Yes," I answered.

He exhaled into the receiver.

"Tell him to meet me at Flagler Steak House on the island. I'll be at the bar."

I pulled the cash out of the RV and stuffed it into two large garbage bags.

I was surprisingly calm as I drove toward my destination. No matter what happened to me, my family would be safe and secure.

I left the money in my trunk and entered the restaurant.

Steiger was at the bar celebrating already, gulping down shots of Crown Royal, as I sat down on the stool next to him.

He smiled and asked with a stale whiskey breath, "Where is it?"

"Let's walk," I said.

He left a few bills on the bar, and we exited quickly.

We got to my trunk, and I put the key in and turned. Steiger stuck his head inside, opened the bags, and counted quickly.

I placed my hand on the Glock nestled in my waistband as I watched him shuffle the bills around.

He finally pulled the heavy bags out and smiled.

"I didn't think you'd go through with this after what happened to your boyfriend. I tried to tell Jeff not to do it, but he was angry. He comes across as a decent fellow, but he's got a hair trigger."

"That's the way I figured it. We're good now, right?" I said.

"No more trouble from me."

"Do you have more diamonds?"

"How many?"

"Ten."

"That's not worth my effort," he said as he slammed the trunk so hard the car shook.

"Come on. I just made you whole, and that took a lot of effort. I need a favor."

He hesitated and then said, "Okay, but I'm making solid plans to leave the country. I won't be around much longer. Meet me tomorrow at noon at the IHOP across from the airport. We'll make the exchange and never meet again. One hundred thousand, not a dime less."

"Come on. Can't you give me a discount?"

"You know they're worth a lot more. This is already the deal of a lifetime."

"Give me your phone number so we can stay in touch just in case either one of us runs late."

"I never run late."

"What about me? I have all kinds of things going on in my life." I rubbed my stomach.

He was reluctant but finally gave it up.

Denny was home when I got there, and I was happy to see him. He asked what I had done all day, and I said, "Nothing much. Same old stuff. I went to the beach, and I was thinking about taking up golf."

111

I didn't have the money I promised Steiger, and I had no plans to meet him at IHOP either.

I wasn't going to give him anything. As a matter of fact, I was planning to take whatever he had and give it to Gallagher. He was robbed of his inheritance, and I wanted to make it as right as I could. It would be only a portion of what was due him, but it would be better than nothing. I was sure Steiger had killed Trevor, and I wasn't convinced that he didn't have anything to do with Sally's or Gates's deaths either.

But for some reason, he didn't scare me.

I called him in the morning and said I was ready to meet earlier, and I was in the neighborhood and suggested we meet on the beach in the vacant lot next to Gates's old house.

He didn't sound suspicious, and he agreed without a problem.

He was standing in the middle of the lot when I approached, carrying my backpack and a bottle of water. The private beach in front of us was vacant. Sea grapes covered both sides of the empty lot, blocking anyone's sight of the area.

We were all alone when I faced him.

"Toss your gun." He pointed.

I pulled the .38 revolver out of my waistband and threw it in the sand.

He had the SIG, semiautomatic, and he held it up to my temple as he pulled me close and searched my body.

"Can't be too careful," he said as he lowered the SIG down by his side.

I dropped my backpack into the sand and then bent over to pick it up. As I did, I fisted my hands together and struck Steiger between the legs. He fell to the ground and vomited.

And then I kicked him twice more in the same area. He moaned each time.

When I was sure he'd passed out, I kicked him hard in the solar plexus, and all the air left his lungs. When his mouth opened to suck air back in, I loaded it with sand. His body squirmed around as I added more.

His brain instructed him to breathe, but that was his death sentence. He suffocated on the sand.

I watched for a few seconds, and then I picked up his SIG along with my pistol and stuffed them into my boots, one in each.

He finally stilled, and I took an easy breath.

Steiger was dead, and his family had the money to do whatever they wanted to without him. Everyone was better off.

I searched his pockets and found the diamonds. Ten, just like we agreed upon. And I took them. I pulled his wallet out and grabbed his cash. A little over eight hundred dollars, and I took that too.

I left Steiger dead in the sand and walked to my car.

I pulled a blanket from the back and covered the seat and the floorboard before getting in and driving home. I didn't want any evidence sticking to me that would tie me to this evil man's death.

After showering, I took the Volvo to the carwash and asked for the deluxe.

I dropped the bag of my clothes and boots into a trash bin, and then I took an Uber to Tractor Supply and purchased another pair of Fatbaby Boots.

After my car was clean, I went to see Herman Chase, and he was delighted to see me. It would take a while, but he was sure he'd get top dollar for those twenty beauties, ten from Steiger and the ten that were supposed to go to Upton. Roughly thirty grand apiece on the low end, totaling at least six hundred thousand.

I searched the Internet for information on Gallagher Weekly. I found his address on the property appraiser's website, but it was also listed in the general population of the county jail. He'd been convicted of DUI, and apparently, it wasn't his first offense.

So making things right with him would have to wait.

CHAPTER 112

Things finally settled down, and Denny and I had two full months of tranquil but fulfilling happiness.

It was getting harder to exercise, so I took some time off until the baby came. But I still attended Mr. Foo's self-defense classes. He'd saved my life by schooling me, and I would be forever grateful.

I had yet to determine who Kaitlyn's father was, but my desire to know had waned.

Ellie and Beth were planning something for dinner, but I wanted some alone time with Denny. The baby would be there before we knew it, and our lives would change.

Denny made reservations at the Flagler Steak House, and we got ready and headed out. The last time I'd been there, I'd handled some risky business, but that didn't bother me. I was satisfied with how it ended.

We were seated at a table for two, and I ordered the rib eye with duck-fat-roasted fingerlings, and Denny had the prime rib with mashed potatoes.

The salad came first, and Denny ate as I pushed food around my plate. My gut felt like it was on fire.

We talked about the baby and where she was going to fit into our lives. And I finally began to relax.

Kaitlyn was due in less than a month. At first, we'd keep her with us in the big room. After that, we'd have to work things out. I didn't want her to stay too far from us. But the only rooms available were on the other side of the house.

"We could convert part of the attic into a loft and make it a nursery," I said.

"That's a great idea," Denny agreed.

"It's getting tough to drive. My stomach's getting in the way."

That made him laugh. His bright blue eyes sparkled in the dim romantic light.

I took a bite of steak, and it was fantastic, but I wasn't in the mood to eat.

I wanted to tell him about the horrors of the past few months, but I knew I would never be able to do that. If I told him everything, it would bring an avalanche of issues that could break our world apart.

After twenty more minutes of small talk and discussing plans for the nursery, the waiter dropped by and asked if he could clear the table.

He wrapped my steak, and Denny ordered coffee. I asked for a refill on my water, and then we got back to ourselves.

Denny asked, "Have you decided if you're going back to work after the birth?"

My stomach ached at the thought, and I shrugged. I enjoyed working and the rewards of a paycheck. But I knew I would never return to the Boat. Too much had happened.

"I was thinking about doing something different."

"Up to you." Denny smiled, and I knew it would please him if I didn't go back.

"You know I'm afraid of what I've done to this child." I recalled the story about the trip to Europe that Dr. Jones had told me and repeated it to Denny.

He picked up my hand and said, "This is our baby. Whatever trips we take will be together. You made the right decision to have her. You should never doubt that."

And I realized just how much I not only loved but also respected this man. He was so forgiving and humble, accepting me and all my faults without question. I didn't know if I could ever be as good as him, but I was going to do my best. I never wanted to live without him.

I wanted to trust him with my secrets, and I almost told him about my trips to Rapid Testing and the deals I'd made with the Russian and killing the Canadian, but I held back. And I knew then I would never tell him. We were making memories, and this was a good one.

A few blocks from the house, my phone rang. It was Ellie, and she sounded weak and frantic.

"Someone's outside," she whispered. "They tried to open the door. I looked in the viewer and saw a man. I think he headed around back."

"We're on our way," I said.

CHAPTER 113

Denny had his gun out as we approached, and I had my key ready to unlock the door. He stopped to examine indentations, chipped wood, and pits on the door from the recent attempt to force it open. A brick lay on the doorstep.

I handed him the key, and he opened the door. The alarm beeped as I bent down to pick up the brick.

Things happened fast after that.

Three shots fired rapidly from behind us.

I leaped into the house, and Denny fell on top of me.

And then there was another blast of gunfire.

As Denny rolled off, Ellie grabbed the handle and slammed the door behind us. But not before I got a glimpse of the guy with the gun.

And then I noticed blood spurting from Denny's neck.

Beth bolted the door as I heard Ellie on the phone to the emergency operator.

As the pool expanded around Denny, I put my finger in the hole in his neck and found the source. I pressed on the nick in his jugular vein to stop the blood from draining from his body.

Ellie screamed into the phone, "Someone's been shot, and we need an ambulance!"

There was another round of gunfire; three more shots slammed into the door.

The alarm beeped, begging for a code.

As Ellie responded to a series of questions, I tried to stop Denny's blood from spurting through my fingers.

"We're inside, and bullets are breaking through the door!"

Ellie turned on the speaker and put the phone down.

"I've alerted the police and fire rescue," the 911 operator stated. "They're on the way. Don't hang up."

The alarm horn screamed and caught me by surprise. Beth finally entered the code, silencing the deafening noise.

Denny's skin was white, and his eyelids were twitching.

It wasn't long before I heard the sirens and saw the red-and-blue lights flash through the bullet holes.

The wooden door slammed open, and men in green and blue uniforms were everywhere.

The paramedics took over, and I moved away. I saw what was happening, but it didn't seem real. It was a nightmare.

They started an IV and stabilized Denny. One paramedic had his hand, covered in latex, in Denny's throat, as two more lifted him onto a gurney.

I heard words coming from everywhere but couldn't understand what was being said.

"I need to go with Denny," I answered without caring about myself.

A paramedic slapped a blood pressure cuff on my arm, and I tried to pull away.

A cop held me by my shoulders and said, "He's in good hands. After we make sure you're all right, I'll take you to the hospital. Now let him take your pressure."

The paramedic nodded and said, "She's good. A little high, but under the circumstances, nothing to worry about."

I heard someone talking to Ellie and Beth about leaving and finding somewhere to stay.

"Where are your keys?" one of the cops asked. "We'll need to investigate, and I'll make sure you're locked up when we're done."

I picked up the keys from Denny's pooling blood and handed them over without a thought.

"Let's go," he said, and we were out the door.

On the way to the hospital, the cop asked, "Do you have any idea who could have done this?"

I glanced his way, and for the first time, I actually saw him. He was dressed in a suit, not a uniform. He had a gun in a holster on his hip, and a badge clipped to his belt, a gruff-looking man with sunken cheeks and light skin. And he had big oversize hands. He was a small guy, maybe five six, but his hands looked like they belonged to a much larger man, and he reminded me of the Russian.

His voice was soft, in conflict with his rough appearance.

"What's your name?" I mumbled without really caring.

"Nathan Smythe. I worked with Denny when he was in homicide."

"Homicide," I repeated his word as it echoed in my head.

"I'm here because of Denny. Not because of any other reason. He's a good friend. We've known each other for years, and he told me about you."

I shook my head slightly, wishing the ride would end. I wasn't interested in having a conversation, and I was sorry I'd asked his name. All I wanted was to get to the hospital and make sure Denny was going to be okay.

"Do you know of anyone who would want to hurt Denny?" he asked.

My mind was a sieve. Information was leaking out everywhere.

"It's important that we know where to begin," he insisted.

I forced myself to focus.

"I didn't see him," I lied.

I began putting it together in my head. Another flowchart, but I didn't need any yellow pad for this one. Everything finally made sense, and the missing pieces of the puzzle fell into place.

"Sally and Gates," I whispered.

"Who?"

I hadn't realized I'd said it aloud.

"Nothing," I said.

The rest were just collateral damage. A snowball of deaths, Mik, Sam, Trevor. All because of deals made with a few strangers from somewhere up north.

I knew it would never stop until I ended it. And then Denny would recover, my family would be safe, and we were going to have a baby. We would live happily ever after, just like in the movies.

Nathan drove me to the emergency room entrance and stopped by the double sliding doors.

"I'll park and then be in to make sure everything's okay."

I rose out of my seat in a daze. I didn't even remember closing the car door and probably didn't.

My stupor continued as I walked into the ER waiting room. I stopped and looked around, confused about what to do.

Nathan reappeared, took my arm, and led me through the double doors that opened automatically for him as he showed his badge.

Denny lay on a gurney in a trauma room, much like the one where I watched Sally die. Doctors and nurses worked feverishly. Just like they did with Sally.

I placed my hand on my stomach, swallowed hard, and whispered, "Our child."

"What?" Nathan asked.

"Our daughter, Kaitlyn," I murmured.

I watched as they labored on Denny, but it wasn't as frantic as I'd seen them with Sally, and I took that as a good sign.

It wasn't long before Nathan left, and I was alone.

My thoughts zoomed around in my head, crashing against my skull. This was a long horrible nightmare that just wouldn't end. Finally, I calmed myself, breathing in and out slowly as I watched a nurse remove an empty bag of blood and hang another on the IV pole.

And then Nathan was back.

Suddenly, everyone was on the move. Doctors and nurses pushed the gurney. Someone held the IV pole, and another flopped a machine on top of Denny's lap. The door opened, and the team moved like an organized mob past me and down the hall toward the elevator. And I floated behind them.

We couldn't all fit into the crowded space, and Nathan flashed his badge again.

A doctor held up three fingers.

It must be nice to have that power, I thought.

We took another elevator to the third floor and met the group as they unloaded.

A man dressed in green scrubs met us in the hall. He was tall, fair-skinned, with thinning hair that started high on his forehead. Spatters of Denny's blood dabbed his shirt.

He held out a hand and said, "I'm Dr. Wicker."

I picked up my hand to shake but froze. It was covered with red blood, drying to brown. I pulled my hand away and took a deep breath.

Dr. Wicker withdrew his hand and asked, "Relative?"

Nathan answered for me, "This is Annie. And the guy you have on your gurney is Denny McCaffery, her husband. He's also a detective with the Palm Beach Sheriff's Office."

Husband. It was still a strange word.

"I know you're concerned, but let me assure you that your husband is in good hands," Wicker said. "He's stable and going into surgery to repair the nick in his jugular vein."

"So much blood," I said. "Spurting everywhere."

"Yes, well, the jugular is relatively unprotected by bone or cartilage. It makes it very vulnerable."

I knew this. Mr. Foo had said the same thing, different accents, but the words were similar.

Dr. Wicker continued, "Large volumes of blood flow through these vessels." He took a breath.

"He'll be okay?" I asked.

"At this point, it looks good. However, your husband lost over 50 percent of his blood volume before he came in. And that's a major concern."

"What kind of concern?"

"A loss of this magnitude can cause hypovolemic shock. And that's where we are now. We're doing all we can. We're pumping in blood as fast as he's losing it. It shouldn't take long to close the wound. We'll know more then."

He looked me up and down and then motioned to someone behind me. He told a nurse, "Fix Mrs. McCaffery up with something to wear, please." And then he turned and hurried away.

The nurse looked at my stomach and said, "Go to the bathroom at the end of the hall and wash up."

After I rinsed off, she gave me a pair of green scrubs, size large, to fit over my belly. And then she cut a few inches off the legs so I wouldn't trip.

I emerged from the bathroom, for the most part, free of Denny's blood.

Nathan said I looked better, and I probably did, but I didn't feel it. My head was aching, and I was concerned and worried about everything. I didn't know if anyone was safe around me.

Nathan said goodbye outside the waiting room. "I need to get involved in the investigation. The sooner we find out who did this, the better."

He left just as Ellie and Beth walked through the door.

We sat down together in the waiting room.

"Mom, you look terrible," Ellie said.

"Things have been better," I said, and we did our best to smile.

"Seriously, are you all right?"

I nodded, hoping the subject would change.

"What happened?" Beth asked. "Do you know who did this? Are we all in danger? What are you wearing?"

"It's the latest fad—hospital scrubs." I chose to answer the last question and nothing more.

"Why would someone shoot up our house?" Beth asked.

"They're investigating."

"Who would have done this?" Ellie asked.

"They're investigating," I repeated.

"Has to be someone from that terrible place that you work," Beth said.

"I haven't worked there for months, Beth. They don't know anything for sure." But I actually had all the answers. The bullet that hit Denny was meant for me.

"You need to be more selective with your friends. Mom said the same thing."

I was fed up with her but didn't say anything. I needed my strength for more significant battles.

I folded my hands in front of my face and prayed to God that Denny would live. Then I silently repented my sins and promised to live a good and decent life from that point on if he spared the ones I loved.

I opened my eyes, and Beth was staring at me. "What are you doing?"

"Praying."

"You never prayed in your life. You're not even religious."

I unfolded my hands and sat up, but only because I was finished. It had nothing to do with Beth's observation.

I opened my mouth to respond but couldn't speak. I felt the room spinning, and I was floating somewhere above the heartbreak and sorrow.

"I'm sorry, Annie," Beth cried. "I don't know why I say things like that."

Beth had her hands over her face, hiding like she did all her life. It reminded me of the myth about ostriches with their heads in the sand. If Beth covered her eyes and didn't see it, everything would be okay.

I put my arms around her, and she wept as she said she was sorry again.

After that, we sat in silence for what seemed like hours.

Finally, I saw Dr. Wicker step off the elevator, and I hurried toward him.

He began talking without a greeting of any kind. "He's out of surgery, and we've moved him to ICU. You can see him when you're ready."

"I'm ready now."

"I'll walk you down."

CHAPTER 114

Dr. Wicker and I got off the elevator, and we walked into a sea of uniforms and detectives dressed in sports coats standing outside of the ICU.

A short Hispanic woman stepped toward me. She had brown eyes and a heart-shaped face, and her hair was curly and fell to her shoulders. Her waistline was thin compared to her oversize thighs and butt. And she said her name was Gina Martinez, *Denny's partner*.

I lied and said I was glad to meet her. But actually, I couldn't have cared less. A few months ago, I wondered why we hadn't met. But at that moment, I just wanted to be with Denny and to be left alone.

She said she was sorry about what happened, but the doctors seemed to think he would be all right.

I thanked her for the information and then weaved my way through the crowd toward the ICU.

A doctor edged up to me and introduced herself as Dr. Gabriella Cohen. She placed a hand on my shoulder. She was shorter than me, not even five feet tall was my guess. Her hair was dark and looked like a batch of loose wire. It was everywhere and wild. And she had a huge nose that seemed out of place on her small face.

"Mrs. McCaffery? How are you doing?" she asked.

"I've never been so low," I whispered.

"I'm a neurologist here in the ICU. Your husband is stable but in a coma."

"How long before he wakes up?"

"We don't know," she replied frankly. "Could be an hour, a week, month, or longer."

"Just before they loaded him into the ambulance, his eyes were open, and he was alert."

She exhaled and said, "On the way in, he went into cardiac arrest twice, and they brought him back. We thought we lost him in the OR. He was without a pulse for just under four minutes. So there can be other issues."

"Is his heart damaged?"

"We have to wait and see. His brain function appears healthy, and that's always an excellent sign. You can visit him as often as the ICU allows. It's limited to ten minutes every hour. Talk to him. Sometimes it helps."

"Thank you, Dr. Cohen."

She wrote her number on a small pad and handed me the page.

"Call me if you have questions."

I nodded and then entered Denny's room. Ten minutes an hour was all the time allotted, and I wasn't going to miss one second of it.

Denny was hooked up to beeping machines and monitors. Fluid and blood dripped from bags on a pole into his veins. His skin was still ashen, but he seemed peaceful, and he looked like he was asleep.

There was brain activity, and that was good. The rest would come along. I knew Denny was going to make it. His heart was beating. If the heart beats, there's always a chance at life.

I didn't care how long it took for him to recover; I would be at his side.

I sat for ten minutes with my head on his chest, listening to his heartbeat, making sure blood pumped through his veins. Half of his blood had been replaced by pints from good people, strangers who donated.

The bandage on his neck was white as snow. His lips were dry and cracked from the lack of fluids. His skin was waxy and white. Lighter than it had been. Lighter than it should be.

I stayed longer than ten minutes. The ICU nurse had mercy on me and allowed me more time.

Afterward, I walked through the sea of cops and went back upstairs to Ellie and Beth.

Ellie greeted me at the door of the waiting room. "I don't know what to do. I feel so sorry for you, and I don't know what to do."

"You're doing fine, Ellie. Why don't you go home?" And then I remembered that they had to stay away until the investigation was complete.

I handed her my debit card and said, "Get a couple of hotel rooms. Use this card for whatever you need."

"Sure, Mom. We'll do that. I'll come back in the morning."

And then I was alone.

CHAPTER 115

Gina Martinez drove me home in her patrol car the next day.

On the way, she said, "They took pictures and got everything they needed, and we got someone in there to clean up, and we have a carpenter coming over to fix your door," she said without taking a breath. "Nathan is going to meet you there," she added.

"Any developments?" I asked.

"He should be the one to talk to you because I'm not entirely in the loop. He's the detective handling everything."

Two Hispanic men were working when we got out of Gina's patrol car. The doors were repaired and rehung, and they were attaching hardware.

Nathan stood in the foyer, and we followed him inside.

I looked around. Things seemed reasonably normal, and it was almost like nothing had happened. Like no one shot up the house and nearly killed Denny. The blood was gone, and the bullet holes were patched up.

"Thank you," I whispered.

"It's the very least we can do," he said. "We all love Denny. I consider him my brother, and he's been through hell. When he met you, he changed. He was happy. I was worried about him for a long time. But he fell in love with you, and it changed his life."

My eyes welled up, and that angered me. I needed to be strong for my family, and I blinked away my tears.

"For a while, I didn't think he was going to make it. He was on a self-destructive path. He picked himself up and got on with life. But even then, he was just going through the motions. And then I noticed he was different. Not so stoic, not so sad. And I asked him what was up? He told me about you, and he smiled. First time in a long while that I'd seen it."

"He saved me. Did he tell you that?" I asked.

Nathan shook his head. "All he said was you were wonderful. That you were good. Just plain fantastic. And he was so happy when you agreed to marry him and have his baby."

He'd claimed my child in public to his friends, and I imagined that he told his family too.

"Any suspects?" I asked.

"Nothing yet, but I'll keep you informed. We'll keep a unit outside for as long as it takes to make sure you and your family are protected."

"Thank you, but we don't need anyone outside," I said. "We'll be okay for now. No one will be returning here until this is over."

"Let me know when you do, and I'll make sure you're safe."

He left me alone as I showered and changed. I packed a few things in a bag and drove back to the hospital.

CHAPTER 116

After a few days, the sea of uniforms and detectives had disappeared, and all that was left was Gina.

She greeted me with a somber stare. "How are you?" she asked awkwardly.

"Ready to slow down," I answered without a thought.

"Take care of yourself. If you need anything, call me." She handed me her card. "I'm on duty, so I have to leave, but call me anytime. Even if all you want to do is talk."

I thanked her and then skirted into Denny's room, just like I'd done before. Everyone knew me by then, and I had been able to come and go pretty much as I pleased.

I held Denny's hand, told him about what was happening, and then babbled on about things in my past.

I had called his mother, and she would be making her way down later that week.

I felt his pulse, and it was strong. I leaned my head on his chest, held his hand, and listened to his heartbeat. He was alive, and somewhere in there was the man I loved.

And then I felt his hand move. It was sort of a squeeze, but not quite. It was more like a robust twitch, and I took it as an excellent sign.

I was there an hour before Dr. Cohen came in.

"He moved," I said.

"Really?" she asked.

"I was talking to him and holding his hand, and he squeezed it."

She looked into his eyes and volleyed a penlight back and forth, checking for pupil reaction.

I could tell by her blank expression that she wasn't impressed. "I don't see any change. Sorry."

"I know he moved."

"Coma patients twitch sometimes. But the good news is that his body is recovering. Kidney function is back within normal limits, and brain functions also improved."

She looked at my stomach and asked again, "How are you doing?"

"Any day now. I'll be happy to meet this child. I need to know that everything is all right with her." *And if I was going to Europe first class or backpacking.*

"I remember feeling the same way when I was in your condition."

She had no idea, and I knew she couldn't possibly feel the same as me because she probably didn't drink alcohol and take drugs while pregnant.

"The staff says you spend a lot of time here. This could be a long haul, and you need to pace yourself."

"My family is okay, so I'm here as much as I can be."

"Don't wear yourself out. You're going to need your strength for that child."

"She's good too. Just gave me a big kick in the ribs."

She left, and I got up on my haunches and placed my head on Denny's chest. I listened to his heartbeat as I had before. But the beat wasn't as steady as it had been. Instead, it was weak and slushy.

I brought my head up and looked at the monitor. I didn't know exactly what I was looking at, but I thought maybe the EKG's upswings didn't reach as high as they had before.

I put my head back on his chest, and it was the same, no change.

I approached the nurse's station and asked the male nurse behind the counter, "Is Dr. Cohen still here?"

"She's gone home. What can I help you with?" he asked.

"I don't think Denny's heart is beating right. Can you check it, please?"

He looked at a monitor and said, "It's fine. Sometimes they go through periods of rest, and the heart slows down. I'll keep an eye on it."

I had a feeling he was humoring me, but there wasn't much I could do. So I went back to his room, sat on my legs, and listened.

There's something about the separation of life and death. When a heart is beating within a chest, there is life and all the possibilities that come with it. As long as you can take air into your lungs and keep breathing, there's hope.

When Denny's heart stopped, I felt him leave. I drew my head away from his chest and knew he was gone. All that was left was a body that didn't belong to him anymore. And my soul seeped out through the bottoms of my feet.

Buzzers and bells rang out, and people crowded into the room.

I backed up to the wall and watched as the horde of medical professionals worked hard at pumping his chest and calling "Clear!" and shocking him and seeing his body jump.

Nothing was important. Nothing mattered to me at that moment. Denny was gone, and so was I. Numbingly, I watched them pound and shock and pump for nearly half an hour with no response.

The EKG was flat, and nothing changed throughout the ordeal.

Finally, a doctor stepped back and said, "Let's call it."

A voice stated the time, and I knew what it meant, but I refused to acknowledge it. The time of Denny's death had been the second his heart stopped beating with my ear to his chest.

CHAPTER 117

I hadn't told anyone that I'd recognized the shooter, but I knew.

I left the hospital and drove to the nearest Walmart, where I purchased an XLG hoodie, baggy warm-up pants, gloves, and sneakers, all black. I picked up a blanket, and a small duffel bag, used the self-checkout lane, paid with cash, and hurried out of the store.

I changed my clothes in a dark corner of the parking lot.

As I drove toward Gallagher Weekly's house, I reviewed the plan in my head.

I parked three blocks away and packed the bag with my Glock and pick set. I tucked my hair into the back of the hoodie and pulled the top over my head.

I hoped no one had an outside video camera because I was sure my extended stomach would be a dead giveaway. And it would not take much to put two and two together.

As I walked past the house, I saw a thin light shining through a slit in the drapes.

I didn't linger. I kept my pace slow and casual as I made my way through the yard to the back.

I peeked through a slit in the blinds and saw that the TV was on, but there was no sign of movement.

I used the pick and had the lock undone in no time. As I opened the door, my heart raced as I expected an alarm to blast. But nothing happened.

I stepped inside and faced a full-grown German shepherd.

I slowly slipped off a glove and held my hand out. The dog licked the back of my hand and wagged its tail, an excellent sign, and I began to breathe again.

I found Gallagher Weekly lying on the couch in the living room. His eyes were closed, and a vial of pills lay on the coffee table in front of him next to a sweating glass of amber liquid, and I thought, *Maybe he had beat me to it.*

I removed the Glock from my bag and touched his hand. He didn't move. I placed a finger on the side of his neck and felt a pulse, *slow and steady.*

I picked up the vial, diazepam, and there were plenty of pills left, and I tried to think of a way I could force these things down his throat. But couldn't come up with much.

In the kitchen, I zeroed in on a knife set in a butcher block.

The dog whined behind me, and I nearly fainted. I calmed and searched the cabinets until I found a box of large Milk-Bones. I pulled one out, and the dog sat down.

I gave him the treat, he took it gently, and headed for a corner to chew. His fur was soft, and it was evident that he was healthy and well cared for. This was a good animal, and I wished I could take it with me when I left. But that would be impossible.

I pulled out a paring knife, small and sharp, but wasn't sure it would do the trick. I placed it back into the block and chose the larger slicer. It was long, thin, shiny, and sharp.

I remember hearing once that it was nearly impossible for a person to commit suicide by stabbing themselves, but there's always the exception. Hopefully, the coroner would say that he must have been very determined to take his own life that way. Especially when they discover the gun used to kill his own father, Sally Grover, and Denny. He had sealed his own fate, and I was here to deliver.

Why he didn't use the gun instead of a knife was a question that might be asked. But he must have been insane to have committed these crimes in the first place.

I returned to the couch, and Gallagher had not moved one iota. I tried to recall if he was right- or left-handed. I had seen him at the tables holding drinks and cards and throwing chips into pots but couldn't remember which hand he used.

So I picked up both of his hands and wrapped them around the knife's handle.

As I held it high, Gallagher's eyes flickered, and then I used all my force to cram the knife into his throat.

His eyes opened wide as blood spurted out all over the place, including me.

I quickly stepped back so I wouldn't disturb the spatter patterns enough to cause concern for the crime team.

His body spasmed and shook and then came to rest.

I hurried back to the kitchen and washed my hands and face.

The dog was still in the corner. I tossed him another Milk-Bone, and he wagged his shaggy tail with thanks.

I took one last look at my handiwork and panicked when I noticed my bloody footprints on the tiled floor.

I removed my sneakers and used wet and dry paper towels to wipe the mess up as well as I could. After I was confident that they were gone, I washed and dried the area one more time.

As I stepped toward the back door, I stopped and thought about how the scene would be viewed by a trained detective's eye.

I realized the pills on the table didn't make sense. *Why stab yourself when you could take the pills and just go to sleep?*

I returned to the sofa and tried my best to avoid any blood. I snatched the vial of pills and stuffed them into my bag.

I left through the back door, carrying the bag and my shoes, and locked the handle.

It was difficult not to run back to my car, but I knew that would draw attention to me, and that was something I couldn't afford to do.

Halfway there, I felt a pain in my stomach that bent me over. It only lasted a few seconds, and I whispered, "Not now."

As I finally opened the door to my car and spread the blanket over the seat and floor, I got hit with another pain, and I knew it was time.

But there were still things left to do.

I had to work at maintaining my speed within limits because I was near panic.

I stopped on the bridge over the Intracoastal, the same place I'd dropped Mik's phone and the Sig that belonged to Steiger, and emptied the vial of pills. I ripped the label off, wadded it up, and threw each in separately.

Three more pains hit me as I drove, each one more agonizing than the previous one. I had to pull over when the last one hit and breathed deep until it subsided.

I tore off my blood-spattered clothes and blanket at my back door and crammed everything into a black garbage bag.

I hurried through the house and upstairs, where I showered and shampooed my hair.

As I dressed, another pain bent me over, and I ended up rolling around on the floor.

I whispered, "Please wait."

On the way to the hospital, I searched for a neighborhood with trash cans on the street, all the while getting hit with pain. Each time I dismissed the urge to scream.

I found a street with garbage cans at the curb, but the first few I looked in were full.

I finally found a can with enough room, and I crammed in the big plastic bag full of evidence of my crime.

Before I could get back into my car, I got a pain that brought me to my knees. I moaned and instantly regretted it.

I took quick, short breaths as I climbed back behind the wheel.

I rubbed my stomach and said, "We just gotta get away from the evidence, and we'll be okay."

As I drove away, I hoped I had escaped unseen.

I finally pulled into the hospital parking lot. The feeling of dread hit me as Mr. Foo's words repeated in my head, *Before you embark on a journey of revenge, dig two graves.*

I had crossed that line. I had let my anger channel me and taken Gallagher's and Steiger's lives for revenge.

But the dread abated as the pain took over and made me scream. I took short breaths, and as soon as it eased up, I hurried to the front door and bolted to the elevator. Once inside, I pressed the button to bring me to the second floor.

As the doors closed, another pain struck, and I fell to the floor, grunting and moaning.

The door swept open, and I crept toward the gap and reached a hand out to prevent it from closing until I was able to stand.

I rushed to the nurse's station but didn't have to say anything. The nurse on duty had seen the look on my face many times and knew just what to do.

CHAPTER 118

"How far apart are the contractions?" the nurse asked as she rolled me away in a wheelchair.

"Not far, maybe a minute or less," I moaned.

Several people appeared, picked me up, and placed me on a table with a bright light overhead. And it was only a matter of minutes until it was finally over.

After she was born, the nurse took her away and did whatever they do to newborns to clean them up, make them cry, and ensure that things worked the way they should.

I mumbled, "Everything okay?"

The nurse smiled and said, "So far, so good. The rest is up to you."

Shock waves zapped my brain. *Up to me?* The words echoed in my head. She said something else, but I failed to understand anything more.

It couldn't possibly be up to me. *That was a mistake.*

She held the bundle toward me, but I turned away, exhausted from the fight. I didn't want anything to do with any of it. There had to be someone else more capable.

I closed my eyes and nodded off.

119
CHAPTER

Ellie picked me up the next day and took me home. I went up to my room, fell back to sleep, and didn't wake up for two days.

I vaguely remembered Ellie spieling out plans and asking for my approval because things had to get done. But I had no idea what.

When I opened my eyes again, my mother was sitting on the bed next to me. She ran her fingers through my hair and massaged my shoulders.

"You know I love you, Annie," she said. "And when you were little, I knew you were special. I had such high hopes for you. I knew you would become something important. All this time, I was angry, and I'm sorry. I was disappointed that you didn't achieve what I thought you were capable of. But I've finally realized that you didn't need to become exceptional. You already are."

I didn't move or acknowledge her presence. After she left, I got up and went to the bathroom, drank water from the tap, and then went back to bed and slept some more.

The next day, Ellie forced me out of bed and into the shower. She dressed me in black and led me outside to the graveyard in the back of the house.

Hordes of people were there. Police officers dressed in uniforms, a few on horseback, and friends and family stood solemnly. Ellie led me to a chair in front of a casket draped with an American flag across the shiny lacquered wood. Someone spoke, but I didn't know who or what was said.

The flag was folded and placed in my lap. I stood up, and Ellie grabbed it before it hit the ground.

A baby cried, and I thought it odd for someone to bring an infant to an event such as this.

Someone handed me a white rose, and I laid it on the casket as "Taps" played in the background. The service ended as bagpipes screeched out "Amazing Grace."

After it was over, people crowded into the house, where food was laid out on tables.

I hadn't eaten in days, but the smell of nourishment sickened me. I drank a bottle of water without stopping and then returned to my room, lay down without changing, and went back to sleep.

I dreamed of being trapped in the pit, but I wasn't alone this time. I was with a beast, and it was devouring my soul.

I lay down and just let it happen.

CHAPTER 120

The next day, I got up.

I looked down at my clothes and wondered why I was dressed in black. Everything was a blur.

I pulled off the dress and dropped it to the floor. I dressed in jeans, a worn thin Northwestern T-shirt, and drew my Fatbaby boots onto my feet.

I pulled the bag of cash out of the bottom drawer and laid it on the bed.

I sat for a while, trying to sort things out, trying to understand what was happening to me, but I became frustrated. *There were no answers.*

I looked down, out of the overhead window, and saw Beth preparing something in the kitchen.

Ellie rocked in a chair, holding a bundle of something.

I exhaled.

I couldn't really say why, but I was sure that my family would never be safe around me.

I counted the money, just over twelve thousand dollars, and I thought there should be more.

My life was in shambles. I could end it at any time without a problem. But that was the coward's way out. Pills would be my choice if I decided to go that route. And I would make sure it looked like an accident. For Ellie's sake.

I stuffed the cash into my boot and then grabbed my cell. I pulled up my bank account and transferred the balances to Ellie.

I grabbed my snub-nosed .38 and thrust it alongside the money. I shoved the Glock into the other boot. Not because I needed protection, just because I didn't want anyone else to find the weapons and cause more heartbreak. What kind of heartbreak? I hadn't a clue. But I knew there had been too much of it.

I slowly made my way downstairs.

Ellie stopped when she saw me and probably had no idea what to say. *What could she do? What could anyone?*

I asked, "Everything okay here?"

She nodded.

"I need to go away for a while. Sort things out," I said.

"It's okay, Mom. We've got things covered. Take as long as you need."

I walked out the back door and found a fresh tomb without a headstone, but I couldn't recall who had been buried recently. I stood for a moment, trying to remember. And then I saluted.

I grabbed the keys from the garage, climbed into the captain's motor home seat, fired up the engine, and drove away.

SCREAMING ECHOES

I awoke with the sun seeping into my darkness, and it annoyed me. Another day of nothingness. Another day of not remembering.

I arose and stretched as I looked out at the vastness of trees and sky. Rays of light bled into my darkness. I blew out a breath of chilly air, and it clouded the space in front of me.

Somewhere in the night, the cold leaked in, and I chose not to acknowledge it. Just like most everything else, I'd decided to ignore.

A slight memory flashed, and I shook my head, trying to rid myself of the snippets from the past. But my brain seemed not to be behaving—it was unwinding instead.

I rubbed my forehead, trying to remember, but trying harder to forget.

I dressed quickly in sweats and Nikes purchased by someone else and didn't belong to me—or maybe they did by now—and then exited the motor home.

I stood just outside the door and inhaled the cold air. Leaves fell all around me, and I paused to take in the beauty of the changing seasons. The green was changing to red, yellow, and orange. Leaves fell from trees that would soon be bare and then covered in snow.

But I would be okay. My motor home had a heater.

I ran up the path toward the hilltop like I had done for one hundred days before. *Limping.* I favored one leg or foot or ankle. I didn't remember why, but I knew I hadn't always listed to one side. It was due to an injury somewhere in my past.

I counted each day as if it would soon be over, but I didn't know when or how long it would take.

I ran like a well-oiled machine. The first weeks were hard. But I continued to work at it, and now it was easy. Moving fast for a mile, then another, and another after that. I ran until there was no more path. And then I made my own way up the hill until it became a mountain.

After nearly an hour, I reached the top. It had taken longer at first, but now I was in good shape. *Physically, at least.*

I stood at the top and looked down at the valley that was once green. It seemed like yesterday that it was endlessly emerald with trees and brush. Now it was flaming with the colors of fall. Different, yet okay. Lovely, even beautiful

I filled my lungs with air and *screamed.* When I finished, the echoes came back—*snippets of something.*

I turned and ran back down the mountain.

Memories were coming back like screaming echoes from the valley.

ABOUT THE AUTHOR

Skyler Kent is an award-winning author living in South Florida.